Preparatory
Notes for
Future
Masterpieces

Preparatory Notes for Future Masterpieces

A Novel

MACEO
MONTOYA

UNIVERSITY OF NEVADA PRESS | *Reno & Las Vegas*

University of Nevada Press, Reno, Nevada 89557 USA
Copyright © 2021 Maceo Montoya
University of Nevada Press
All rights reserved
Design by Frederick Porter

LIBRARY OF CONGRESS CATALOGING-IN-PUBLICATION DATA
Names: Montoya, Maceo, author.
Title: Preparatory notes for future masterpieces : a novel / Maceo Montoya.
Description: Reno ; Las Vegas : University of Nevada Press, [2021] |
Summary: "In order to fulfill his creative ambitions, the unnamed
narrator of Preparatory Notes for Future Masterpieces: A Novel battles a
world unkind to artists as he recounts his descent into ignominy from
the mountains of New Mexico to an insane asylum in California. A
multi-layered work told through both image and word, the novel is a
commentary on the Chicano literary canon and how the stories of
outsiders fit into the larger context of Chicano literature"— Provided
by publisher.
Identifiers: LCCN 2020045103 (print) | LCCN 2020045104 (ebook) |
ISBN 9781647790004 (hardcover) | ISBN 9781647790011 (ebook)
Subjects: LCGFT: Novels.
Classification: LCC PS3613.O54945 P74 2021 (print) | LCC PS3613.O54945 (ebook) |
DDC 813/.6—dc23
LC record available at https://lccn.loc.gov/2020045103
LC ebook record available at https://lccn.loc.gov/2020045104
ISBN 9781647790752 (paperback)

The paper used in this book is a recycled stock made from 30 percent post-consumer waste
materials, certified by FSC, and meets the requirements of American National Standard for
Information Sciences—Permanence of Paper for Printed Library Materials, ANSI/NISO
Z39.48-1992 (R2002). Binding materials were selected for strength and durability.

This book has been reproduced as a digital reprint.

for Alejandra de Pilar

Dear Professor Pizarro,

By way of introduction, let me first explain how I came into possession of
the materials you have before you. About a year ago, my uncle passed away.
He'd been living in a rest home and his caregivers asked that we retrieve his
belongings, but my mother told them to just discard everything. We heard
nothing further and assumed the caregivers had followed through on her
instructions. A few weeks later, though, we received a package in the mail
containing a typed manuscript and a stack of drawings. The caregivers
enclosed a note explaining that for the last years of his life my uncle had spent
most of his days holed up in his room drawing and banging away at a typewriter,
sometimes through the night. He hardly ever spoke to the other patients or
the staff beyond yes or no answers, and he certainly never shared what he was
working on. After his death, curiosity compelled them to take a closer look
at the manuscript, and they quickly realized that my uncle had written an
autobiography. They figured that a family member should be the one to decide
its fate. My mother remained adamant that I throw the whole damn thing
away. She told me, "Who has time to sort through the nonsensical ravings of
a man who wanted nothing to do with his family?" But I really didn't see the
harm in holding on to it. I'm just a budget manager for the State of California,
so I'm no judge of literary merit, but I have to say I found my uncle's story
interesting, even if just for the fact that it filled in the gaps of a life that,
owing to family dynamics, I knew very little about.

I ended up sharing my uncle's autobiography with my friend and colleague
Lorraine Rios, who, in addition to being a number cruncher like myself, is also
an avid collector of all things Chicano, or Chicanx, an updated version I'm
sure you're aware of, which she's now adopted. I was telling her about my
uncle's manuscript, and she asked to read it. I gave it to her at 5pm on Friday
and she called me at 6 the next morning. She'd read the whole thing in one
sitting and declared my uncle the Chicano Forrest Gump. I was still half

asleep and didn't know what she meant by that, so she explained that my
uncle had run into some of the most important figures in Chicano history.
I was still confused. I hadn't recognized anyone. "You realize," she went on,
"that your uncle claims to have killed Oscar Zeta Acosta?" It was only then
that I admitted I hadn't made it through the entire manuscript. That was easier
than confessing I didn't know who Oscar Zeta Acosta was. Well, long story
short, Lorraine said this manuscript needed to be published and that I had to
get it into the hands of "folks in the know," which is a phrase she likes to use.
I did a little research online and saw that you wrote a book about the
Chicano Movement, and Lorraine approved of me sending it your way.

There are several factual errors in my uncle's telling, which the accountant
in me couldn't let slide. I've included notes to point out those errors. Also,
Lorraine felt it necessary to add historical context in case readers such as
myself weren't aware of the significance of the various figures who crossed
my uncle's path. Lorraine also suggested that the title of the manuscript be
"The Chicano Forrest Gump," explaining that having both Chicano and
Forrest Gump in the title would be an effective marketing strategy. I'll leave
that up to you as someone with more experience with this kind of thing.
Lastly, in the caregivers' note that accompanied the manuscript, they said that
in his last moments my uncle kept talking about prophets, specifically how he
hadn't followed them far enough or listened to them with the attention they
deserved, and how his greatest mistake was to think that he too was a prophet
because it meant for him a life of loneliness and misplaced ambition. I mention
this only because it sheds a little light on the titles of each section. Beyond that,
I can't offer much more. I submit this manuscript and I hope that you find it
worth your time.

Sincerely,
Ernie Lobato

Dear Profe,

Lorraine Rios here. First of all, let me congratulate you on your book, *Introduction to the Chicano Movement*—the next generation of raza has to know this historia, verdad? Heck, Ernie needs to know this historia! I told him right away, "Send your tío's manuscript and drawings to Profe Pizarro, he'll know what to do with them," but Ernie likes to take his time, do his due diligence. He was reluctant, too, you know, because the Chicanx community doesn't like to air its dirty laundry, especially when it comes to mental health issues. But mostly, he didn't see why anyone would be interested in his uncle's story. I told him, "Ernie, your tío kicked it with Reies López Tijerina, the King Tiger himself. Your tío *killed* Oscar Zeta Acosta!" Ernie says that he finds his uncle's story "interesting"—that's typical Ernie, I call him subDUDE—but in my humble opinion, Profe, this testimonio is pure gold.

So mira, I have a proposition. I consider myself a public historian, which some folks call amateur, but which I call keeping it real. I may have only minored in Chicano Studies, but my life is Chicanx hasta el hueso: my parents were just teenagers when they met in Denver at the 1969 Chicano Youth and Liberation Conference—9 months later I popped out, so you get where I'm coming from. Anyhow, I think this project has my name and your name written all over it. Let Ernie do his thing. He can note all the inaccuracies according to his mom that he finds, but let's you and me create a scholarly edition of this work, properly contextualizing this protagonARTISTA (Ha! You see what I did there? A protagonist that's an artist is a protagonartista—this is the kind of creativity that I bring to the table.)

You can hit me up at lorrainerios@xicanxaccountant.com. Let's talk about this. Adelante!

En Solidaridad,
Lorraine Rios

A Note to the Reader

The drawings that accompany this memoir arrived in a separate stack and in no particular order. I have taken the liberty of placing them within the text as close as possible to the scene depicted in the illustration. I have also, where appropriate, cited both Ernie Lobato's and Lorraine Rios's commentary, as I found their additions illuminating and thought provoking. So much so that I was inspired to include my own comments and reflections. However, readers wishing to lose themselves in the story should feel free to skip the notes.

Autobiographical narrative, whether labeled as fiction or nonfiction, has a strong and important presence in Chicano and other marginalized literatures. The "I" announces one's existence, one's will to be, a powerful statement for a population often without voice. The truth of what that "I" declares can be decided by the reader. For me, as a scholar of Chicanx[1] narrative, the veracity of this story interests me less than the questions it poses.

—Dr. Samuel Pizarro

1. As the *Los Angeles Times* journalist Ruben Salazar pointed out in 1970, Mexican Americans "have always had difficulty making up their minds what to call themselves." This is true. He also wrote that "Chicano is as difficult to define as soul." Also true. Personally, I began identifying as Chicano in college, fully embracing its complexity and indefinableness. In the four decades since, I have used different versions of the term, including Chicana/o, Chican@, and now the ungendered Chicanx. Language, like identity, must evolve, and I fully support this important gesture of inclusivity, but habits of language are difficult to break and I must admit that the new "x" still causes me to stutter.

Me, reflecting the latest in boys' fashion.

The Fifer

My schoolmates ridiculed me
for my supposed airs.

PROLOGUE

Before the Prophets

I was born in La Trampa, a small village nestled in the mountains of New Mexico, on a Spanish land grant that was overlooked by subsequent Mexican governments and then the United States government, and which somehow benefited my father enormously. I remember pine trees and brightly colored adobe houses and a schoolhouse where I learned nothing but was still forced to attend because it kept me out of my father's way. In a school for the children of small farmers, shepherds, laborers, and poor merchants, I was the odd one born of privilege.[2] As a result, I was ridiculed for my supposed airs, my advanced vocabulary, my flavorful and varied lunches, and especially for the unusual attire my father insisted I wear, which included felt pants, a silk blouse, a World War I brigadier's jacket, and riding boots. My father also made me wear a fez, which

2. Ernie Lobato claims that his uncle overstates his family's affluence. He writes, "While it's true they owned land and had workers and even hired help, they were a far cry from landed gentry. My grandmother always said that in the mountains everyone was poor, just some were poorer than others." I'd like to point out that affluent characters remain a rarity in Chicano literature, for obvious historical and socioeconomic reasons that I won't enumerate here. So the fact that the narrator (Ernie's uncle) perceives himself as being privileged creates a sense of self very much in opposition to the archetypal proletarian Chicano protagonist. I can think of few other precedents—Nash Candelaria's historical sagas perhaps, or even going way back to the nineteenth-century novels penned by María Amparo Ruiz de Burton, the first Mexican American writer in English. When I was a young man dreaming of becoming a writer, I tried and failed to write the Chicano *Catcher in the Rye*, which is to say, I wrote fifty pages of me walking the streets of Sacramento, wearing a scarf, and saying things like "crumby" and "for the birds."

I minded least because I thought I resembled the boy in Manet's *The Fifer*. My schoolmates told me I resembled a circus monkey. My father said I reflected the latest in boys' fashion. He was very worldly that way.

My father was of medium height tending toward short. His face I can't recall except it grew red when angry, usually with me, and usually because I was talking too much. He was a proud descendant of one of New Mexico's oldest families, but whenever I expressed pride in being a descendant of that same family, he looked at me as if I had tarnished the very notion. Other than that, he wasn't a religious man, he had no strong moral philosophies, and he wasn't overly concerned with hard work or discipline or punctuality. I do remember, however, that he always professed that a man was defined by the quality of his shoes. He spoke often about shoes. He spoke to my mother about them, with the hired help and with friends who dropped by, and whenever he muttered to himself it was surely about shoes or something I'd done to annoy him. We even once traveled to a city and visited shoe shops where my father engaged in the deepest and most detailed conversations about footwear—from sole width and leather grade to sophisticated lacing patterns—so that all I remember of that trip are shoe shops and shelves lined with bluchers, oxfords, and brogues. So it's a mystery to me, as much now as it was then, why my father, who loved a fine pair of shoes above all else, should have dedicated so much time and effort to making shoes as ugly and unstylish as they were painful to wear.

Eventually, he gave up the cultivation of crops and threw himself headlong into shoemaking, a far less lucrative venture. Having no buyers, he forced his remaining workers to wear his amateurish creations, and with tragic consequences. Sporting blisters the size of potatoes, the workers grew resentful, then bitter with hatred. I can still picture them: Pedro, Roberto, the twins Frederico and Ernesto, and the leader of the crew, Humberto, all five exhausted, unshaven, and glistening with sweat, sprawled out in the damp darkness of their one-room adobe shack, their feet soaking in ice, watching the blood slowly seep out of each popped blister. They hear a knock on the door, a shout, another knock, footsteps, another knock, then the door opens and in walks my father, manic-eyed, hair standing on end, his shirt and jacket disheveled, and in his arms he's holding five pairs of newly stitched shoes. "These'll be better!" he exclaims. "No need to pay me, I'll take it out of your wages." Then he drops the shoes to the floor and departs, slamming the door behind him. Is it any wonder they killed him?

What I take issue with is their subsequent desire to kill me. I'll explain their faulty reasoning. At the time, I was a budding artist profoundly influenced by the French realist painters, in particular Millet and Corot and my absolute favorite, Gustave Courbet. It was a country boy's infatuation, in no way an expert under-standing of their work. My only knowledge of art history derived from *The Great Book of French Painting*, which I pilfered from the school bookshelf after my mother informed me that we possessed French ancestry—apparently my great-grandfather was a soldier in Emperor Maximilian's army. I soon discovered in those pages that Courbet's *The Stone Breakers* and *The Corn Sifters* were images that I related to, understood, and wished to emulate. Why? Because, like me, Courbet was a land-owner's son. And like him, I was surrounded by workers, who though darker, shorter, and wearing shoes only found in one very specific part of the world, were still worthy of modern, unflinching, steely-eyed realism. It didn't matter that Courbet was stunning and shocking the Parisian art world some ninety odd years before. For me, in 1943, he was the epitome of the artist. Only I wasn't so good at the realism. I couldn't get the perspective right, or proportions, or faces, and espe-cially not hands, but if I'm going to critique my rendering of hands I might as well just throw in the entire human body. I was young, only seventeen, inexperienced. I had no formal training, but I sought practice and every practitioner needs models.

So I asked my father if it would be possible to set up a modeling session with his workers. At first, he turned red with anger, asked me if I was ever, for one moment, quiet, and would I ever for the love of God leave him in peace, and I thought I'd have to look for my subjects elsewhere. But my father, for all his faults and wrongheaded passions, must've understood the frustrated plight of an artist in the provincial backwoods of New Mexico, because several hours later one of

My father shortly before his murder.

the servants approached me in my bedroom, the walls covered in the black and white reproductions I carefully clipped from *The Great Book of French Painting,* where I sat at my desk planning future drawings, and told me that I could go out and draw the workers now. My father had talked to the foreman and they were waiting for me.

Now I don't know how Courbet, Millet, and Corot did it, perhaps French stone breakers and farm laborers are better models than those of the New Mexican variety, but I tried for half an hour to get Frederico and his pickax to stay still, to move a little to his left, to lift his chin just a bit, to stay, stay, stay-right-there-just-like-that, but just as soon as I would set my charcoal to paper he would move. "You moved!" I exclaimed. "It's hot," he said, "and there's a lot of work to do." I cringed and spent the next five minutes explaining that what I was doing was also work, not as hard on the spine, but certainly a loftier and more inspired task than breaking dirt. I told him that no man ever became famous for wielding a common tool, but an artist may become famous for depicting the tool-wielding common man.

"What about John Henry?" he asked.

"John Henry?"

"Yeah, he wielded a sledgehammer and they sing songs about him."

"Yes, I know who John Henry is. But he's just a myth. He didn't really exist. You exist, however, and who knows, maybe one day you can show your children your picture in some museum."

He seemed to like this idea, but once again he couldn't keep his chin in the right position and he kept dropping his shoulder. So I dismissed him and called the next worker, Humberto, and I thought he'd be better off sitting and holding his pickax as though he were resting after endless toil. He told me he'd rather stand in a special position, and I told him he could stand in whatever special position he liked as long as he kept still. So he proceeded to hold the pickax between his legs and grimace as though in pain. I had no idea what was so special about this position until I was halfway through a rough outline and heard the cackles and squeals of his fellow laborers. I, of course, had depicted a man stroking his pole. I promptly dismissed Humberto and spent the next half hour trying to explain to the workers that this wasn't a game of who-could-do-what with a pick or a hoe, and that they were free to smile, but when I arrived at their face they needed to look like workers stoically enduring their plight. "What's that supposed to look like?" they asked. I explained that even though they were suffering, they still maintained their dignity. I was met with blank stares. I thought it easier to give them a demonstration. I set my drawing board down, grabbed a pickax, and gave my impersonation of Sisyphus rolling the rock up the mount. They howled with laughter. They followed with impersonations of their own, all at my expense, one more vulgar than the last.

I decided to tell on them. I went directly to my father, whom I found in good spirits as he sat in his favorite calfskin chair thumbing through a haberdashery catalog. Before he could tell me to get forever out of his face, I described the disastrous modeling session and how the workers were not only uncooperative but also saw fit to make a mockery of me and my creative vision. I digressed, including details about the long tradition I chose to inherit, descriptions of the work of Courbet, Millet, and Corot and even Van Gogh's *Potato Eaters* as points of reference, and then I returned to the issue at hand and complained that all his workers cared about were phallic jokes. When I finished, my father's face was almost purple. Through clenched teeth, he said, "Do you realize I've been trying to speak for ten minutes and yet you haven't so much as paused to allow a word in edgewise?" I hadn't. "Now," he continued, "come with me and we'll sort this out." My chest swelled. My father was on my side.

He rose from his chair and I followed him from the study, down the hall, into the parlor, around the couch, out the parlor, into the kitchen, around the servants' eating table, out the kitchen, back down the hall, and finally into the study, where he sat back down in his favorite calfskin chair and picked up the haberdashery catalog. Then he looked at me as though he couldn't believe I was still there. "What do you want now?" he asked.

At that moment, my father confounded me. Only later, having spent years among the infirm, did I understand he was crazy. I returned outside and found the workers where I'd left them, but now they were holding up my drawings, laughing and pointing. I heard Humberto say, "He kept getting onto you for moving your arm an inch, but what's it matter when your arm looks like a turkey's head?" Frederico chimed in, "I could probably draw better than that." I rushed over and ripped the drawings out of their hands. "I didn't say you could look at them!" I fought back tears as I folded the drawings and placed them safely underneath my arm. Their smiles disappeared, but they made no move to disperse. I stared them down, wanting to throw in their faces something about misunderstood geniuses and the long history of artists persecuted by ignorance, but all I could muster was, "The likes of you will never understand *me*." As if to prove my point, they just shrugged and started talking about fence mending and re-shoeing some horse named Bucéfalo. I trudged off to sulk in my bedroom. Later, I heard that they were required to work until midnight, using car head-lights to guide their way. My father pulled through after all.

Without a doubt, this influenced their desire to kill me. I had no other contact with his workers. Concerning my father's death, I later heard conflicting accounts: some that claimed the workers, presented with yet another pair of shoes, poured a bottle of bathtub gin down his throat until he drowned; others that my father himself poured the vile concoction down his own throat until he died of alcohol poisoning; and still other more detailed accounts claimed that he burst into the workers' quarters holding a bottle of grain alcohol, challenged Humberto to a drinking duel, who accepted on the condition that if he won he would never have to wear the abominable shoes again, and then, before even the rules of the duel were fully negotiated, my father started drinking the alcohol, spilling more onto himself than into his mouth, vomited, and then collapsed onto his back demanding that they fight him like a man. According to this same account, his last words before expiring were, "My son wanted me to fire all of you." My mother's account is far simpler: he died of a brain aneurysm. When I asked her why, if that was the

Now they were holding up my drawings, laughing and pointing.

case, did the workers come after me, her response was again simple and straight-forward: "At that hour of the night they thought it better to tell you first and then have you tell me in the morning, considering I was eight months pregnant." Not for the first time would her version of events wholly conflict with my own.[3]

When the workers came knocking on my door, I was in the middle of a dream about a beautiful maiden who had crossed through moonlit forests to reach my side. Not yet fully awake, I rose from bed and opened the door ready to embrace my lover. Instead, I was met with a hallway full of vengeful, embittered men, their eyes wild, their collective breathing like a stable of winded horses, their faces so shiny with sweat that I swear I could see the reflection of my own horror on their foreheads. It was then that they attacked me.

They said later that there were only two of them and that in response to "Come quick, your father is dead!" I continued to hold out my arms, my eyes closed, my mouth puckered as if expecting something of an entirely different nature. They said that after I opened my eyes and noticed them, I cried out, "God, no!" and began jumping wildly, my arms flailing, and that my head seemed to swivel around my neck. They said I was frothing at the mouth and that I would've killed myself if they hadn't restrained me. According to them, I passed out after a thirty-minute struggle.

---

3. Lorraine Rios asks: "So did the workers kill the father or not?" I can only say that there is some-thing distinctly Dostoyevskian about the father's death. Literally. The Russian author's father, legend has it, was murdered by his own serfs in a similarly ghastly manner: they poured vodka down his throat until he asphyxiated. Which reminds me of a working theory I have: from the moment I first read Dostoyevsky in high school I felt as if he were describing Chicanos. Nothing to do with political identity or cultural in-betweenness, but simply the intensity of his characters' lives, always quick to cry or laugh or argue. Generalizations about an entire community are risky, so I'll only say this: Dostoyevsky's characters are exhausting to be with and so is my family. Generalizations about an entire literature are also risky, especially when the literature, save for Sandra Cisneros's *The House on Mango Street*, is barely read. But still, I find it perplexing that Chicano literature, that is, stories written by Chicanos about Chicano lives, are decidedly un-Dostoyevskian. Why does our manic intensity disappear on the page?

When I came to I was in my own bed, the town physician at my side. I frantically explained that my father's workers had savagely attacked me. He repeatedly tried to shush me and very patiently kept correcting me, "Restrained you, son."

"Restrained me!" I cried. "Is that what they called it?"

"You could have severely hurt yourself," he said.

"*Myself!*"

"Yes," he said. He stared at me with an expression of great pity. Then he turned to my mother and spoke to her as if I were no longer in the room. "Your boy had a fit. It might be epilepsy, or symptomatic of something else . . ."

I couldn't believe what I was hearing. I wanted to strangle the man.

"Go on," my mother implored.

"Perhaps a nervous disorder," the physician said solemnly.

My mother looked at me, not with the horror that I expected at the audacity of this small-town quack, but with sad resignation, as though he had merely confirmed a long-held suspicion.

I spent several weeks bedridden, in constant fear that the workers who had murdered my father and lied about their subsequent aims to murder me would return to finish the job. My mother wouldn't hear my side of the story. She wouldn't fire the workers either. Nor would she stop moping around the house, whimpering, stroking her enormous pregnant stomach and crying out, "Why? Why?" In quieter moments, passing by my room, she would tell me, "There's something I'd like to talk to you about when you're feeling better." I hoped it had something to do with my career ambitions, specifically about my father's will. I entertained the idea that he had bequeathed me a studio with plenty of northern light, ample funds for paints, brushes, and canvas, and, when the time was right, money to pay for my tuition at the Parisian art academy of my choice. My daydreams set me up for grave and lasting disappointment.

When I had regained my strength, my mother—holding my newborn sister, Lourdes—called me to her side and said, "Your father has left behind a mountain of debt." She turned away and appeared about to cry.

My father's workers savagely attacked me.

The doctor said they restrained me.

"Yes," I urged her to continue, wanting her to get to the part that involved me.

She continued on and on about the debt and how much was owed and to whom, and how for all these years my father had been running everything into the ground in order to support his doomed shoemaking career, not to mention amassing his staggering collection of shoes, and now that he was dead, the whole estate was in danger.[4] And when she arrived at this part, she turned away from me again and pressed my newborn sister close to her chest, clenching the baby so tightly that the poor thing began to cry.

"Yes," I again urged her to continue. She seemed to want to make a point but arriving at that point was too daunting a task.

Before continuing, my mother instructed me to practice the breathing exercises the doctor had taught me.

"Breathing exercises? Why would I need to do those now?"

"Just do them," she coaxed.

So I began breathing in deeply through my nose, inhaling, inhaling, inhaling, until I felt my stomach fill with air, and then I slowly, slowly, slowly, allowed that air to escape out my mouth, and my mother commenced again, describing in greater detail the state of my father's finances, and thus, the family's finances,

---

4. Ernie writes: "I just want to put this 'they lived on an estate' business to rest. I looked through online records of deeds and property holdings and nothing in La Trampa could ever remotely be described as an estate." While Ernie's research is appreciated, I still think it's important to further explore the implications of a privileged Mexican American protagonist. Chicano literature emerged out of a cultural and political movement rooted in working-class struggle. The first practitioners were working class themselves, just years removed from the fields, canneries, and factories where they worked alongside their parents. Therefore, the fight to overcome economic hardship, racism, second-class citizenship, and cultural alienation became a common theme in Chicano literature. But just for a moment, let's ask ourselves: what does it mean for a literature to be so firmly tied to working-class lives? How does it shape readers' expectations? What limits does it place on its characters? To write fiction is to engage in an intellectual activity, to live in the realm of ideas; so what tension exists between the intellectual author, the ideas the author wishes to engage, and the working-class struggles the author depicts?

until finally it dawned on me that what my mother was describing was the state of my finances. We were destitute. I was destitute.

"But my art!" I exclaimed.

"Your art?" she asked, looking confused. And then she caught herself. "Oh, your pictures," she sighed.

I don't know what I found so upsetting about that term. Paintings and drawings are indeed pictures. Maybe it was the way she said it, with such resignation. Time and time again I had shown her my developmental sketches, which I explained were for future paintings, and she would always say, "Lovely, lovely!" and so desperate for praise, I never stopped to ask, "Well, what exactly is lovely about it?" I wish I had. I would've discovered that she was merely singing my praises because that's what mothers do. At least, that's what mothers do when they're not fretting about widowhood and the doomed state of their finances. Once they are widows, and once they are broke, and once they are left alone with a newborn, they no longer sing the praises of their almost grown sons. Instead, they say the following: "You realize, don't you, that you're going to have to get a job and support us?"

This is what she wanted to tell me the whole time. If only she'd come right out and said it, I wouldn't have wasted weeks in bed dreaming about Paris, of carefree days drawing from ancient marble statues and evenings carousing at bohemian haunts. I went to bed that night deeply troubled. The truth is, up until that point of my life my mother hadn't played too large a role. Yes, it was to her that I owed my French blood, which allowed me to claim a direct lineage to the French realist painters, but it was my father who had always dominated my existence, constantly yelling at me for speaking out of turn, for slouching, or for smiling when there was nothing to smile about. My mother seemed, well, just there. A nice soothing presence who occasionally told me to wash behind my ears. She was loving, I won't take that away from her, but I see now that very early on she must have sensed the genius in me, and by genius, I mean all that conventional society rejects and scorns and repeatedly tries to squelch in its mediocrity. But my mother tried her best, she did. I see her now, her youthful face, her patient dark eyes, only a slightly furrowed brow betraying her concern as she watches me at my drawing table writing out longhand descriptions of sketches that I hoped to get around to sketching. If only I weren't such a methodical planner. If only I were drawing circles for heads and sticks for limbs, she might not have worried so. But now that my father was gone and forever silent, my mother's presence grew infinitely louder, and not just because she was saddled with my newborn sister who cried incessantly, but because after having acquiesced throughout my entire childhood, disappointed that I was not like other boys, she was now asking the impossible: that I be like other men. A job?

The entire night I tossed and turned and worried about my mother's request. Was it a request? Or was it a demand? Was she telling me to get a job *or else?* Or else what? What would happen if I didn't get a job? Suddenly, an image flashed in my mind. I saw my mother holding Lourdes, luggage in tow, leaving our home for the last time. Where were they headed? I could only picture some tuberculosis-ridden boarding house in the city. There they would wait for a handout, charity, any sign of hope. It broke my heart to imagine this: my sister born into a world of uncertainty, my mother suffering this cruel fate. When I saw the situation so clearly, my decision was obvious. I was the one who could save them, shelter them from a life of hopelessness and destitution. The sweat off my back alone could be the difference in their lives. Another image came to me: I am wearing dirty, grease-covered overalls, I am absolutely drenched with sweat, I am more muscular than I ever thought possible, and I have a mustache. I am also wearing large rubber gloves. What job I'm performing, I have no idea, but this, *this* was the image of me as savior. The man who selflessly provides for his mother, for his newborn sister, for his family! I was so moved by this image of myself that I actually began to cry there in bed, tears of joy and pride, knowing what generosity of spirit I possessed.

But by the time I woke up the next morning, my family fealty had waned owing to one nagging question: why, after all these years, did my mother decide to have another child? How much easier and clearer the situation would be if there weren't an infant involved. My mother could support herself as a laundress or something, and I could work if I chose to. But the presence of a baby only increased the weight of my responsibility. So over breakfast I asked my mother, "Why is there a baby involved after so many years without one?"

"Involved?" my mother said, setting down her tea saucer. She sighed and turned toward me.

"Yes, why, after all these years, did you decide to have another child? You know it places a huge burden on me now."

"I didn't *choose* to have a baby," she said. "It just happens. Your father, as you know, had his peculiarities. He swore off all intimacy for years and then suddenly he couldn't be satisfied—"

I cut her off immediately. "Please spare me," I said. "What I meant—" I stopped. I didn't know what I meant. Did I wish Lourdes gone from this earth? No, of course not. Did I wish for a sibling closer to my age to help shoulder this burden? I hadn't considered that. Did I merely wish to know how it was that two children of the same mother and father were born seventeen years apart? Maybe. My mother, however, seemed to intuit exactly where I was going with all this.

She asked, "Do you feel incapable of work?"

There it was again, the tone in her voice. Was it exasperation? Here I was only ten months out of high school and I had enough developmental sketches to keep me busy for a lifetime in the studio. How had she not noticed the hours I spent alone in my room, never straying far from my drawing table? Did she not see my hands covered in silver lead? I was the most meticulous and diligent of workers, and the thought of that not being recognized filled me with rage and I cried out, "Art is work! Don't you understand that?" And I rose from the dining table and went to my room and slammed the door.

I didn't leave for four days. I sat at my drawing table and began a new process. Instead of developmental sketches I began writing exhaustive outlines for proposed sketches, or "preparatory notes" as I came to call them—*a tall sinewy man bathed in morning sunlight wrestles a bull dark as the night, dust envelops them both; a frail child with hollow eyes and a button nose, an expression of hopelessness on his face, looks up at a dark and mysterious tree whose brittle branches have begun to perilously sway; a mother and child shrouded in black stand above a shallow grave, its simple cross casts a shadow a hundred feet long.* Meals were left at my door with a knock and entreaties to come out, which I ignored. In the meantime, the creditors' henchmen came and removed every article from the house. They left my bedroom, I assume according to my mother's wishes, for last. Then, without knocking, without even so much as acknowledging my presence, two men with matching handlebar mustaches entered the room. First, they took my bed. Then they took my drawing table. Then they took the chair I so often sat in. Thankfully, they left me my developmental sketches, my extensive preparatory notes, my pencils and erasers, and they even overlooked the several strips of canvas on which I had yet to paint. They also left me the excised pages of *The Great Book of French Painting* along with what remained of the book. When they were gone, I felt utterly and completely alone in the world. That was when I felt my mother's hand on my back and the soft cooing of my baby sister pressed against her chest.

"I'm sorry, my son," she said.

I turned toward her. She looked worn and tired.

"We have to leave now," she said. "The house is no longer ours."

"Where are we going to go?" I asked.

"I found a room for us in a boarding house in Albuquerque," she said. "Just until we can get on our feet." Then she added. "Until I can figure out a way of making ends meet..."

I understood this to mean that I was no longer required to get a job. And so I learned it was possible to feel both wretched and relieved at the same time.[5]

---

5. So our narrator's affluence, whether real or perceived, was short-lived. But he remains an artist, less a rarity in Chicano literature than one might think. In fact, much of the canon consists of coming-of-age novels about children becoming the writer who now tells the story at hand. There's nothing wrong with this, literature is replete with bildungsroman, but a variation of my earlier question about working-class subjects could also be posed: what does it mean when a literature cannot escape the preternaturally wise and sensitive children found in its coming-of-age stories?

I felt utterly and completely alone in the world.

PART I

The Unsung Prophet—Enrique Hurtado

CHAPTER ONE

Albuquerque revealed so much to me. For one, I learned that there was a war going on. Of course, I had heard talk of a war, but among citizens of my small mountain community, for whom Santa Fe might as well have been another country, a war on the other side of the world didn't enter into everyday conversation. But the city was different. Every newspaper headline mentioned the war, every diner conversation alluded to the Western Front or the Pacific, and every kid my age was talking about enlisting. I didn't talk much with kids my age, but I often overheard them, and it seemed all they wanted to do was go kill some Jap or Kraut. For my part, I learned that I was medically exempt from the draft, which my mother said I owed to the physician's diagnosis.

Albuquerque also taught me that there were two kinds of people: there were decent white people, and then there were Spics, Beaners, Greasers, and Mexicans. And despite my privileged upbringing and venerable lineage, my cultivated tastes in clothing, not to mention my traceable French blood, I belonged exclusively to the latter grouping. No one cared to listen to my explanations that I was a descendant of one of our state's oldest families and that my great-grandfather had been a soldier in Emperor Maximilian's army.[6] In certain stores and restaurants, I was

6. Lorraine writes: "You know what gets me? This dude's insistence on his French heritage and his claim to be from one of New Mexico's oldest families, read: Spanish. I've been to Santa Fe, and everyone I met claimed to be from one of New Mexico's oldest families. If you ask me, this is typical of certain Mexican Americans who think that if they're just white enough or European enough that Anglo society will accept them just as they did the Irish and the Italians. I say be

treated suspiciously. Fair enough, I had no money with which to buy anything. But the look in their eyes! As if I wished to rob them of house and home and merchandise. Then there was the occasion I wasn't allowed entry into the community swimming pool. I was told that I had to come back on Tuesday. "Why on Tuesday?" I asked, my towel in hand along with the current issue of *Boy's Life*, whose feature article—"So You Think You're an Artist?"—I was anxious to read. "Because Tuesday is for Mexicans," the attendant said, pointing to a sign that read, "No blacks, no Indians, no Mexicans, and no dogs."

"On Tuesday?" I repeated. I was at a loss for words.

"That's right," he said. "Because Tuesday come closing time is when we drain out the water."

I walked away dejected. I understood their motivation to start fresh, especially when I considered the general standard of cleanliness of the snot-nosed, grubby-cheeked children in our three-story boarding house. What bothered me was my inclusion in that bunch. I wasn't blind to our fall from grace. As much as I wished to view my destitution in romantic terms—Courbet painting landscapes from a jail cell, Van Gogh painting in an attic in Auvers-sur-Oise, Gauguin holed up in some remote jungle enclave—I understood that if you're surrounded by the downtrodden, chances are you're either among them, not too far behind, or lost.

We lived in a cramped one-bedroom apartment. To my dismay, we shared a toilet with everyone on our floor. To my further dismay, there was no shower or bathtub, so we could only wash in a basin. We had a stove, but my mother was a lousy cook, so we paid the neighbor to make us meals. The bedroom was mine;

---

brown and proud." I'm not disagreeing with Lorraine's characterization, but we must strive to approach a work of art on its own terms, not the ones we choose. My students often make the mistake of viewing (and often condemning) characters through their own specific lens, which is only natural. It's also partly the fault of their instructors, and I include myself. In fact, I seek to teach Chicanx novels that students can relate to, that allow them to flesh out their own moral and political values; otherwise, how else to get them to talk? The easiest way to get students to engage a text is to place primacy on how they *feel*. What might be positive, validating pedagogy, however, doesn't always foster the best literary analysis; it can also hamper our literary canon.

the living room belonged to my mother and sister. I insisted on calling my room a "studio" until I realized that it upset my mother. She wouldn't tell me why. She just moaned and whimpered pitifully. Finally, I demanded that she tell me what was wrong. She first asked that I perform my breathing exercises, and then she explained, her voice trembling, that I had "yet to make one picture." When I showed her my copious preparatory notes for future drawings and paintings, she burst into tears.

"What are those?" she cried. "I don't understand what those are! You say you're an artist, but you're always writing notes. Those are just words! I don't understand. If you're an artist you should draw!"

"I'm a meticulous planner," I explained.

My answer didn't reassure her. She continued crying until she fell asleep. I found that her work cleaning houses all day left her exhausted and emotional.

The boarding house was a former hotel. It was full of workmen, who, when they weren't working, seemed always to be drinking, singing, and playing the guitar. Most were single and lived piled on top of one another. Some were married, and their wives stayed at home and took care of their throngs of children, whose sole source of entertainment was chasing each other up and down the stairs for hours on end. There was also a schoolteacher, a typist, a nurse, and a tailor and his family. Per agreement with my mother, I watched my baby sister during the day. It wasn't so hard. Lourdes was even-tempered, and it was easy enough to ask one of my many neighbors to watch her in exchange for running an errand. Usually, the errand gave me an excuse to leave my studio for a few hours, my sketchbook in hand. I took in the sights, the people, the cars, the buildings, the commotion of a big city, and at times I was able to convince myself that I was strolling around the Latin Quarter of Paris.

It was on one of these prolonged "errands" that I ran into a boy my age who lived in our building. He was selling newspapers, calling out some headline relating, as always, to the war. I had noticed beforehand that he was scrubbed clean and well dressed. He wore brown slacks, a white silk shirt, a black vest, and a

We lived in a cramped one-bedroom apartment.

I insisted on calling my room a "studio" until

I realized that it upset my mother.

"You've yet to make one picture," she said.

fedora pulled stylishly low over his left eye. I also noticed that he, like me, was not a soldier. After I had crisscrossed his corner several times, he was the first to break the ice.

"You live in my building, right?" he asked.

"That's right," I said. "I've noticed you, too."

He flushed red when I said this and smiled awkwardly. I clarified that I was impressed with his attention to contemporary fashion; it was obvious that he appreciated the finer things in life. He quickly explained that his father was a tailor and that he and his siblings' entire wardrobe consisted of clothes that clients had failed to pick up. "Meaning," he said, "I can't really take credit for the fashion choices of others, just their neglect." I acknowledged his self-effacing wit.

Then he asked me, "You eighteen yet?"

"Yes," I said, knowing the inevitable next question.

"How come you're not enlisted?"

I was about to invent an excuse detailing my avowed pacifism when I looked into his eyes—dark, sensitive eyes that were partially obscured by the longest eyelashes I'd ever seen on a boy. He looked almost feminine. I knew in that split second that he wouldn't judge me for my medical waiver. He wouldn't think me less of a man. Plus, he wasn't enlisted either. So I told him the truth.

"They say I'm not well," I said.

I braced myself for the follow-up question. I didn't want to tell anybody about my epileptic attack or supposed nervous disorder. I refused to accept it myself. But he didn't ask, and I knew then that we were destined for friendship. Instead, he answered, "They say the same thing about me."

"What's wrong with you?" I asked.

He hesitated. "A bad heart," he said. He seemed on the verge of tears. "They said I displayed *undesirable proclivities*—"

"No, no, don't listen to them," I said. I placed my hand on his shoulder. "Those medical examiners think they know everything, but they don't." He smiled in return, and I smiled, too, and he said, "Thank you for that," and I replied, "No, thank you, my friend," and when I said those words I realized that I'd never had a friend before, and that there was something truly wonderful about it, to feel understood, to exchange compliments, to say reassuring things to each other. It made me want to spend the rest of the day exchanging pleasantries, and I was about to compliment him on the tilt of his fedora hat, when he told me that he had to get back to work selling papers. I told him that I too had to get back to work, and I held up my sketchbook. "Drawings to do," I said, knowing that he would understand. He wouldn't ask, "*Oh*, and what kind of work is that?" He wouldn't say, "*Oh*, wouldn't we all want to have fun doodling in a little book." His response, when it came, was one I had been desperate to hear my entire life.

"I knew you were an artist," he said, smiling. Then he bent down and picked up a stack of papers and began hollering something about the Germans and the Western Front.

His name was Enrique Hurtado. He would become my most loyal friend. He was the first to believe in my greatness as an artist, so much so that he began documenting our time together, diligently noting all that I said and observed, and doing so without ever having seen one of my drawings. He *just knew*, he told me. It was immensely flattering to have a champion. He listened intently to my stories about Courbet, asking questions I didn't have the answers to, but which I answered anyway. He nodded understandingly whenever I bounced some new theory off him, theories on painting mostly. I can see him now, his head continually nodding, his small grunts of "uh hum" so reassuring, always prodding me forward. And forward I went, talking endlessly, unable to stop as long as Enrique was there listening.

Life was much better with someone to pal around with. We had fun together. I felt more at ease with a sympathetic soul at my side. I even felt brave, courageous. I realized that one man alone was merely that, a man alone, but two men, well, that was the start of something great. I began to see Enrique as Courbet must have seen Baudelaire, a fellow genius, and I encouraged Enrique to see himself as

I was able to convince myself that I was strolling

around the Latin Quarter of Paris.

I knew that he wouldn't judge me for my medical waiver.
He wouldn't think me less of a man. Plus, he wasn't enlisted either.

He would become my most loyal friend.

such: as Baudelaire in Albuquerque, in 1943. When he asked what Baudelaire was like and I didn't exactly know, I told him that Baudelaire believed in Courbet's genius and wrote about it so that the world would know too. Also, I told him, Baudelaire was a poet. But all I really knew about Baudelaire was that Courbet included him in *The Painter's Studio,* which of all Courbet's paintings captured my fancy most vividly, because I could only imagine what it'd be like to have a studio so large, so full of compliant models—fellow artists, workmen, children, dogs—even a naked woman watching over my shoulder as I painted a landscape. In *The Great Book of French Painting,* the caption made special note that Baudelaire was the figure in the far right corner reading a book. I showed it to Enrique. I told him, "That is you." He seemed pleased. He even wrote down Baudelaire's name on a notecard. "I'd like to find his poems," he said, smiling from ear to ear.

With Enrique at my side I ceased to bemoan my father's untimely and ghastly death and our resulting circumstances. In fact, that's what I called them, merely our "resulting circumstances," which sounded better than "our wretched fate," which was my mother's description. I realized that if my father hadn't been murdered[7] I would have remained, for who knows how many more years, in the

---

7. Ernie writes: "My grandmother always said that her first husband died of 'natural causes.' When I asked her once what was a natural death for a man in his forties, she replied that in the mountains people used to die all the time and at all ages and that it was just a part of life, which is to say, natural." I welcome Ernie's attempts to set the record straight, but for me, how the father died, natural or otherwise—and this may sound cynical—is less significant than the power of personal narrative, the stories we tell ourselves to make sense of our lives, compounded by an artist's penchant for self-mythology. An art historian colleague once told me that he prefers to write about subjects who are dead because then they can't interfere, obfuscate, or obstruct his research. In other words, they can't counter *his* version of their lives. Are we not all sums of multiple, competing narratives? In my humble opinion, Chicano literature has always been too chained to "realism," that is, a depiction of reality without stylization. Sure, there are examples of magic and myth—Anaya's *Bless Me, Última,* Ron Arias's *The Road to Tamazunchale,* or Ana Castillo's *So Far from God*—but I'm talking more about the narration, the way the story is told. It's one thing to read about an eccentric character, it's an entirely different experience to read an idiosyncratic voice.

backwater village of my childhood. Already I had started to erase the place from my mind. There was nothing memorable about it. Pine trees, beautiful sunsets, sufficient for a few landscape paintings. Other than that, a smattering of adobe shacks, horses and burros, poor workmen, poor laborers, poor merchants. Even Courbet moved beyond his beloved stone breakers and corn sifters. The city was good for me. It was a new world. It fed my creative soul. It gave me a friend. Even my epileptic attack became a distant memory.

I felt that I was finally inching closer to starting my first paintings, but just as I was about to unroll my sacred strips of canvas, my mother learned that I wasn't, in fact, watching my baby sister while she was away at work. One of the neighbors had finally complained to her that she couldn't afford the extra mouth. "What extra mouth?" my mother asked. "Why, your baby girl!" the neighbor told her. I can only imagine my mother's shock, but by the time she brought it to my attention she was eerily calm. She sat there quietly, rocking Lourdes in her arms, never once looking in my direction. She was very pale. I could see her jaw clenched tight. She looked haggard and drained. She looked old. At that moment, it entered my mind that maybe my mother hated me, that my very presence made her want to scream. What I learned the following morning confirmed my suspicions. I awoke to an empty apartment. She'd left a note on her pillow. It read: "I've taken your sister with me. If you don't contribute to this family, you are just another mouth to feed. You are grown now. You need to find your own place. I'm sorry, but you've given me no other option. I love you, Your Mother."

I could've accepted that. I didn't expect my mother to understand that what an artist doesn't contribute to his family he contributes to humanity. I could've even accepted her embrace of tough love—"push him out of the nest," I imagined one of her workmates telling her. But what I couldn't accept was the note that I found crumpled in the waste bin. To this day I wish she had ripped it to shreds, poured water over it, and beat it back into pulp, because what she wrote, all these years later, still creates an empty feeling in the pit of my stomach. No, that is an understatement. It creates inside me the deepest, darkest, most profound hole, an abyss where nothing matters, where life has lost all meaning. It read: "My son, I believe, like your father, that you need to be admitted to an asylum. Your father should have been protected from himself. I blame myself for his death. I should've committed him when I had the chance, but I couldn't bear the thought of him being dragged away against his will. Nor can I bear the thought of that happening to you, but I know that your delusions will only get worse with time. It starts with believing you're a shoemaker or an artist, and then one day, just like your father, it will be too late . . ." The letter broke off there.

I understood that I had neglected the care of my sister. I know that for non-creative people it is often hard to understand the ebbs and flows of the artistic process, to comprehend that quantity should never be mistaken for quality. So I hadn't made much progress on the painting side of things. So I'm a lousy care-taker of children. Did that mean I was delusional? Did that mean I deserved to be put away? I knew my mother had written the letter in a fragile state. She had only recently lost her husband; she was tired and overworked; she had spent years living in comfort and now spent her days maintaining the comfort of others; and her son, admittedly, had let her down. But wasn't her response just a little extreme?

I hastily returned the note to the waste bin, as if by returning it to its original state I could pretend that I hadn't read its contents, which had shaken me to my very core. But that was when I found in the waste bin another crumpled piece of paper. I smoothed it out. Yet another piece of writing she should've ripped to shreds or burned in the stove or swallowed whole or at the very least kept in her own pocket rather than risk the chance that I might see it. It was a questionnaire from a mental institute called Dry River Sanitarium. In response to "Examples of Subject's Delusional State," my mother refused to acknowledge that my father's workers had murdered him; even worse, she cited as "delusional" my insistence on referring to my "restrainers" as "attackers." Unsurprisingly, she also exposed her ignorance of my creative process. "Though he insists that he is an artist," she wrote, "the only time he actually does anything resembling drawing is when he squints his eyes and moves his head as if he's mentally tracing what he's viewing." The most alarming part was yet to come. Referring to me, she wrote:

> At night he paces back and forth for hours at a time. When I ask him what he is doing, he doesn't hear me or pretends not to hear me. Rather, he holds whispered conversations with a man named Gustavo Corbay, always saying both names, and sometimes other men are there too, Coro or Millay, I think they're called, and he tells them, sometimes angrily, that he no longer wants to paint country landscapes or the French working class. Sometimes he adopts another voice, the voice of one of these men, and he says that he can paint whatever he wants as long as it's the truth. These conversations with himself go on for hours and never rise above a whisper.[8]

I was sure that my mother had gone crazy. Wouldn't I know if I held nocturnal conversations pacing back and forth like a madman? Wouldn't I wake up tired, my voice hoarse? Wouldn't I have some recollection of these long discourses with

---

8. Lorraine writes: "I don't know how historically relevant this is, but I think the mother should be commended for taking proactive measures regarding her son's mental health. Maybe he's schizo-phrenic, maybe he just needs to talk through his trauma. All she's doing is seeking help. Nothing wrong with that. I'd take this whole family to my therapist if I could, Ernie included." Lorraine is, of course, speaking in a clinical sense, but I'm reminded of Alicia Gaspar de Alba's essay on cultural schizophrenia, specifically how it relates to our narrator's obsession (can it be called anything else?) with Courbet and the French realist painters. Could this be a result, as Lorraine argued earlier, of internalized Eurocentrism, or could he simply admire the artists' work? Is that "simply" even possible for artists of color? The Chicano Cultural Renaissance, which developed in tandem with the Chicano Movement, emerged as a backlash against the suffocating effects of whiteness and a dominant North American culture that sought to stamp out difference. For Chicanos, then, a cultural ethos emerged articulating the idea that everything brown was good and everything white was bad, but that dichotomy always oversimplified the true position of Chicanx artists: do they work within, outside, or against Western tradition? To paraphrase the great Benjamin Alire Sáenz, the ever-present dilemma of the Chicanx artist is to not know what tradition they rightfully inherit.

What she wrote, all these years later...

creates inside of me the deepest, darkest, most profound

hole,

an abyss where nothing matters

where life has lost all meaning.

To this day I wish she had ripped it to shreds.

such artistic luminaries? I didn't believe it for one second, but there it was on the application, stated as indisputable fact. Now on top of everything I had to worry that my mother had already taken steps to commit me. What if this was just a draft and she had already sent off the polished final? What if, unable to bear watching me being dragged away, she had told the doctors at Dry River Sanitarium exactly where I was going to be (at the boarding house) and what time I would surely be there (asleep until at least midmorning)? Maybe orderlies in white suits were on their way now, straitjacket in hand. I would have to depart. I looked around frantically. What would I need? Immediately I found my sketchbook, my strips of canvas, and my drawing utensils, and I ran out the door, only to remember that I would be lost without *The Great Book of French Painting*. I returned to collect the pages I'd pinned to the wall, as well as the remnants of the book itself.

I bounded down the stairs, not even stopping to pick up a dropped pencil. Both hands full, I banged on Enrique's door with my forehead. His mother opened the door just wide enough so that I could see an eyeball and her nostrils. "What do you want? Enrique's not here," she said suspiciously. That was when I remembered it was Wednesday and Enrique would be selling newspapers on the corner of Tenth and Union. I ran down the steps, out the door, and turned one last time in case orderlies in white outfits were entering the building just as I was fleeing.

The second I saw Enrique, immaculately dressed as usual, his fedora pulled stylishly low over his left eye, I called out to him, "We need to go! We need to go now!" He stopped yelling out the headlines and turned in the direction of my voice. The expression on his face, the radiant happiness, his great joy at seeing me so unexpectedly, instantly reassured me that I was going to be okay. My mother no longer wanted me around, but someone did. My mother was ashamed of my singularity, but Enrique wasn't. His devotion was palpable.

"Where are we going?" he asked, his complicity assured.

I didn't know where we were going, I hadn't thought about it yet. But in that instant I had a revelation: Albuquerque was too small for us. It was a city, sure, but what we needed was something grander, some place where worlds converged, where ideas were exchanged, where history was written. It was so plain to me then. I don't know why I even had to think about it. Our destiny was before us.

"We're going to Paris!" I said.

"Paris?"

"Yes, Paris!"

To his credit, the smile did not leave Enrique's face—it was obvious he didn't want to quash my enthusiasm—but he was always of a more practical bent. All he said was, "Well, I have enough saved for the two of us to get to Los Angeles."

"But that's in the opposite direction of Paris!"

"We'll figure it out from there," he said, placing his hand on my shoulder and giving it a little squeeze.

I accepted that compromise. It was his money paying our way after all. I was ready to head directly to the bus station when Enrique asked me where my clothes were. I told him that all I needed was what I held in my hands. He glanced momentarily at the rolled strips of canvas, the sheets of paper, the remnants of my personal bible, *The Great Book of French Painting,* and my little box of drawing utensils, and he smiled. "You should really get some clothes. We'll be gone for a while."

"Forever!" I said. "We're gone forever."

"All the more reason why you need a change of clothes."

I explained somewhat incompletely that I couldn't return home because my mother had banished me. Enrique thought for a moment and then said that he had an idea. He would visit his father's tailor shop and rummage through the bin where his father kept miscellaneous articles of clothing. He would find a few outfits for me and then he would stop by his place to see if his mother wouldn't pack us a lunch. I worried that he would run into the orderlies, so I cautioned him about returning to the boarding house. "Maybe it's best to steer clear," I said. "There might be people looking for me." Enrique eyed me strangely, but then said, "I'll be on the lookout." He took off.

I waited for him there on the corner, looking around me, still expecting the orderlies from Dry River Sanitarium to be on my trail. Forty-five minutes passed, and just as I was sure that my pursuers had captured Enrique and were pressuring him into confessing my whereabouts, he appeared in the distance, saddled with two bags. He was also now wearing two fedoras, his black one and on top of that a gray fedora with a burgundy band. I rushed to greet him. He handed me one of the bags and said, "This is full of clothes. I grabbed what was there." I peeked inside and to my delight found articles made of the finest fabric: a few slacks, a white linen dress shirt, a heavier cotton dress shirt, and a pair of suspenders.

"What's with the two hats?" I asked.

Enrique smiled and took off the second fedora. "This," he said. "Is yours. I found it lying about. No one will miss it."

He placed it on my head. I was instantly overcome by a head-to-toe tingling sensation. I felt as if all my life I had been tottering back and forth and that this hat, this wonderful short-brimmed 100 percent wool fedora, had restored my balance. I felt complete, I felt whole. I felt as if all my life had led to this point—this escape, this departure—and all of my life following would flow from it.

We took the Greyhound to Los Angeles. I talked almost the entire way. Several passengers in front of us and behind asked if I would be quiet so that they could sleep, but I couldn't stop talking as long as Enrique urged me to continue. He listened, hanging on to every word, every "um," every brief dramatic pause. I told him about my mother's letters, how delusional she was about my delusions, how I almost wished for a confrontation, measuring my perspective with hers, and that I would only refuse such a confrontation because the world had proven itself over and over again unkind to free thinkers and visionaries. As I spoke, Enrique recorded what I was saying in his notebook, emitting encouraging "uh hum"s every few seconds, as if he knew exactly my meaning. I believe he did. I had convinced him that this trip was going to be something special, and we agreed that every aspect needed to be recorded.

Eventually the passenger in front of us, a fat man with a pinkish bald head who had covered his face with a handkerchief and kept banging the back of his head against his chair and groaning, turned around and said, "Boy, it's dark out and we all trying to sleep. Will you please shut yer mouth?"

I don't think I even paused. I was in the middle of a point and I could see that Enrique was really enthusiastic about that point and I didn't want him to miss a word, or to lose my train of thought. I continued talking even as the man in front of us stood up from his chair and raised his Coca-Cola bottle over me. Then he began to pour it. I can still hear the slow *glug* as, unable to move, I felt the liquid soak my shirt and pants.

"That'll teach you to quit yer blabbing, you goddamn Spic," the man said.

It did. I was quiet for a long time after that. Soon the stickiness seeped through both my shirt and pants and plastered the small hairs of my body to my skin. Every time I breathed I felt as though I were ripping them out one by one. All I wanted was for the bus ride to be over so that I could wash myself. I was glad that Enrique had brought me a change of clothes. Being dirty made me anxious, wearing soiled clothing even more so. I felt suffocated, and I began to breathe more heavily, gasping for air. I remembered the breathing exercises the doctor had taught me, and I started inhaling, deeply, deeply, deeply, forgetting, of course, that the small hairs of my body coated with syrup were clinging to my skin. I whimpered in agony. I don't think Enrique noticed my pain. If he had he surely would've waited to pose the following question:

"What are we going to do when we get there?" he asked quietly.

Until then I hadn't thought about what we would do once we arrived. Of course, I imagined myself painting in a studio with plenty of northern light, working from a live model, maybe even a beautiful aspiring actress, while Enrique sold newspapers on a street corner. But that would happen eventually, once we were settled in. But upon immediate arrival? I had no idea, and apparently neither did Enrique because his next question was to ask if I had any money.

"Not a penny," I said.

"That'll teach you to quit yer blabbing, you goddamn Spic."

The envisioned palm trees.

The envisioned flophouse full of colorful characters.

That was when he informed me that all the money he had left wouldn't buy us two plates of ham 'n' eggs. When I asked him what we were going to do for lodging, he shrugged. Then he said, "It doesn't even matter. It's California. We can sleep on the beach if we need to!" His voice rose, but he quickly quieted when the passenger in front of us stirred. He began again, "And tomorrow we'll go looking for work. I'm sure there will be plenty, and we'll have enough for a room in a flophouse, at least." Then he added another "at least!" for emphasis, as if I hadn't heard him the first time. This is what "at least" looked like to me: a rat-infested hotel frequented by prostitutes, pickpockets, and drug users where we would survive like rats on little more than stale bread, moldy cheese, and water. And here I had thought Enrique was the practical one.

In addition to the stickiness, I was now drenched in sweat. So focused on my discomfort, I hadn't even registered Enrique's comment about the two of us getting jobs. Slowly, it dawned on me, and I waged battle trying to push it from my mind. If the first three-quarters of the trip flew by, the last quarter dragged on interminably. I thought we would never get off that bus. I thought I would endure this nightmare forever, drenched in both sweat and Coca-Cola, with the canvases that were my destiny to paint forever moving farther from my reach. "Can't an artist just paint?" I cried. I looked at Enrique. He had fallen asleep. I waited for the man in front to turn around and pour yet another bottle of soda pop over me. He was asleep too. I waited for someone else to shush me. But all was quiet. Maybe I hadn't said it. Maybe it was just a silent cry in the night.

Out the pitch-black window I saw a promising glow in the distance. I woke up Enrique. "Look! We're getting close." He rose from his seat and peered out into the night. His expression was not very enthusiastic. All we could see at that moment were the waves of lights, the infinite sparkling expanse that was to be our new home, at least until we made our way to Paris. He muttered something about thinking there would be more beaches and palm trees. He probably realized that finding a quirky little flophouse filled with colorful characters was not going to be easy in such a megalopolis. Just moments before I had been the one fearful of ending up in a rat-infested hovel surviving on a pauper's diet, but now I was the optimist. "Don't worry," I reassured him.

When we arrived at the bus station, I jumped up from my seat and headed straight for the exit, pushing ahead of the other passengers, ignoring their complaints and insults. I leapt from the top step, and as soon as my feet hit the ground, I inhaled deeply as though with this new breath I was accepting my future. All I got was a gust of diesel exhaust. Should that have been sufficient forewarning? Should I have jumped back on that bus and headed to its next stop, in Bakersfield? I ignored the omen and continued forward through the crowd, both our bags slung over my shoulders, my gray fedora with burgundy band tilted just to the left. I was a man on a mission, and Enrique struggled to catch up.

Once we were inside the brightly lit bus station, I saw more clearly the fear in Enrique's face. He looked helpless. I understood that I needed to lead the way. I decided the first order of business was to freshen up and change my clothes. We found the bathroom, and I quickly stripped down to my briefs. In the mirror, I noticed that Enrique blanched white and turned away. "What's wrong?" I asked him. "You feeling queasy?"

"Yeah, a little," he said in a high-pitched voice. "But I'm fine."

"Well, hurry up my friend and pick me out an outfit. I gotta get this darn soda pop off me."

While he rummaged through the bag, I took my shirtsleeve and placed it underneath the faucet. There was a bar of soap on the counter, and I rubbed it against the sleeve until I formed a decent lather. Then I began to clean myself, wiping first my stomach, and then between my thighs, until I had to lower my underwear a little and vigorously wipe all areas where that syrupy mixture had worked its way. Then I removed my underwear, folded them nicely, and asked Enrique to hand me a fresh pair. Instead, he leaned forward and placed his hands on his knees. I rushed over to him. "You all right?"

"Yes," he said. "I just need some fresh air."

Just then a man opened the restroom door, saw me naked consulting my sick friend, and quickly closed it, but not before saying, "Goddamn fairies!"

I worried that someone else would come barging in, so I quickly reached into the bag of clothes and pulled out the first articles I could find: a pair of finely knit wool slacks, a stiff-collared dress shirt, and suspenders. I dressed quickly, feeling the clothes were a little large for my narrow frame, but at that moment more focused on reviving Enrique and getting out of the bathroom before our presence was again misinterpreted. Enrique slowly raised himself, holding onto the sink for support, but he was still unstable. "I'm really dizzy," he said. I draped the bags over one shoulder and then placed his arm around my neck. "I have you," I told him, and I felt a surge of pride. There I was, out in the big wide world bearing the burden of weaker souls. I was in charge of this adventure. Without doubting my purpose, I carried Enrique out of the bus station and into the Los Angeles night.

I don't know what direction we went. I don't know how long I carried him. I just know that the farther we walked, the more dangerous and sinister the city became. We passed whores, hardened thugs, hustlers, and men with vacuous faces. We passed drunks and beggars. I heard threats, promises of payback and vengeance. Even the buildings were ominous, dark and crumbling. I kept hearing windows break, followed by screams. Finally, a thief stopped us and demanded all of our money. I explained that we had none, and then I asked if he would be so kind as to recommend a cheap flophouse full of colorful characters. He told me to go screw myself and proceeded to take our luggage. I offered little resistance. I was almost relieved. Between carrying Enrique and the two bags, I was on the verge of passing out.

The thief disappeared into the night. The commotion seemed to do Enrique some good because instantly he became more alert and was able to walk on his own. "Where are we?" he asked. I told him I had absolutely no idea. "Where are we going?" he asked. I again told him that I had absolutely no idea. "Then why are we here?" he cried, his voice rising. Again, I couldn't provide a reason. "I just

I don't know what direction we went.

I don't know how long I carried him.

I just know that the farther we walked,

the more dangerous

and sinister the city became.

kept walking in hopes of finding something promising," I said. We looked around. We were anywhere but promising. I rushed to shift the blame: "If you hadn't practically passed out in the bathroom, we could've planned things better."

"So you walk off into the middle of nowhere," Enrique cried shrilly. I had never seen him so upset. "We should've at least asked someone if they knew of any flophouses!"

"I did!" I said.

"And what did they say?"

"Well—" I was on the defensive. I tried to shift the blame: "These clothes you picked out, they're all much too large!"

He snapped back, "If it weren't for those clothes you'd still be covered in soda pop!"

I was about to critique the loose cut of my shirt when Enrique began to sob. We were having our first fight. We were tired. Both of us had experienced severe nausea or outright fainting spells. We had no money, and we had just been robbed. Our predicament had quickly grown nightmarish. And it only got worse when Enrique asked me, "Where—where—where are your drawings?" It was then that I remembered that the bags contained more than just ill-fitting clothes. My developmental sketches, my years of diligent preparatory notes, my strips of canvas, my drawing utensils, everything that mattered in my life, everything was gone. Even *The Great Book of French Painting* was in the hands of that thief. I suddenly experienced physical pain, a sharp jolt from my shoulder to my chest and then up to my neck just behind my ear, knowing that that man, that despicable thief, was in possession of years of work. And not only that, he wouldn't even know the true value of the treasure he'd plundered.

"He's probably already dumped it in some alleyway trash bin. Let's go!" I clutched Enrique's arms and gave him an abrupt shake. "We have to get that bag back!" And I took off running in the direction I thought the thief had gone.

What happened next remains muddled. For my part, my panic and fear, my realization that our great escape was getting off to a horrible start, the sinking feeling that years of developmental groundwork would never see the light of true creation, the awareness that even if all worked out and I found the bag and my work was safely inside, we would still be without money, without a flophouse to rest our head, and our only hope of survival would be to find paying jobs, a burden that was the very reason for our departure in the first place, all came over me at once, midstride, and contributed to my breakdown. I was running very fast, but I lost my sense of direction, my sense of up and down, in other words, my balance. The gray fedora with burgundy band had lost its power over me. I was stumbling around, calling out who knows what nonsense. I had no idea where Enrique was. I was lost in the great horrible expanse of the Los Angeles night, overwhelmed by my own failed ambitions, and that was when I felt a great urge to swallow my tongue and my eyes rolled back in my head.

The last words I heard were, "Is that boy sauced?" Followed by, "No, that's not sauced, that's—"

Then I remember seeing white. I felt hands on me. I saw more white. Just a jumble of white.

According to Enrique, who had struggled to keep up with my manic pace, he rounded the corner and witnessed the following: six sailors on top of me, two holding my legs, two holding my arms and shoulders, and another trying to keep my head from spinning around like a top. The other was trying to pull my tongue out of my throat so that I wouldn't choke to death. When he had succeeded, I began yelping savage wails that pained Enrique to hear. It also brought the attention of a group of young men from down the street. These young men were not sailors. They were dressed in oversized suits with shiny pants that ballooned outward. They wore suspenders. They wore fedoras with feathers in the band. They sported gold jewelry. Minus the feather in my hat and the gold jewelry, they were dressed just like me. What had been an accident on Enrique's part—not checking to see if the clothes he removed from his father's tailor bin were of the appropriate size—identified me as a fellow zoot suiter. I didn't know anything about zoot suiters, but what I knew wasn't important. What mattered was that a group of zoot suiters saw a gang of sailors apparently beating one of their own in the middle of the street.[9]

So the zoot suiters came to my aid, fending off the sailors who had done the exact same thing, come to my aid. They attacked each other, becoming a tangle of limbs, breaking noses and jaws and splitting open flesh. Blood splattered onto pristinely starched drapes and dress whites. And there I was, unconscious, splayed out in the middle of it. When the melee ended, sirens approaching in the distance, zoot suiters and sailors gathered their broken brethren off the concrete, and Enrique emerged from the shadows to drag me to safety in a concealed alleyway. He then went in courageous pursuit of our bags. He was sure the thief had looked inside, found nothing of interest, and discarded them. Enrique scoured every dumpster and alley in a mile radius, stealthily avoiding the dangers lurking on every corner, then found his way back to me like Theseus in the maze of the Minotaur.

When I awoke the next morning, Enrique was at my side, my bag in his arms. It was a miracle. It was a testament to his loyalty, his faith and determination. He wouldn't allow my work to be lost to history. He was still distraught, however.

"But you found the bags," I reminded him.

He was inconsolable. He started to cry, tears hanging onto his impossibly long eyelashes.

9. Lorraine writes: "I told Ernie that given the year, 1943, it's possible his uncle was collateral damage in the so-called Zoot Suit Riots, when American servicemen prowled the streets looking to beat up and strip naked any brown or black youth wearing oversized clothing." I'll add that the zoot suiters, or the pachucos as they called themselves, would later become important symbols for the Chicano Movement. They were the first generation to rebel—in language, attitude, and style—against both American and Mexican culture. Like later Chicano activists, pachucos embraced their differences, their hybridity, and proudly laid claim to an outsider status. Chicano artists made them the heroes of their work; José Montoya's poem "El Louie" and Luis Valdez's play and film Zoot Suit are the foremost examples. Our narrator—mistaken for a zoot suiter but dreaming of art school in Paris—seems like an outsider of an entirely different ilk.

They attacked each other, becoming a tangle of limbs, breaking noses

and jaws and splitting open flesh.

Blood splattered onto pristinely starched drapes   and dress whites.

And there I was, unconscious, splayed

out in the middle of it.

"What's wrong?" I implored. "What's wrong?"

He looked at me. "They took all your drawings!" he cried. "I looked through the bags and all I found were a few very lightly drawn sketches and pages and pages of notes. All of your drawings. Gone. The thief *did* know what treasures he had stolen!"

I grimaced, unable to confess to the one person who believed unflaggingly in my genius that everything was still there, that not one page of my oeuvre had been touched. I told him it was okay, everything was okay; I told him I would draw even better works—"Much better works," I said—and I vowed to myself right then and there to begin immediately on my masterpieces. No more developmental sketches, no more preparatory notes, no more methodical planning. I needed to draw, I needed to paint. For me, the whole experience was an artistic break-through. As for Los Angeles, though we'd been there less than twelve hours, I knew that we had to get out of that godforsaken city.

CHAPTER TWO

I knew now that I was unwell. I couldn't deny it. Yes, I still blamed my father's workers, the physician, and my mother. But that only answered the *why*. It didn't change the facts: I was prone to horrendous brawl-provoking breakdowns. Our plans for Paris would have to be put on hold. Enrique's mother wired us money and we left Los Angeles, heading in the direction from which we had come. We admitted to ourselves that we hadn't planned well. You can't just head out into the unknown and expect to land in conditions ripe for creative activity. We would return to Albuquerque, where we at least knew of half a dozen flophouses, and Enrique would find a job while I spent the time necessary to rest and recuperate. Once I was well again, and once we had saved enough money for more than just two bus tickets, we would set off again, avoiding Los Angeles—its thieves and its tensions between sailors and zoot suiters—at all costs.

We found a room together on Union, not too far from our former boarding house. It was a small but sunny place on the second floor of a mechanic's garage. We had our own little kitchen, and although we had to share the bathroom with two other boarders, not to mention the mechanics with their forever grease-covered hands, it was just across the hall, so we could at least pretend it was ours. Enrique managed to convince his parents to loan him some money, but it would cover us for only a few months, so very quickly he returned to his job selling newspapers. He also picked up an evening gig as a busboy. As far as my own work, I finally decided that what I needed was structure; more to the point, I needed someone watching over me, demanding I produce results. I was too much of a perfectionist. I could plan for years and keep putting off my master-pieces. I'd completed pages and pages of preparatory notes, but when it came to posterity, I needed something more tangible. I imagined History to be very unfair to those who don't produce, so I began looking for a master to study under, a relentless ruler-wielding disciplinarian who would demand results of the highest caliber.

Early in my convalescence, while lying in bed thumbing through a hobby magazine that Enrique had snatched from a barbershop, I came across an adver-tisement for the Salon des Refusés Art Academy in Brooklyn, New York, which offered instruction by mail. In twenty courses, through one-on-one correspon-dence, I could study with a master draftsman. The advertisement seemed to call out to me. Next to a painting palette and a happy-faced mime wearing a beret were the words, "Why travel to Paris when Paris can travel to you? Study now with one of the great draftsmen of our time!" I was already filling out the appli-cation form when I saw the master's name. If I hadn't been convinced already, I was when I learned that I would be studying with Jean-Jacques Millet, described as "the grandson of one of France's greatest artists."

On the application form, it asked that along with a letter of introduction I also include an example of my "best" work for purposes of evaluation. The letter of introduction was the easy part. I described my influences, my love of Courbet, Corot, and Jean-Jacques's grandfather, Jean-François Millet. I also made clear that as soon as I saved enough, I was heading to France to make my mark on the Salon. But when it came time to submit my "best" work, I was confronted with the dilemma that had plagued me since the carefree days on my father's estate in La Trampa. Without compliant models to draw from, models who understood the importance of standing still, how could I draw the unflinching realistic portraits that so appealed to me? Later that night, I mentioned this to Enrique after he arrived home from the restaurant, and he said, "Well, you could always draw me. I am a laborer, too, you know." I noticed a slight tremor in his voice, as if he feared I would reject his offer out of hand.

I examined my friend's fine features, his smooth olive skin, his eyelashes like a woman's, and I was about to say something dismissive, such as that Courbet painted laborers with faces chiseled out of stone and hands as rough as sandpaper, but decided that beggars could not be choosers. Courbet, after all, had painted his friend Baudelaire, and wasn't Enrique the closest I had to a like-minded poetic soul? We decided that it would be best if he posed just as Baudelaire did in *The Painter's Studio,* reading a book, leaning against a table, a glint of light touching his forehead. We had to adjust our lone bald light bulb, and our rickety aluminum folding table wasn't the same as the elegant wooden one in the painting, but we made do. Once Enrique was situated, and the light just right, I picked up my sketchbook and my favorite pencil and began a rough outline. I stopped, however, when I noticed Enrique trying his darndest to mask a smile.

"Why are you smiling?" I asked.

Without looking up, Enrique said, "I'm just so happy to be the subject of one of *your* drawings."

I was flattered, but suddenly Enrique had upped the stakes. This couldn't just be any sketch. Not only did this work need to impress the grandson of Jean-François Millet, it also had to be my first masterpiece. Why? Because Enrique had, in his way, decreed it. And if it was going to be my first masterpiece, then I needed to plan it out just right. A masterpiece never happens by accident. So I turned over the page and began taking notes. I addressed issues of line, of composition, of shadow and light. I referenced other great works that set important precedent, and I described the contours of Enrique's pose in case we needed to return to it for subsequent studies. I recorded shadows, highlights, and midtones; I noted proportion. I even attempted, for the first time, to describe the unknowable, the expressive depths of my friend's gaze. After a while, Enrique said, "It looks like you're writing rather than sketching."

"Yes!" I said. "I've decided I need to be more methodical about this work. It's going to be something special—it really is. First a few notes, then I move on to drawing."

We decided that it would be best if he posed just as Baudelaire did in "The Painter's Studio," reading a book, leaning against a table, a glint of light touching his forehead.

Enrique flushed red. He had arrived home exhausted and drained, maybe even a little saddened. Working two jobs was taking its toll, and he seemed daunted by the idea of taking on a third in order to pay for my mail correspondence course at the Salon des Refusés Art Academy. But now his spirits had enlivened, his energy returned, and I knew he could hold Baudelaire's pose for half the night. I don't know how long he ended up posing, maybe three, four hours at most. By then I had ten pages of notes, and I had convinced myself that not only would Millet's grandson accept me into his art correspondence course, he would pave my way to Paris. I was also convinced that my preparatory notes alone would convince Millet's grandson of my unequivocal talent. Why was I going to risk placing a precious drawing in the care of the United States Postal Service? Better to send my detailed description, which I could copy out longhand.

I didn't allow Enrique to see the result of his modeling session. Nor did I tell him that in all those hours I hadn't transitioned from note taking to drawing. He wouldn't have understood. He was so happy to be my subject, my model, I knew that he would only be disappointed, and it wasn't yet the moment for discouragement. He needed to continue working those two, soon to be three, jobs, I needed to continue on the road back to wellness, and Jean-Jacques Millet needed to recognize my genius.

I sent off my application packet and waited desperately for a response. In small print I read that I would receive a letter notifying me of my status within four to six weeks. But I needed an answer immediately. After three days waiting at the window, watching countless cars come and go from the mechanic's garage, I started hounding our mailman, convinced that he had lost it, convinced that he had damaged it, convinced that he had never even sent my application just to spite me. After a week, I was once again bedridden, and Enrique had to apply cold compresses to my forehead. After two weeks, I couldn't muster the energy to get out of bed. After three weeks, I had a mild fit and temporarily lost use of my left hand. In my darkest moments, I feared that Millet's grandson would consider my application so absurd, so beneath him, that he would return the first installment of my tuition and say that my work wasn't even worth evaluating. At slightly better but still dark moments, I worried that Monsieur Millet would accept me as his student just for my money and then, using the same judgment as my mother, consider my notes useless slop and ignore me altogether. I realized then how maddening was the artist's need for acceptance, and this a mere correspondence course! Finally, after four weeks, my health regressing to frightening levels, I received my reply.

Bonjour Monsieur Artiste,

Thank you for your interest in the Salon des Refusés Art Academy *By Mail*. We received your application packet, as well as the first installment of your tuition. You are officially a student in Jean-Jacques Millet's Art Academy *By Mail!* Félicitations!

Monsieur Millet has asked me to share some words with you. He says that you have "an excellent eye for observation." However, he continues, "This is a drawing course, not a course in prose." Nevertheless, he would like me to add that he (Monsieur Millet) "felt as if he was in the room with you as you were recording the young man with "eyelashes like the wingspan of a great heron." In conclusion, he strongly recommends that you, in his exact words, "take those details and express them, express them, express them!" Lastly, he wanted me to tell you, in case it wasn't clear, by express, he means *draw*.

Bonheur!
Stuart Gall
Assistant to Monsieur Millet

P.S. Monsieur Millet would also like to remind you that at the moment Paris is occupied by the Nazis. He recommends that you sit tight there in New Mexico.

My initial reaction was euphoria. The grandson of Millet had recognized the value of my notes. He knew that I was a true observer. He just wanted me to draw, which was reasonable, this being a drawing course. I also wanted to draw, and as soon as I was done planning, I would. In fact, when Enrique arrived home that night, I intended to pick up my favorite pencil and begin the process of converting my precisely observed notes into visual form. But then I noticed that enclosed with the letter was another sheet of paper. It read: "First Assignment: Sketch a crowded café."

My euphoria quickly disappeared. I had finally found a model who could stand still for hours and hours, and I was ready to use that model, use him until he could stand no more, and now Monsieur Millet was asking that I discard those preparations and draw a crowded café full of bustle and movement. How was I going to get all those people to sit still? From *The Great Book of French Painting,* I knew that café scenes were popular among French painters, but they also lived in a society that appreciated great art and the artists that produced it, so those café dwellers wouldn't have thought twice about holding a pose, say, a tea cup to their lips, for several hours while the great Manet or Degas or Renoir did what they did best. I broke into a cold sweat just imagining myself trying to convince the ruffians at the billiard hall down the street to sit still for a few moments longer.

When Enrique came home, his clothes covered in soot, his eyes half open, his long eyelashes casting a shadow halfway down his cheek, his shoulders stooped with exhaustion, I shared the news of my long-awaited acceptance and then explained my dilemma. Champion of mine that he was, he didn't even flinch. He murmured, "You can do it, you can draw anything," and then he fell fast asleep. I waited for more, I even tried to wake him, but he was gone to the world. It was his third job sorting coal at a factory (which factory, I never knew) that really put him over the edge. He just didn't have the build for that kind of heavy labor. Nevertheless, with Enrique's vote of confidence, I decided that I would at least attempt a sketch of a crowded café.

The following morning, I took my sketchbook, my favorite pencil, and a protractor to measure angles down to the billiard hall. On our street, it was the closest we had to a café. I also knew that Van Gogh's *Night Café* prominently featured a billiard table; so if Monsieur Millet was pedantic about what qualified as a café and what didn't, I could at least establish a worthy precedent. On entering the billiard hall, a cavernous place filled with rustic wooden tables and overhead lamps made of stained glass, I was disappointed to find only one patron, who was drunk. His head of matted black hair was resting on the table and his swollen eyes were half open, and he was mumbling what sounded like a song about his mother and a life spent dealing in contraband. It was only eleven-thirty, and I figured things really didn't get going until late afternoon, but this gave me an idea. What if I drew the customers as they trickled in, one or two at a time, rather than wait until I had to wrap my creative powers around a large, rowdy crowd? I started drawing the drunk first, who was actually compliant. He remained in the exact same position, only his lips slowly moving as he mumbled the lyrics over and over. I had lightly sketched in the torso when the bartender asked me what I wanted to drink.

"Oh, nothing," I responded, not taking my eyes off my subject.

"Well, you gotta have something. Customers only."

I still hadn't turned away from the drunk, so afraid that he would move and I would lose the pose forever. I continued, lightly rendering important aspects of directions and weight, resisting the urge to take notes.

Lost in concentration, I wasn't aware that the bartender had left his station behind the counter and walked over to my table near the entrance. I was startled when a voice right next to me said, "What are you doing? Are you drawing?"

I looked up. The bartender was a burly, bald man with a thick mustache, his sleeves rolled up to reveal large forearms covered in a mass of black hair. "I'm sketching," I said.

"It doesn't look like there's anything on the page," the bartender said.

I looked back at my drawing. My mark was indeed hesitant, as I was just getting started. An expert would call it a delicate line. "Well, I'm lightly sketching to get everything in and make sure it's precise," I said.

The bartender squinted his eyes and drew closer. "But I can't see a thing," he said.

"Well, it's dark in here," I said.

"Bring it over to the light. I want to see it."

I hesitated. I looked over at the drunk, who had passed out completely and was no longer mumbling to himself. He wasn't going anywhere. His pose was safe.

"Look, I'll let you hang around," the bartender said, his voice oddly imploring. "I just want to see your drawing. I've never met a real artist before."

I couldn't deny his request now. I rose from the table and brought my sketchbook over to the counter where sunlight streamed in through a window. It was only then that I realized just how lightly I had been sketching. I could barely make out what was there. The bartender kept squinting and drawing closer to the sketchbook, so that his nose almost touched the page. "I can't see barely nothing," he said.

"Well, you're blocking the light," I said.

He backed away and continued squinting his eyes. "I think I see it now," he said. "Oh, yes, now I see it. Definitely."

I explained that I had only just started the drawing and that I would slowly darken it. He nodded his head, still appearing unconvinced.

"So that's how an artist starts a drawing . . . very lightly. I always wondered."

"Yes," I said.

He seemed pleased. To my surprise, he told me that I could sit there all day if I wanted, and then he repeated what he'd said before about never having met a real artist. He asked me if I had studied picture making. I told him that I had attended the Salon des Refusés Art Academy. The name seemed to impress him greatly. I returned to my table, took up my pencil, and resumed the drawing of the drunk at the other end of the billiard hall. Shortly after, the bartender brought over a pint of beer and set it in front of me, careful to wipe away the moisture from the bottom of the frosted glass. "This is on the house. Let me know if you need anything else, Señor Artista!"

I was honored. I took a sip of the beer and was instantly overcome by a feeling of elation. I had really misjudged billiard halls! Soon after, two more patrons came in. I overheard the bartender explaining to them that I was an artist and that I would be sketching them. They looked in my direction and nodded unsurely, but when beers were brought to their table they lifted their glasses and said "Salud!" I set down my pencil and enthusiastically returned the toast. One of the men called out, "Let us know if we need to sit still." I smiled and gave him a nod of assurance. Slowly, the billiard hall filled with patrons—workmen in soiled clothing, store clerks, cowboys, a half-breed Indian who brought his own cue stick—and upon each entry the bartender would make special note of my presence. More beers were purchased for me. More toasts. More questions of "Am I sitting right enough for you?" Even the billiard games seemed to progress at a snail's pace, as each player asked, "Can I take my turn or do you need me to stay like this?" Unfortunately, the more I felt appreciated, the more pressure I felt to rise to the occasion. No longer could this be a simple sketch. No longer could this be viewed merely as Assignment #1 for Master Millet. This had to be a work worthy of their expectations. I was wrong about billiard hall ruffians. They didn't scorn artists; they'd just never met one. And here I was, an artist among them, and they were more than willing to assist my efforts. I couldn't let them down.

Of course, when faced with immense pressure, when the expectations were so great, it was all too easy to fall back on comfortable habits. In other words, I ignored Master Millet's directives and abandoned my delicate sketching for preparatory notes. When I'd had too many beers to count and could barely read my own writing, I decided that it was time to leave. I had enough for fifty paintings of billiard hall society. But I worried that the men surrounding me, who had all been so supportive of my work thus far, wouldn't understand that I had not, in fact, been drawing them; that instead I had been taking notes for *future* drawings and paintings of them. I imagined confused faces, furrowed brows, looks of disappointment mingled with disgust. I wondered if they would feel betrayed. Even worse, would they demand that I pay for all the beers to which I had been treated? I wasn't about to find out.

When I was confident that all eyes were off me, I rose from my table, carefully closed my sketchbook, placed my pencil in my ear and my protractor in my pocket, and scooted along the wall toward the exit, stopping momentarily when someone appeared to glance in my direction. I believe I would've escaped if it weren't for the drunk who raised his head from the table and yelled, "Hey, are you done drawing me?" Turns out he'd been posing all along! Well, a roomful of heads turned in my direction, and they beckoned me forward and demanded, ever so politely and cheerfully, to see the results of their collective modeling session. "Don't be shy!" I heard. Someone else called out, "Look how humble he is." To my right I heard a man tell his friend, "It *has* to be good, all that time he's put into it."

My back against the wall, figuratively and literally, I clutched the sketchbook to my chest and tried to think of an excuse.

"Let us see, Señor Artista," the bartender pleaded, waving me forward. He came closer and placed his hairy arm around my neck as if we were old friends, and pulled me toward the center of the room. I heard seconds and thirds, "Let us see!"

I quickly imagined the horror of the situation if I revealed my preparatory notes when what they wanted was unflinching, steely-eyed realism. I wanted that as well. But process is process, and my preparatory notes always came first.

An idea came to me. "An artist doesn't show his work until it is completely done!" I blurted out.

My adamancy momentarily stunned them. The men around me, many of them holding both billiard sticks and beer steins, stared at me blankly, not quite understanding or not wishing to understand, such was their desire to see my depiction of them. The center of the room was heavy with smoke, body odor, and the smell of cheap beer. I felt weak and alone in the world.

I think they would've allowed me to leave, satisfied with my rationale, if it weren't for one fat walrus of a man, who said, "How do we know you weren't sitting over there making funny pictures of us?"

Two weasel-faced men at his side seconded his charge. I looked at them in disbelief. In truth, the trio would have been impossible not to caricature, but I pleaded my innocence: "I wasn't! Why would I do that?" I said. "I'm an artist, not a cartoonist!"

The bartender, who had seen my lightly rendered version of the drunk, came to my rescue. "No, he doesn't draw funny pictures! I saw his work already. Well, I saw it before he really got started, but it's good! He studied at an art school in France, isn't that right?"

I nodded my head. "Yes," I said. "The Salon des Refusés Art Academy."

I saw a few nods of approval as if they were familiar with the institution. The walrus was unconvinced. "Let us have a look, just a little part," he said.

Someone else agreed. "Just a little part!" I heard seconds and thirds.

I decided to indulge them a little. "It's true," I said, "that an artist should never show his work until it is absolutely done—it's bad luck otherwise!—but how about I describe to you what I've drawn so far. Would that convince you?"

The walrus turned to the weasel at his left and then the weasel to his right, and the three men nodded their assent.

I asked that no one stand behind me. To make sure, I leaned against a billiard table. When I was certain that the contents of my sketchbook were safely concealed, I began to read from my notes, uncertainly at first but quickly gathering steam as I fell into the rhythm of my own words. What's incredible is that the previously jovial, boisterous men, three and four beers in, if not many more, visibly quieted. It wasn't just the silence of the room—you could actually hear a fly buzzing against the window and the low whir of an electric icebox—it was the visible calm that descended on each and every one of their faces. They truly believed I was describing a detailed drawing of them, their friends, their fellow patrons, and the room in which we were all gathered . . . the grain of a beer-stained tabletop, the wafting haze of smoke, the golden light glancing off a forehead, a receding hairline, a cowlick, an uneven part, the bunched wrinkles of a silk shirt, the crosshatched weave of a leather belt, the number of folds in a short man's linen pants, a perfect crease in another's khakis, shoes with round laces, leather boots covered in a film of fine dust.

The more I became aware of my audience's rapt attention, the louder my voice rose, until I felt like god decreeing that the world be as I saw it. My description moved around the room, from left to right, starting with the drunk. I described their faces, the broad bridge of a nose, nostrils the shape of a pinto bean, untrimmed nose hairs, an eyebrow with a scar through the middle, brown eyes speckled with green, black piercing eyes, the sharp plane of a cheekbone, sunken eyes, a pronounced chin, wide jowls, a pockmark, a mole, a stray mustache hair, chapped lips, skin the color of red earth, ruddy skin, wrinkled skin. I described the room's minutest details, the reflection of a ball formation in a man's glasses, the crisscrossing shadows on the splintered wood-paneled floor, the downy texture of green felt, the eight ball's crosslike highlight, a hint of white chalk on a black fedora, two-toned shoes, an untied shoelace, a silver timepiece. I described it all, the shadows, the highlights, the midtones, thick lines giving way to thin ones, the prominent details supported by the insignificant, more details than they could ever process, but they tried. They tried hard. Even though I was describing *them*, in the billiard hall that we still occupied, my description seemed to transport my subjects so that they were imagining men in a billiard hall thousands of miles away.

When I finished there was silence. I waited for their reaction. I looked at the walrus and his two weasel friends. I turned to the bartender. They all had the same look on their face, and if I may interpret their expression, it said: "We would really like to see this drawing, but we are content not to see the drawing, because we understand it is bad luck to see an artist's creation before it is finished, but we are still happy to know that such a drawing exists." So surprised by the effect my description had on the crowd, I actually thought of giving in and showing them the drawing. I had to remind myself that there was no drawing to show.

The silence was broken by the fat walrus, who said, "Well, when you're finished, when you're completely done and it's no longer bad luck to show others, I'd like to buy it." Then he turned to the rest of the room and challenged them, "I'll match any man's price!"

The bartender responded, "No, we'll all buy it together, and we'll put it up on the wall. That's what we'll do. It's of all of us, so we should all be able to enjoy it!"

They truly believed I was describing a detailed drawing
of them, their friends, their fellow patrons, and the
room in which we were all gathered.

The more I became aware of my audience's rapt attention,
the louder my voice rose, until I felt like a god decreeing
that the world be as I saw it.

Several other men voiced their agreement.

The walrus recognized the value of the proposition and agreed. The weasels quickly approved as well. The room broke into a lively discussion, and before I could say anything to discourage such talk, they had all agreed to chip in five dollars each. There were at least twenty-five men in the room. Times five that would be one hundred and twenty-five dollars. Would I agree to that price? Dumbstruck, unable to imagine such a quantity of money, I agreed, once again forgetting that I had no drawing to sell them. I began worrying that my execution of said drawing would not compare to the description I had so confidently read aloud. But before I could refuse they took up a collection and paid me half up front. In my hand was placed a half-year's rent. I was rich!

I left the billiard hall that late afternoon full of love for my fellow man. I even entertained ideas of rushing back inside and returning their hard-earned money. I would tell them, "I create for you, not for personal gain!" I imagined myself reverently laying the drawing on the green cloth of a billiard table and walking away before their praise and gratitude could reach me. The idea brought tears to my eyes, tears of joy but also of sorrow because I only wished that I had a thousand drawings to give to men in every billiard hall in the world. My mix of joy and sorrow wore away, though, as I reminded myself once again that I had no drawing to speak of, and as successful as my preparatory notes were, notes were not drawings and a drawing is what they had paid for. As this reality set in, I felt weaker and weaker. The wad of money in my pocket seemed to get heavier with each step, until it felt as if I were carrying a sack of millstones. I barely made it home.

I didn't tell Enrique about the money or the commission. I was sure he would have some encouraging words for me and at that moment I didn't want encouragement. I wanted someone to tell me that I was a miserable excuse for an artist, an artist who wasn't even an artist, for how can I be an artist if I don't make art? I was a fake, a phony, even in a roomful of compliant models, kind and gracious men who were happy to hold a billiard stick in a shooting position for twenty minutes. Even then I was incapable of setting pencil to paper except to write preparatory notes. I was angry with myself and I wanted someone to be angry with me, disgusted, revolted by my presence. And that someone was not Enrique. He would come home drained, covered in soot, his back hunched, his poor delicate hands so stiff that he was unable to uncurl them, and I would know that he endured this exhaustion for me, sacrificing his every waking hour for his belief in my creative genius. So how could I ever expect him to suddenly berate me for the lowlife imposter that I was? It was then that I remembered that that was exactly why I had enrolled in the Salon des Refusés Art Academy. A stern lecture from Master Millet would surely jolt me into action.

So I sent him my preparatory notes of the billiard hall. No excuses, no apologies. He had asked me to *draw* and I had not. I deserved whatever punishment came my way. I was even willing to accept expulsion, if that was possible in a mail correspondence course.

A week later I received my response. It thrilled me as much as it confounded me. It was from Mr. Millet himself and read as follows:

Monsieur Artiste!

The other night after reviewing countless pages of ill proportioned, poorly rendered, amateur dribble, I opened your envelope and was pleasantly surprised to encounter your beautiful work of art. It singlehandedly restored my faith in drawing as an art form. Now, clearly, it isn't exactly a drawing. In fact, you disobeyed my request to draw (tisk, tisk!), but what you have described—this exquisite billiard hall—is a drawing and only a drawing and only ever will be a drawing even if it is only the suggestion of a drawing. Does a drawing only become a drawing once it is drawn? Is a drawn drawing still a drawing if it is never seen? To the former I say no. To the latter I say yes. So you describe first what you intend to draw. Fair enough. I recognize that as process. Michelangelo used to make a hundred sketches of a man's calf muscle before ultimately covering it with a robe. Then he would destroy the drawings by stomping on them in a mud pit. Does the fact that those drawings no longer exist mean that those drawings never existed? No, of course not. What I'm saying, Monsieur, is that I read your notes and saw the drawing that was to be. It was finished already! Carefully rendered, volume precisely modeled through light and shadow, details raw and inviting. I felt as if I was there in the billiard hall with you, having a draught! Now the question is, and as the grandson of Jean-François Millet I have to ask, are you able to execute your notes, and by execute, I mean, are you able to draw not write your every observation? If yes, then do so. If not, and something in the perfection of your laborious methodical process tells me that you have not been able to move beyond the developmental stage, then we must work on doing so. We must commence at once. These descriptions of drawings must become drawings! We will work on making this so. Are you ready for this challenge? I eagerly await your response. Enclosed pleased find your next assignment.

Sincerely,

—JJM

He spoke to me as no other person had before, with complete and utter understanding. Yes, Enrique would have nailed himself to a cross for me, such was his devotion, but how could he truly understand me if he didn't know my process? But Monsieur Millet knew; he intuited, he empathized. He saw that I had a gift, and he saw that I had trouble unleashing that gift. He was offering to help me unleash it. He would guide the way. My preparatory notes would soon become the masterpieces they were destined to be.

I sent Monsieur Millet an immediate reply. On the back of a postcard we had lying around, which featured an old adobe village, I wrote the following: "You're exactly right. I was beginning to lose hope. Your words have resurrected that hope. I am your humble and willing pupil. If I might add, the last true drawings I made were the result of a disastrous drawing lesson which led to my father's murder followed by an attempt on my own life. Perhaps we can start sorting that out. I sense a breakthrough just around the corner!"

When I think back to those optimistic words, I am reminded of just how dangerous and damaging hope can be. A breakthrough did happen, but not "just around the corner," unless you consider the phrase in generational terms. I was a young man when Mr. Millet and I embarked on overcoming my fear of setting pencil to paper, and I was still a young man when I finally did so. But it wasn't because of Mr. Millet. It was also five years later. Yes, five long years I studied under Mr. Millet, and for five long years we traded ideas on art and draftsmanship and, above all, on the merits of preparatory notes. Reflecting on our correspondence, it seems that at some point Mr. Millet merely settled for treating my preparatory notes as the drawings themselves. In fact, our discussion of actual drawings and supposed drawings and intended drawings became so muddled that I don't think either of us could've spotted a drawing if Michelangelo himself had taken one of his thousand actual drawings and shoved it in our faces.

I never got close to executing the billiard hall painting. I chose to live in fear, cautiously avoiding any workman I saw on the street. I was afraid I'd be dragged to the billiard hall and forced to pay back every dollar, which I kept untouched, sewed in my pants, in case that ever happened. Even with Enrique working like a dog, I felt that it wasn't my money to spend. Five years slipped away like this, five years of tuition payments and countless stamps, and I had nothing to show for it. My correspondence with Millet's grandson served only as a good cover when Enrique started to doubt that his round-the-clock sacrifice was paying off. "I'm tired," he would say. And I would merely point to Monsieur Millet's letter praising yet another finely rendered drawing, and say, "We're getting closer, Enrique. We can't stop now." Of course, supportive and devoted friend that he was, he couldn't help but wave the white flag of understanding.

Was I unfair to Enrique? Was his sacrifice of working three jobs that paid the rent, bought the food, covered my mail correspondence course as well as the occasional movie ticket greater than my sacrifice, that of peace of mind? Wasn't life easier working and getting paid? As opposed to working and *not* getting paid. And when I did work, it wasn't really considered work. Why?

Because it was unconventionally executed, and by that, I mean it was written rather than drawn. I don't know. I'm still conflicted. It's easier to side with Enrique, to see the world in black and white, good and evil, exploiter and exploited, but what about Devoted Friend & Creative Patron in league with Struggling Artist? Far more nuanced, but also closer to the truth. Thankfully, Enrique agreed with me. For the most part. He whimpered a lot, and was always trying unsuccessfully to massage his aching muscles, but he never, not once, asked to see a finished drawing. He didn't need proof. He simply believed. He worked and worked and encouraged me and even gave me updates on my mother and her growing family.

Yes, Enrique was in touch with my mother, or rather my mother was in touch with Enrique's mother who asked Enrique news of me so that she could report back to my mother. After she abandoned me or I left her, or she made it clear that I was to pack my bags and go, life improved significantly for her and my baby sister. She married a successful businessman named Francisco Buenrostro, and he adopted my sister Lourdes. Then he proceeded to impregnate my mother three more times in as many years. She was too old to be having so many babies, and through Enrique, who told his mother who told my mother, I let her know just that, and my mother replied, through the same channels, that her new happiness had restored her youth. It made me want to throw up.

Some nights, unable to sleep, I would speak to my father's memory and tell him that I would avenge his honor, but the truth is I didn't have anything against Mr. Buenrostro. If anything, I was thankful that he took my mother and sister off my hands. I wasn't ready to be a provider; Mr. Buenrostro clearly was. Also, for all I knew, he wasn't aware of my existence. Maybe if he knew I existed, he would embrace me with open arms and tell me I was the grown son he never had. In fact, I used to bounce this idea off Enrique, who would remain quiet and give no indication whether he agreed or not. He would just mumble, "Maybe so," but I could tell that there was more he wished to say. Eventually, I pressed him to confess his true thoughts.

"If you think your stepfather would embrace you with open arms," he said, "then why don't you ask him if he could give you some money? You know, to help with the rent, and then maybe I could work just the two jobs."

I'm not sure what the expression on my face betrayed, but as soon as he said it, he apologized. He told me it was a horrible idea and insensitive to suggest that I should solicit help from the new husband of the mother who'd abandoned me. But despite my initial disgust, I knew I had to go. Enrique had asked very little of me over the years. If he thought my stepfather would help us financially, then I had to at least ask. I wanted to make life easier for my devoted friend. An artist was supposed to struggle, but Enrique was merely an artist's best friend.[10] For him, I would take this first step toward reuniting with my family.

10. Lorraine writes: "I find it hard to believe that this was an exclusively platonic friendship. They lived together five years! Enrique may have believed in his friend's genius, but what's more believable: he worked three jobs to put food on the table for his homie or for his lover? I'm just saying." Lorraine's observation is interesting, but we can only speculate. In John Rechy's 1963 novel *City of Night*, about a half-Mexican gay hustler, there is no reading between the lines: gay sexuality is front and center. As a result, the novel was perceived to deal with non-Chicano themes and was left out of the Chicano canon. There has always been this factor in Chicano literature. Some themes count, some don't. Who decides? Chicano scholars and educators? Editorial boards of small Latino presses? Compilers of anthologies? Chicano readers? To what extent are the themes determined by the white literary establishment—the particular tastes of literary agents and editors at commercial publishers answering to the all-important market? There's no conspiracy here. My point is that our stories (those that get published, at least) are too often determined by factors outside the quality of the literature itself. In my experience, Chicano literature is expected to (1) teach outsiders about Chicanx/Latinx life, and (2) simultaneously reaffirm Chicanx/Latinx identity. Where does that leave our outliers and outcasts?

I knew I had to go.

Enrique had asked very little of me
over the years.

I wanted to make life easier for my devoted friend.

CHAPTER THREE

Enrique's mother gave Enrique my mother's new address. She now lived in a large white stucco home with a terracotta roof in the nice part of town. The quiet street was lined with trees and seemed devoid of dirt, which was the exact opposite of the dilapidated, dusty street I inhabited, always alive with workmen, screaming children, and the shouts of cart vendors. I imagined how much easier it would be to concentrate on my work on a street like this. I pictured a small bungalow studio in a shady backyard, nothing but peace and quiet, not a grease-covered mechanic in sight. I had to fight the urge to daydream about my mother bringing me ham sandwiches just like she used to. In this first encounter, I had to be tough, firm. I was asking for money, but I wasn't begging for reconciliation. She had to know that I had struggled these last five years, survived but not without difficulties. I hadn't bought a new shirt or pair of pants in all that time, mainly because Enrique swiped clothes from his father's tailor shop, but I had been deprived of one of life's supreme pleasures: entering a shop and purchasing something off the rack. My brown leather shoes were secondhand, and water seeped in through the soles. I wouldn't have traded my gray wool fedora with burgundy band for any other hat in the world, but that wasn't the point. The point was I lived in abject poverty while my mother lived the good life on the good side of Albuquerque, and somehow that just didn't seem fair. It's not what my father would've wanted.

I arrived at my mother's home and found above the door a ceramic tile sign with the words, "Welcome to the Buenrostros." Children's toys were scattered about the front yard, and I had to walk around a bright red wagon in the walkway. I felt a lump in my throat as I pictured my sister and half siblings being pulled around in this shiny red wagon, laughing with delight, while I awoke every morning to the sound of scattering cockroaches and bleating car horns. I wondered if I would recognize my sister. The last time I saw her she was a shapeless infant whom I blamed for driving a wedge between my mother and me. I wondered if I would see a familial resemblance in my half siblings. If so, would that warm my heart to them? I preferred to imagine them as spoiled brats, arrogant and mischievous.

Just as I was about to knock on the door, a woman who was not my mother walked outside. She was small and dark and wore all white. She was pushing a stroller made for three, and there they were, my half siblings, staring up at me with frightened eyes. I also startled the woman, for she yelped and pressed her hand to her heart. "Who are you?" she asked. I explained that I was looking for my mother, Señora Buenrostro. The woman's eyes grew wide before she poked her head back into the house and called out, "Hurry up, Lourdes!"

"My sister!" I told her.

"I didn't realize Señora Buenrostro's son was so grown up," she said.

"Oh, well, yes," I said, amazed that she knew I existed.

"Señora Buenrostro is not in right now—she's at the market. But shall I call Don Francisco?"

At that point, my little sister rushed to the door, wearing a bright yellow dress and shiny red sandals and carrying a small plastic purse over her shoulder. "I'm reeeeady," she said in a singsong voice. She wore sunglasses on top of her head, keeping her hair in place. She looked positively cosmopolitan, and for a six-year-old I was greatly impressed. She reminded me of myself as a child, always dapperly decked out and confident, secure of my place in the world. How my fortunes had changed since then, I thought, as I stood at the door like a hobo in tailored scraps, doubting my footing as an artist on the verge, and about to ask for money.

What made matters worse was that my little sister didn't even recognize me. I realize she was only an infant when we lived together, and even then I mainly gave her to the neighbors to watch; but still, the complete lack of recognition on her angelic face filled me with shame, knowing that in five short years I had become unrecognizable to my family.

I was ready to turn around and run back to my one-room hovel when I heard a deep friendly voice call out, "Now, don't leave without giving Papá a kiss! All of you, and that means you, Lourdes. I don't care how big you've gotten." A large man appeared in the doorway, his body shaped like a pear. He wasn't fat, but he had large womanly hips accentuated by brown wool slacks pulled well above his waist. His mustache was thin and groomed, as were his eyebrows, which looked almost unnatural. His hair was slicked back with plenty of pomade, except for a few stray curls. His large eyes were as friendly as his deep voice, and the second he saw me he broke into a wide smile that left me speechless.

"And who is this?" he asked in a goofy tone, directed more at his children than at the nanny or me. "He looks a bit lost, wouldn't you say, kids?" Then he added, "Can we help this young man find his way?"

"He probably wants money," my little sister said, her eyes narrowing. She crossed her arms as if to emphasize this assessment. Of all the people gathered in the doorway, Lourdes was the only one who should've known me and yet she was the wariest of my presence.

Finally, I found my voice. I introduced myself, explaining very quickly that I was the son of his wife, the brother of his adopted daughter, the half brother of his own children, and an artist. I thought that would be enough to assuage my little sister's suspicions. I thought she would come rushing into my arms. Instead, she put her hand on her hip and again narrowed her eyes as though full of suspicion. Then she said, "I told you he came for money."

This, a girl of six, and my own sister! Who had filled her head with such ideas? I could only assume my mother, and the thought made me want to flee. I wanted to run all the way home and wait for Enrique to arrive so that I could yell at him

"He probably wants money," my little sister said.

My sister.

Of all the people gathered in the doorway, Lourdes was the only one who should've known me and yet she was the wariest of my presence.

for his stupid idea. But then I realized that my sister was right—I had come to ask for money. My quarrel was with the tone of her voice. She, the little brat that had benefited from five years of Mr. Buenrostro's wealth,[11] was judging me for simply asking for my share. We were of the same flesh and blood. Why was she entitled to comfort and not me?

I ignored my sister's glare, which was easy enough because Mr. Buenrostro was all smiles and joy. His eyes widened, and a grin spread over his face that flipped the arc of his thin mustache.

"What a miracle!" he boomed. "Oh, if only your mother were here right now. To see her surprise. Children, this is your brother. He has returned to us!"

Flattered and overwhelmed by his obvious joy, I was also somewhat perplexed by his triumphant hailing of my so-called return. I guess it was true: I had *returned* after being kicked out, abandoned, banished under threat of institutionalization. But something in his voice told me that what he meant was, "Children, your brother left of his *own* accord and has *now* returned." It's a minor distinction, and my half siblings and the little snot that was my sister couldn't care less, but for me, it was important. Before I could quibble over the difference, Mr. Buenrostro

11. Ernie writes: "This is not an overstatement. My adoptive grandfather was indeed a successful businessman, and, unlike my mother's family, the Buenrostros had the documents to prove they were actual descendants of one of the original Hispano families of New Mexico." Perhaps it's not surprising that Ernie, an accountant, would be fixated on who is and who isn't actually wealthy in this story. As a scholar of Chicano literature, can I do anything but fixate on this story as it relates to my subject of expertise? I have a confession to make: I find Chicano literature as a whole wanting. It exasperates me. I want more from it. Despite my most generous intentions, I want every Chicano novel to be great; instead, I find only poignant passages. Back in late eighties, I dropped out of my English PhD program determined to write *the* great Chicano novel. I lived in my parents' basement and imagined myself either as the narrator from Dostoyevsky's *Notes from the Underground* or Ralph Ellison's *Invisible Man*. I failed in my endeavor and burned all my drafts. For one, I wanted my novel to be some version of another literature's masterpiece. Two, I aspired to write a masterpiece, not because of any burning creative drive, but because I felt the need to fill a gap in our literature. Again and again, the problem with Chicano literature is that its writers and its readers, myself included, demand it satisfy their own expectations.

stepped forward and embraced me. The strong smell of his cologne tickled my nose and made me lightheaded at the same time that it made me wish I had a bottle of my own.

Two of the babies began to cry.

Mr. Buenrostro let go and exclaimed, "The gardens will wait! We shall stay here until your mother returns."

Immediately my sister clenched her little fists into balls and stomped her foot. "But I've been waiting to go all morning! You said we were going to the gardens." And she stared at me with disgust as if for five years I had conspired to coincide my arrival with her morning jaunt. I tried to win her favor:

"Please, don't wait for me. I arrived unannounced. I can return another time."

"No, oh no, your brother has returned," Señor Buenrostro said, grinning, leaning down to Lourdes's eye level. Obviously, he saw my sister's attitude as a child's whim. The look on her face told me otherwise.

We sat in a large parlor with leather couches surrounding a wood-fired stove. Tapestries with Indian motifs hung on the walls. I wasted no time explaining my dire situation. I began by apologizing for my tattered clothes and beat-up shoes covered in automobile grease. "I live in a room above a mechanic's garage, that's why," I said. I saw Mr. Buenrostro's forehead crease in concern. "Oh my," he said.

"What's your job?" my sister asked. She was supposed to be playing with the other children, but she decided to stand at the front window and wait for my mother's arrival.

"My job?"

"Yes, do you have a job?" Her arms were still crossed and her eyes still narrowed, and I thought that she resembled my mother, which would make sense, it was her daughter after all. But what I mean is that she looked not six but forty.

"Well . . ." I looked to Mr. Buenrostro with his creased forehead and sympathetic eyes. I didn't want to lose that sympathy. "I sell newspapers," I heard myself say. His brow creased even tighter, as though trying to imagine a life lived hawking papers. I continued, unable to stop myself, "And I bus dishes at a restaurant." Mr. Buenrostro pursed his lips on hearing this and groaned, as though recalling his own days as a poor industrious young man. It was only natural that I continue. "I also . . . I work—I work at a coal factory."

Mr. Buenrostro grimaced as if it actually pained him to hear this news. My sister, on the other hand, knit her little brow and asked, "Why aren't you there now?"

"Where?" I said.

"At your jobs."

It was a logical question, and I had a logical answer.

"It happens that I've been fired, just yesterday."

"Fired!" Mr. Buenrostro exclaimed. "From which one?"

"From which one?" I repeated. I glanced in my sister's direction. I detected a twinkle in her eye as she awaited my answer. She had also decided to start hopping on one foot, as though playing an imaginary game of hopscotch.

"Well, from all three," I said.

"All three? Whatever could've happened?"

Before I could answer, my mother appeared in the entranceway. I didn't even hear the door open. I just looked up and there she was, my mother, radiant and youthful and more beautiful than I remembered. If one's health is any indicator of having made the right life decisions, then abandoning me to my fate and marrying Mr. Buenrostro had proven wise. The last time I saw my mother, she was pale and gaunt, her eyes lacked spirit, her hair was not exactly dirty but dull and limp, and if someone had told me that she was suffering from consumption I wouldn't have doubted that someone. But now . . . now! My God, she looked like she'd emerged from a department store catalog.

I looked at her, and she looked at me, her eyes wide, mouth slightly open, and I wondered whether I should mention what I had found in the garbage bin immediately or wait until after we said our hellos. I hadn't forgotten her crumpled letter or the application to Dry River Sanitarium. I hadn't forgotten her wish to commit me to a mental hospital, or her desire to hide me away while she escaped with my darling little sister to a life of bubble baths, sundresses, garden jaunts, and all the other trappings of bourgeois prosperity. But I was momentarily stunned, unable to speak, waiting for her to do what mothers do when they see their long-lost sons. Rush into my arms. Shriek with joy, then faint. Fall onto her knees and thank God. But the expression on her face I knew all too well. It said: "What are we going to do with you?" And she looked to Mr. Buenrostro with pleading eyes, as though begging his forgiveness for whatever might happen now. Then, adding insult to injury, my sister Lourdes blurted out, "He wants money." That was when my mother burst into uncontrollable sobs.

When she recovered, my mother tried to make amends for her breakdown, but not before Mr. Buenrostro himself tried to excuse it, exclaiming in his booming voice, "Oh, the emotion after all this time. The relief!" But all those gathered in the room knew that if there was any emotion in her sobbing, relief was small part of it. Nor was there much joy. Her healthy radiance was gone, and if that same someone had again appeared out of the woodwork and said she was dying of consumption, I would've found no cause to doubt it. She sat with me on the couch, sniffling, dabbing her eyes with a silk handkerchief, holding my hand, then gently stroking my forearm, attempting a motherly display of affection that felt forced and awkward, as if I were an armadillo or an opossum.

Mr. Buenrostro disappeared into the other room and returned holding glasses of lemonade. My sister remained at the window, occasionally twirling around so that her yellow dress twirled with her, a perfectly six-year-old activity, but then she would stop and say something sarcastic like, "He works at a coal factory, coal factory!" Then she would burst into giggles. I thought that already I might hate her. My mother looked into my eyes for a long time, as though she were trying to ascertain whether I was crazy or not. But then she surprised me. "It's so good to see you, my son. Why—why did you disappear?"

"Disappear?"

"Yes, why did you run off?"

"Run off?"

"Yes."

I thought she was joking—I really did. A cruel, sick joke and completely out of character, but what else could it be? Me, run off? Me, disappear?

"You abandoned me!" I said. "All because I wouldn't get a job and support you and my sister."

My mother's eyes widened, and she drew her hands away from mine and covered her mouth, as though aghast that I would have such thoughts.

"That's not true," she said. "I—I was upset. Changes had to be made. But when we returned to the apartment you had already left and taken all of your pictures and drawing utensils. When I asked around, I heard from Enrique's parents that you had left for Los Angeles—"

I tried to remember the chain of events. We did leave quickly, mainly because I worried that orderlies from Dry River Sanitarium were on their way to get me. I reminded her of her steps to commit me. "I'll have you know," I said through clenched teeth, "I saw the application to the sanitarium. Isn't it true that you wished to put me away?"

"Put you away? No, I couldn't bear it. But your condition had become worse, so yes, I did weigh the option, but in the end, I couldn't do it."

"My *condition?* What condition are you talking about? They don't just commit people because they'd prefer to paint rather than go out and get a lousy job!"

Mr. Buenrostro interrupted at this point. "And how is your painting going? I've heard great things."

I knew very well that he was just trying to change the subject, but for a brief second I imagined that Mr. Buenrostro, a successful businessman with infinite connections in high-up places, had some knowledge of the Salon des Refusés Art Academy and that perhaps Monsieur Millet himself had informed him of a "young, up-and-coming talent from Albuquerque, New Mexico." I even thought that maybe Mr. Buenrostro knew one of my patrons at the billiard hall and had somehow put two and two together and understood that I was the very artist that had brought a room full of ruffians to the edge of their stools, and then left them

My mother's eyes widened

and she drew her hands away

from mine and covered her mouth,

as though aghast I would

have such thoughts.

there. But I caught myself. I looked over at Mr. Buenrostro's kind, jovial face, and I realized that his "I've heard great things" was just something that people say. I wouldn't be baited by empty flattery.

"My time to paint has been limited owing to the fact that I've had to work three jobs," I said.

"Ah, yes, of course," he said.

I turned back to my mother. "I found your letter and the application in the trash bin and I read every word, and for five years I've been unable to forget, so hurtful was it. You wanted to hide me away! I didn't fit into the life you wanted. No son should have to endure what I've had to endure—"

I stopped because my mother began crying again. I saw it as admission of guilt, and I found satisfaction in this. She wouldn't admit to who had abandoned whom, but the letter and the application, she had written them, and I had found them, and there was no denying this. But then, shaking her head slowly from side to side, tears streaming down her now pallid face, she said, "I had already watched your father deteriorate . . ."

I couldn't take it anymore. I shot up from the couch. I thanked my mother for her time, then I turned to my sister and told her that she should treat her elders with more respect, to which she responded by twirling around and around and singing, "Can we go to the gardens now? Please, please, please?" Then I turned to Mr. Buenrostro and said, "You seem like a wonderful man. I thank you for the good care you have taken of my mother and my sister and my half siblings, whom I haven't had the pleasure of getting to know, but I really must be off—"

He cut me off abruptly. "Be quiet!" he shouted. I quieted immediately. He rose from his seat, clutching the back of the chair as though to balance his great height and unnaturally wide hips. "Now, come into the other room," he said. His voice had calmed, but his face was dead serious. Without another word, he turned and walked down the hallway. I felt I had no choice but to follow. I glanced in my mother's direction, and she peered up at me. She looked frightened. I turned to my sister, and even she had paused her twirling game to look at me with mouth agape. Only my half siblings in the other room playing with the nanny continued to babble and fuss.

I found Mr. Buenrostro in his office. While the rest of house was full of light and color and lots of lace curtains, his office was dark and windowless. It smelled like an ashtray. He turned on a lamp, and then struck a match to light a cigarette. He squinted his eyes and took a long drag. His lungs full of smoke, he asked, "Do you want one?" I felt I couldn't say no. I knew he would've thought less of me. So I took one from his little tin container, and he handed me the matchbox. I sat down in a leather armchair across from his desk. I broke two matches before I could light one, and then I couldn't keep the flame going long enough to light the cigarette. I had seen people perform this task a million times, but I never thought it would require so much coordination. Finally, Mr. Buenrostro said, "Stop it. Please, stop it."

I looked up at him, the cigarette still between my teeth. I thought of just pretending it was lit.

"Throw it away," he ordered as he nodded in the direction of the waste bin.

I threw it away.

He was studying me, his elbows on his desk, his hands held together in the shape of a steeple. I felt I had no choice but to study him as well. His sympathetic, kind expression was now a distant memory. We'd known each other less than an hour, and already I'd seen two distinct men. The happy-go-lucky accommodating Papá, and then this man before me: agitated, impatient, and all business. Even his thin little mustache, which before had so closely followed the contours of his smile, now looked like two exclamation points following the contours of his frown.

Finally, he spoke, "What is it that you want?"

"What I want?" I said.

"Yes, that's what I asked. What do you want?"

"I don't want anything. I came to see my mother, that's it, and suddenly she starts talking about my condition. She's probably told you all about my delusions. Well, I'll have you know I'm not crazy—"

"Stop it! I don't want to hear it. You have your version of events, she has hers. Fine. I don't care." He leaned back in his chair. "Your mother's nerves are fragile. When I first met her she was on the verge of a breakdown. She was like a broken little bird. But she grew stronger. Together we grew stronger. She brings me happiness, I bring her strength—"

"I'm thrilled that you have found marital bliss, but what—"

Mr. Buenrostro groaned loudly. It was clear he didn't like being interrupted. His voice rose over mine. "As her husband, my job in this world is to protect her, you understand? Protect her from those who may bring her harm, do you understand?"

"Yes."

He closed his eyes resignedly. "So I ask you. What is it that you want?"

It was clear what he was getting at. As her husband and guardian, it was his duty to protect her from harm, in this case, from me, and by repeatedly asking what it was that I wanted, he was essentially asking what I wanted in exchange for keeping as far away as possible. I couldn't believe these were the terms. Was I really such a threat? Was my very presence alone going to lead to my mother's deterioration? I replayed the last hour spent in the Buenrostro household. None of my actions seemed egregious. Why was he so prejudiced against me?

"What have I done to you to deserve this?" I asked, my voice quivering.

"Deserve what?" he said.

"To be treated like a bum off the street. I've been on my own all this time. I've made it by myself in this world, and I'll continue to make it by myself. I don't need anything from you or my mother."

"So why come? Why appear out of the blue?"

"She's my mother. My sister is my sister. Do I not have a right to see them?"

"Then why lie to me about your jobs?"

"Lie to you? I haven't lied to you?"

"You've never worked at a coal plant. I can tell by your hands, your finger-nails. If you worked at a coal plant, you certainly didn't touch one piece of coal. I don't want to hear any other lies from you, understand? I only want one thing: straight talk. You're a horrible liar, you know that? The minute you start to say something untrue, the corners of your mouth curl up, like you're telling a joke."

I didn't know this. I quickly tried to replay all the lies I'd told in my life but now with an odd, creepy grin on my face. It didn't make sense. Why would the corners of my mouth conspire against me? I decided to test it.

"I really do work at the coal plant. I don't care what you say. This morning in preparation for coming here, I scrubbed by hands and fingernails for hours."

"Nope!" Mr. Buenrostro exclaimed boisterously, clapping his hands together. His jovial self was returning. "Your mouth curled up. You're lying." He chuckled and shook his head, then sighed deeply. On a dime, his face turned serious. "Now, tell me what is it that you want."

I didn't know what to say. I felt stymied. I had no desire to go around lying to people. I couldn't even remember why it felt so important to lie to Mr. Buenrostro about my jobs in the first place. Then I remembered: my sister had asked what I did for a living. That question and all the judgment that came with it had struck a nerve. I decided to come clean.

"It's my friend Enrique who works at the coal plant," I said. "He's also the one who sells newspapers and washes dishes. He works around the clock in order to support us. He's killing himself because he believes in my talent as an artist. I keep hoping for a breakthrough, but . . . but . . . well, it hasn't happened, and I fear for his health—"

"So you have come for money?"

"I've come for help."

"Help in the form of money. It's okay, admit it. You're an artist. I know very well you can't eat your paintings. Have you tried selling them?"

I thought of the never completed billiard hall commission. "Once," I said, "but it didn't work out."

"How come?"

"How come? Well, I guess the conditions just haven't been right."

"What kind of conditions? Your living conditions?"

I thought about this for a moment. What conditions was I talking about? I had two routes to follow that wouldn't cause the corners of my mouth to curl upward: I could describe my inability to move beyond extensive preparatory notes, but I was sure Mr. Buenrostro wouldn't understand this. Or I could describe my poor working conditions. Feeling little choice, I chose the latter. I began describing the cramped, cluttered room above the mechanic's garage. I also added that I was crippled by my dependency on Enrique. "As long as he's killing himself in the service of my art, I feel too much pressure to produce something worthy of his sacrifice, and I just can't, it seems." I had never articulated this before, and I thought that maybe my mouth had formed into a smile, revealing my lie. But Mr. Buenrostro didn't protest. So it was true. The pressure was too great.

Mr. Buenrostro was quiet, and he stared somewhat absently at the ceiling. I tried unsuccessfully to surmise his thoughts. After a pause, he reached around himself and pulled from his back pocket a billfold. For a second, I thought I would have to suffer the indignity of Mr. Buenrostro handing me whatever cash he had left in his wallet and telling me to scram as though I were a street corner beggar. I would've taken it, but I would've hated him in addition to my sister. Instead, he pulled out what looked like a business card and said, "I have a place for you. A studio, maybe. It's not an artist studio, exactly, but it will work, I'm sure. Plenty of light, which I hear is important."

I hadn't expected this. I rose to the edge of my seat. "A studio?"

"A humble one," he responded.

I pictured a small house in the backyard, a miniature version of the main house, with white plaster walls and a red tile roof. I imagined a gigantic window with bright northern light flooding the room and bouncing off spotless floors. I already pictured myself wearing my artist's smock, wiping my hands clean of paint and linseed oil, and heading inside to join my mother, my sister Lourdes, my joyful half siblings, and my benefactor and patron, Mr. Buenrostro, for lunch or afternoon tea. I imagined that Mr. Buenrostro's influential friends would swing by the house *just to see* the artist at work. Maybe they would even purchase a painting or two. I couldn't stand the suspense. I wanted to see my studio right away. "Can we look at the backyard?" I asked, already rising from my seat.

"The backyard? Sure, but what for?"

"To see the studio," I said, hardly able to contain my excitement.

Mr. Buenrostro smiled, his groomed eyebrows rising either in confusion or amusement. Then he began laughing. "Oh, no, it's not in the backyard. No, not quite. Whatever led you to believe that?"

"Where is it then?"

"Here, take this number," he said, reaching across the desk to hand me the card he'd pulled from his wallet. "Call this man. Leyva. He works for me. Tell him you need a ride and where you need to be picked up. He'll take you to your studio. If you like it, it's yours."

"Mine?" I said. "How do you mean?"

"I mean yours. Yours to use. Yours to make that breakthrough."

It took me a moment to process this new reality. I was going to have a studio, my very own studio. I thought I'd died and gone to heaven. I reached across the table and held out my hand. He shook it, then attempted to draw his hand away, but I held on tightly. "I'll owe my future masterpieces to you," I said.

He chuckled good-naturedly.

Specializing in small metal parts, the TSSS factory rested on the far outskirts of Guadalupe, a town thirty-five miles from Albuquerque. The factory boomed during the war years, but had fallen on hard times once the war ended. When producing at maximum capacity, the factory had a labor force of fifteen hundred men and women. Situated miles from town, they all needed housing, which the workers themselves built down the road from the factory on a dirt lot.

The Painter's Studio

The grand bargain: I was going to have a studio, my very own.

The homes were built in a matter of days with whatever scraps of wood and aluminum they had around. The roofs were aluminum, the walls were aluminum, the doors were wood, the porches were wood. The windows were glass, of course, but if broken they were repaired with wood or aluminum, and most of them were broken. The homes were less than two feet apart, some closer. At the end of the workers' camp there was a slightly larger home—though shack is really the more appropriate word for all these structures—that stood on a cement foundation and so was taller than the rest. This house didn't have a porch, or steps. Those had crumbled away. In order to enter the front door you either had to bring your own stepladder, find some crates and create your own steps, or walk around on stilts. The driver, Mr. Leyva, informed me that this was my studio.

He had been dead silent from the moment he picked me up at the mechanic's garage until we showed up at the factory, but as soon as we entered the grounds he transformed into a tour guide, a role he filled rather naturally. He recounted the history of the factory—the good times, the bad times, and the current times, which were even worse than the bad times. He had been informed that I was an artist, and he asked what kind of pictures I painted. I told him I painted people. "What kind of people?" he wanted to know. "All kinds," I said, "stone breakers, grain reapers, gleaners, spinners, laundresses, nymphs." He looked confused. He turned toward the dilapidated structure.

"Well, this is the place. You gonna live here, too?"

I didn't answer him. I could only stare at the shack in disbelief. It leaned to the left, and the smaller shack next door leaned to the right, so that they looked like two old lovers ready to expire. *This* was where I was supposed to live and work and create masterpieces? I was speechless. My legs felt weak. The night before I had been so excited I could hardly sleep. I kept Enrique up for hours describing my new studio, how I was going to set it up just right, for an artist and only an artist, and Enrique didn't mind because I also reassured him that he could finally quit his three jobs. We would remain roommates, he could live rent

I could only stare at the shack in disbelief.
This was where I was supposed to live and work and create masterpieces?

free, and he could relax after all his years of selfless toil. But how could I bring Enrique to this dump? I had promised him a smaller version of Mr. Buenrostro's home (my only frame of reference), not a shantytown.

I wanted Mr. Leyva to drive me back to Albuquerque immediately. In fact, I wanted him to take me directly to Mr. Buenrostro so I could spit in his face. The mechanic's garage was luxurious by comparison, not to mention it was in the city, close to diners and billiard halls and other bohemian haunts; this place was a ghost town after the apocalypse. This is where artists went to die, and that is exactly what I told Mr. Leyva when I regained the ability to speak.

"How do you mean?" he asked.

"How do I mean? This is absolute squalor! This is worse than a dumpster in an alley."

"But you haven't even seen inside yet," he said.

He was right. After setting up a stepladder conveniently pulled from the trunk of his car, Mr. Leyva took out a set of keys, tried two before finding the one that worked, and opened the door. He waved me in, and I quickly followed, practically leaping from the stepladder to the doorsill. Once inside I made three immediate observations: first, Mr. Buenrostro wasn't exaggerating when he said that there was plenty of light. Practically the entire north side of the shack was composed of windowpanes. Second, the place was actually quite spacious. And third, it was, except for the wall of windows, almost an exact replica of Van Gogh's bedroom in Arles, which I knew because it was one of the few color reproductions in *The Great Book of French Painting*. The walls were painted a pale violet and the wood floors a bluish-green color. In the corner was a sturdy wooden bed painted yellow, complete with a scarlet bedcover, and next to it were two yellow chairs with green cushions.

Mr. Leyva pulled an envelope from his breast pocket and placed it on a small table. "That's for you," he said, tapping the envelope for emphasis. "From Mr. Buenrostro. Now I must be leaving." He opened the front door.

I rushed to pick up the envelope. I peeked inside and saw several twenty-dollar bills. I found a note, too, which read, "Make that breakthrough. F. Buenrostro."

His generosity caught me off guard. I felt a surge of emotion. By then Mr. Leyva had already climbed down the stepladder and was outside. I rushed to catch him. "Wait! You're leaving me? But how do I get my stuff?"

"I don't know. My instructions were to drop you off. I have a busy day ahead."

"What about Enrique? I have to get Enrique."

"Who's Enrique?"

"My friend. He's going to live here, too."

"All I know is I have to get to my next meeting. I won't be heading back to Albuquerque until tomorrow. I can give you a ride then."

"It's okay. I'll just take the next bus back to the city. Do you know the schedule?"

Mr. Leyva began laughing. "There's no bus!" he said. "Well, only to Guadalupe, the pueblo down the road, and it only runs on Fridays, comes back on Sundays."

I allowed this piece of information to settle in. I may have had Van Gogh's bedroom in Arles with a perfect amount of northern light, which I owed to Mr. Buenrostro, but I was also stuck in the middle of nowhere, which I also owed to Mr. Buenrostro. I slowly began to understand. He would give me what I wanted most—a studio to work—and he would get what he wanted most—me as far away from my mother and sister as possible.

My gratitude quickly turned to anger as I contemplated these conditions. I imagined my family sitting around the warm parlor, telling each other stories, laughing at the little ones' antics, while I dangled precariously at the ends of the earth.[12]

12. I've learned that artists, not unlike academics, often feel persecuted and misunderstood. For artists and academics of color, this feeling is only compounded by the fact that they are indeed frequently misunderstood if not as often persecuted (although many would argue that they are just as often persecuted). Creating in this atmosphere can be overwhelming. Constantly defending one's worth can be stifling. I'm reminded of Gloria Anzaldúa's lines, *"Who am I, a poor Chicanita from the sticks, to think I could write?... How hard it is for us to think we can choose to become writers, much less feel and believe that we can. What have we to contribute, to give?"* Stripping our narrator's words from context for the sake of metaphor, what Chicanx artist has not felt as if they are dangling from the "ends of the earth"?

This wasn't generosity, this was coldly calculated convenience, and I cursed the family who treated me like a parasite. I was once again ready to instruct Mr. Leyva to drive me back to Albuquerque so that I could spit in Mr. Buenrostro's face when Mr. Leyva remembered that he needed his stepladder back. He retrieved it from the front entrance and grumbled something about there being plenty of stackable crates around, or I could always just climb if I was limber enough. Then he opened the trunk of the car to place the ladder inside.

"Oh, I almost forgot," he said.

He set the stepladder on the ground, then reached into the trunk and pulled out a box of pencils, pens, and paint brushes and handed them to me. Then he reached back in and grabbed a box of paints and painting mediums. These he placed on the ground. Then he reached back into the trunk and pulled out a roll of canvas, which he leaned against the bumper. Finally, he pulled out a stack of quality drawing paper, struggled to find a place for it, then decided to place the stack on top of the box I was holding.

"These are for you," he said. "Again, from Mr. Buenrostro. He must really believe in you."

Before I could find the words to thank him, to ask him more questions, to find out how I was to return to Albuquerque and retrieve my preparatory notes, or how I was to let Enrique know that I wouldn't be coming home for the night, he took off, leaving me in a cloud of dust, holding my precious new art supplies, which I soon dropped because the stack of paper was so heavy. His last words had warmed me to Mr. Buenrostro once again. I really couldn't pin that man down.

I gathered the supplies and hoisted them into the shack, and then went around the back of the building and found two wooden crates, which I stacked and used to climb back into my studio. Once there, I looked around and noticed a door I hadn't seen before. I thought to myself, "Another bedroom," and then immediately, "Enrique's bedroom." As large and spacious as the studio was, I couldn't decide where Enrique's bed would fit. Already I had mentally designated one corner of the room for drawing, another corner for painting, and another corner for moments of deep concentration. I considered placing Enrique in the kitchen area, which consisted of a small wood stove and a rusted sink. He would be warm next to the stove, I thought. He wouldn't even have to step out of bed if he wanted a drink of water. When I saw the door, however, I thought I had my solution. He would have his own bedroom. After all, didn't Gauguin have his in Arles? But I swung the door open only to find the same endless terrain, the vast blue sky, and yet another entrance without steps. Disappointed, I secured the door shut and turned my attention back to the studio. I decided to examine my new art supplies.

It's difficult to describe the rush of feelings as I sat cross-legged in the middle of the floor, holding the array of paint tubes in my hands, unrolling the canvas so that the bluish-green wood floor was covered in the material of my future masterpieces. My heart was pounding, I remember that. I kept glancing up from reading the paint labels—linseed oil, stand oil, alizarin crimson, phthalo blue, cadmium red, cadmium yellow—to marvel at my wall of windows. Perfect northern light. I could hear the occasional bird chirp and the wind blow like a soothing whisper, but other than that I was surrounded by quiet. I unpackaged the paper and placed one sheet in front of me. I stared at it, afraid at first, intimidated by its whiteness, as though it were a void into which I feared disappearing, but then, almost unthinkingly, I reached for the box of pencils and charcoal. I pulled out a stick of charcoal. I didn't even look at it. I didn't want to pull my eyes away from the white void. I now wanted to disappear into it. I wanted to be part of it. I wanted to exist in that pure whiteness, for it to envelop me.

At some point, I placed charcoal to paper. I say at some point because I don't remember drawing. I don't remember moving the charcoal across the paper, feeling its grit between my fingers, feeling in control of my movements. I just know that the northern light had all but disappeared, and before the room fell into darkness I rose from the floor and looked in every drawer until I found a box of matches and several candles. I lit them, and the room was now cast in a beautiful warm glow. I picked up one of the candles and carried it over to the center of the

A breakthrough.

I stared at it,
afraid at first,
intimidated
by its whiteness,
as though it were a void
into which
I feared disappearing...

room. It was then that I saw what I had done. My drawing. My breakthrough. It was as easy as that. No preparatory notes to be found. This wasn't even a sketch. It was a fully realized masterpiece, and I say this objectively because I can hardly claim to have been there at its moment of creation. I had stepped outside of myself. I brought the candle closer. My hand was shaking.

At first, I thought it was a woman, but now I saw clearly who it was. It was a boy with impossibly long eyelashes, fine thin lips, his hat tilted rakishly, casting a soft shadow over his forehead. I had drawn Enrique, my dearest and truest friend. I had fulfilled my promise after all. I couldn't help but realize, though, that I had drawn the Enrique of five years before. Now he was at least fifteen pounds thinner, his eyes hollower, the bones of his face more pronounced, and he had even taken to trimming his eyelashes because the coal dust would settle on them, obscuring his vision. But here was the proof that his years of sacrifice had not been in vain.

I stared at the drawing for hours. What would Monsieur Millet think of this? I wondered, smiling to myself. Mr. Buenrostro would certainly feel this an invest-ment well spent. My mother wouldn't dare call this a mere "picture." I began chuckling as I imagined the awe on my little sister's face when she saw what her big brother was capable of. I thought about all the years that had passed since my father's death, all those years and not one drawing. There was no doubt that I had improved, that I had become what I always felt myself to be: a master draftsman capable of steely-eyed realism. I realized then that the physical act of drawing was only a small part of the process, that my preparation these many years had amounted to something, something spectacular! I fell asleep that night in the cen-ter of my new studio, among my art supplies, next to my first masterpiece. I slept soundly, full of contentment. I only wished that I had blown out the candle.

Only part of the page burned. I must have rolled over the fire and put it out myself without waking, but candle wax covered Enrique's face. All you could see were his hat and his ears. I also rolled back and forth over the drawing the entire night because my whole left side and back were covered in burgundy candle wax and charcoal dust. In desperation, I lifted up the page and tried to pick off the wax but only ended up tearing the paper. I decided to leave it. I had already damaged my first masterpiece enough. I figured that someone, somewhere, must know how to remove candle wax from paper. I picked up the candle and worthless candleholder, opened the door, and threw them both outside. Obviously, I was disappointed that I had created my first masterpiece only to immediately destroy it, but I felt assured that my breakthrough had indeed been just that, a watershed moment, and that there were many more masterpieces to come. In other words, my second masterpiece would be a suitable replacement for my first, and my third for my second, and so on.

More importantly, I discovered that all along what I needed was a place of my own. It was that simple. By myself, surrounded by both quiet and art supplies, I had at last made the leap from preparation and procrastination to execution. The hard part would be breaking this discovery to Enrique. I pictured the disappointment in his eyes as I explained to him my desire to live on my own, and I just couldn't bear it. He had been too good a friend. Loyal, dedicated, he had stuck with me through the darkest of times. And now I was about to abandon him. I felt like the most wretched person on earth. I tried convincing myself that I was doing Enrique a favor. After all, without me to support, not to mention covering my tuition at the Salon des Refusés Art Academy, he could return to working just one job. I even briefly wondered what he would do with all his free time.

Later that morning, Mr. Leyva arrived to pick me up. We traveled back to Albuquerque in almost complete silence. We shared one exchange. Out of the blue, he asked, "How was it?"

"Transformative really, in fact I—"

"Do you intend to stay at the TSSS factory?"

"Yes, I think I just might," I replied.

After a short pause, he said, "I ask because once you retrieve your things, how do you plan on getting back?"

"I don't know," I said. "Might you be able to give me a ride?"

He scoffed and shook his head. "Look, I have an errand to run. Then I can give you a ride to the bus station. But that means you got only about an hour. On Sunday there's only one bus leaving for Guadalupe." Then he asked me what it was that I was holding so tightly. I looked down and realized that I was clutching the smudged, candlewax-splattered drawing of Enrique.

"Nothing," I said, sighing deeply.

The closer we got to Albuquerque the more I thought of the conversation I needed to have with Enrique and the tighter I clenched the drawing. By the time we arrived at the mechanic's garage, my throat felt so constricted that I could barely respond to Mr. Leyva when he instructed me not to dawdle. "I don't have all day to wait around for you," he barked.

"Okay," I managed as I shut the car door. I watched him drive off.

I was relieved to find our apartment empty. I wasted no time. First, I collected my developmental sketches, which predated my father's murder, and then I gathered and sorted through my extensive preparatory notes as well as five years of Master Millet's commentary and stuffed them all in a bag. Then I took down the pages of *The Great Book of French Painting,* which were pinned to every square inch of wall space, and tried to put these in some order: by year, then by artist, and then by favorite artist to least favorite artist. At some point the task became overwhelming. I gave up and stuffed the loose pages and remnants of the book in my bag. The important things packed, I then gathered my clothes, a pillow, and a blanket. Enrique still wasn't home.

I don't know how long I sat there, certainly less than an hour because Mr. Leyva hadn't returned, but I kept watching the door, waiting, expecting Enrique to enter at any moment. When he didn't, I became worried. It was Sunday, his day of rest because the factory was closed, which meant he sold newspapers in the morning and then had the day free until he bussed dishes that evening. He would usually be in bed sleeping. Why wasn't he home? A troubling thought suddenly entered my head: maybe Enrique was the one to abandon me. I stood up and began pacing back and forth, pausing briefly to stare out the window, hoping to spot him as he arrived, but the potholed, oil-stained lot was empty: no mechanics, no cars, no Enrique.

Maybe all he needed was to taste one night of freedom. Liberated finally from supporting me, he was off to better things. I was no stranger to abandonment. Hadn't my own mother, despite her denials, left me when she had the chance? Was it such a stretch to imagine Enrique doing the same? Yes, of course it was. Enrique was my most loyal and devoted friend. He was my only friend. I was *his* only friend. I agonized for twenty minutes before finally deciding that Enrique hadn't abandoned me: he was probably visiting his mother. But I peered into the waste bin just in case. I wanted to see if he had left any crumpled notes of his own. The bin empty, I returned to waiting.

I sat back down on the bed and began to unravel the drawing I'd made of Enrique. I had to do so carefully because the candlewax kept sticking to the page. I placed the paper on Enrique's bed, smoothing it out as best as I could. I gazed hard at my work, straining my eyes until my vision blurred, and that was when, through the wrinkled paper, smudges, and wax, I saw my friend's countenance. Yes, the drawing was undeniably ruined, but careful observer that he was, Enrique would recognize his likeness. He would know that his portrait had been recorded from memory. I found a scrap piece of paper and wrote him a note. "Enrique, here is my first masterpiece. As you can see, I did spill candle wax on top of it, and smudged the charcoal, but if you can find someone to remove the candlewax you'll see just how expertly I've drawn you, my friend." I hesitated to write a final line: "Meet me at the TSSS factory."

I couldn't do it. I thought of the previous night, the peace and quiet, the solitude I needed to create, and then I imagined Enrique in my studio as well, moping around with not a task to distract him. Better that he not come, I thought. I was doing him a favor, I reassured myself. He could rest after so many years of toil. So I signed off: "We'll see each other soon!" I felt guilty, but also immensely relieved.

A short while later, Mr. Leyva picked me up. As we drove out of the parking lot I thought I saw Enrique. I can't be sure, and yet I am sure. For all these years I've carried this image with me, the last glimpse of my friend: he's still a block away, his head down as he carries a bag of groceries in either hand. Groceries for us. He looks up and immediately stops. He's frozen in place. Did he see me driving away? Did he know then that I had abandoned him? Was it even Enrique? Of course, it was, and yes, and yes.

I can't be sure, and yet I am sure.

For all these years

I've carried this image with me,

the last glimpse of my friend.

PART II

The Itinerant Prophet—Reies López Tijerina

CHAPTER FOUR

Mr. Leyva dropped me off at the bus station. It was two in the afternoon; the bus to Guadalupe left at three. The waiting area was full of people. It was hot and stuffy and seemed to grow louder by the minute. Finally, the bus arrived and the doors swung open. I leapt up from my seat, anxious to escape the crowd, and was surprised when everyone else lined up to board as well. Where could they be going? I wondered. The stuffiness and noise only increased once we were all on the bus. Everyone was dressed up—men in dark buttoned-up suits, women in long dresses and wrapped in shawls—as though they'd just come from church. Children seemed to emerge from every direction, poking their heads over the tops of seats, around seats, and even from the bottom of seats. Men and women spoke across the aisle. They called to one another from the front of the bus to the back of the bus. It seemed as though everyone knew each other. Every passenger carried multiple bags of goods filled to the brim. The bus smelled like a produce market. The lady next to me kept leaning over to share her purchases with her friend in the other aisle. "And look at this, comadre," she'd say, and her comadre would respond, "Oh my, look at that comadre, and how much did you get that for?" And all the while the woman was rubbing her right forearm and stomach against me. I kept staring at the seatback in front of me, hoping the trip to Guadalupe wouldn't be long. It took two and a half hours.

When we arrived in Guadalupe, I expected everyone to disperse. I hoped never to see these people again in my life. But they all lingered, as though they couldn't bear to end the party. They continued sharing their new purchases, stretched their legs, or got a bite to eat from the snack shack. I didn't see any signs for a bus to the TSSS factory, so I went inside the station and inquired with the ticket vendor. "It will be here shortly," he said, not even bothering to look up.

"Thank you. I just want to make sure because there's so many people here. I don't want the bus to come and leave without me realizing it."

Now he looked up and peered at the crowded station. "You see all these people?" —he pointed behind me—"They're all going to the same place."

And so they were. When the rickety TSSS factory transport bus arrived, everyone around me lined up with shopping bags and children in tow. I tried to recall the previous day at the work camp. There hadn't been a soul around, and I didn't even think to ask Mr. Leyva where they were. Now I knew. They'd been shopping in Albuquerque. The bus ride to TSSS was even more uncomfortable. I was smashed between two sweaty grandfathers holding grandchildren much too big to be held on grandfather's lap. The kids kept saying, "Grandpa, who is that? Grandpa, Grandpa, who is that?" and pointing their sticky fingers in my face. The grandfathers didn't even acknowledge their questions, or my presence. They just kept talking about horse breeding and ointments for backaches.

It was almost dark by the time we arrived at the TSSS factory. I worried about not being able to find my way, so I hurried to my studio at the far end of the row of shacks. I was desperate to flee from these people and their incessant chatter. I had heard more about the good purchases to be made in Albuquerque than I ever cared to hear again. I found the wooden crates that served as my front steps and carefully hoisted my bag of belongings onto the ledge. Then I fished in my pocket, found the key, and strained to reach the lock, worried that the crates would slip out from underneath me and I'd fall crashing to the ground. The door finally open, I lunged inside and slammed it behind me. I pressed my back against it. I felt as though I were still on the bus. I could hear the deafening whir of fifty voices talking at once, each one growing louder, demanding to be heard; I could hear the screams and squeals of children ringing in my ear. I couldn't get the combined smell of onions, parsley, overripe fruit, and chicken feed out of my nose. I experienced a

The occasion of meeting my new neighbors.

Children seemed to emerge from every direction.

The bus smelled like a produce market.

strong feeling of claustrophobia, as though I were still smashed between the sweaty grandfathers, their sticky-fingered grandchildren, and the comadre rubbing her girth against me. I rose from the floor, reached for my bag, and removed *The Great Book of French Painting*. I needed a soothing distraction.

I pulled out a few of my favorite paintings, which included Millet's *The Angelus*, which depicted two peasants praying, and Corot's *The Bridge at Mantes*, a painting of just that. Both were calm, quiet scenes, just what I needed at that moment. I also started my deep breathing exercises. I stuck my fingers in my ears to drown out any noise. I took a breath, held it, then slowly breathed out, and I imagined myself with Millet's peasants, praying with them, hands clasped, the smell of hay in the air as the sun set over the French countryside. But the peasants too closely resembled the horde of factory workers out my door. I kept imagining them finishing their prayers and then rehashing all the bargains to be made at Sunday market. So I switched my thoughts to *The Bridge at Mantes*, a peopleless landscape, and instead of incessant chatter I heard the crisp fall wind, the crinkling of leaves, and water lapping against the bank. This calmed me. I felt my heart begin to slow. I said to myself, "You are alone here. This is your studio and your studio only. You are here to work, to make your masterpieces." And with that I felt fine. I breathed easier and removed my fingers from my ears.

For a second all was silent. But then I heard what sounded like two girls playing pat-a-cake. It was so clear, so close, that I was certain they were in the room. But they couldn't be. My studio consisted of one large room, and I was the only one inside it. I moved toward the sound, straining my ears, and now I heard not just two girls playing pat-a-cake, but also pots and pans clanging together, more children giggling, a woman's voice scolding someone, a man's voice demanding quiet, and all of it as if it were taking place inside of my studio, as if I were listening to the ghosts of past occupants.

Then I saw it. I had a window on the left side of my studio that faced nothing but the shack next to me. Because the window was covered with a dingy violet curtain that blended in with the dingy violet wall, I hadn't paid it much attention.

The window must be open, I thought, and I hurried over to shut it. I drew the curtain back and discovered that not only was my window open but so too was the window next door. Not only that, the two windows were almost touching on account of my studio leaning left and the shack next door leaning right. We practically shared the same house. I could reach out and touch the girls playing pat-a-cake. And when they turned and saw me standing there, that's probably what they assumed I was about to do, because they looked up at me with eyes full of terror and began shrieking.

I quickly slammed my window shut and closed the felt curtain as tightly as I could, as though it were enough to block out all the sounds in the world. It wasn't. I could hear the girls sobbing, and the woman's voice scolding them, "Get away from the window! Didn't we warn you? Play on the other side of the room."

"Looks like a sissy," a man's voice said.

Was he talking about me? I pressed my ear against the felt curtain.

"Well, better safe than sorry," the woman said.

"Don't worry, he probably just wants to play pat-a-cake with the girls." The man began laughing boisterously at his joke.

I heard further tittering. "Well, at least we don't have to worry about him taking advantage of Ella," the woman said.

"Yes, that's one man who won't be. If only there were more sissies in this camp, we wouldn't have to keep her cooped up all day. Well, it's partly her fault. She brings it on herself."

"She's just innocent. She doesn't know any better."

"That sissy better—"

I couldn't take it anymore. I moved aside the dingy violet curtain and found that my window had slid back open. I poked my head outside, which meant that I was now inside my neighbor's shack.

"I can hear you over here as clear as can be!" I exclaimed.

Children began shrieking, a woman screamed, a pan dropped, and the man cried, "Good God, man!"

Their shack was significantly smaller than mine, but it also looked to have an extra room, so it could've been bigger. To one side five or six beds were lined up as in a hospital ward. There appeared to be at least two kids on each bed. Some were asleep; others were red-faced and crying and pointing at me. The two girls, already recovered from their fright, had resumed their game of pat-a-cake. The man, probably in his late thirties or early forties, was lying on one of the beds with his shoes and shirt off and his belt buckle undone to allow room for his protruding belly. On seeing me, he rose onto his elbows. The woman, his wife I assumed, was busy scooping up from the floor whatever she had been preparing in the dropped pot.

"You can't just be barging in here," said the man. "You scared my wife half to death. Look, she dropped our dinner! Give us our privacy!"

"I didn't barge in here," I said. "I'm still in my house—"

"And mine!"

"Well, I can't poke my head out my window without poking my head into yours, and . . . and would you mind speaking in lower voices? I'm an artist and I need peace and quiet."

"I don't care what you are. This is my house and I'll speak however I damn well please."

"Oh, this is just great. First the bus trip, now this." I ducked back into my own place and tried to shut the window, but it wouldn't cooperate. It kept rising and I kept pulling it down only for it to rise again, until finally I drew the curtain in defeat. I could hear the man say, "Can you believe that?" and his wife respond, "What are we going to do about dinner, Javier?"

I placed my fingers in my ears. I was going to have to do something about this. Nail the window shut and build some sort of barricade. Tomorrow first thing, I thought. I pictured myself building a brick wall. I could spare the studio space if it meant peace and quiet.

I suffered through that night, cursing unchecked procreation and large families altogether. I heard children whimpering, a baby cooing, the man's snores; I heard

We practically shared the same house.

The two windows were almost touching
on account of my studio leaning left and the shack next
door leaning right.

the collective breathing of a family of ten. I cursed the builders of this ramshackle complex. There was plenty of room in every direction; why couldn't they have built the shacks at least a few feet farther from one another? After tossing and turning for hours, I decided to get up and go in search of barricade-making materials.

My task was infinitely more difficult in the dark. Using the moonlight as my guide, I made my way to what looked like the factory dump, a pile of rusty machines and scrap metal that I had noticed on the ride in. I wanted to create a fortress, and this was exactly what I needed. Unfortunately, most of it was too heavy to cart away, and after startling a third feral cat that in turn startled me, I settled on a woodpile that would hold me over. Nails were driven through most of the planks, which saved me the task of searching for those. I gathered what I could carry and returned to my studio. Once I'd hoisted all the wood inside, stacking it neatly in front of the window, I searched for something to hammer with. Finding nothing in my studio, I climbed down the crates and quickly found a large rock with a flat side.

By the time I'd climbed back in, I was breathing heavily and feeling drowsy and was starting to think that maybe a few hours of sleep would do me good. But I also relished the thought of hammering the planks to the wall and waking up the man, his wife, and their ten children. I imagined the man telling me to knock off that racket, and I would tell him, just as he'd told me, "This is my house and I can do as I please!" So I picked up my hammering rock, found a plank big enough to cover the window, and started to remove the felt curtain.

The first thing I saw were her legs, perfectly smooth and pale in the small bit of moonlight that found its way between the two shacks. I quickly shut the curtain, afraid that I would set off shrieks and accusations of being a Peeping Tom. But I heard nothing except for a contented sigh and then a quick return to the uninterrupted sounds of deep breathing. I pulled the curtain back. She was reclining in the windowsill. It was a woman. A young woman. A woman about my age, I determined. She was wearing a slip. A thin slip. A slip so thin that I thought she might be naked. I shut the curtain again. My heart was pounding.

What if she should wake up and find me staring at her? But wasn't I simply gazing out my window? Nothing wrong with that. Is it my fault that she chose to sleep in the window right next to my window and that our windows were practically touching on account of poor design and even poorer construction? I felt justified in pulling the curtain back again.

To my relief, she was still there. For a second, I thought that maybe in my exhaustion, my lack of sleep, my delirium, I had invented her. But she was as real as our windows were close, and not only that, the cool morning air had given her goose bumps. But who cares about goose bumps when through the thin fabric of her slip I could see dark nipples surrounded by the milky white skin of her breasts. The artist in me wanted to observe her. The young man in me wanted to touch her. I knew that I shouldn't. I knew that it was wrong. I knew that no good could come from it. But this whole window-abutting business was driving me insane. It was as if she were in my very own home. How could I resist?

So I slowly poked my head out the window and reached out my hand. What I was reaching for exactly, I don't know. I was letting instinct guide me. But just as I was close enough to feel the energy radiating from her living, breathing body on my fingertips, she stirred. She was probably just shifting her position on the windowsill. After all, it couldn't have been very comfortable. But my trance was broken, and I pulled back quickly. Too quickly. I hit the back of my head on the window frame. Hard but not so hard. Hard enough to propel my head forward so that I hit my face against the windowsill. And that was hard enough to knock me out cold. Before I lost consciousness, I got one last glimpse of the girl sleeping in the windowsill, and I knew I was in love.

"Is he dead?" I heard someone say.

"I don't know. He's been lying like that for hours. When I went to shut the window this morning I saw him there. He hasn't moved since."

"Should we call the doctor?"

"Of course not. It's none of our business."

I opened my eyes and tried to figure out where I was and what had happened to me. My head hurt and I tasted blood. I feared I had suffered another epileptic attack. I turned to my left and noticed the planks of wood I had gathered to barricade the window. Then I remembered the girl in the windowsill. I remembered trying to reach out to touch her. I hadn't succeeded. I felt a wave of relief, as I imagined the situation if I had. There would've been hell to pay with her father or brother or uncle or whoever the man was. I turned toward the window and my neighbor's curtain quickly closed.

I rose to my elbows and saw that I was covered in dried blood. I touched my nose. It was tender. I stood up and felt lightheaded. When I regained my balance, I decided to move the planks of wood out of the way. I wanted to avoid stepping on an exposed nail. It dawned on me that I wasn't going to be using the wood anymore. I couldn't barricade my window as long as there was a chance that a beautiful girl in nothing but a slip could be found sleeping just outside that window on a nightly basis. I could hardly wait for her return. But first I had to get through a day with a splitting headache and what felt like a broken nose.

The children next door seemed to multiply. There were the two girls playing their endless game of pat-a-cake, then at least four boys alternating between games of cops and robbers and cowboys and Indians. Then there were sets of toddlers and infants that took turns crying, babbling, and knocking things over. I heard thuds and crashes, followed by cries of, "Oh, no!" There were older children, too, trying without much luck to corral the younger children. I observed all of this through my open window abutting their open window. At some point their curtain was pulled back and the window opened by one of the children, and it remained that way. I could have tried shutting my window again or at the very least my curtain and maybe achieved some respite, but that would have meant missing a glimpse of the girl in the windowsill. As long as their window and curtain were open, I would be a fool to shut mine. I wanted to make sure she hadn't been an apparition or a particularly vivid dream.

Meanwhile, I tried to draw. My thinking was that if the girl was real, and there, and happened to look through my window, best that she find me drawing rather than holding an icepack to my tender nose. But the children made it hard to concentrate. They were loud, full of hysterical conversations, squeals, giggles, and all manner of cries, and when they weren't loud it was because they had poked their heads out their window and into mine and were watching me, quietly, waiting to see what I was going to do. I was about to set charcoal to paper when a heavy silence compelled me to turn my head, and there they were: five, six, seven small faces, brown and ruddy, dirty, sticky, sweaty, and, above all, curious. "Whattaryou doing, thir?" they asked.

"I'm drawing," I sighed.

"Oh," they said.

Minutes passed.

"Whattaryou doing, thir?" they asked again.

I lost my patience. "I'm trying to draw, but I can't with all of you poking your head into my house and disturbing my peace! Leave me alone, please!"

So they left, and I heard them discussing their childish thoughts on the situation.

"He say he drawing."

"What he drawing?"

"What's dat, what drawing?"

"Drawing, he like drawing. You know drawing. Like a picture of something."

"A picture of what?"

"Like horses or—"

"He drawing horses! I want to see!"

I had to interrupt. "I'm *not* drawing horses!"

And then it started all over. Slowly, quietly, they poked their heads back in again, eyes wide, mouths agape, as if they'd never seen a man standing in front of a sheet of paper holding a charcoal stub. I couldn't focus. Because of them, true, but also because I couldn't stop thinking about the girl in the windowsill. Finally, I asked them outright: "Isn't there like a girl who lives with you, like your older sister. Is she around?" The heads disappeared, and they returned with one of the pat-a-cake girls. I asked her, "Do you have an older sister? I saw her last night in the window—I mean, I just happened to see her through the window. I thought maybe I'd like to have a word with her." She seemed to know exactly whom I was talking about. She left for a moment and my heart surged. But then she returned with her pat-a-cake partner, who looked annoyed that their game had been interrupted. She looked old enough to have a frank discussion.

"I saw a girl around my age that lives with you," I said. "Is she around?"

"Nope," she said.

"But is there a girl around my age that lives with you?"

"Well, how old are you?"

"I'm twenty-five."

"Nope."

"Nope what?"

"Nope, no girl lives here who's twenty-five."

"Maybe she's a little younger, then. What I mean is, she's *around* my age, give or take a few years."

The girl eyed me carefully. "If you're twenty-five, how come you're not at work?"

"What does that have to do with anything?"

"My daddy says that you're a sissy and that's how come you don't work."

I sighed. "I'm an artist, this is my studio, as you can see." I gestured to my art supplies. "I make drawings and paintings, which one day, very soon, I will sell to collectors and museums. And if you must know, I'm simply working here, biding my time until I can make it to Paris. *That* is what I do."

She looked stubbornly unconvinced, and I was about to elaborate on the nature of art and the distinction between everybody else's work and an artist's work, when she said, "Ella, she's twenty. She works at Mrs. Ordoñez's today.

Tomorrow she'll be here watching us." Then she ducked her head back into the room, leaving me to mouth the name of my beloved over and over. Ella, Ella, Ella. Tomorrow I shall meet her, I thought. And I imagined seeing her through the window; or rather, I imagined *her* seeing *me* through the window, busy at my task, immediately impressed by my talent and dedication. What would we say to each other? How would I break the ice? At that moment I was actually grateful for the abutting windows. It was as if we lived together already. *Not* talking to each other would almost be unnatural.

The day passed slowly, and by the end of it I wanted to inflict pain on each and every child next door. I put up with them only because they were the very children Ella would be caring for and I wanted to make a good impression. I learned from them that she wasn't their older sister but the younger sister of their mother, so their aunt. I also learned from the children that Ella sleepwalked and that sleeping in the windowsill was a frequent occurrence.

"Does she really?" I exclaimed, unable to control my exuberance.

The older girls eyed me warily. Admittedly, my inquiries hadn't been very subtle—from the family tree I jumped straight to sleeping habits. But I had the information I needed, and I looked forward to that night with great anticipation.

As soon as my neighbors drew their curtain, blew out their candles, and settled in for a night of snoring, deep sighs, and heavy breathing, I sat by the window anxiously awaiting any sound of movement on the other side. I imagined being able to stare at Ella each and every night as she slept in her transparent slip. I would fight the urge to touch her. I would only admire, I promised. I don't know how many hours I waited by the window, but I heard nothing except the family's collective breathing, which grew almost symphonic. Several times my anticipation got the best of me, and I frantically pulled aside the curtain only to find disappointment. I grew tired; my eyelids became heavier. I nodded off, but then quickly awoke at the thought of missing my opportunity to gaze at the girl's body. Soon, out the north wall of windows, I noticed the sky getting lighter. I collapsed with exhaustion. I don't know when I finally fell asleep.

When I awoke it was almost dark. Confused and disoriented, it took me a moment to realize that the entire day had passed, and I had slept through it. I had missed her. The man and woman and their ten children were making a racket, and I didn't dare pull aside the curtain to see if I could catch a glimpse of Ella. I kept waiting to hear her voice, but all I heard were children chirping and whining and crying and the mother squawking and the father grumbling. After having slept all day, my only consolation was that I was now sufficiently rested to spend the entire night awaiting her arrival in the windowsill. But again, my vigil was in vain. She didn't come.

The night hours were interminable. I distracted myself by snacking on cans of tuna and sardines, and ordering and reordering the reproductions from *The Great Book of French Painting*. I hadn't left the house in three days, and I was starting to feel stir crazy. I thought of taking a walk, explore the camp and its sur-roundings and breathe some fresh air. But just as soon as I opened the door, I would hear a creak at the window. I'd scramble to see what it was, grasping for the curtain to pull it back, only to realize that I had probably created the sound myself. At other times, I grew tired and climbed into bed, only to toss off the blanket a minute later, beset by the thought of missing her.

It was maddening. I was trapped by desire, obsessed with seeing the girl in her night slip as she slept in the windowsill. I am ashamed to admit that this con-tinued for three more nights. Which meant, of course, that I also slept through three entire days, missing my opportunity to meet Ella properly, fully clothed and awake. I didn't attempt a drawing that entire first week. I had my studio, my supplies, my solitude, but now I was plagued by man's greatest distraction, and that distraction had really thrown off my sleep schedule! I even grew accustomed to the screaming children next door, much as I had grown used to the constant bleating horns and backfiring engines of the mechanic's garage.

It was the mailman who finally interrupted my daytime slumber. He wasn't really the mailman, but just the man that the work camp had designated to distribute the few pieces of mail that arrived at the end of every week. He knocked loudly at the door. At first I ignored it, assuming the children were up to some new antic, but the knocking continued and I realized it was coming from a different direction than usual. I rose, groggy and blurry-eyed, and opened my door.

I looked down and saw an older gentleman in a dirty straw cowboy hat, his white mustache browned from cigarette smoke. "A letter for you, young man." He handed it up to me as I leaned down to receive it. I was curious to know who knew of my whereabouts. For a second I hoped it would be from my mother, asking that I soon pay her a visit, or maybe Mr. Buenrostro informing me that my mother missed me terribly and would I come for dinner at once. But it wasn't. I recognized immediately the elegant script. I saw the all too familiar return address. The letter was from Enrique, and I couldn't bear to open it. I imagined page after page asking me to come back to him, or pleading for an invitation to live here with me, or, in martyr-like fashion, he would flagellate himself wondering what he had done to deserve this complete and utter abandonment. No, I couldn't bear to read his words, not then at least. Later, I told myself, when I had my sleeping schedule back on track.

As I decided whether to place the letter underneath my bed or in my sock drawer, I heard a voice next door. A woman's voice, pleasant and melodic. Something told me it could only be hers. I was finally awake. She was awake. I tossed Enrique's letter into a corner. Eventually that corner would fill with unopened letters from him. They would remain unopened for the same reason that first letter remained unopened: given the choice between reliving the guilt for having abandoned my truest friend and enjoying the charms of a beautiful woman, who in his right mind would opt for the former? I heard her voice again and wasted no time. I pulled the curtain aside and there she was.

She was shorter than I remembered. Uncommonly short. Strange short. For a second, I thought this must be the dwarf version of the girl sleeping in the window-sill and that the normal-sized version would soon appear. But then I recalled that when it came to measurements, her height from head to toe had hardly concerned me. Now it did. And just as quickly as I opened the curtain, I closed it, thinking to myself, "That can't be her!" Curiosity forced me to open the curtain again. I think I hoped to find her true height restored. But her true height had never been lost. It was as solid as her low center of gravity. She was at least an inch shorter than the pat-a-cake girls, which I noticed because they were also in the window, looking at me wide-eyed and afraid as if beholding a madman.

I closed the curtain again, turned my back to the wall, and slumped to the ground. I pulled my knees to my chest and rocked back and forth, wondering what to do. I had fallen for Ella the moment I gazed on her body in the moonlight, but now that same body had betrayed me. That's how it felt: not that *I* had been mistaken; not that *I* had failed to pay attention; not that *I* had seen only what I wanted to see, namely, her dark nipples through the sheer fabric of her slip, but that I had been betrayed, tricked, duped. And I vowed right then and there that I would never again fall in love with a woman unless I first saw her standing up straight. But what was done was done. It was too late to go back, I knew that. I couldn't get her sleeping face out of my mind, peaceful and angelic. Her sighs of contentment. The smooth skin of her legs. Her ample chest. I had already fallen for her. I rose to my feet and pulled the curtain aside with such force that the metal rod fell from the wall. There would be no closing it again.

She was now sitting in the windowsill. She didn't seem surprised to see a man standing before her, breathing heavily and holding a ratty felt curtain in his hand. She just looked up and smiled. She had large green eyes that sparkled. Her hair was golden and wavy. Her cheeks were pink, and her lips painted a sultry red. Focused exclusively on her face I could almost forget that just moments before I thought she was a dwarf.

"And just what are you doing?" she said, in a voice so smooth that I was reminded of a beautiful actress I'd once seen in a Bogart film.

"Why, I'm just standing here looking out my window," I said, attempting to sound as cool and collected as Bogart himself.

"So you're the artist I've heard so much about."

"Oh, is that right?" I said.

"Yes, all the children keep talking about is our new neighbor, the famous artist heading for Paris. Is it true that you're bound for Europe?"

"Yes, it's true!" I exclaimed, immediately abandoning my Bogart impression.

"Well, if you need a model, just let me know," she said. She smiled, and her large green eyes seemed to sparkle even more, and I thought to myself something grand: I want to stare into those eyes forever.

That night she came to the window. I was awake, how could I not be? I was thinking of her, imagining the two of us arm in arm strolling the streets of Paris. I pictured her in my studio, a studio not unlike the one in Courbet's allegorical painting, and she was nude, of course, holding a white sheet to her chest, watching me complete a landscape. Then, as though divining my thoughts, Ella appeared. At first, I thought she was awake, so I whispered "Hello!" but she didn't respond. She merely made herself comfortable as she leaned against the frame and placed her foot on the sill. I saw that her eyes were closed and she was breathing deeply, her chest rising and lowering perceptibly. Realizing she was asleep, I allowed myself to stare. Now that she was in her slip once again, her bare leg revealed, I saw why I had been mistaken. Determining a woman's height when she's reclining in a window frame is next to impossible.

I watched her for untold minutes before I was struck with an idea. I wanted to draw her. She hardly moved. She was asleep and would be unaware that I was drawing her, meaning she would have no expectation of the result. The pressure was off. She was the perfect model. I tiptoed across the room, afraid that I would wake her, and found some sheets of paper and a piece of charcoal. Then I tiptoed around some more, looking for another candleholder. I found one, and luckily the matches were not too far away. I lit the candle and made sure it was secured. I tiptoed back toward the window and set the candle down beside me. On my knees, a sheet of paper on the floor, I looked up, admired once again the beauty of my subject, and started to draw.

I traced the contours of her legs, her hips, her arms, her shoulders, her neck; I shaded the volume of her calf, her thighs, her stomach, her breasts; I mapped each and every feature of her peacefully sleeping face. I made five drawings and was about to commence a sixth when she stirred. Scared to be discovered, without thinking I reached for the candle and put the flame out between my fingers, which I'd seen done but had never tried. It was infinitely more painful than I expected. I let out a yelp and then covered my mouth to suppress another. I stuck my fingers in my mouth and tasted the grit of charcoal dust but felt some relief. I tried not to move.

When enough time had passed, I fumbled for the matches in the darkness and relit the candle. I looked up to find her gone. She had returned to her bed. I felt a pang of disappointment. I missed her already. But when I looked around myself, I found her again. I had captured her five times over. I was exhausted, and I struggled to keep my eyes open. I wanted to lie down right there on the floor and sleep, but remembering the mishap with my first masterpiece, I mustered the energy to collect the drawings and place them safely on a table before I dragged myself to bed. I blew out the candle and closed my eyes, dreaming of Ella, my muse, in my arms.

I slept through the entire next day, which hardly mattered. I knew that Ella was at Mrs. Ordoñez's, and I needed my rest if I was going to keep awake that night. I didn't know for sure she would return to the windowsill, but I had to be prepared. On waking, I examined the drawings I had made the night before. I felt a range of emotions as I absorbed what I had created. Ella was there in all her glory, and I wanted to show someone my masterpieces, but I fought the urge, realizing that showing someone would mean revealing my nocturnal drawing sessions with an unconscious subject. Plus, it would also mean sharing Ella's opulent body, her ample breasts, her sturdy legs, her well-proportioned hips, her radiant face, with another, and that I couldn't do. She was mine and only mine, and I even thought of destroying my masterpieces if only to prevent others from

On my knees,
a sheet of paper on the floor,
I looked up,
admired once again the beauty
of my subject,
and started to draw.

gazing on her as I had. But that would've been foolish. What if I destroyed the drawings and she never reappeared in the window? No, I would keep them for myself. Safeguard them, at least until I could have her completely.

That night she appeared again, and again I drew her. Although she was sound asleep and didn't even stir when I knocked over a chair, I felt somehow that we were both complicit in this game. Yes, she had slept in the windowsill wearing nothing but a slip long before I arrived—the children had confirmed this—but weren't children always lying? I preferred to believe that a powerful magnetic attraction had compelled her to rise from bed searching for me, beckoned by my presence. She wanted to reveal herself, to be captured by an artist's hand. As I completed one drawing after another, I became convinced that she was the puppet master and I the puppet. Wasn't that a true muse after all, one who commands attention, insists on being listened to? Well, I listened, I obeyed, and by the end of that second night I had fifteen more drawings to add to the previous five. I fell asleep on the wood floor surrounded by them, exhausted, my hand unable to hold the charcoal any longer. It was a beautiful feeling, to be inspired, to love, to create, to be surrounded by one's creations. In all my life I had never felt more fulfilled.

The next morning, I awoke to shrieks. "Look at what he did! Look, Javier, look at this disgrace!"

I raised my head from the floor, momentarily unsure where I was. Through bleary eyes I saw that the woman next door had poked her head out her window and into my studio. Her entire torso was leaning into the room. She kept pointing and saying, "Look! Oh my God, look!" I saw her husband behind her trying to pull her back into their house. "Come on, woman," he said. "Calm down. Let me see." He finally managed to pull her away. Now it was his turn to be shocked. His eyes opened wider and wider as though he were trying to take in all the drawings at once.

"A pervert!" his wife called out. "A pervert! Our neighbor is a pervert! Can you see them, Javier? Can you see them? Can you see them?"

The dumbfounded, wide-eyed expression had not left Javier's face. He quickly closed the curtain, and I heard him say, "Don't you dare open this curtain. I don't want the children to see what I'm going to do!"

"Teach him a lesson he'll never forget!" was his wife's reply.

"I'm telling you, don't open that window curtain!" he yelled again. Then I heard their door squeak open and slam shut, and a second later I heard pounding at my door. Still half asleep and a little bewildered, it took me a moment to realize that I was the pervert she was talking about. I quickly scooped up the drawings as though I could hide the evidence, but then I stopped. I had already been caught. Javier had seen everything, and now he was coming to teach me a lesson. I was about to turn and head for the back door, the door leading to nothing but open country, when my front door swung open and I saw my neighbor struggling to pull himself inside as he balanced on the wobbly stack of crates.

"Pssst!" he whispered. "Listen to me. I'm not going to hurt you, I swear. Help me up."

I thought this was some sort of trick to catch me without a chase, and I continued toward the back exit. He whispered again, "Seriously, I mean it. Help me up!" Then in a loud deep voice he cried out, "I'm going to kill you, you sissy!" Then he held his fingers to his lips and whispered, "I don't mean it. That's just for her sake," and he pointed vigorously toward his shack as though to make his purpose clear.

I was very confused. I continued backing up, eyes on him as my hand reached for the doorknob.

"Wait, please!" he mouthed imploringly, just as he found his footing on the crates and hoisted himself into the house. "Just pretend like I'm hurting you," he whispered. Then he cried out, "You ingrate! I'll kill you!" And he reached for a chair and knocked it to the ground. "Squeal like you're in pain," he said. "Do it, or I'll really hurt you," and his eyes bugged out and he clenched his teeth as though to show me he was serious.

Fearing violence yet finding myself unable to run, I felt compelled to play along. I cried out, "No! Please!" He picked up the chair and threw it across the room.

"Let me have those drawings," he whispered heavily.

"Why? To destroy them?"

He shushed me. "No, because I can sell them like *that*," he said, snapping his fingers. "Now cry again."

I cried out in pain and yelled, "Don't hurt me!"

He pounded his foot on the ground and then slammed his hand against a table. "Just give them to me and every guy in this camp will pay a week's worth of wages for one."

I eyed him unsurely. "You mean like an art dealer?"

Javier knit his brow in confusion, mulled it over for a second, and then nodded his head. "Yes, why not? Call it whatever you want." Then he leaned down and picked up one of the drawings of Ella in the windowsill. He stared at it admiringly, almost in awe, and for a moment I was never more convinced of my genius. Even this poor laborer living in the middle of nowhere could see the value of my work, and what's more, wanted to represent it. But then his expression of admiration became more specific. He stared as if looking at a foldout in a nudie magazine. It was a gaze full of lust. Then he said, "What I'd give for a night with—"

I gasped. "This is a work of art!"

"You can say that again," he said, not taking his eyes off the page.

"No, I meant this"—and I pointed to the page—"the drawing itself."

Now he looked up. "Well, yes, that's what I'm saying, too. You're good. You're very good. Which is why I know that men will be lining up to buy these. By any chance do you think you could make smaller drawings, like a size to fit in a wallet?"

I was conflicted. To my mind, it still wasn't clear whether my neighbor recognized the expert rendering of the subject or if it was simply the subject itself that caught his attention.

"Doesn't it bother you that this is your wife's sister?" I asked.

He glanced up at me, his brow furrowed, and then he looked back at the drawing. "My wife's sister? You mean Ella?"

"Yes, your wife's sister. That's who it is!"

"But this doesn't even look like her!"

"Yes, it does," I said.

He began shaking his head. "No, this isn't her. For one, Ella is much shorter than this girl here."

"Well, she was reclining in the windowsill, which makes it hard to tell how tall or short someone is."

Javier stuck out his bottom lip as though considering this possibility, and then shook his head again. "I'm sorry, it doesn't look like her. But why were you drawing my sister-in-law in the windowsill anyway?"

"I don't have many models to draw from, and she was—well—just there, not moving or anything."

He continued staring at the drawing. "This woman here—she's . . . she's exquisite. Ella, she just thinks she looks like a pinup girl, with her fake blonde hair. I'd be careful if I were you. She flirts with every guy who crosses her path. All she wants is to get her hooks into someone—anyone."

I didn't like hearing this at all. Ella was my muse. I wanted to believe that she was reserved for me and me only.

"Hand those drawings over," he said. "You don't have much choice. My wife is going to drag your name through the dirt. She's a God-fearing woman who doesn't abide pornographers. You're going to be a pariah in this camp. You might as well make a quick buck for your troubles."

I don't know what was more upsetting: the negative light in which he had portrayed Ella, or the fact that he didn't recognize his own sister-in-law in the drawings. So much so that he was willing to sell the drawings to strangers.

"No, I won't give you these drawings!" I blurted out. Then I rushed over and gathered the sheets of paper as quickly as I could. I directed my voice toward his wife's ears on the other side of the window. "I didn't make these drawings for fornication!" I cried.

His eyes widened and then turned angry. Before I could turn and run, drawings safely in hand, he bounded toward me and slapped me across the jaw. The drawings went flying. I tried catching them all at once, but was so staggered by the blow that I grabbed only air before falling to the ground and striking my face against the wood floor. Already tender, my nose began to pour out blood.

"You pervert!" he screamed, his face beet red. "You're lucky I don't kill you for shaming my sister-in-law!"

He kicked me in the side, and I heard a rib crack. When I raised my head, his fist slammed into my cheek. I reached for two or three drawings that had settled nearby. I grabbed onto the corners, but soon felt my grip loosen. Then everything went black.

When I awoke, Ella's face was gazing into mine. I thought for sure I was dead and in heaven. She was caressing my cheek and softly singing a lullaby. I became aware that my head was resting on her thigh.

"You're alive?" she said.

"I think so," I said. I breathed in deeply and pain shot through my body. I struggled for air. I winced as every breath pressed on my rib cage.

"You're just a little banged up," she said.

I turned my head to the side and saw my drawings scattered everywhere. Some were crumpled, one appeared ripped, another had blood on it, but most seemed intact.

"I like your drawings," she said.

"You do?" My breathing momentarily eased.

"Yes. Who are they of?" she asked.

I groaned and tried to lift my head from her thigh, but I fell back in pain. "Oh, forget it," I said. "Just forget it." And I consoled myself with the fact that I had drawn these works with only a candle to guide me. Distortions were bound to occur.

"I'm just kidding," she said, giggling. She reached for my head and repositioned it comfortably on her thigh.

"What do you mean?" I asked.

"I know they're of me."

Following my beating...

When I awoke, Ella's face was gazing into mine.

I thought for sure I was dead and in heaven.

"You do?"

"Well, yes. Who else was sleeping in the windowsill last night?" She smiled, then added, "I also heard you tell Javier before he attacked you."

"Oh," I said, my disappointment returning.

"I think they're very good."

"You do?"

"Of course I do. But you're the artist. What do you need my opinion for?"

"You're right," I said. And she was right. I was the artist. How had I let Javier shake my confidence?

She looked around.

"How did you find me here?" I asked.

"I crawled through the windows," she said matter-of-factly. "They're so close to one another."

"They are. It's like we practically live together."

"That's true!" she said. "I didn't even think about that." Then after a pause she asked, "So you really live in this giant place all by yourself?"

I turned to look at my surroundings, wondering if we were looking at the same room. "It's not exactly giant," I said. "This is just my studio. I *grew up* in a giant home."

"Oh? Is that where your family is?"

"I have no family," I said. "My father is dead, and my mother wants nothing to do with me."

"I'm so sorry. I know what it's like. I'm an orphan, you know. That's why I live with my sister." She sighed. "It's not easy, living with all of them. So many children, it's impossible to sleep with five, six of us to a bed. That must be why I get up in the night. And Javier . . . well, you know Javier. He can be such a bully. I still can't believe what he did to you." As she said this, she placed the palm of her hand over my forehead. It was soft and cool. Then she gently combed my hair into place. It was a gesture as pleasurable as it was painful, because as she did it I breathed in deeply, causing spasms throughout my body.

"I'm sorry!" she cried.

"It's okay," I lied.

As my breathing eased, she looked toward the window mournfully. "When I opened the curtain, I saw Javier throwing you around like a rag doll. I told him to stop, but he just kept throwing you about, then pouncing on you. Your tongue was hanging out and your eyes had rolled back in your head. I thought for sure he was going to kill you . . ."

Based on her description, I realized that I had suffered another epileptic attack. I wasn't about to admit this. In fact, I was thinking of something completely different. She lived with a sister who overworked her, a brother-in-law who wouldn't recognize a likeness if he was staring at himself in the mirror, and ten insufferable kids. Now, my studio wasn't exactly spacious, but it was just me, all alone except for some paints, some canvas and paper, and a yellow wooden bed in the corner. As I stared into her twinkling green eyes (she was still describing my beating in great detail), it almost didn't seem fair. I knew that I had just abandoned my one and only friend Enrique after learning that in order to create masterpieces I needed absolute solitude. But love changes everything. What I needed now was Ella.

I'd been conscious only five minutes, but I was inspired. I imagined myself asking her to live with me, telling her that her days sharing a bed with extended family were over. She would no longer be at her sister's beck and call; she wouldn't have to suffer her brother-in-law's lustful gazes; she would have peace and quiet and could decorate however she saw fit. She may have been a poor orphan girl reliant on the generosity of family, but that would all change. I would be her guardian. I kept imagining her excitement and gratitude, and the thought of her pleasure was overwhelming. So much so that I heard myself ask, "Why don't you live with me?"

She stopped describing my beating. A smile came to her face, and her cheeks turned several shades of red. "Live with you?" she asked.

"Yes, live with me," I responded, my inspiration only growing. "Here in my studio. You will be my model and my—" I was about to say "muse," but I stopped myself. It didn't seem proper. "My roommate," I finished.

She laughed. "Your roommate? Is that what you want me to be?" Her voice was playful, and I almost came right out and said "lover." But I opted for something more chivalrous. "Yes, you won't have to worry about a thing." I felt a great surge of emotion as I grasped the meaning of the words already out of my mouth. I would be her provider, her protector—as soon as I'd healed from my wounds, of course.

She lifted my head off her thigh and settled it gently on the floor. She rose, a childlike smile on her face. She wore an ankle-length white cotton dress that clung tightly to the curves of her body. As I stared up at her, she almost seemed tall. She spun around as if doing a waltz. "There is so much room, it's like a dance floor!" she squealed gleefully, spinning some more, her dress rising just enough to reveal the back of one of her calves. Seeing just this bit of skin caused a tingling in my loins. Never mind that the night before I had made fifteen charcoal drawings of both her legs, bare all the way up to the top of her thigh. That didn't matter. The night before she was in a windowsill, close, but not close enough. Now she was inside my room, spinning around, laughing, and even though my rib was broken, and most likely my nose, too, and I had suffered both a beating and an epileptic attack and accusations of being a pornographer, there was joy in the room. Pure unadulterated joy.

When she stopped waltzing, she placed her hands on her hips and caught her breath, her chest rising and lowering. The smile hadn't left her face. If I could have stood up I would've rushed to embrace her, to cover her mouth with my own. Instead I lay prostrate on the floor, feeling very much the invalid.

"I'll be your roommate," she said. "Just let me get my stuff."

As easy as that, we ended up living together. In retrospect I wish it had been more difficult. We should've had a trial period, gone on a few dates, maybe even spent an hour or two alone in my house just talking and feeling each other out on certain domestic issues, potential bones of contention, such as what was the appropriate amount of talking in any given hour. Even though Javier had beaten me up and left me for dead, and Ella's sister thought I was a pervert, I wish that the two of them had sat us down and explained the difficulties of cohabitation. After all, they were more experienced. But they were just happy to be rid of Ella, one less mouth to feed, and she still watched the kids, so it was no loss for them. Ella even convinced her sister not to tell the whole camp about my lewd pictures. They gave her an extra blanket as well as some dishes and silverware, which were welcome because I'd taken to scooping food out of the pot with my hands.

I quickly learned that Ella talked a lot more than Enrique. She especially liked to ask questions. At first, I answered willingly and in great detail. For instance, she wanted to know how I became interested in drawing and painting. So of course, I delivered my general philosophy on steely-eyed realism, dropped a few names, Courbet, Corot, Millet, and was really getting to the heart of where I situated my work in the Parisian art world of eight decades before when she interrupted me to ask another question: "What's the farthest place you've traveled to?"

So I told her about my sojourn to Los Angeles with Enrique. Just as I was getting to the part about being robbed, she interrupted to tell me that all she wanted to do in life was travel far away and never live in one space longer than a year. "That's very nice," I said, and then I quickly finished my story about finding my luggage and preparatory notes discarded in a dumpster. Her response to this miraculous story was to ask if I preferred apple pie or peach pie. Her questions about pies made me recall a long-suppressed memory from my childhood having to do with a family picnic. As I was reminiscing, searching for the details of this admittedly vague, potentially mundane story, she asked why I hadn't fought in the war, which caused me to abandon the picnic memory and begin elaborating on the capricious nature of military exemptions. It's true that, when asked a question, I've never had much restraint, I can't help answering in great depth, but the problem was Ella didn't seem to care about my answers. She just enjoyed coming up with questions. So it would go on like this for hours. Her asking, me answering, then her interrupting, until I became exasperated, at which point I would say, "Why don't you let me finish my story?" And she would quickly apologize and say something immensely flattering, such as, "It's just that I want to learn everything about you, I can't help it!" So we'd continue.

Until my ribs and face were healed, I remained in bed and Ella took care of me. She cooked and cleaned and even organized and reorganized my art supplies. Other than that, there wasn't much for her to do. She sat around and asked me questions, and when she tired of asking questions, she gazed out the wall of north-facing windows and sighed loudly every few minutes. As distracting as her sighs were, I tried to ignore them. I feared that if I asked why she was sighing it would lead her back to asking questions, and I needed rest from answering. Plus, I needed to work. I leafed studiously through the reproductions in *The Great Book of French Painting*. I laid out several of the drawings of Ella and made preparatory notes for the paintings I planned to make once I had fully recovered. I also tried to draw. Ella brought me my drawing board, and I propped it against my knees. She sat in a chair several feet away, and I began sketching her. Every thirty seconds she asked, "What part are you drawing now?" I told her and she would respond with a giddy squeal. Her excitement pleased me, but after the tenth time I informed her that her question was breaking my concentration. She apologized and became quiet, almost morose. The joy gone from the room, I found its absence equally distracting. So I would make amends and tell her, "I'm drawing the graceful slope of your shoulder." All joy returned.

The truth is I wanted to make Ella happy. I tried to indulge her whims even when those whims ran contrary to what made me happy, like when she told me she was bored and asked if three of her nephews and nieces could visit for a few hours. I consented. They crawled through our adjoining windows and right away started using my brushes and paints and ruined several sheets of paper before I made her send them home. They left, but not before one of them jumped on a tube of red paint and caused it to explode. Red paint was everywhere, on the walls, on the floor. Even after repeated scrubbing, the room looked like a crime scene. Twice a week Ella helped Mrs. Ordoñez, and I had to admit I felt some relief when

My convalescence.

Ella brought me my drawing board, and I propped it
against my knees.

She sat in a chair several feet away,

and I began sketching her.

she left the studio. Even though I had lived with Enrique for years, he was mostly gone at work for fourteen, fifteen hours a day, whereas Ella and I were never out of each other's presence. I felt suffocated, and I think she did, too, hence the repeated sighs as she longingly stared out the window. Soon all she talked about were the adventures we would have once I was fully recuperated from my beating. She had plans to travel to Albuquerque, Santa Fe, and El Paso, and she even mentioned Los Angeles and San Francisco. She wanted all sorts of adventures, and she felt that those were finally possible now that we were together.

Our being together remained an uncertainty. I had asked her to move in with me, and many God-fearing people would understand that to mean that we were now together as a couple, and soon to be man and wife if we didn't want to rot in hell. I know that's what her sister thought. She now smiled at me and affectionately called me brother-in-law. I know that's what her husband Javier thought, too. Once when I was alone he poked his head through the window and told me, "I told you so, and you didn't believe me. She was just waiting for someone to get her hooks into." But when it came to Ella, I could only assume that when I said "roommate" she understood it literally, because at every opportunity she referred to me as just that, her "roommate," and variations thereof, such as "roomie" and "bunkmate." Nothing was said otherwise. I had asked her to be my roommate, and so we were.

That's not to say my desires had disappeared—they most definitely had not. But my broken rib prevented me from doing much of anything about them. It was difficult sleeping together in the same bed. We had separate blankets, so that created some proper distance. Even though my mattress was small, for a girl accustomed to sleeping with multiple nieces and nephews, all limbs intertwined, sleeping with just one person was a luxury. She slept soundly. She still slept in her slip, but now she was more discreet. She would change with the candles out and awake in the morning with the blanket pulled around her. I kept hoping she would rise in the night and sleepwalk, but she did this only once. I watched her, straining my eyes to see in the dark. By the time my vision had adjusted, she was already reclining in the windowsill. But now, instead of facing me, her womanly attributes there for me to admire, all I had was a dim view of her back. I lay awake that night frustrated and full of regret. I was in love with the girl I'd first seen not on my windowsill but the neighbor's windowsill, meaning, facing me, the silent muse I could draw without interruption. I wasn't so enamored with this Ella, the roommate who wouldn't stop with the questions and the sighing and the talk of all the places she wanted to visit.

When my broken nose and rib had healed, I remained in bed because I didn't want to accompany her on those adventures. I finally had my studio, I had a model to work from, and I wanted to draw and paint and become the famous artist I was destined to be. Plus, Mr. Buenrostro had given me only finite funds, and if I blew those on trips to Albuquerque, Santa Fe, and El Paso, I would have to start thinking about getting a job, and that had to be avoided at all costs. So I would get up and walk around only on the days when Ella was helping Mrs. Ordoñez. I didn't do much that I didn't already do in bed: I leafed through the pages of *The Great Book of French Painting,* made preparatory notes, stared at the unopened letters from Enrique in the corner and imagined the guilt I would feel on reading them, and reorganized the art supplies that Ella had already ordered so neatly, and then put them back in the same order so that she didn't know I was up and about. But it felt incredible to have the space, the quiet, the solitude, and I felt more and more certain that I had made a mistake inviting Ella to live with me. Could I possibly send her back to live next door with her family? I didn't think so, but I certainly fantasized about the idea.

Then one day I was caught. Sometimes, through our abutting windows, the children would see me walking around my studio, and they would ask me when they could come back to play. I didn't think much of it, but later, Ella was talking to her sister and was explaining how I was still too delicate to get out of bed, and her sister informed her that the children saw me walking around all the time.

Ella rushed over to confront me. "What? You don't want to work? Is that why you pretend to still be hurt?"

"What do you mean?" I asked. I was in bed after a relaxing day by myself.

She recounted the conversation with her sister. The ruse over, I rose from bed to finally have the "talk" about our living situation. I was momentarily stunned, however, because now that I was standing I again realized just how short Ella was. Weeks in bed gazing up at her, I'd almost forgotten her diminutive stature. She must've noticed me eyeing her strangely, because she said, "Don't look at me like that."

"Like what?"

"You know exactly what I'm talking about."

I didn't, or at least I wasn't sure. Was it clear that her height disappointed me?

"There's plenty for you to do to contribute to this household," she began. "For one, we need stairs to be built rather than crates. It's just too hard for me to get up and down. We also need to get rid of all these wood planks with rusty nails sticking out. Someone is going to step on them one of these days. Also, we need to go into Albuquerque to run errands. I'm tired of cans of sardines . . ."

And she continued to list off all the things we had to do—*I* had to do—now that my convalescence was over. I should've told her that this wasn't the life I wanted for myself, that I was an artist who needed solitude in order to produce the great works of art I was destined to create, and after years of seeking that solitude I had finally found it, only to give it up too soon. I should've told her that I was happiest on the days when she was gone working at Mrs. Ordoñez's; that was when I felt inspired to work, and it was only through my art that I was going to go anywhere in life. I was about to tell her this, but while I was building up the courage, her long list of chores came to an end, and she stopped and said, "And now that you're better, we can do this, you idiot."

Before I could ask her what "this" was, she reached for the bottom of her dress and pulled it over her head. A second later her slip was off as well. Seeing her stark naked in broad daylight was almost too much for my virgin eyes. I couldn't breathe. I didn't know what to look at first. Her full round breasts, her smooth, pale midriff, the dark patch of pubic hair, her firm thighs. Her short stature was clearly not an issue at this point! Her body inspired me, and because it was in my nature, I found myself reaching for a piece of charcoal and a sheet of paper.

"No, no," she scolded. "No drawing right now." And she rushed in my direction, practically tackling me, and threw me onto the bed. I quickly learned that my rib was not fully healed. I gasped for air, but she was on top of me, kissing my mouth voraciously, pulling off my nightshirt, ripping off my pajama bottoms, as though she were hungry for me, and all I could think of was the previous weeks, all that time, in the same room, sleeping in the same bed, growing increasingly dissatisfied with our living arrangement, and I never once thought that what we needed to do was *this*. She was right, I was an idiot.

Things improved remarkably after that. While it's true I had a whole lot of chores now that I was the man of the household, I did them gladly knowing what was awaiting me that night, or that night and the following morning, or the following morning and that coming afternoon. Ella's appetite was insatiable, and I fed her willingly. Even when I was exhausted, not an ounce of energy left, and still she wanted more, I found deep inside me a carnal reserve. I didn't want to disappoint her, physically or domestically, especially when both were intertwined. In fact, my first household chore was to build a wall to cover the window through which I had first glimpsed her. She told me that she didn't want her sister and brother-in-law and ten nieces and nephews to hear us. When I told her that the walls were thin and that I'd have to build a concrete wall to block out our moans and screams, she told me to just build it and stop complaining. When I told her that I wasn't complaining, that I was merely stating a fact, she simply repeated what she'd said. "Just build it and stop complaining." So I built a wall, not out of cinderblock but out of wood. I could still hear her brother-in-law Javier's snores at night, but she was satisfied, so I was satisfied.

I soon entered the most productive period of my life. I drew and painted Ella over and over, and every drawing and painting completed I placed at her feet as if it were a sacred offering. She had me build her a large trunk to place at the

"No, no," she scolded. "No drawing right now."

And she rushed in my direction...

Even when I was exhausted, not an ounce of energy

left, I found deep inside me a carnal reserve.

THE ITINERANT PROPHET—REIES LÓPEZ TIJERINA

foot of the bed, where she carefully placed my growing body of work. I suspected she wanted the trunk for our future travels, but I kept putting off those plans, explaining that I was finally inching toward my masterpieces and couldn't break my momentum now. Paris, our ultimate adventure, was just around the bend. She relented, but not without heavy sighs and periods of sulking. The farthest we traveled was to run errands in Albuquerque, but I kept thinking I saw Enrique on every street corner, so soon she went alone. I preferred to stay in my studio all day, working, where the outside world couldn't disturb me.

I continued to receive letters from Enrique, all of which remained unopened and tossed into the corner. I wasn't yet ready to face the fact that I had abandoned him. Better to ignore his pleas. I also received letters from Mr. Buenrostro containing money and nothing else. I kept hoping for a letter from my mother, but the most I ever got was a note in Mr. Buenrostro's hand letting me know that my sister had asked for me: "She wants to know if you have found a job yet!" He must have found this very funny. In an entire year that was the only news of my family.[13]

13. Most Chicano literature situates its characters squarely within the family or the community, placing special cultural emphasis on familial or communal values. There's a political component to this. Early Chicano nationalists saw individualism as an American value to be shunned. In fact, José Antonio Villarreal's 1959, therefore pre-Movement, novel, *Pocho*, was criticized upon its reprinting because of its central protagonist's alienation from his family and community. I don't believe Chicanos hold any monopoly on family or community values, just that we're constantly expected to talk about them, as if our work can't be divorced from our tíos, tías, and abuelitas. If Tolstoy were Chicano, he would have to write: "Chicano families, whether happy or unhappy, are all alike."

CHAPTER FIVE

One afternoon, I was in my studio sketching another portrait of Ella while she sat by the wall of windows, sighing every two minutes, her face glistening with perspiration as she gazed out on our barren surroundings, when we heard a loud commotion outside our door. It sounded like a crowded bus station. I glanced up from my drawing and Ella turned away from the window, and we looked at each other, confused. "What's that?" I asked. And before she could venture an answer, we heard the voice. Rather, I felt the reverberations of that voice from my head to my toes. I was drawn to it, hypnotized. I couldn't even hear what the voice was saying—that seemed inconsequential. The voice made me stand up. I set my drawing board aside, and, because it was closer, walked out the back door rather than the front.

"Where are you going?" Ella asked. I didn't answer her.

Once I was outside, the voice was louder but no clearer, but the booming cadence, rising and lowering, rising and lowering, beckoned me forward. I heard other less impressive voices calling out expressions of pleasure or agreement. "Yes, sir!" "Tell it!" "Ah hmm!" "Preach to us!" I could now see that the large crowd was gathered right in front of my studio. This gave me pause. Before rounding the corner, I stopped to listen more carefully to the words being spoken.

"This is a house of sin, of wayward children, of God's ill-fated creatures, lost in a wilderness of fornication and desecration. Like Eve who snatched the apple off the tree, temptation will always doom the weak. Here in this house of sin we find the weak, succumbing to moments of lust and desire. They know not the eternity of hellfire in store for them. What do we tell these sinners? What, I ask you, do we tell these sinners living under one roof without the blessing of God?"

It took me a second to realize that the man was talking about Ella and me. Apparently, the preacher had arrived on foot at the TSSS factory work camp along with his wife and child and immediately started preaching, which I would learn was his preferred style. Don't let people ask questions, don't let them busy themselves with other tasks, don't let them run inside and close the door and draw the shades; just start preaching eternal damnation. He had asked those gathered around who among them was living in sin, but instead of fessing up to their own misdeeds, my neighbors decided to take the preacher directly to my studio. They told him that a girl named Ella and a strange man hardly anyone ever saw were living together and succumbing to the pleasures of the flesh, which indeed we were. Guilty as charged. But the preacher's words weren't important, nor the fact that they were directed at me. No, what impressed me most was the passion in his voice, and that passion was contagious. I felt it first in my feet, from where it moved up my shins and rattled my knees, then in my fingers, the tingly sensation rising to my elbows and then all the way to my ears. Never mind that a large group of people had congregated at my door and were working themselves into a red-faced frenzy as they called out "Sinners! Sinners repent!" I emerged from my hiding spot on the side of the house and sidestepped around the gathering, inching my way closer to that magnetic voice.

When I finally saw the preacher in the middle of the crowd, I felt that I had found my long-lost twin. I can acknowledge now, with the perspective gained over the years, that perhaps it was an instance where I wanted so much to emulate him that I drew comparisons only I recognized. For the preacher was tall and barrel-chested, with strong forearms; he had heavy eyebrows, a large nose, and piercing eyes, and when he spoke his face contorted every which way, as though a higher authority were forcing the words through him against his will. I was at least two inches shorter; his build tended toward robust, mine toward a diet of canned sardines; his hair was thick and wiry and slicked back, with not one hair out of place; my hair was an afterthought, constantly disheveled. But how can I deny my thoughts on seeing him for the first time? "There is my long-lost twin," I said, and felt a twinge of regret as I conjured an image of my childhood self, impeccably dressed, playing alone by a creek bed.

Because I rarely left my studio, and tried to do so when everyone was working at the factory, no one really knew what I looked like. My precautions as I walked around the crowd were unnecessary, and as I drew closer and closer to the preacher, I moved people aside. "Excuse me, excuse me, coming through," I said. They glanced at me without recognition, quickly turning back to direct their cries of "Repent, sinner" at my front door. I watched the preacher in awe. I had never met someone so eloquent. He used words like a swashbuckler, moving nimbly forward and back, side to side, his sword extended, and when he thrust that sword, the blade of his passionate fervor went clear through you. We were his opponents, an army against one, but as long as he kept talking we were defenseless.

I moved closer, nudging people aside, ignoring their petty grumbles, until I stood right next to him and could tell just how tall he was, just how broad his chest and shoulders were, and just how handsome. At once I had a desire to be him. "This man is a genius," I thought to myself. And in that same moment, staring up at the preacher, watching him gesticulate and spit and hurl invectives at my studio, I saw all my failings. Wasn't an artist supposed to inspire emotion? Who had I inspired other than Ella's lascivious brother-in-law? Who had I moved to tears? I had not moved anyone to do anything, while the preacher, in just ten minutes, had convinced all of our neighbors to hate us. That was tangible evidence of his gifts. I had no evidence of mine, except maybe a trunk full of drawings, but this man, by God, he was working the crowd into a manic state. They had ignored us for months, but now they were pushing closer and closer toward our door, unable to contain their cries of "Repent, sinners!" They grew louder and louder, and I even found myself chanting along with them. "Repent sinners, repent!" Then I felt the

"This is a house of sin, of wayward children, of God's

ill-fated creatures, lost in a wilderness of fornication

and desecration."

It took me a second to realize that the man
was talking about Ella and me.

preacher's large hand on my shoulder, and I looked toward him and our eyes met, and he was saying, "Repent and accept the Lord into your heart, brother!" And I cried, "Brother, yes! Repent and accept the Lord into your heart!" We both turned toward my studio, and I half expected to see someone resembling me emerge from the house to accept whatever fate God had in store for him.

Instead, Ella emerged. I stared up at her, and then I panicked and quickly looked away, afraid that she would recognize me in the crowd. But she wasn't looking for me. When I peered up again, I saw that she was staring at the preacher, matching him piercing gaze for piercing gaze.

"What have you to say for yourself, sister?" the preacher cried out. A handful in the crowd repeated his question. Others called out "Sinner!" "Disgrace!" "Shameful!" "Harlot!" I felt the preacher's hand still on my shoulder, and he seemed to squeeze it. I thought he was encouraging me to call out something as well, and I felt incapable of disappointing him. So I said the first thing that came to mind. "I love you!" I cried.

Ella knit her brow and frowned. She looked for my voice and very quickly spotted me standing next to the preacher. She looked confused, but only for a moment. She turned her attention back to the preacher, who had followed my declaration of love with some necessary context. "This man says he loves you, as God loves you, for He loves all His children. We are all sinners, we are all wretched, we are weak, but we have a choice. To continue down this path of sin or to find redemption in the eyes of our Lord, Jesus. This man says he loves you! Well, we all love you, sister. I love you, my wife loves you, my child loves you, because we are all the children of God exiled from Eden and we must find a path through the darkness. We must find the light, understand me, we must find it together. So, sister, answer me, why do you choose the path of darkness, why do you live with a man who is not your husband, when matrimony with the blessing of the Lord promises nothing but righteous communion?"

Again, the preacher's voice had me enthralled, its rising and falling cadence. When the voice rose, I rose. When the voice lowered, I lowered. I was almost annoyed when Ella interrupted him, and I wanted to cry out, "Let the man speak!" But her voice silenced his, as it did the rest of the crowd.

"I don't want to ever get married," she said, cutting right to the chase. "You want to know why? Because then I'd be stuck, just like everyone here. Like my sister, like you Lupe, Maria, Elisa, Susy. You should all be ashamed of yourselves—you should just go home to your miserable lives. You'll die here, and if you don't die here, you'll die in a place just like it. I'm going to explore this world, live wherever I want, and do whatever I please. I'd rather live in sin than live a slave. And you—" her face was angry now, and she pointed, and at first I thought she was pointing toward me in order to out me to the crowd, but to my relief she was pointing at the preacher— "you don't know who I am. You don't know the life I've lived. What I've seen or what I've suffered." And then she began to cry. She fell against the doorframe, her pale, round forearm covering her face as she tried to hide her sobs.

The crowd remained silent. Soon they began to disperse, backstepping and sidestepping, looking down at the ground, repositioning their hats, checking their watches, pretending that they were merely bystanders to Ella's grief. I followed their example. I tied my shoelaces and then helped carry an umbrella for two old women as they walked away. I feared that the crowd, on learning that I was the lustful man preying on this poor young girl, would regain their furor and direct it at me. Better that I return when things cooled down. But the farther I walked from my studio, and the more I heard my neighbors, men and women alike, muttering to one another, "Who's miserable? I'm not miserable! Clearly, she's the miserable one," or "I sure don't envy the man she marries," I couldn't help but reflect on her words. She'd never told me any of this before. I knew she wanted to go on adventures. I *also* planned to go on adventures. Wasn't I always telling her, "When we're living on the Boulevard Saint-Michel, we'll do *this* and *that*"? And what was that about never marrying and wanting to be free to do whatever she wanted, whenever she wanted, and to go wherever she pleased? Was she already tired of being my model and muse?

I walked for five miles. I know because I arrived at a sign that said TSSS FACTORY 5 MILES. I turned back. By the time I reached the work camp, it was dusk. I had run through all the reasons Ella might be unsatisfied with our life together, and I kept coming back to an incident a few days before. Ella had been thumbing through a magazine her sister had given her, and she'd held up a photo of a balding artist standing cross-armed before a paint-splattered canvas. "Maybe you could do something like this," she said, her eyebrows raised expectantly. "It says here he sells a lot of paintings." At the time, I hadn't taken her seriously, but now I saw that maybe her suggestion had been made in earnest. I decided I must sit her down and explain not only why I couldn't fall prey to contemporary fads, but also why steely-eyed realism in New Mexico was as relevant today as it had been in nineteenth-century Paris. I was formulating my arguments when in the distance I saw a man and a woman sitting on our front steps.

As I approached, I saw that the woman was actually standing and it was Ella. She was wiping her eyes with the palms of her hands. The man at her side was the preacher. He was seated with a foot on one step and the other foot on another. His suit jacket was open, and he was gesticulating with his hands. I could hear his voice. He was talking about all the places he'd been, by foot mostly, up north, out west, back east, nothing but a suitcase full of clothes and his Bible. His wife and child walked with him. And when they tired, they stopped. And when they stopped, he spoke to people about faith and hope and justice. He spoke to them about Jesus. He had been to a thousand towns and a hundred cities, and he'd spoken to thousands of people, and every day was different, and every night they slept in a different place, but the road was beautiful, he said, and ever changing.

I heard Ella's voice say, "Your wife and boy must get tired."

And the preacher laughed. "Yes, yes, they do. The road is not for everyone."

They now looked up to see me approaching. Ella said something to him that I couldn't hear, but in response the preacher stood up quickly, dusted off his hat and placed it on his head, and already had his hand extended to shake mine. He looked much younger now that he wasn't preaching. He had a boyish air about him, and he was grinning from ear to ear. But then he must have recognized me from the crowd, because his smile disappeared and was replaced by a confused frown.

"Weren't you—?"

"Yes, he was, right next to you," Ella said. Then she turned toward me. "Where were you just now?"

"I walked five miles that way and then came back," I said. "I was thinking about what you said and how you didn't want to marry me, and . . . well"—the arguments I had been rehashing became muddled and I stumbled over my words—"I mean, is it because you'd rather that I adopt a more contemporary style? Perhaps these would sell better, but—"

"Stop it," Ella said, cutting me off. Her voice was low and sharp. Then she turned to the preacher, the same man who hours before had brought her to tears, and in a kind, melodious voice said, "Thank you for your words. They meant a lot to me."

"Yes, and again, I'm sorry for what happened today," he said, bowing his head. "It was not my intention. Sometimes . . . these things . . . like I said, I meant no harm." He held out his hand, and Ella shook it. Then she gave me a wary glance and turned and stomped up the steps and into the studio. I started to follow her, but the preacher grabbed my arm. He nodded solemnly. "Give her a moment," he said.

The door closed behind Ella. I stared after her, wanting to follow and knowing that I should, but I felt as though I were the stranger and the preacher her confidant. They certainly seemed to have developed a nice rapport in my absence. Hell, I thought to myself, after today's outburst and meltdown, the whole factory camp knew Ella better than I did. I wanted to follow her inside and demand that she tell me everything. What life had she lived before me? What travails had she endured? Could she be more specific about the adventures she wished to have and her timeline for such adventures? Is it true that she preferred the childlike finger paintings found in flashy magazine spreads? But the young preacher continued to hold on to my arm, and I was torn. My initial impressions of him returned, and they beckoned my attention. Hadn't I declared him a genius, a man to be emulated? How could I not take advantage of this opportunity to remain at his side?

"Come, let's go for a walk," he said. "Give her some time."

"What did she tell you?" I asked.

"Tell me? She told me nothing. I spoke to her. I wanted to apologize for what happened this afternoon. When she broke into sobs, I realized I had erred. I was the sinner, the aggressor, the wrongdoer. Vanity had blinded me to the harm that I was capable of. I seek to lead men to Christ, not to lead men against one another."

"Did you convince her to marry me so that we no longer live in sin?"

The preacher laughed. We began to walk away from the studio and into the encroaching darkness. "No, in fact, we mostly spoke about being orphans."

"Did she tell you I was an orphan, too," I said.

"No, she didn't. I'm sorry. Then you, too, have walked this earth alone after your parents' death?"

"Yes. Well, my mother is still alive."

The preacher stopped. "If your mother isn't dead, then you're not an orphan," he said.

"She has abandoned me, and has no desire to see me, so it's as if she's dead."

The preacher's thick brow furrowed.

I continued: "My father was killed unjustly, his land taken from him, and my mother, my baby sister, and I were forced to live in unimaginable squalor. Her only way out was to marry again. But to do so she had to abandon me to my wretched fate."

"So this man she married, he is not a good man?"

"No—well, he's a good man in the sense that he sends me money every month, and gave me painting and drawing supplies, and he set me up in this studio to paint."

"Sounds like a very generous man."

"Yes, if you look at it like that, in terms of giving. But he also wants me as far away from my mother as possible."

The preacher nodded his head and said, "I see. It sounds very complicated. But you're not technically an orphan unless both your parents are dead."

"Are both your parents dead?"

"I'm not an orphan. My mother died when I was young, but—"The preacher hesitated. He looked deep into my eyes as though sizing me up, unsure if he wanted to take me into his confidence. "Come to think of it, I know what you mean. My father is still alive, but it's as if he's dead—"

"Yes, exactly!" I cried.

"He is a weak man," the preacher continued. "He has lived his entire life like a caged animal, and he has suffered both physically and spiritually. He has never been able to stand up for himself. A man like this, a man who cannot stand up against the master that abuses him day in and day out, is as good as dead."

"So is Ella an orphan with both parents dead or with one parent dead and one parent as good as dead?" I asked, feeling that I now understood the distinction.

"Both parents dead," he said.

"Oh."

We were quiet for a long time after that. As we continued walking, the preacher appeared lost in thought. Finally, he started speaking again. He told me about his great-grandfather killed by Anglos in Texas, who then stole his land. He told me about his life as a migrant farm laborer and the squalor in which the workers lived, how the white farmers would run them out of town after all the work was done so that they wouldn't have to pay their wages. He told me about the time a group of vigilantes came and strung a noose around his father's neck because they wanted to steal his corn. He gave me a detailed account of his mother's early death, when he was just six, and how it was she who had given him the greatest gift, the belief that all of earth's wrongs would be righted, that justice would be meted out, the poor made rich and the rich made poor, the abused would judge the abuser, and the dispossessed would find their way home.

I listened, enthralled, but I had to interrupt, the suspense was killing me. "Do you think we look alike?" I asked.

"How do you mean?" he sputtered.

"I mean, do we look alike?"

"I don't think so."

"Oh," I said, disappointed.

The preacher was quiet, with a baffled expression.

"What is your name?" I asked to break the silence.

"Reies López Tijerina," he said.[14]

"Okay, Reies, what does this have to do with me?"

"With you?"

"Yes, why are you telling me all this?"

"All what?"

"What you were saying just now."

"Oh, I was telling you about justice."

"Why?"

"Because I believe in it and I want you to believe in it, too."

"Justice for what?"

---

14. Lorraine writes, "This is where I about fell out of my chair. Reies López Tijerina was once the most famous (or infamous depending on what side you were on) man in New Mexico. In the 1960s, he founded La Alianza, which sought to reclaim Hispano-American land stripped away by whites after the Mexican-American War ended in 1848. His tactics included marches, citizen arrests, and taking over Kit Carson National Forest and declaring it a sovereign state. Long before he became a hero to Chicano activists across the country, he was just a young evangelist preacher crisscrossing the country." Lorraine is exactly right. In what can only be described as a Forrest Gumpian moment, our narrator inadvertently crosses paths with an important historical figure. The question is, important for whom? Tijerina was a larger than life personality, polarizing, inspiring, a prophet to many. His big dreams fit squarely into his time: Chicano activists may have clamored for a metaphorical homeland, but Tijerina and his followers laid claim to a physical one. But who today knows Tijerina's name? To be a Chicanx scholar, to know its historical figures and events, its cultural documents, is to speak in code or gibberish or to feel as if you've made everything up. Or worse: it's to speak legibly and make up nothing, only to realize that no one cares.

"For all of us who suffer."

"I have a confession to make," I said. "You are an incredible orator, but half the time I have no idea what you're talking about!"

"Thank you," Reies said. A smile crept across his face, and for a moment he looked like the teenager that he was. Then he broke into a high-pitched nervous laugh. "But I *want* you to care what I'm talking about. Otherwise it is a skill gone to waste."

"Well, I'm sure that most people do. I was wondering if you could tell me your secret. How did you learn to speak like that? Today when you were talking, I thought to myself that I would give up all my God-given talent to speak as you do, to move crowds like you did today!"

"It's passion," he said without hesitation. "A passion for justice."

"I have passion," I said.

"For justice?" he asked, reaching out to clutch my arm.

"No, for my art."

He let go of my arm. "Tell me about your art then," he said.

I gave him a brief rundown of my history as an artist, going back to my days in La Trampa on my father's estate trying to draw the workers who were unwilling or unable to stand still for longer than a minute. I told him about my time in Albuquerque trying to satisfy my teacher, the grandson of Jean-François Millet, and the Salon des Refusés Art Academy, and how we had only recently lost touch after my move to the TSSS factory. I explained my preference for the French realists, my love of Courbet, my desire to be Courbet in New Mexico, my desire to paint unflinching portraits of stone breakers and grain workers, and finally, my desire to go to Paris and gain entry into the Parisian art world.

Reies stopped me at this point and asked, "Why do you want to gain entry into the Parisian art world?"

"Why?" I scoffed. "Why? Why?" And I repeated that a few more times before I threw the question back at him, "Why do you want justice to triumph?"

"Because it is God's will," he said without hesitation.

"Well, it's God's will that I gain entry into the Parisian art world."

After that we were silent again. I was annoyed that such a silly question had been posed—*why* would I wish to gain entry into the Parisian art world?—and I was annoyed at myself for answering that it was God's will. It wasn't God's will. It was my will, my desire, my wish and my wish only, and so many years had passed and I was no closer to getting to Paris than when I had been as a teenager frolicking in the mountains. In fact, it seemed that God's will was to *prevent* me from getting to Paris.

I confessed this to Reies. "It is my will only," I mumbled. "God seems set against it."

"I know what you mean. I feel the same way about justice. Everywhere I turn it is the poor and the Spanish-speaking people of this land who continue to suffer. Mexicans, Hispanos, *our* people!" He again reached out and shook my shoulder as though to emphasize this last part.

"Our people?" I asked. All I could think of was the workers back at the camp who had called me and Ella fornicators and wanted to tear down our house of sin.

"Yes, *our* people. We seem destined to suffer our entire lives. But the Lord works in mysterious ways. These are only His tests."

"Tests of what?"

"Of our faith. Don't lose faith, my friend."

"Thank you, Reies," I said, feeling that at the very least I had met a kindred spirit. Of course, I used to say the same about my dearest Enrique, but his only passion had been for supporting us, and now, it seemed, it was for writing letters that I couldn't bring myself to open. But Reies's passion rivaled my own, and he was right, the road was filled with tests created to kill that passion. But we would endure—I was sure of it—we would not be defeated. Having met Reies, I felt a little less alone in my quest, and I wanted to give him something, a token of gratitude, something to acknowledge this fortuitous meeting. I decided to give him one of my drawings.

It seemed that God's will was to prevent me from getting to Paris.

"Everywhere I turn it is the poor who continue to suffer."

"These are only His tests."

"Test of what?"

"Of our faith."

"Reies, I want to give you a piece of my art, if you'll accept it. Something to remember mc by."

He eyed me hesitantly at first. "Are you sure?" he asked.

"Yes, I'm sure. Why would I not be sure?"

"It's just that Ella said—"

"Ella won't mind. Yes, I've given every drawing to her—she's my muse after all—but I'm certain she'd want you to have one as well. Come on, let's get back to the studio."

We turned and made our way back to the workers camp. Reies kept saying that he should get back to his wife and child, but I wouldn't hear of it until he had one of my drawings in hand. We found Ella where I assumed she'd be, staring longingly out the window, sighing. I rushed in and went directly to the trunk at the foot of the bed. "I'm going to give Reies a drawing as a token of friendship," I told her. "He's not such a bad guy, you know? This afternoon was all just a mis-understanding. Anyhow, let me see—"

"I should be going," Reies said. "My wife is waiting for me."

"One second, Reies," and I picked out a drawing of Ella sitting in her slip on the edge of the bed, staring forlornly at her hands in her lap.

"I can't accept that," Reies said. "I—I—it wouldn't be proper."

"It's a work of art, what wouldn't be proper about it? It's a depiction of beauty, isn't that right, Ella?" I turned to her.

Ella remained silent. She was staring at me with pursed lips and wide eyes. She was fuming. Why was she fuming? Could she really not bear to part with one of her drawings?

"Don't worry, my love, it's just one. I'll make plenty more for you."

"I can't accept it, I'm sorry," Reies said. "And I really should be going." This time he didn't wait for my consent. The door was already open, and he slipped out. I heard his footsteps bound down the steps and then hit the dirt.

I turned back to Ella. "What's wrong with you?"

That was when she exploded. "Auuuuuuuuuuuuuuuugh!" she screamed at the top of her lungs, her mouth open so wide that I glimpsed her tonsils. "I don't want any more drawings of me!" she yelled. "I'm tired of posing! I'm tired of being your muse. You can't draw anything else. All you draw is me, and I'm sick of seeing myself over and over and over!"

I was stunned. "Where is this coming from? Why didn't you just say so? I can draw other things."

"No, no, you can't," she whimpered. She had quieted and her chest was rising and lowering. I didn't think any more screams would come out of her. I was mistaken.

"Auuuuuuuuuuuuuuuugh!" she screamed again.

"Shhhhhhh! Calm down, calm down. There's no need to get upset over this."

"No, there is," she said. "I've been living with you for an entire year now, and all you do is talk about going to Paris and becoming a famous artist, and you look through your giant book of pictures and you talk to them as if they're your best friends. I actually believed you. I thought we really were going to Paris, or if not Paris, then somewhere, anywhere, other than this dump."

"It's just a matter of time," I said. "Look how productive I've been! All these drawings of you, and even a few paintings. You should be honored, grateful!"

Ella scoffed. "Grateful?" She picked up one of my drawings from the floor. "For *this?*" she said, her brow arched in disdain. She let the drawing fall, and then she stood up and walked toward the door. She looked very short at that moment, disgustingly short, and because she had aimed to hurt me, I aimed to hurt her.

"You look like a dwarf," I said.

She stared at me, her big green eyes full of disappointment and maybe even hatred, and shook her head. The door closed behind her. I wanted to call after her, to apologize for calling her a dwarf, already I regretted it, but I half hoped that she too regretted her cruelty and would return to beg my forgiveness.

I waited for her all night. I lit all the candles and examined the trunk where most of my drawings were, all for Ella and all of her. She said that I couldn't draw anything else, but why should I? She was my muse, and I had been content, fulfilled for the first time in my life. Sure, I wasn't in Paris, but I was making do. I was in love, I was making my art. I didn't need anything more. But then I thought of that love—me happy, Ella miserable—and I plunged into a deep depression. I fought against it. I grabbed a piece of charcoal and a sheet of paper and started making dark, heavy marks. "I can't draw anything else, you say? Nothing but you, huh? Well, how about this!" And I drew a dark swirling cloud. I stared at it. I admired it. It was there, a drawing of something other than Ella. I set it aside, waiting for Ella to return. I would show her this drawing. I drew another and another, one dark swirling cloud after another, warding off the depression that was closing in on me. I felt as though if I stopped drawing, the depression would consume me. I drew dark swirling clouds until I ran out of paper, and still, Ella didn't return. I looked for more paper. The depression wrapped its arms around me. I began drawing on the walls, nothing but dark swirling clouds, and when I finished with the walls I began drawing on the floor. I drew until I ran out of charcoal. The depression took hold and began to squeeze and squeeze, and just when I could take no more, Ella returned.

She found me in the center of the floor, in the last square foot of space without a dark swirling cloud. She looked at me, her face exhausted. She had been crying. I wanted to apologize then and there for saying that she looked like a dwarf, but instead I cried out, "Is this what you wanted? A drawing of something other than you!" She looked around. Her mouth parted as if she had just now become aware of the charcoal storm she had entered. Eyes wide and eyebrows arched, she looked like she was ready to unleash another scream. She didn't though. She collected herself, and said, "You're right, these drawings aren't of me."

"Of course they're not," I cried. "Of course they're not!" And I felt vindicated. But instead of being able to bask in my small victory, I felt my body begin to spasm. I lost control of my arms. My right leg jerked wildly. I couldn't focus on anything, and soon I was thrashing back and forth. I was still conscious, wholly aware that an attack was upon me. I tried to fight it. Not now, not now, I told myself, willing my body to stop. My only consolation before blacking out was that surely an epileptic attack would scare Ella into feeling sorry for me. It would awaken her maternal instinct. She would want to take care of me, to nurse me back to health. She would realize that I was a poor, delicate soul who needed her love and care. My very last thought was a happy one. I imagined her there when I woke up, my head resting on her lap and she gently stroking my hair.

I was wrong. When I came to I was alone, surrounded by swirling charcoal clouds serving only to remind me of the dark cloud of depression I had tried in vain to keep at bay. I rose with a heavy weight on my chest. I found it difficult to breathe. I thought for a second that maybe Ella had returned home to her sister next door. I spent the next hour or so dismantling the wall I had built to cover the window, only to discover that her brother-in-law had erected a similar wall, probably for the same reason: to block out the sounds of our lovemaking. The thought of those sounds made the weight on my chest even heavier; I recalled the days and nights when Ella and I spent hours satisfying our carnal needs. I didn't know what to do with myself. I waited for Ella to come home, but as the hours passed, I became sure that she had left and had left for good. I was no stranger to abandonment. The question was how long I would wait before I went looking for her.

I waited four days. I didn't eat, I didn't bathe; I did nothing but stare at the door and hope that at any moment she would open it. I didn't even scrub the charcoal off the floor, and because it was too difficult to sleep in our conjugal bed, I slept on the floor and was soon covered head to toe in soot. On the morning of the fifth day, the mailman disturbed my abject misery. He knocked on the door, and I rushed to open it, thinking, of course, that it had to be Ella. When instead I saw a little old man with a yellowed white mustache carrying a bundle of letters, I fell to my knees and began to weep.

"Good god!" he cried. "Was there a fire? You look like you've been charred in the embers of hell."

I felt as though I had been. I wanted him to ask me what was wrong. I wanted to tell him my story of abandonment, of love gone sour, of drawings made and not made. I wanted to ask him if he had heard news of Ella. Instead he handed me a letter, which I assumed was from Enrique, and left. "Wait," I whimpered after him, but he was already gone. I rose from the floor and tossed the letter into the corner along with all the others. Ella had once asked me why I didn't open them, and instead of answering I simply covered her in kisses. That was my answer. Given the choice between the desperate pleas of an abandoned friend or the pleasures of a beautiful woman, the latter always won out. But now that I too had been abandoned, now that I too was desperate, now that there were no pleasures of a beautiful woman to be tempted by, I decided to examine the pile of letters. First, I counted them. Fifty in total. A nice round number. Then I noticed that in my haste, I hadn't seen that one of the letters was from Master Millet and that the most recent wasn't from Enrique, but from my mother.

Although I had long been desperate for something from my mother—a letter, a request to see me, a visit, any sign that she cared—I couldn't help but entertain the idea that perhaps Master Millet was writing to inform me that a gallery in Paris was interested in my artwork and wanted to give me a solo exhibition, all expenses paid, and was even willing to set me up in an apartment in Montmartre. That would really show Ella, I thought. My spirits lifting, I tore open the envelope, leaving charcoal smudges on everything I touched.

My hopes quickly turned into further disappointment. The letter informed me that Master Millet's Salon des Refusés Art Academy *By Mail* was being shuttered on account of fraud. As a condition of the settlement, the school had to return a portion of tuition paid, and write the letter I now had in hand, stating that he, Stuart Gall, was not Master Millet and that by impersonating Master Millet he had inflicted grave harm on his all-too-trusting victims. He now realized the error of his ways and was committed to undoing much of the harm he had caused, though he realized that that harm was irreversible. He wished for me, his longest standing student, to accept this check of ten dollars, a small amount when compared to the tuition paid, but it was all that he had left to be divided. He also apologized for the delay in locating my current address.

"But Stuart Gall was Master Millet's assistant!" I cried. "Impossible." I ripped the letter and the ten-dollar check to shreds, as though that were enough to preserve the integrity of my artistic education.

I turned my attention to my mother's letter.

Hers was very short. It said. "Son, please come to visit us soon. We have some grave news about your friend, Enrique. I understand that the bus leaves the TSSS factory on Friday. We will expect you sometime this weekend."

A little perturbed that Mr. Leyva, the driver, wasn't being sent to retrieve me, I nevertheless resolved that I needed to get to my mother as soon as possible. In my vulnerable state, waiting three days for a bus was an unbearable torture. If something had happened to Enrique, I needed to know immediately. Of course, I could've read his forty-eight letters and gleaned some information, but I wasn't quite in the mood for reading, especially letters that were probably long. Not only that, I had always been certain that the letters were full of laments about how I had abandoned him, how I had used him for years, how I had made him work three jobs around the clock, and then, when I'd found something better, I had left without even an explanation, and how instead of a real masterpiece I'd given him a smudged masterpiece covered in candle wax, and on and on about how miserable he was and how it was all my fault. I wasn't prepared to shoulder that burden, not now.

I set out at once walking toward Albuquerque. I thought that eventually some-one would offer me a ride, but maybe because I hadn't slept in days, and was covered in charcoal dust, and my facial hair, never very thick, had quickly grown long and wispy in the manner of a Chinese sage, cars just sped by as if I were a roadside hobo. I kept walking, stopping to rest when my feet could take no more. The landscape was impressive, so open and vast. The sky was cloudy and seemed to stretch on forever. I continued on until I collapsed from exhaustion, my feet in excruciating pain. As I lay there with my back against the hard earth, the sun high in the sky peeking out from a gigantic cloud, I felt something in my pocket. I looked down and realized for the first time that I had brought Enrique's letters with me. Unable to rise, stranded in the middle of nowhere, for I had long veered off the main road, not a car or a person for miles around, I decided that I might as well open one of the letters and see what my dear old friend had to say about how miserable a dear old friend I was.

I chose a letter at random. So weak was I that I found it difficult to rip open the envelope. So I tore it open with my teeth. Inside, I found two pages. Neither of them had the appearance of a letter. No "Dearest Friend" or kind salutation, just words and lines irregularly placed. I looked for a third page, but there was none. I held up one of the pages, blinked and strained my eyes to focus, and saw that Enrique had written a poem. "A poem!" I exclaimed to the rocks and dirt and open sky, and I laughed as I recalled trying to convince him that if I were Courbet then, logically, he must be Baudelaire. I stopped laughing, however, when I started reading.

It was a beautiful poem about two poor men sharing a room above a mechanic's garage, and how late at night they discussed nothing but their love of the light at dusk, the colors of the seasons, and the surreal magic of dreams. I was in a wretched state. Heartbroken and abandoned, sleep deprived, physically exhausted, my face covered in soot, my feet aching from blisters, and yet my spirit was lifted by the words. I found myself rising from the ground, and soon I couldn't help but recite the poem aloud, and not just aloud but actually screaming the words to the immense openness that surrounded me. Enrique's words filled me with hope. Once I finished that poem, I moved on to the next envelope and discovered more poems. He hadn't sent letters after all; he had sent me poetry! I only wish I could share those poems now. What I have is only the memory of that discovery, that my friend Enrique was a genius, a poet for the ages. His words lifted me off the rock-strewn arid earth and gave me the energy to finish my journey. I wanted to find Enrique. I would throw myself at his feet and beg his forgiveness. I had forsaken him. I had followed a selfish path, and where had it led me? Truthfully, where I deserved. Abandoned by the woman I loved, my artistic talent in question. Well, I didn't need her as long as I had Enrique. I continued walking full of purpose, full of excitement, reading and rereading his poems, reciting my favorite lines aloud, and soon I was on the outskirts of Albuquerque.

I debated whether to go directly to Enrique's or to my mother's. Then I remembered my mother's letter. She told me she had grave news about Enrique. I hadn't even considered what that grave news might be. I had assumed, just as I had about the letters, that somehow this grave news involved my abandonment of him. But if I had been wrong about the letters, then perhaps I was also wrong about the grave news. I pictured Enrique in a hospital room suffering from tuberculosis. I would nurse him back to health, I thought, and I was almost moved to tears as I imagined myself ladling spoonsful of soup between his pale blue lips. I was now running toward my mother's neighborhood, and soon I was on a quiet shady street, perfectly manicured. Compared to the TSSS factory workers camp, this was a slice of heaven. Compared to the young couple that passed by, walking arm in arm, scrubbed clean and wearing only the finest clothes, I looked like a sewer rat. I didn't have time to worry about my appearance. I ignored their expressions of revulsion tinged with fear and pushed on. I found Mr. Buenrostro's house and knocked on the door.

The maid answered and let out a scream.

"I'm here to see my mother," I said.

The maid slammed the door in my face. I knocked again. This time Mr. Buenrostro answered it, full of aggression, ready to pounce on the intruder, but after a moment he recognized me, and the expression on his face softened. "You came," he said. "We expected you later."

"I received my mother's letter," I said.

He nodded his head solemnly and led me into the parlor. "Wait here," he said. Then he looked me up and down and asked, "What did you do, walk here through a fire?"

"It has been a very difficult time for me," I confessed.

When he returned, my mother was at his side. On seeing me she burst into tears, which I anticipated. But whether her tears were tears of joy, tears on account of seeing me in such a sorry state, or tears of guilt for casting off her first born to the ends of the earth, I couldn't yet tell. Two small children followed behind her. "Hello!" I said to them. They ran away crying. Soon my sister Lourdes entered the room, and even though she walked in full of haughty confidence, most likely ready to deride me and call me a hobo, a beggar, and a good-for-nothing, her attitude changed when she saw that I indeed looked like a hobo, a beggar, and a good-for-nothing. After all, what sport was there in kicking a man already on the ground?

"Oh, my God," she said. "What happened to you? Do you really work in a coal factory now?"

"This is charcoal," I said. "I've been drawing."

My mother wiped her cheeks and walked toward me. "Sit," she said, and she placed her hand on my arm. I wanted to hug her, but just as I was about to sit down on the sofa and melt into her arms, she asked that I sit on a wooden rocking chair so as not to soil the fabric.

I was nervous. Except for the children crying, everyone was subdued, almost mournful. Mr. Buenrostro was quieter than I remembered. My sister didn't seem as sassy. My mother's tears, I determined, were tears of sorrow.

"Why the long faces?" I blurted out. "Did someone die?"

"Yes," my mother said.

"Yes, what?"

"Yes, someone died."

"Who?"

"Enrique."

"Enrique? No, that can't be, he has consumption—" Then it hit me. This was the grave news. "He's dead?" I asked, my voice weakening.

My mother nodded. I looked to Mr. Buenrostro for further confirmation. He nodded. I looked to my sister. She was looking behind me. "You're going to knock over that vase," she said. I turned around. She was right. I was rocking so forcibly that the chair had slid dangerously close to a large porcelain vase full of colorful papers flowers. I stopped rocking and picked up the rocker and moved it back toward my mother. Then I stood up and said, "I really should be going now!"

"Wait," my mother said, rising with me. "Don't you want to know how he died?"

"Died? Who died? No, I don't want to know anything about anyone dying, good God, what morbidity!" And I started laughing. I thought that if I didn't hear anything more about Enrique that I could pretend he was still alive. I could pretend that I would see him soon, that we would resume our creative partnership—me the great painter, he the great poet—sharing a room above a mechanic's garage. A year had already passed without my seeing him, but he had still been living and breathing, writing me poems that I assumed to be letters. If I didn't see him for five years, he could just as easily still be alive. Does a tree crashing in a forest make any noise if there's no one around to hear it? Does a tree in a forest even fall down if there's no one around to witness its fall? If I never saw him again, he could just as well be alive, just as I was alive and not seen by him. I was making absolutely no sense to myself, but as long as I was lost in my own muddled reasoning, I could ignore what I'd just learned, and I could ignore the sad faces gathered in the room.

"He killed himself," my mother said.

"Oh, very good," I said. "It has been a wonderful visit, and I do wish you all the best. I had long been hoping for an invitation to dinner or to one of your many parties, even your birthday, little lady," I said, patting my sister on the head.

"My son, stop—"

"Very well!" I cried, trying to drown out the sound of my mother's voice. I extended my hand to shake Mr. Buenrostro's. "Good to see you, sir!" He reached for my hand and then pulled me toward him. He wrapped his arms around me in an embrace.

"I'm sorry," he said.

I tried releasing myself, but Mr. Buenrostro was a large man and I was helpless. I squirmed in place. He placed his lips next to my ear and whispered, "It's okay to mourn. We are here for you."

I found the strength to free myself. "Something I'd like to address," I cried. "If I needed consoling, this is the last place I'd come to. In an entire year, you've never visited me once!"

"You know you are always welcome here," my mother interrupted. "We were just a bus ride away."

"No, I *didn't* know I was welcome here, which is why I didn't come until I was summoned by your note. When asked, I came, very simple."

"We thought you wanted your privacy," my mother said.

"As I was saying, there is nothing I need to be consoled about!" I was still hoping to delude myself. My sister had other ideas.

"Yes, there is," she said. She crossed her arms and gave me a look as if a gauntlet were about to be thrown down.

I wasn't going to fall into her trap. "Aren't you a strange little girl," I said. "What do you know about anything but dolls and pretty dresses?"

"I know that your girlfriend left you for a preacher and now you're all alone."

This hit hard. How would she know this? How would she know anything about Ella? Mr. Buenrostro answered my question. "Worker chatter gets back to me," he said. "We heard you were living with a woman. We were happy for you. We thought this was a good thing—"

"We even hoped you would bring her to meet us, when you were ready, of course," my mother chimed in.

"But then I heard the other day," Mr. Buenrostro said, his eyes looking at me sympathetically, "that she took off with a preacher."

"With Reies? With my friend, Reies?" I started chuckling. "No, no, that's not true either! Oh, my God!" I was laughing uncontrollably. In my weakened state this seemed my only defense. This was all too much information. I wasn't ready

I'm told of Enrique's death.

"He killed himself," my mother said.

Mr. Buenrostro wrapped his arms

around me in an embrace.

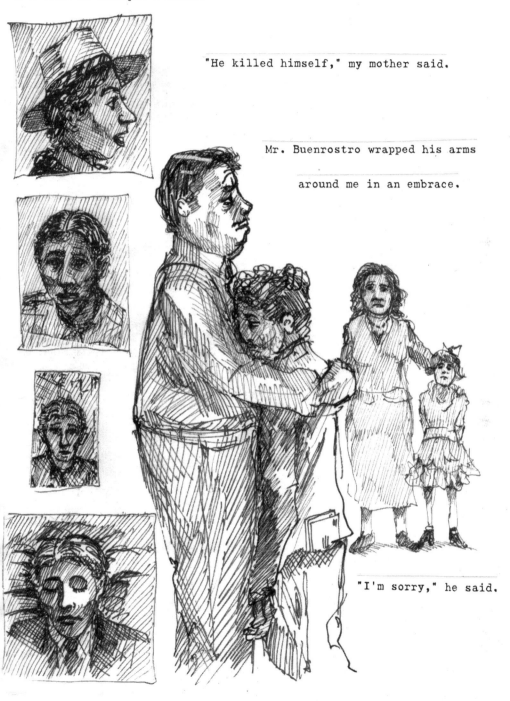

"I'm sorry," he said.

to accept Enrique's death. Nor was I ready to accept that Ella was gone and wasn't coming back. The sooner I got out of this house full of people who wanted nothing more than for me to feel sorry about my life, the better. I ran toward the door, ignored my mother's pleas to stop, opened it, and just as I was about to slam it behind me I heard my little sister say, "He's even crazier now."

Maybe I was. I made it back to the TSSS factory and don't even remember the journey. My feet were bloody when I arrived. I still had Enrique's stack of poems. They were stuffed in my pockets. Once I was back in my studio, I pulled them out, smoothing each page, and began reading. His voice was alive, and if his voice were alive then *he* was alive. As I read, Enrique was in the room with me. I could hear his breathing after a long day's work. By the lamplight, I could see his smooth olive skin and the spidery shadow cast on his cheek by his impossibly long eyelashes. I could see his excitement as I described my next drawing, which would be of him, of course! I read one poem after another until I fell asleep. "Of course you're alive" I kept saying to Enrique. "Of course I am," he kept saying back to me.

CHAPTER SIX

The next morning, I awoke and decided that I must go in search of Ella. According to worker gossip, Ella had departed with Reies, but I wasn't going to so easily fall prey to rumors and innuendo. Sure, she had left her sister's house to be with me, but that didn't mean she had left my studio to be *with* Reies. Reies was a man of God, and married to a good woman. Even though we hadn't spent much time together and he didn't accept one of my drawings and left without saying goodbye, I considered the two of us friends, kindred spirits if not long-lost twins, and I didn't believe he would betray that trust. But as I looked around my studio, the walls and floors covered in swirling charcoal dust clouds, I was a little less certain. Ella was unimpressed by my artistry, but Reies, he inspired and moved people, and what's more, he didn't just dream about traveling the world, waiting for his passion to guide the way, he actually did so. Reies could give her what I could not.[15] My resistance to the worker gossip quickly dissolved.

15. Lorraine writes, "I know this was sixty years ago and Ernie's uncle is from a different generation and all, but his sexism, yes, I said it, is preventing him from recognizing that Ella is a prophet in her own right. She's a free spirit who won't be chained down and she sure as hell won't stand to be someone's muse. I wonder whether her name was really Ella or if this dude was simply referring to her as *ella*, 'she.' Makes my blood boil." Ella could be short for something like Isabella. It also wasn't uncommon in this era for Mexican Americans to take on more American sounding names. But that's not really Lorraine's point. Does our narrator reveal sexist bias in overlooking Ella's visionary attributes? If so, how do we judge him? To my mind, Chicanx scholarship, which places queerness and feminism at its core, is at a crossroads. The Chicano Movement and the activists, artists, and scholars that emerged from it were certainly tainted by the sexism and homophobia of their time. Do we "allow" for that larger context—it wasn't just Chicano men who were sexist and homophobic, but society as a whole, as it continues to be—or do we sweep these men into the dustbin of history?

Without packing my bags, my art supplies, my preparatory notes, or *The Great Book of French Painting,* or even cans of food, I walked out of my studio convinced that Ella had left me for a worthier man. I carried nothing but Enrique's poems, which I had again stuffed into my pockets. I was now impervious to the pain in my feet. I walked over rocks, burrs, pieces of glass, and hot pavement. Nothing deterred me. I vaguely recalled that Reies had said they would be heading west. I had nothing else to go on, so I walked toward the setting sun, expecting at any moment to come across their camp.

It took me five days. By then I was delirious. I had alternately convinced myself of Reies's goodness and of his complete depravity. I imagined him persuading Ella to return home to me, as a good friend would do. Then I imagined that he had somehow orchestrated Ella's breakdown in order to give her an excuse to leave with him and become part of his Jesus-loving harem. I cried out at these moments and swore vengeance on Reies, on Ella, on his wife, and even the helpless child. "I'll punch you all in the face!" I cried. But then an hour or so later my desire for retribution was replaced by a desire to talk to Reies, to seek his counsel, to ask his advice on relationships, to see if he might impart some of his oratory skills so that I too could sway crowds. "We are long lost brothers, Reies!" I yelled at the top of my lungs. I would feel bad for having such horrible thoughts about him, and when I noticed those thoughts returning, I would fight back, attempt to repel them, but always in vain. I was truly of two minds.

When I finally found Reies, he was in the middle of giving a speech. Not to a crowd, but to his wife. He was standing on top of a rock, and she was standing below him, and the kid was crawling around in the dirt, crying.

"You say you're tired of me giving away all our money. You say you're tired that every time a congregation of followers gathers money together to help us on our way, I decide to give it to the first beggar who crosses our path. You say you're tired of not having enough to eat, of sleeping on dirt, of walking twenty miles every day. You say you're tired of living like Indians. Well, I tell you I'm tired of all the same things, but would I take away the money from the beggars, would I abuse the trust and faith of my followers and take their hard-earned money for my own profit, would I sleep comfortably on a featherbed while my brothers and sisters live like the Indians you scorn, nothing but their own poverty guiding them from miserable job to miserable job?"

"Just once, Reies! Just once!" his wife said, her hands on her hips. "Why should the beggar spend *our* money on booze when all I'm asking for is milk for your son?"

If I had been in a better mood I would've looked for Ella, and, not seeing her, inquired as to her whereabouts. But for the last half hour I had been stumbling forward swearing vengeance on Reies and all those who kept his company. I stood stunned for a moment, unable to believe that the first people I'd come across in five days of walking through such vast and empty territory were the very people I was looking for. They didn't notice me, focused as they were on their marital spat. In fact, with their speechifying and the baby's cries masking my footsteps, they noticed me only when I dragged Reies down from his rock pulpit.

"You took my Ella!" I cried as I tried wrestling him to the dirt. "You took her, and I thought you were my friend!"

I moved and thrashed and heaved and pushed until I realized that Reies was on top of me, pinning my arms to my sides. Later, he would explain that he thought I was hugging him in gratitude or relief, and only when he heard what I was saying did he realize I had attacked him in anger. By then we were sitting around a fire, and I was slurping down a steaming bowl of beans, and his wife was nursing my feet, which were bleeding and covered in sores.

I told Reies what had happened, how because he and Ella had left at the same time, the workers in camp assumed that Ella had left with him, to be with him, to break up his marriage, and how even though I didn't believe it for one second, I let my emotions get the best of me. That was when Reies explained that Ella *had* left with them, not to be with him, but to accompany them on their journey. But after two days she grew tired of walking. "Of course, you realize," he explained, "five steps for us are like twenty steps for her."

I stood stunned for a moment, unable to believe that the first people I'd come aross in five days of walking through such vast and empty territory were the very people I was looking for.

They didn't notice me, focused as they were on their marital spat.

I didn't realize this. Except for back and forth in my studio, I hadn't seen Ella walk much. "How do you mean?" I asked.

"Well, her legs are quite short!" Reies said, chuckling. Even his wife, who had been sullen faced, broke into a smile.

I acknowledged that they were. "That's one of the things I feel really horrible about," I said. "Upon parting, I told her she looked like a dwarf. Imagine, those were my last words to her! That's what she has to remember me by."

Reies furrowed his brow. "But she is a dwarf."

"She's just short," I said. "Many women are short. That doesn't mean they're dwarfs."

"No, she's a dwarf," Reies insisted. He was about to launch into a long explanation—I could tell because he always began gesticulating when a discussion required it—but his wife cut him off. "Reies, enough," she said sharply.

He looked at her, confused, as though unable to comprehend why this conversation merited censure, but he quieted and we changed subjects.

He explained that Ella had decided to head west on her own, and that if I cared to I was more than welcome to join them, as they were heading west as well. "It's not easy," he said. "My wife María will tell you that"—I heard her scoff. "We are seeking the *Lord's* comfort, not physical comfort." Then he quoted a few passages from the Gospels about the virtues of asceticism. His voice grew louder, and I realized that he was directing these words at his wife, who had walked away to nurse the baby.

I would quickly discover that their squabbling was constant, that the marital dispute I witnessed when I caught up to them was their normal banter. When we awoke the next morning, they were arguing about breakfast. Reies was fine sucking on stones. María wanted scrambled eggs. Reies recited more Gospel passages. His wife allowed the baby to cry as though hoping to drown out her husband. I kept quiet. I was Reies's guest and it wasn't my place to intervene, though I wanted eggs too and was even hoping for some bacon. Still, the stones weren't so bad, and it wasn't too long before the grumbling in my stomach ceased. But I understood his wife's frustration. After walking for hours in the hot sun, the hunger pains returned, and despite throwing some smooth pebbles into our mouths, we were all very parched. We came across a farmer who offered us water, but Reies, to prove a point, refused the water. He wanted to prove to the Lord Jesus Christ that he would suffer as He had suffered. I thought he did it to spite his wife. She must have thought so too, because for the rest of the day she wouldn't even look at him.

That evening we arrived in a small town on the border of New Mexico and Arizona. First matter of business was to ask if anyone had seen Ella. When no one showed any sign of knowing an Ella, Reies asked them if they'd seen a very pretty thing about yay high with golden hair and green eyes walking through all by her lonesome. Reies held his hand just above his belt. I was about to contest the yay high part when a man told him that he'd been visiting his cousin up north and a short little thing matching that description had passed through, and no one would have paid any attention except that she was trying to sell drawings of a woman sitting in a windowsill wearing nothing but a slip.

This was a bitter pill to swallow. I hadn't even thought to take the drawings at the bottom of the trunk! Now I learned that *she* had taken them and was hawking them for a quick buck. In my eyes, she might as well have been turning tricks.

"How much was she selling them for?" Reies asked.

"Twenty dollars," the man said. "And she sold every one!"

Reies thought this news would cheer me up. "Some artists die without ever having sold a picture. You've cleaned up in just one town!"

I started to weep. Without skipping a beat, Reies began delivering a sermon to the gathered crowd. He used me as an example, the first but certainly not the last time he would do so. He pointed to my bleeding feet, my tattered clothes, and my unshaven, unkempt face, as proof of God's absolute power. Because God had given me love, he had also taken it away. He had also given me the pain in my heart, just as not too long ago he had given me its joy. I felt everyone's eyes on me. I couldn't stop crying. All I could think about was Ella selling my drawings for twenty dollars a pop while I traveled on foot penniless. She could travel by bus to San Francisco and back on that money. For that matter, she could probably buy passage on a steamer to Paris! I would never catch up to her. "I'll never find her!" I cried, momentarily interrupting Reies's sermon. Unfazed, he yelled back, "But you will find God in every new breath!"

When he finished his sermon, we returned to the road, heading north. We found shelter in an abandoned barn, and then were off again before sunrise. By nine o'clock the next morning we arrived in the town where Ella was said to have sold the drawings. Reies started preaching, and when he had a sizeable crowd before him, he began asking who among them had purchased pictures of a woman sitting in a windowsill in nothing but her itty-bitty slip. Silence reigned. He persisted, but no one claimed to know what he was talking about. Who wanted to admit to a man of God that they'd purchased lewd pictures, however well drawn? But I didn't need verbal confirmation. I could see it in their faces. They'd seen my drawings of Ella; they'd admired her curves, her voluptuousness, and the dark coloration of her nipples through sheer silk. I cursed my attention to detail. I decided that it would be too painful to see those drawings again, I wanted them no longer, and I inched my way closer to Reies and whispered in his ear to change the subject, which he did on a dime.

We traveled to the next town and the next and the next. When it came to their incessant arguing, I now sided with his wife. Every town we entered, people became so enamored with Reies's words that they treated him like a celebrity. They invited him to their houses for dinner. They offered him and his family a room to sleep in. They gave him gifts—jewelry, small gilded statues of Jesus on the cross, silverware, china, whatever they had that might be of some value—so that he could more easily travel and spread the Lord's message. He could've made a killing! But according to Reies, the Lord's message and easy didn't go together. So he returned their gifts, or if they insisted and he risked offending them, he accepted the gifts only to give them away to someone in desperate need. You would've been hard-pressed to find anyone more destitute than us, but we *chose* our destitution, which meant we were

Who wanted to admit to a man of God that they'd purchased lewd
pictures, however well drawn?

But I could see it

in their faces.

nourished by our spiritual communion with God. As I said, I sided with María, and though I kept my distance from their marital tit for tat, I personally hoped that one day she would knock some sense into her husband. God knows we didn't ask for much. All I wanted was a pillow, some ice cream, and maybe even a Friday outing to the picture show. Reies would have none of it.

As I began to comprehend that Ella was farther and farther away and that catching up to her was less and less likely, I became hopeless, vulnerable, and desperate. I sought answers. Any answer might have done the trick, but there I was, traveling with a preacher providing answers left and right, and with such eloquence. His message boiled down to this: If you have no material possessions, then nothing can be taken from you. If what you possess is inside your heart, then no man can take that from you. If no man can take anything from you, then you are stronger than that man, and if you are stronger than that man, then you are stronger than all men, and if you are stronger than all men, then you are strong enough to lead men. Reies wanted to lead men toward goodness. I had no desire to lead men or to be stronger than any man or to be impervious to anyone taking my material possessions, which constituted only *The Great Book of French Painting* and my years' worth of preparatory notes, and I had already left those behind. I didn't consider Enrique's poems. I just wanted Ella back. But Reies explained to me that Ella was a physical possession stripped away, and that I only *felt* that I needed her back in order to be whole again. "Whatever you need to feel whole is inside you, my friend!" When he said this, he pressed his hand to my chest and then pounded it very hard. I became his best convert.

I sucked rocks. I ate dirt. I refused shoes. I didn't bathe. I gave away the billiard hall money that long ago I'd sewn into my pants. To whom, I have no idea. I walked and walked and walked, and even when my feet were swollen to twice their size, I still denied myself bandages or the pleasure of soaking them in hot soapy water. When I did eat, it was only because Reies's wife begged me to. Or rather, she begged Reies to beg me to eat. Reies would sit me down and explain that death was not the answer, that it was a way out, an escape, and that the greater sacrifice was to survive another day. At the same time, he praised my asceticism and told me about the monks who traveled to the middle of the desert and constructed towers to sit on and ate only what the birds accidentally dropped from the sky and drank only the rain that so rarely fell, and how their only thoughts were meditations on God and His greatness. As he whispered these soothing words, he slowly spoon-fed me beans and tore off strips of tortilla that he placed on my tongue. María, who complained nonstop about my stench, told Reies that he hadn't found a convert but a man hell-bent on destruction.

I awoke one night to the two of them speaking in hushed tones. We were on the edge of a cotton field underneath a gigantic oak tree. Reies had given three sermons that day, and none of them had gone well. The people were impatient. They lost interest. A crowd of twenty had quickly become ten, then five, all of them old women. Poor Reies, always so confident, was worried that he had lost his touch. María saw it differently. "It's him!" she whispered loudly. "He scares people off. You think he looks like Jesus with his long hair and beard, but all they see is a crazy man, skinny, dirty, sickly looking. And when you start talking he shakes his arms and legs, and his eyes flutter and roll upward, and people stop listening to you to watch him! And then you start praising him, how he's the perfect example of a man who has given up worldly pleasures. Who wants to follow your wisdom when it results in looking like that?"

Reies was quiet for a moment before responding. "I understand what you're saying, love, but what can we do with him? He's chosen us. God has his reasons."

From that day on, I feared that eventually María would convince Reies to abandon me. I would awake at night with a start, worried that they had packed their belongings and left. But they were always there, asleep on the other side of the dwindling campfire. Reies grew colder toward me. He no longer praised my asceticism. He no longer told me about the monks in the middle of the desert. Instead, he made comments like, "A bath would do you good!" or "How 'bout a shave, old friend!" or "We should find you some shoes, your feet don't look too good!" or "Another helping of beans won't upset your stomach too much!" But

I always responded, "But I'm at peace, brother." Reies would laugh nervously and glance at his wife with an expression that said, "I tried," and she would glare at him as if he weren't a leader of men but hardly a man himself.

Their squabbling, which I had learned to tune out, became harder to ignore. Instead of fighting about the discomforts of the road, they fought about me. They probably figured that I was in such a fog, limping along after them, trying to stuff yet one more pebble into my mouth, that they could speak about me as if I weren't there. I understood that María hated my guts—she wouldn't even look in my direction, and she would shriek whenever I tried to play peekaboo with the baby—but as long as Reies was on my side, I knew that I wasn't going anywhere. That's not to say he defended me. He just didn't have the heart to tell me we had to part ways. He felt responsible for the state I was in. He told his wife that if they left me to fend for myself, I would die in the middle of nowhere and be eaten by vultures. María was unmoved. "What's there to eat?"[16]

We continued west. I lost track of time, one day blurring into the next. I hardly paid attention to our whereabouts. I heard the names of towns in Utah, Nevada. I saw desert, open plains, rock formations. I sensed an incline. It grew colder. I saw the valley behind us. I heard Reies say we were in California. We spent the night freezing under the cover of pine trees. We walked on. I fell behind. I struggled to

---

16. I keep thinking of Lorraine's comment. Is our narrator sexist? Quite possibly. He's also flawed in other ways, but his vantage point, however limited by life and experience, is what he has. It's all anyone has. We can strive to account for other vantage points, but we still stare out from our own tiny peepholes. Harder to decide is what to do about a controversial figure like Reies López Tijerina, whose rap sheet includes accusations of anti-Semitism, sexual abuse, and a messianic complex? Do we simply pretend that Tijerina, already on the verge of oblivion, never mattered? Some would argue that we should seek out overlooked subjects, the unsung men but especially the women who contributed to La Causa, and I agree. But seeking out the unsung needn't come at the expense of our imperfect leaders. I feel like a dinosaur when I say this, a romantic nationalist far behind the times, begging my colleagues and students not to dismiss all that came before. Why do I even care whether Tijerina is remembered or forgotten? *Why do I even care . . .* I repeat this question like an endless refrain.

keep up, but my legs wouldn't move faster. Occasionally, I would see Reies turn around to see if I was still there. I waved. He waved. I saw María castigate him, and he turned and kept walking. Eventually the incline ended and the decline began and the walking grew more difficult because I couldn't slow myself down. I kept tumbling over, scraping my knees and the palms of my hands. Finally, the terrain became less steep. It was warmer. We passed through a town. We walked down the main drag. At some point, something caused me to pause and turn. I stared at my reflection in a storefront window. My beard reached down below my chest. My hair had formed into clumps. My clothes, what were left of them, hung like tatters. My feet looked chiseled out of old wood. I recalled my days in Albuquerque where the thought of walking outside without perfectly pleated pants and shoes shined to perfection would have made my knees weak. As I stared into the storefront window, I saw Reies's reflection join me. He placed his hand on my shoulder.

"Look at you," he said.

"Yes," I said, feeling proud.

"No, this is no longer a good thing."

"Of course it is," I said. "Worldly pleasures and comforts are no longer important to me. Only the spiritual."

He sighed. "That would be fine if that were actually the case, brother. But are you spiritually at peace?"

"Yes," I said.

"No, you're not."

"Yes, I am."

He sighed again. "If you continue like this you will be dead. And it will be my fault. I did this to you. You listened to me, and at first I was happy to be leading you. But now I see that I have led you astray. Only vanity would keep me from telling you this. But I'm able to admit when I am wrong, and I was wrong to lead you down this path."

"No, you weren't! I'm so happy!" I said. I had to remove the pebbles from my mouth because they were making it difficult to speak. "I'm happy," I repeated.

"No, you're not," he said. "Look, do you remember that night when we met and you told me about your passion? It was your art, right? Well, you need to follow that passion. You can't follow mine any longer."

"But I want to follow your passion."

"You already have, for too long, and it has led you to this." And his reflection pointed at my reflection.

"Yes," I said, finding satisfaction in the Christ-like figure before me.

"You walk, you eat, you sleep, but you don't exist," he said. "Before, when I met you, you existed. You were alive. You loved, you hurt, you created! But now you are a ghost following my family from town to town. A ghost that has begun to haunt me."

I stared at our reflections in the storefront window. At once, as though a spell had been broken, the two of us transformed. Reies, my wise friend and spiritual guide, suddenly seemed just a boy. His face so eager, his smile so innocent. Just a young newlywed kid! Then I looked at myself. I became the ghost he described. I cut a frightening figure. No wonder María kept me as far away as possible from the baby. I tried fixing my hair in the reflection, combed out my beard a bit with my fingers, stood up straight, but to no avail. I had left the world of the living. Reies was right: I didn't want to be among the walking dead. I didn't want to be numb. I turned to him and saw that he had tears in his eyes. "Goodbye," he said. "I must leave."

"Can I follow you to one more town?" I asked.

"No," he said. "We must part ways now."

"Can I say goodbye to your wife and your baby boy?"

Again, he shook his head. "My wife—she . . . she . . . well—" he couldn't find the proper words to describe María's hatred for me.

"It's okay," I said.

We embraced, and Reies walked away without turning around. In the distance I saw his wife carrying the baby. I waved. She didn't. I looked down and realized that Reies had handed me a few dollars. I understood. *I* was now among the

"I'm happy," I said.

    "No, you're not," he said.

      "You can't follow my passion any longer."

"But I want to follow your passion."

       "You already have, for too long,

        and it has led you to this."

        "You are a ghost

        that has begun to haunt me."

needy. I no longer chose my destitution; there was nothing spiritual about my predicament. I was poor and alone, and I had no idea where I was or where I was going.

I walked around town and ignored the stares of passersby. I found a park, and in that park I found a shady patch of grass and fell asleep. Soon I was dreaming, and in that dream Ella came to me. I was lying in her lap and she was combing my unkempt hair. She washed it in warm water. Then she shaved me. Then she bathed me. Then she fed me tomato soup. And all along she was singing a song about two young men living above a mechanic's garage who late at night would talk about their love of the light at dusk. I recognized the words from Enrique's poem. Now Enrique appeared in my dream. He looked sick. He was pale, and his eyes were dark and sunken, and his tongue hung loosely from his mouth. When I tried talking to him, he just shook his head and pointed to the sky, and the sky was a gigantic canvas dripping with gesso.

When I awoke it was cold and dark. I heard a voice barking questions at me that I couldn't understand. I looked up, straining my eyes to see my interlocutor. It was a policeman, and he was poking me with his billy club. Poking me and poking me. I kept saying, "Please stop poking me," but the poking continued and so did the questions.

"What is your name?"

"Where are you from?"

"What is your business here?"

I remember thinking it important to safeguard my identity. I heard myself telling him that my name was Gustave Courbet and that I was from Paris and I was looking for my wife, whose name was Ella, and that my best friend and the only person who ever understood me was dead. Then my eyes began to flutter and roll back in my head, and I couldn't control my tongue and knew that an attack was upon me, but I didn't fight it. I had the feeling of being transported, and that when I awoke I would be in a better place.

PART III

The Mad Prophet—Martín Ramírez

CHAPTER SEVEN

When I awoke it was dark, and I was lying on a bed. I felt a pillow underneath my head for the first time in months, and I was reminded what pillows were for. Comfort. The mattress, too, was soft, and it seemed to hug my body as if I were a long-lost friend. A blanket covered me, and it was warm and felt so good that I immediately disavowed all of Reies's theories about self-sacrifice and the denial of life's comforts. I spoke to him: "You are wrong, friend. Sleeping night after night on a bed of dirt and rocks. If God didn't want us to have pillows and blankets and mattresses, he would not have made them feel so amazing!" Later, of course, I would recant. I would return to Reies's teachings when I realized that the bed, the pillow, and the blanket were not so comfortable after all, that I could feel the springs in the mattress and that it smelled of urine. The blanket was rough and itchy and smelled of disinfectant, and the pillow hardly merited being called a pillow, just some cotton balls sewed into a T-shirt. I would learn that all the patients at DeWitt State Hospital hated their mattresses, their blankets, their pillows, and the sanest among us would clamor for better mattresses, softer blankets, and more substantial pillows, clamor to the point of desperation. Just as Reies had forewarned. Comfort only breeds the desire for more comfort, and more comfort only breeds a stronger desire for even more comfort, until you don't even know what comfort is: all you know is that what you have is not comfortable enough. But that first night I still didn't know I was in Dewitt State Hospital, and the bed felt as if it had been heaven sent, a special gift of thanks for my long journey through spiritual darkness.

I tried pulling the blanket over my shoulders so as to snuggle better, but found it stuck. I pulled harder but without success. I didn't want my head to leave the soft pillow, but I needed to free the blanket. I rose onto one elbow, and that was when I saw a shadowy figure sitting at the edge of my bed.

"Who are you?" I cried out.

"Shhh!" the figure responded. "You'll awake the others," he whispered in Spanish.

"What others?" I whispered.

"The others."

As I looked around and my eyes adjusted to the darkness, I saw that I was in a large room full of beds.

"Where am I?"

"You'll find out soon enough," the man whispered. "I have one question for you, one question only."

"Go on!" I cried.

"Shhhh! Do you want to wake Mr. Stanley?"

"What is your question?"

"Are you crazy?"

"What do you mean, am I crazy? What kind of question is that to ask a man you just met? No, of course I'm not."

"Look, I'm going to be straight with you. This is a place where the weak survive and the mighty are broken. I've seen a man as sane as day enter, all his wits about him, only to end up babbling nonsense to himself in a corner while he sits in his own urine. The people who run this place are in the business of craziness. If you're not crazy, then they make you crazy. Do you understand?"

"Absolutely not," I said. "I'm not crazy and nobody is going to make me crazy. There's been some mix-up."

"That's the kind of attitude that will get you medicated and hooked to the wires. Listen to me," and he scooted forward on the bed and leaned closer so that I could feel the warmth of his breath. "When they first found me, I was in a

bad spot. I was lonely. I was out of work. I lived in a room the size of a closet with six others. I missed my family, my wife, my kids. I hadn't been home to Mexico in years, and it was just killing me. So sometimes I would drink too much and talk to my wife as if she were actually there with me, and sometimes, just for some peace and quiet, I would take to sleeping outdoors, in city parks mainly, just like I used to when I was a kid. Well, one day the police arrest me. I'm not causing any problems, but they don't want to deal with me. So they bring me to a hospital. The hospital takes me in, they ask me a whole bunch of questions, and I don't answer them, because, well, they're in English. So they wait for a translator to come, but the translator never shows up. They're busy with all the other crazy people coming in every day and soon they forget about me. I'm quiet, I don't cause any problems. I was happy. I had three square meals a day, a roof over my head. I hadn't slept so well in years."

The man paused and then scooted even closer so that it felt as if he were about to either cradle my head in his arms or smother me with a pillow. He began again. "Days passed, weeks, and I started to notice something. I was observing the newcomers, just something to pass the time, and I saw that a new guy would be brought in talking about how there had been some mistake and he wasn't supposed to be there and how his family was out to get him or something like that. He'd be taken away, and when he returned he looked like the life had been sucked out of him. Looked like he'd been beat up, but with all the bruises on the inside. After that the guy wouldn't talk about there being a mistake. Wouldn't talk at all. He would just sit quietly, saliva coming out of his mouth, and I'd feel sorry for him because I believe a man's word. If he says he's not crazy, well, he's not crazy. Now, I also observed that they'd bring in a crazy son of a bitch, talking to invisible friends, yelling at the wall, always scratching himself and complaining about the bugs crawling all over him, and I'd think to myself, 'They're going to take that guy away any minute now and he's going to come back drooling and pissing his pants.' But guess what? They'd leave that man alone. So I learned. If they think you're crazy, I mean really certifiably crazy, then they don't worry about you. You're in the right place. The world makes sense and they leave you alone. But if you fight them, if you tell them there's been some mistake, well, then, they try to help you see things their way."

"But I'm not crazy!" I whispered. "I don't want to be here longer than I have to."

"I'm not crazy, either," the man said. "But the question is, do you want to remain sane in a place for the insane? Or do you want to be insane in a place for the insane?"

"I don't want to be *in* a place for the insane!"

The man chuckled under his breath.

Just then a door opened and a bright light shone in the room. My bedside visitor quickly ducked down, freeing my blanket. There was a silhouette of a large man in the doorway. I couldn't see his face, but he had the steady bearing of someone carefully making sure everything was in order. When he shut the door, I waited for the visitor to return. I wanted to continue our conversation. I had so many more questions. But he didn't return, and soon, the bed feeling so comfortable, I fell asleep, wondering if maybe the conversation with that shadowy figure was all a dream.

The next morning, I awoke to a ward full of men dressed in white hospital gowns. Beds lined either side of the long, narrow, barrack-like room. It smelled. I detected urine, body odor, and bad breath. I stretched my arms. I let out a long, satisfied yawn, and when I went to cover my mouth I realized that my beard was gone. My mass of long tangled hair that so disgusted María had been shaved off as well. I spent a few moments touching my smooth face and rubbing the stubbles on my head. I felt gaunt and vulnerable, but certainly less itchy. I looked around for my old clothes, and briefly panicked that they'd been thrown out along with Enrique's poems stuffed in the pockets. I was distracted by a man at the far end of the ward hollering something about his mother. Another man, his head shaved to the skin revealing bright red boils, was snapping his fingers in rapid jerking movements and giggling. Two old men had hiked up their hospital gowns, baring all. Another man told me, very nonchalantly, kindly even, that if he found out I was the one fucking his wife he would slit my throat. I nodded my head in understanding and told him that I too was looking for my wife. Then I felt the need to explain that she wasn't my wife and that we had just lived together. The man backed away and started speaking to an empty chair.

I looked around, curious to find out who had spoken to me the previous night. The darkness had prevented me from seeing any distinguishing characteristics. He spoke Spanish and said he was from Mexico, so I looked around for a Mexican. I found one, an elfish looking man, still in bed. He was curled up in the fetal position and staring off into the distance, with a face so absent that I assumed he had to be insane. "That can't be him," I thought, recalling the lucidity of our exchange.

A giant pink-faced man dressed all in white entered. He had a buzz cut. He was tall and his muscular arms filled out his short-sleeved shirt. I heard rumblings and one or two squeals of "Mr. Stanley." He started barking at everyone to get dressed for breakfast. Then he walked over to me, leaned down, and said in a low deep voice, "You. Stay. Understand?" I could smell bacon on his breath, and it made my stomach growl. I hadn't had bacon in years!

"Yes, of course, but would it be possible to speak to the man in charge? I believe there's been some mistake. I'm also a little concerned as to the where-abouts of my clothes. Will they be returned? And will I be allowed breakfast before my discharge?"

Mr. Stanley's eyes bulged momentarily, but then he leaned down again, a strained smile on his face, as if I were trying his patience. "I'm the man in charge," he said, "so you can direct all questions to me. Your clothes are safe, don't worry. And you'll get your breakfast soon enough."

I watched the other patients, now wearing robes on top of their gowns, file past the long line of beds and toward what looked like a cafeteria. I again observed the elfish Mexican, who shuffled forward on his tippy-toes, hands in his robe pockets. I called out to him, "Are you the man who spoke to me at my bedside last night?" He didn't even glance in my direction.

I am introduced to
DeWitt State Hospital

It smelled. I detected urine, body odor, and bad breath.

My beard was gone.

I felt gaunt and vulnerable,

but certainly less itchy.

Mr. Stanley.

Mr. Stanley returned and escorted me down a long windowless hallway. We stopped at a door and he knocked. "Come in," we heard. With one hand on the doorknob and the other on my lower back, Mr. Stanley said, "I'll be seeing you shortly." Then he opened the door and shoved me into the room.

The sun was pouring through two large windows, and it took my eyes a moment to adjust. I saw seated three silver-haired men in matching white coats whom I assumed were doctors, and a nurse, a thin, almost skeletal, black woman, standing to the side. She wore a very serious expression. The doctors, wire-rimmed spectacles on the tip of their noses, were sitting cross-legged and held clipboards. When I walked in, they didn't look up. They were intently reading whatever was before them with the same thoughtful, concerned look on their faces. Finally, the doctor in the middle glanced up and, without saying anything, gestured that I should sit down in the chair at my side.

"You were brought in last night under circumstances of duress," he began. "Often our patients end up here after a few nights in jail, but you're lucky. I happened to be checking in on another case when I heard several officers discussing your arrest. Apparently, before you were overtaken by a seizure, it seems you introduced yourself as Gustave Courbet. They, of course, had no idea who that was. Your arrest report has you as Gustavo Cortbait. But I'm an amateur art historian. I know Courbet quite well. Is your name actually Gustave Courbet? You are French, I presume?"

"Of course," I said. What I meant to say was that my great-grandfather was French, according to my mother. I also wanted to add that I appreciated French culture, admired its long artistic tradition, and Gustave Courbet was a personal hero, but I was still out of sorts on account of my new surroundings. I opened my mouth to clarify, hesitating momentarily because I didn't want to interrupt the doctors who were scribbling manically on their clipboards. Then one of them abruptly stopped writing and asked, "*Of course*, to which question?"

"Excuse me?"

"Of course your name is Gustave Courbet or *of course* to—"

"Well, of course my name is not Gustave Courbet! As the good doctor has acknowledged, everyone knows he's one of the greatest French painters."

"But occasionally you believe yourself to be this Gustave Courbet?" the third doctor asked.

I laughed good-naturedly. "I mean, don't we all wish to fashion ourselves after the greats in our field? I'm a painter of steely-eyed realism, so naturally I identify with Courbet. I should throw in Millet, Corot, and when I'm feeling bold, Manet."

"You believe yourself to be Millet, Corot, *and* Manet as well?" the art historian asked, his eyebrows rising.

"Well, I believe that I may stand in their company. Not yet, of course, I'm still developing my technique, and I've been on somewhat of a hiatus. But in my studies with Master Millet, he often praised my preternatural ability for observation."

"And where did you study with Master Millet?" the art historian asked as he jotted down more notes.

"At the Salon des Refusés Art Academy."

"I'm not familiar with this institution."

I cringed as I recalled the fraudulent mail correspondence course.

"Nurse Franklin, will you please hand me the cards to your left," the art historian asked.

The nurse handed him a black cardboard portfolio, and the doctor pulled out a stack of letter-sized cards.

"Do you mind if I sit next to you?" he asked.

"Of course not."

The doctor rose and sat in the seat next to me. "I want you to take a look at these cards," he said. "Just sort through them for now."

I obeyed, while the doctor peered over my shoulder in anticipation, breathing loudly through his nose. The cards looked as though someone had spilled ink on them. When I finished, the doctor asked that I look at each one individually and then describe what I saw. I assumed then that he was the creator of these images and that, having an artist in his midst, he was asking for an expert opinion. I felt bad for him. Why was he asking me for a critique in front of his colleagues? I tried to be kind.

"I like how you balance the space," I said. "Compositionally it has a lot of potential."

"What do you mean by *you?*" one of the other doctors asked, shifting in his seat.

"Well, him," I said. "It's you who made these ink drawings, right?"

The art historian looked confused. "No, no, these aren't my drawings at all. These aren't even drawings. This is a test. We just want to see how you respond to each inkblot."

I breathed a sigh of relief. "So you're not asking my opinion of your art work? Oh, thank goodness. At first I thought these were your drawings and that you wanted me to judge their artistic value!"

"I do actually enjoy painting," the art historian said, chuckling. "And not a few claim they're quite good."

"They certainly are," one of the doctors chimed in.

"Thank you, Dr. Livingston," the art historian said. "That's kind of you."

"Who created these works then?" I asked.

"Nobody. Again, these are not drawings or paintings. These are part of a psychiatric test. We want to learn what you see when you see these images."

"I see inkblots," I said.

"Yes, but what *in* the inkblot do you see? What does it remind you of?"

"What do you mean, what do I see? I see nothing more than a simple inkblot. As though someone spilled their inkwell and didn't bother to clean it up."

The art historian glanced over at the other doctors. "But if you were to take a less literal view and perhaps use . . . well, how about that artist's eye you say you have, what would these inkblots remind you of?"

"My artist's eye?"

"Yes, the eye of an *artiste.*"

He was testing me. Did he think that I was mere amateur dabbler just as he was an amateur art historian? Well, I would turn that test around. "Okay, let's see . . . ," I said as I held up the first image. The truth is I saw Ella. The inkblot formed an hourglass, a short, curvaceous hourglass. "To be quite honest," I began, "I'm reminded of a painting by Ingres called *The Turkish Bath*. Do you know Ingres's work?"

"*A*nge," the art historian said.

"I'm sorry?"

"It's pronounced *A*nge, not In-gress," he said, jotting down a note on his clip-board. Then he eyed me carefully. "So you're French, but you don't speak it?"

I hesitated. I still hadn't clarified that I wasn't French. It already felt too late. "I don't get much of a chance to practice," I said, coughing into my hand. Remembering the facial tic Mr. Buenrostro had brought to my attention years ago, I worried that the sides of my mouth would curl upward into a smile.

He eyed me carefully for a moment and then moved on. "Of course. How about the next one?"

This inkblot also reminded me of Ella. Ella naked, still in bed, neck and back arched proudly, her hand on her leg.

"Manet's *Olympia*," I said confidently, but coughing to make sure my mouth didn't betray me.

"That's right," the art historian said, nodding his head, as though he too saw Manet's inimitable mark. "Would you like a glass of water? Nurse?"

"No, no, I'm fine," I said.

The next card I hardly looked at. I didn't want to lie about what I saw. I just searched my memory for an obscure painting. I wanted to stump him. Surely, he couldn't have studied *The Great Book of French Painting* as closely as I had. "Ah! This one is an old favorite. Courbet's *La Bacchante*!"

"Yes, a good one!" the doctor said enthusiastically and without hesitation. "A daring painting, wouldn't you agree?"

"Yes," I said. The truth was the high school librarian had cut out *La Bacchante* from *The Great Book of French Painting*. I knew nothing about it except that it was of "a reclining nude," which was its alternate title. Apparently, she didn't think it an appropriate masterpiece for high school boys to admire. I never knew why *Olympia* and *The Turkish Bath* were spared her scissors or for that matter half the book of female nudes. What was it about Courbet that sent our librarian's heart aflutter? Fortunately for me, this question is what led me to the rest of his oeuvre.

"Are you familiar with Courbet's *The Origin of the World*?" the art historian asked. I detected an eagerness in his voice, and for a second I thought that maybe this wasn't a test at all. Maybe he was simply happy to meet a fellow art aficionado.

"Of course, that is a *beautiful* painting," I said, allowing myself to smile. It was not a Courbet painting I was familiar with. Nor was it one that the librarian had cut out; otherwise I would've at least remembered the title.

The doctor changed his position in his seat. "And just what is it that you find beautiful in the work?" he asked.

"Well, the unflinching steely-eyed realism," I said, feeling confident of this description because it was characteristic of all of Courbet's work. "That's what attracts me most to it. He is not afraid to turn away. He makes the viewer look and keep looking until you feel as though you're completely surrounded by the world he's created. I mean, *The Origin of the World* draws you in so that you almost feel smothered, am I right?"

"That is certainly true," the doctor said. And then he paused and placed his finger to his lip as though he were searching for the words. "So, then, would you say your obsession with Courbet is sexual?"

"Sexual?" I spat out. "Absolutely not. I am an artist, and I admire him for his technique, his vision—his . . . his . . . his steely-eyed realism. Why on earth would you suggest something like that?"

"It's a common enough question," the doctor said. "Let's move on to the next card, please."

I looked at the inkblot. Again, I saw Ella. She was in her slip, sleeping in the windowsill, her mouth parted, her moist lips beckoning me. I didn't want to talk about Ella. I knew it would only lead to more questions, and I wanted to avoid appearing vulnerable or desperate. So I thought of more French paintings. "Hmmmmm, there's a lot in this one," I said, holding the card closer to my face. I also wanted to steer clear of any with nudity in them. I didn't like the doctor's insinuation at all. But it was as if my mind had forgotten all the paintings of stone breakers and millet pickers and peasants in front of hay bales. All I could remember were nudes. So I invented a painting. Or rather, I described one of my own—the billiard hall in Albuquerque (except I placed it on the Rue de Rivoli) that I never got around to painting. I described it down to the drunk passed out in the corner and the whiskers on his cheek.

"Yes, that is a truly wonderful painting," the art historian said, interrupting my detailed description. "But, do you actually visualize all of that in the inkblot?"

"Of course. I told you, Master Millet called my eye for observation preternatural."

"I see," said the doctor, drawing out the syllable while he pondered his next question.

I chuckled to myself. I was sure I'd caught him in a boldface lie. He had called the painting *truly wonderful,* and I had made it up! But then I started to wonder if there was actually a similar painting of a billiard hall in some fancy museum. I turned to the next card and was about to test the doctor again, when he asked, "Do you know why you're here?"

"Here speaking to you or here in general?" I gestured to my physical surroundings.

"Well, both."

"I gathered upon waking that this is a hospital, and judging by the patients I assume this is a mental hospital. I'm speaking to you right now probably so that you can determine whether or not I'm supposed to be here."

"Yes, well said. Very well said. And do you believe that you should be here?"

I remembered my nighttime visitor's advice. If I wanted to remain sane in a place for the insane, then I had to play the part. Leaving was not an option. But these doctors seemed like rational men, and clearly the art historian respected my knowledge of French painting. That had to count for something. I was certain they would respond to reason.

"Look," I started in as calm and sincere a voice as I could manage, "in the last few years, I sought a more spiritual path. But that spiritual path only led me away from my true passion, which is my art. In giving up my art, I had given up a part of myself. I was on my way to finding that when it seems I had some sort of epileptic attack, which I've been prone to ever since my father was murdered, a traumatic event in a young man's life, as you can imagine. When I woke up I found myself here. As much I'd like to stay and speak to you good doctors and learn about your work, I need to return to *my* work as soon as possible."

"And by your work you mean your artwork?" the art historian asked.

"Yes, I'm glad you understand that. So few do."

The doctors all began nodding their heads sympathetically, as though they had also followed winding paths filled with pitfalls and dark moments of uncertainty. With thoughtful pursed-lip expressions, they commenced writing on their clipboards, including the art historian, who was still seated next to me. Out the corner of my eye, I tried to see what he was writing, but his scrawl was illegible. All I could make out was the typed question "Patient's Race or Nationality," under which the doctor wrote "Mexican." When he finished he tapped his pen against the clipboard as if to announce that he was finished, and said to me, "Thank you; this has all been very helpful."

"You wrote Mexican," I said.

"Excuse me?"

"I realize earlier that I said I was French, but I wanted to clarify that my great-grandfather was one of Maximilian's soldiers and my family on my father's side actually descends from one of the oldest—"

"That's okay," he said, cutting me off. He placed his hand on my shoulder and smiled. "We'll have plenty of time to talk about that later."

Then he asked the nurse to inform Mr. Stanley that the patient was ready for him now.

"What do you mean later?" I asked, alarmed. "I shouldn't be here. I need to be released at once. I'm an artist and—"

"You'll be happy to learn that we have developed an impressive arts and crafts program here at DeWitt."

"I don't care about your arts and crafts program. I'm a serious practitioner. There is no need for another conversation!"

"Nurse, please make sure Mr. Stanley comes quickly."

The nurse hurried out, and a second later Mr. Stanley appeared. His presence filled the room. Before, the doctors all seemed old and feeble, and the nurse couldn't have weighed more than ninety pounds. They didn't pose the slightest physical threat. But once Mr. Stanley's pink face appeared in the room, followed by his thick neck, his round shoulders, barrel chest, and thighs that stretched his white polyester pants taut, the room became heavy with impending violence. I felt cornered. The doctors were closing in on me, the little black nurse stepped forward with her right hand holding something plastic and sinister. Mr. Stanley towered over me, his hands now on my shoulders, and because I'd grown used to my body failing me in moments of distress—moments just like this—I thought to myself, "Surely now I'm going to have an attack." I waited to lose control of my tongue, for my arms to start shaking uncontrollably, and for my eyeballs to roll back in my head. I found myself almost hoping for it, because one thing I'd learned about my attacks is that I always woke up in a different place, in a calmer state, surrounded by different people, and at that moment I no longer wanted to be in that room with the doctors, that skeletal nurse, and the imposing presence of Mr. Stanley.

But much as I tried, the attack wouldn't come. I shook my arms, I stuck my tongue out, I let my legs go limp, but nothing. Still, I cried out, "I'm having an epileptic attack!" That was when the nurse stepped forward and placed a needle

... the room became heavy with impending violence.

I felt cornered.

in my thigh. As my eyelids grew heavy and I lost all feeling in my legs, I muttered, "Thank you," and I imagined that when I woke up I'd be in my yellow wooden bed, surrounded by dingy lavender walls, back in my studio at the TSSS factory.

Instead, I awoke slightly groggy with wires attached to my head, and my arms, torso, and legs strapped tightly to a chair.

"Hello, Pancho," said Mr. Stanley.

"You're not supposed to confuse or provoke the patients, Mr. Stanley," a woman's voice admonished.

A man's deep baritone voice chimed in, "Mr. Stanley, please carefully escort the patient back to his bed in Ward 1. He needs to rest for a while longer."

"Whathgoingon?" I managed to ask. My tongue felt thick and my eyes were heavy. I had to fight the urge to fall back into a deep slumber. I was alarmed to find myself still in the hospital, with Mr. Stanley's monstrous pink face following me everywhere I went. This was a nightmare with no end.

A doctor with a boyish face and blond hair parted perfectly down the middle stood over me. "We've administered a treatment," he said as he began disconnecting the wires from my head. I was surprised to learn that the deep voice belonged to him. "We usually wait until your observation is complete, but you were quite worked up. It's called electroshock therapy, and I believe you'll be happy with the results. Many of our patients emerge almost completely rejuvenated, healthy, ready to face the world."

"I don't need treatment, I'm absolutely—" I stopped, unable to remember what I intended to say. "Doctor, I feel like I'm in a fog."

"Of course, that is very common. It will pass," the doctor said. "Don't look at it like a treatment then. It's like doing something for the betterment of your body. Say, a big glass of milk in the morning or some jumping jacks to get the heart racing." Then he patted my shoulder and said, "Trust me."

He sounded convincing. Maybe it was his deep voice and no-nonsense demeanor. Who was I to question this man, his many years of schooling, and the medical field along with it? A glass of milk, he said. Fine. Some jumping jacks. Fine. Some electrical shocks. A bit groggy, but still fine. He must know what he's talking about. I even entertained the idea that the shocks were just what I needed. My time on the road with Reies had all but left me an engine without charge.

"How long will this fogginess last?" I asked.

"Just a few hours," the doctor said, patting my shoulder again. Then he nodded to Mr. Stanley, who undid the series of straps that were keeping my arms, legs, and torso in place and lifted me into a wheelchair.

"See you soon," the doctor said.

I tried to mumble my thanks. Once we were out the door, Mr. Stanley said, "Aren't you worried those shocks are going to make you lose your mind, Pancho?"

"A jump start, that is all it is. And why do you keep calling me that name?"

He started to answer, but by then the fogginess had returned. I heard a ringing in my ears and my eyelids were so heavy that I closed them for a second and fell asleep. The last thing I heard was something about nicknames and all Mexicans being Pancho. When I awoke I was still in my wheelchair. Other men in wheelchairs surrounded me. From a distance it might have looked as if we were having a meeting, but my fellow invalids were either asleep or staring vacantly ahead. My head felt heavy, but at least the fogginess was gone. I looked around and was relieved that Mr. Stanley was nowhere in sight. I observed the rest of the ward. The majority of the patients still wore their robes and gowns, while others had changed into street clothes. Some played cards, a handful were gathered around a small television, a few appeared to be reading. Most, however, seemed to be lost in their own world, pacing back and forth, talking to themselves, or staring off into the distance.

A man who looked like a plucked chicken approached me and said something incomprehensible. I could feel his breath on my cheek, and his bulging bloodshot eyes and raw scabs sickened me. I tried to move away, but the wheelchair was stuck on someone else's wheel. I attempted to stand but was too weak and collapsed back into my chair. I struggled to free the wheel, while the chicken-man aggressively repeated his nonsense. After bumping into the feet of a few comatose patients, I managed to wheel myself to safety. Fortunately, there seemed to be a line the chicken-man wouldn't cross. He stared at me for a few moments and then turned his attention to someone else.

My heart was pounding, and my whole body felt flushed and clammy. I decided to wheel myself so that my back was against the wall and I could monitor the proximity of the other patients. I didn't want to be assaulted again. I wanted to observe the ward in peace. As I caught my breath and my pulse returned to normal, I noticed several patients at a table who looked to be drawing. They were hunched over large sheets of paper, with numerous pencils, crayons, and colored markers. I wheeled closer, and that was when I noticed, at a table all his own, the Mexican I'd seen that morning. He had a gigantic piece of paper before him, three feet tall and five feet wide, much larger than the others, and he was working intently, his eyes not lifting from the page. He was older, in his sixties. He was frail and had the wizened face of an old Buddhist monk. I wheeled closer. He was different from the men at the other table. They looked like children drawing for fun, for something to do, for distraction, because someone like Mr. Stanley had told them to sit quietly and do so. But he had the look of an artist. His intensity was mesmerizing. When I wheeled still closer, I noticed that he was staring at a little plastic cowboy figurine, and drawing from it. I almost laughed out loud. That was his model!

Without thinking I reached over and picked the figurine off the table. "Look, friend, look around you! You have models galore and you choose *this* to draw from? This is for kids!" And I started laughing. I hoped for a rational response, a joke in return, a lively discussion about the merits of live models versus staid busts. Instead, the man cowered and held his arms over his head as though I'd come to strike him rather than engage a fellow artist. He began making strange guttural noises, and before I could place the figurine back where I'd found it, the arts and crafts doodlers at the other table leapt from their seats and surrounded me, grabbing for the little cowboy.

"Leave Martín's charro alone!" one man said.

"Leave Martín in peace. He didn't do nothing to you!" another followed.

"Fine!" I cried, and released the figurine. One of the patients placed it back on the table. Immediately, the Mexican quieted, picked up his pencil, and resumed drawing as though nothing had happened. He didn't even look over to acknowledge my presence. The others returned to drawing, eyeing me carefully.

"Wasn't that a bit of an overreaction?" I asked him.

He kept drawing.

"Your name is Martín, huh? Were you the one that came and spoke to me in the night?"

Martín continued to draw.

"Leave him alone," a man at the table said. "Martín needs to concentrate. His drawing time is of the utmost importance."

"And just why is that?" I asked.

The tableful of men looked up from their drawings and stared at me in disbelief.

"Because he's the best," one man said.

"Because he's famous," another said.

"He has exhibitions in New York City!"

"Who does? *He* does?" I asked. So distracted by the plastic figurine, I hadn't even looked at the drawing. I peered over. All I saw were lines. Patterns of lines. One line after another. A dizzying assortment of lines. But just lines. Nothing but lines. And then smack in the middle was a drawing of the plastic cowboy on top of his horse. I rose from my wheelchair to examine it better. I expected it to be drawn with a master hand, but it looked like the rest of the drawing. Crude. Simple. Repetitive.

"Yes, Dr. Pasto thinks Martín is a genius," one of the patients stopped drawing to tell me.

"Dr. Pasto, huh?" I chuckled. "And just what exactly does he claim makes Martín a genius?"

The arts and crafts table.

He was different from the men at the other table.

They looked like children drawing for fun, for something to do, for distraction...

But he had the look of an artist.

Martín Ramírez.

Again, the tableful turned to me in unison, all with the same expression of disbelief, as though clearly I was crazy to ask such a question. I looked at the drawing again. Were they looking at what I was looking at? I observed Martín. He was oblivious to our conversation. "This old man afraid of losing his plastic toy—he's the genius?" I said. I thought I saw a smile creep onto his lips. I thought it was a smile of agreement, as though he could hardly believe it himself. But then I realized he was smiling because he had completed his drawing. He looked up and said in heavily accented English, "More paper." The men at the table chorused, "More paper! More paper!" And soon an orderly showed up and asked, "Does Martín need more paper?" And Martín grinned. "More paper," he said. The orderly left and returned shortly with several sheets of paper.

"Shall we hang this masterpiece up, Martín?" the orderly asked. "Ready to go?" Martín gazed up at him without seeming to understand. So the orderly mimed placing the drawing on the wall and Martín nodded his head. With the help of two eager patients the orderly gently lifted the paper from the table, and they soon had it push-pinned to the wall. Then they all stood back to admire it as though they were staring at the *Mona Lisa*.

"You've got to be kidding me," I said to no one.

"You think you can do better?" someone behind me asked.

I turned my wheelchair around and found a man in brown-checkered slacks and a turtleneck. He was seated cross-legged, a hospital robe draped loosely around his shoulders. His arms were crossed. He had a thin mustache. He was bald and wore glasses with thick black frames. He didn't look the least bit insane.

"Of course I can," I said. "A thousand times better than that."

"What does better mean in art?" the man asked.

"Better? Well, it means one is better drawn than the other."

"But why is better drawn—more realistic, I presume—necessarily better?"

"Well, because steely-eyed realism captures and reveals humanity for what it is."

"But does it?"

206

"Does it what?"

"Does it really capture humanity for what it really is?"

"That's what I said."

"Hmmm," the man said, as though not quite in agreement, and then he nodded his head and extended his hand. "My name is Lawrence."

"You're not crazy, are you," I said. Save for the robe, he appeared rather well put together in his turtleneck, brown-checkered slacks, and loafers.

Lawrence began to laugh heartily.

"You don't seem so, anyway," I said.

"No, believe me. I am. Completely mad."

"Well, I'm not, and as soon as I can speak to the man in charge I'll be out of here. I need to get back to my studio. An artist must work after all."

"If you're an artist, well, then you must be crazy," and he again started laughing heartily.

I didn't see the humor. He grew serious. "I'd like to see your drawings someday. Will you share them?"

"Of course," I said.

"Well, I should be off," Lawrence said, and he reached out to shake my hand. "Nice to meet you. And go easy on Martín. He's alone and frightened on a journey through the void." And with that he pointed at the drawing on the wall.

I felt compelled to turn and reconsider the drawing. I saw the endless repetition of swirling lines, nothing but lines, and there in the center was the cowboy on the horse, a charro lost in a frightening vortex. I looked at Martín, already back at work on another drawing, his mouth clenched, his concentration unbroken. "At least he keeps at it," I thought to myself. When I turned back to Lawrence, I saw that he had moved away and was already commencing a game of chess with another patient.

That same afternoon Dr. Pasto showed up. When I heard that he was the one who had convinced everyone of Martín's genius, I expected a fraud, a slick wheeler and dealer hawking magic potions. But he looked distinguished, his silvery hair neatly combed back to reveal a large shiny forehead. He was impeccably dressed in slacks and a sports coat. I asked around and learned that he wasn't a medical doctor but a professor at the local university. I was also told that he used to come and work with all the patients and study them, but soon it was all about the Mexican, Martín Ramírez. He would bring art supplies and paper and any other material that Martín requested, and every drawing Martín completed Dr. Pasto deemed a masterpiece. He would collect the drawings and paintings and show them to other artists; he would bring his students from the university; he would send select drawings to curators of museums. On Dr. Pasto's encouragement, people would travel from miles away to see the greatest insane artist the world had ever known.[17] They would come and take notes, observing, not Martín's antics, but his technique: the meticulous, obsessive lines, the way he mixed his colors from crayons, shoe-polish, and fruit juice, the small pieces of paper he would glue together with saliva and oatmeal, and above all his intense concentration.

I couldn't believe what I was hearing. Nor what I was seeing. I watched Dr. Pasto fawn over Martín, observing him from a slight distance, a look of admiration and awe on his face. Then I would look at Martín, lost in his own world,

---

17. Ernie writes: "Neither Lorraine nor I had heard of Martín Ramírez before this, but my uncle's description appears accurate. He's considered one of the twentieth century's self-taught masters. We even felt bad for my uncle when we learned that recently one of Ramírez's works sold for over $270,000, in Paris of all places. Lorraine told me that her entire collection of Chicanx art, books, and memorabilia wouldn't sell for a fraction of that price, so I joked that she needed to find her own Dr. Pasto. 'I don't need some so-called *expert* to validate my collection,' she told me." If Ramírez's work does indeed command six figures, it's no small feat. The art market is a tricky thing. Does a price tag really bestow value on a work of art? No; but we live in a capitalist world; so yes, it does. Save for a handful of Chicano artists such as Luis Jiménez, Carmen Lomas Garza, and Carlos Almaraz, most have not cracked the commercial gallery system. Even fewer museums feature the work of Chicano artists. In recent years, the East Los Angeles–based art collective Asco has received mainstream artworld recognition, but on the whole, Chicanx art is placed in a little box, in a corner, and forgotten. In a way, as an "outsider" artist—a self-taught, naïve artist with little to no contact with the mainstream art world—Ramírez belongs in his own category, but really, the condition of the Chicanx artist is to exist perpetually on the outside.

oblivious to Dr. Pasto, drawing the same damn lines over and over. It was dis-heartening, to say the least. I had spent years apprenticing, learning how to draw, observing life in order to document life, to reveal it in all its beauty and detail, and this guy just drew whatever the hell was in his head, a dizzying array of lines, and if he ever did draw from life, it was of a little cowboy figurine rendered hardly better than with a child's hand, and he was getting attention from learned men, artists, and museums. That was attention meant for me!

After wheeling back and forth across the ward several times in my wheel-chair, muttering my disbelief, I decided that maybe the situation was beneficial. All that seemed wrong could easily be made right. Wasn't I now in a position to piggyback off of this Martín Ramírez? Wasn't I a much better artist than him? Surely Dr. Pasto and his worldly friends would recognize that. Maybe I had ended up in the right place after all. In Albuquerque, I dreamed of Paris. At the TSSS factory, I dreamed of Paris. But whether living above the mechanic's garage or in my studio at the far end of the workers camp, I had no audience, *no chance* for an audience, except for the always exhausted, overworked men and women who viewed me with suspicion and outright disdain, if they noticed me at all. Not an art lover among them. But here, my audience would be brought to me. Artists, scholars, curators, owners of galleries, and patrons of museums. They may come for the so-called greatest insane artist who ever lived, but once they were disappointed to see nothing but lines and more lines, they would turn their attention to me. Before I knew it, my disillusionment had transformed into outright optimism.

I wasted no time. I wheeled over to Dr. Pasto and introduced myself. "Hello," I said. "I see you studying this man here, drawing lines all over the place. I remember there was a time when I enjoyed doing that. Anyhow, I was wondering if you'd be interested in taking a look at some of my work?"

I waited for an answer, but Dr. Pasto didn't even glance in my direction. Instead, he looked around and gestured for one of the orderlies to approach. I repeated myself, again without receiving even the slightest acknowledgement, and when the orderly arrived and said, "Yes, Doctor?" Dr. Pasto, without taking his eyes off of Martín, said, "Can you please keep patients away. My observation is being disturbed."

The orderly, a smaller version of Mr. Stanley, turned to me and as though scolding a child, said, "Do you want to wheel yourself away, or do you want me to do it?"

I wheeled myself a safe distance away, stewing over my mistreatment. I glanced over at the arts and crafts table. All the crazies were hunched over, elbows pinning their paper down as though someone might swoop by and steal their drawings. At that moment, one of the men rose and announced very loudly that he had to go to the restroom. I watched him walk away, but instead of going to the bathroom he sat in an empty chair next to the poker players, and then, as though in a trance, fell asleep. It left an open spot at the arts and crafts table. The thought of sitting among such amateurs made my stomach turn, but I had to do something to gain Dr. Pasto's notice.

I quickly wheeled over, parked my wheelchair, and climbed into the empty seat, a piece of paper already before me. No one looked up to acknowledge my presence. Before I could start worrying about the pressure of creating a masterpiece or the need for preparatory notes, I blindly picked up the first available drawing utensil and began sketching the man across from me. I moved my hand across the page, observing my model—a big, fat, bulbous-nosed man with acne scars, cauliflower ears, and a mouth that hung open to reveal rotted teeth. I didn't look down. Not once. I was a transcriber of reality and reality was in front of me. I felt for every contour. I willed dimensions and volumes to appear on the page. But then suddenly, when I was finished with the man's right ear, my confidence gave way. I worried that maybe I would look down and find Ella's face staring back at me. I needed verification. I looked down.

I had indeed drawn the man's ear. Never mind that it was in crayon, the rendering was exquisite.

"Do you see this? *This* is a drawing!" I said to the man next to me, shaking it in front of him.

The man didn't even glance over. He just protected his sheet of paper as though I were trying to copy his exam. I asked the man in front of me, my model. "Do you see your ear? This is reality." He looked up at me, and I saw in his absent grayish eyes that he could barely see across the table.

I stood up. I saw Lawrence in his turtleneck and brown-checkered slacks playing chess. "Lawrence! Lawrence!" I called out to him. I rose from my seat, knocking against the men drawing on either side of me; both of them groaned and grumbled in annoyance. Lawrence looked up from his game and smiled. He beckoned me over. A friendly, warm, completely sane face in a ward full of idiots. I rushed over to him, leaving my wheelchair behind, my drawing firmly in hand.

"I'd like to share this with you," I said.

He looked curious, amused, maybe even flattered that I trusted his opinion. "What do we have here?" he said.

I pressed the drawing into his hands.

He held it up. He knit his brow and squinted his eyes. He leaned in closer, nodding his head approvingly. "It's clear you have an eye for detail—is that the contour of Wilcox's ear? That's—that's actually quite magnificent!"

"Thank you," I said. I felt reassured. I waited for more praise, but soon Lawrence turned back to his chess game. "Is it my turn?" he asked his opponent.

I left him alone. I returned to the arts and crafts table only to find my seat once again occupied. I looked over at Martín still drawing lines and then at Dr. Pasto, who was still admiring Martín drawing those lines. I looked for the orderly who had threatened me. He was nowhere in sight. I decided to try getting Dr. Pasto's attention again. I was sure crazy patients accosted him all the time. He had become jaded. In order to concentrate, he had learned to tune out their insane blabbering. He hadn't even heard me. Summoning the orderly had merely been a precautionary measure that by now was habit. Instead of addressing him, I would offer him what he appreciated most: a piece of art.

I approached him quickly, and as I passed by I gently let my drawing fall into his lap, or at least that was my intention. The paper glanced off his leg and glided to the floor. He was writing notes. He didn't even look to see what had glanced against his leg. I thought I was going to have to walk by again and be more forceful about getting his attention, but just as I was about to retrieve the drawing, Dr. Pasto glanced at the paper at his feet. He did a double take, and on the second glance his gaze lingered. He reached down and picked up the drawing.

By this time my heart was in my throat. I thought to myself, "This is the moment of judgment! This is the moment I'll look back on years from now and say, 'It all began at that moment of discovery.'" Instead, Dr. Pasto looked for a second longer at my exquisite rendering of that deformed ear, and then just like that, turned back to his observation of Martín, the drawer of lines.

I couldn't believe it. I rushed forward and exclaimed, "You didn't even look closely!"

Dr. Pasto peered up at me, a look of horror on his face, as though he feared physical violence.

"I—I—I," he stuttered. "I—I don't know what you're talking about." He turned around frantically looking for assistance.

"The drawing on the floor," I said through clenched teeth.

By that time Mr. Stanley and another orderly were upon me. They wrapped their arms around my upper body, which, frail as I was, was not hard to do. I squirmed, but could do nothing to wrest myself free. As I was dragged away, Mr. Stanley snarled, "You're trouble, I knew it," and in the distance I watched Dr. Pasto pick up the drawing again. This time he stared at it longer. He pulled it closer, almost to his nose. Even then, I still hoped for an expression of awe to cross his face, an expression that said, "Now I understand what that man was yelling about." Instead, he pushed out his bottom lip, shrugged, and let the drawing fall to the floor, again. At first, the paper softly glided downward, but then it gathered momentum and slid over to where Martín was working. The old Mexican noticed the drawing at his feet. He glanced at it. A smile crossed his lips. He picked up the drawing, found his plastic scissors on the table, and immediately began cutting my drawing to pieces.

Dr. Pasto examining my drawing of Wilcox's deformed ear:

I thought to myself, "This is the moment of judgment!

This is the moment I'll look back on years from now and say

'It all began at that moment of discovery.'"

I cried out, but I was powerless to prevent its destruction. The orderlies carried me outside the ward, down the hall, and I was pushed into a dark room.

"Wait here and keep quiet!" Mr. Stanley said.

Minutes later the door opened and someone entered the room. "Who left you in the dark?" a man asked as he flipped on the lights. It was another gray-haired doctor. I was having trouble telling them apart.

"Mr. Stanley," I said weakly, my eyes adjusting to the bright light.

"Oh, Mr. *Stanley*," he said, as though lightly scolding the tyrant. "He's so forgetful sometimes. But who am I to talk; I'm always forgetting things. Now what seems to be the problem? I heard you were creating a disturbance out there. Now, we don't like that. We don't like to isolate you in a room all by yourself."

The doctor pulled out a pen and then felt the pocket of his white gown. "Look at that, didn't I tell you?" He set his clipboard down on a small metal rolling table and felt his pants pockets. "I forgot my glasses, absentminded me." Then he excused himself. "I'll be right back," he said, opening the door just wide enough to slip out and close behind him. Immediately I noticed that he'd forgotten his clipboard. I rushed over, not knowing how much time I had to review my case. This opportunity would surely not come again.

Under "Description of Patient's Behavior," it read:

Believes himself to be a 19th Century French Artist. After the police directed me to the patient, he introduced himself as Gustave Courbet and told me that he was looking for two people, Baudelaire, "his friend and creative soul mate," and Ella, his muse. In my research on Courbet I have not discovered a mistress named Ella, but I continue to look. Race is Mexican, but has made claims to being French. His knowledge of French painters in the 19th century is mainly superficial, but he knows enough names and details to populate his delusions. Sometimes he imagines that he is Millet, Corot, or even Manet, all French Artists. Seems to believe that everyone is working to prevent him from creating his masterpieces. Became angry and agitated when he believed doctors were not going to allow him to return to his "studio." Feigned an epileptic attack. Appeared to suffer a real attack with officers the previous night, according to arrest report. Unsure whether he suffers from epilepsy or if this is a part of his delusions. Continue to research French 19th Century Painters and see if any suffered from epilepsy, perhaps Van Gogh? Electroconvulsive therapy had positive calming effects.

Below that was "Possible Diagnosis":

Schizophrenic or manic-depressive tendencies. Delusions of grandeur or persecution. Believes that he is a famous figure. Believes that he has unusual powers, those of a master painter or draftsman, though so far there is no evidence of that. Stack of letters found on his person had no drawings. Believes that others, "they," now "us," are out to prevent him from reaching his potential as a great artist.

By the time I had read their indictment of me, the doctor returned with his glasses on. As he opened the door, I staggered back, still in shock. I believed myself an artist, and they considered me crazy. I was living in one reality, and they perceived another. Everything out of my mouth was being used against me.

"Found them!" the doctor said, smiling at me kindly. "Now, let's see . . ." He picked up the clipboard and read through their blasphemous assessment, his kind countenance unchanging. "So you're an artist?" he asked.

I thought long and hard about this one. If everything I was saying was being used against me, then I would have to change my story. As hard as it was to deny my vocation, I had to do so.

"No, I'm not," I said.

This caught the doctor by surprise. "As it was explained to me, you were trying to get Dr. Pasto, one of our generous visitors, to look at your drawing, and when he didn't acknowledge the merits of your drawing, you became quite upset. Is that not the case?"

"It was a misunderstanding. I was confused. I thought he was someone else."

"So, you weren't trying to force your drawing on him?"

"No, why would someone force a drawing onto someone else? It's just a drawing."

"Hmmmm," he said. "I see." He seemed to have prepared himself for a very different conversation. "Well, one of our floor therapists spoke to you earlier, and he said that you were very upset that Mr. Ramírez was getting so much attention. You said that you were a better artist."

"Who did I say this to exactly?" I asked.

"Well, Dr. Kelson."

"Dr. Kelson? I don't remember speaking to anyone by that name. The only person I spoke to was another patient, Lawrence."

"Yes, Dr. Kelson. He's not a patient. You were mistaken."

"But he said—" I stopped, remembering that Lawrence had just laughed in response to my question. I continued, "Yes, I was mistaken, you're right. I was merely surprised that Ramírez received so much attention for his work. They seemed quite infantile to me. When I said that I was a better artist, I meant that many others in the ward were probably better artists, too. The bar is not set very high."

"You know, I completely agree with you! I never understood Dr. Pasto's fascination with Ramírez. The museum exhibitions, gallery shows, the artists coming from all around to visit Mr. Ramírez. Seems rather over the top to me. But what do I know about art?"

I sat on my hands and pursed my lips. It was all I could do to not cry out, "Yes, it is preposterous! Which is why I wanted Pasto to look at my drawing!" But I kept calm.

We continued our chat. The whole time the doctor jotted down notes, his brow furrowing every time he looked down at the page. It was clear to me that he felt a grave error had been made in my diagnosis. And there had been. But not for the reasons he believed. I did my best to project a calm, serious man, lifeless and unimaginative. When he asked me if I was a fan of Gustave Courbet, I answered, "Yes, of course. There's much to admire." When he followed with, "Do you ever believe yourself to be Gustave Courbet?" I looked at him as if I didn't understand. "I'm not following you," I said. He stuttered out an elaboration, "As if, you know, at times do you think that you are actually Gustave Courbet, or, I mean, some other French artist, even—who comes to mind, let's see—Van Gogh? Manet? Degas?" I shook my head. "No, not all. I simply admire much of their work. What I know of it, of course. I studied some in high school."

The doctor nodded his head approvingly. "Lastly," he said, "I have to ask because it's here in my notes. It seems that one of the other doctors wrote that you claim to be French. Is that your background?"

I chuckled. "No, of course, not."

"So you're Mexican, is that right?"

I was about to tell him that I had been born in New Mexico and that I had never been to Mexico in my life, but then I caught myself. I had to remember that everything I said would be used against me.

"Yes, that's correct."

The doctor placed the cap on his pen, tapped it against the clipboard, and then placed the pen back in his pocket. He seemed pleased with our conversation, though maybe a little confused. He seemed to be deciding whether what had previously been written about me was all a mistake.

"Thank you," he said. "Mr. Stanley will escort you back to the ward." Then he opened the door, slipped out, and closed the door behind him. I thought I could hear him speak to Mr. Stanley on the other side. I pressed my ear to the door. Mr. Stanley said, "You don't want any more treatment, sir? But you said before—"

"I know what I said before. But let's just continue to observe him."

A minute later, Mr. Stanley entered the room. He looked disappointed. "Time to go back," he said. "Chow time soon. You gotta get your beans and rice, Pancho."

I resisted the urge to challenge his snide comment. "Thank you," I said. "I was getting hungry."

He grunted in response.

I went to bed that night deeply troubled. Having uttered, "No, I am not" to the question "Are you an artist?" was eating at me. I couldn't get the idea out of my head. *Was* I an artist? I had nothing to show for it. Nothing to prove it. And every time I tried to be simply what I thought myself to be, an artist, something prevented me, thwarted my attempts. It was as though I wasn't meant to be an artist because I couldn't do what artists do, and that is make art. If I *made* art, then I wouldn't have to prove anything. I would just be. But because I didn't make art, I was placing myself in a position to repeatedly prove myself, and really, the pressure was just too great. It was crippling. When the doctor asked me, "Are you an artist?" and I said no, a feeling came over me, a feeling that only grew as the day progressed, and that feeling was relief. A sad relief. An utterly miserable, deeply troubling relief. I had said I wasn't an artist, and so I wasn't.

I lay in bed, my neighbors on either side of me, fifty beds in one direction, fifty beds in another, all sleeping soundly, snoring, breathing deeply, with an occasional congested whistle or flatulence, and I found myself yearning for the sleepless nights back at the TSSS factory trying to tune out the sound of my sleeping neighbors. The days before Reies, the days before Ella, the days when all I had troubling me was my father's murder, my mother's abandonment, and the feeling of guilt for having abandoned Enrique. What I would've given to return to that innocent time. What hopes and dreams I had then. Now I was among the sick, the deranged, my hopes and dreams quickly slipping away. While all of this raced through my mind, I settled into bed, nestling into a mattress that wasn't meant for nestling. It was only my second night and already I desired something more comfortable. When I tried to pull the blanket over my shoulder, I found that it was stuck at the foot of the bed. I pulled harder but to no avail. I lifted my head and saw once again the dark silhouette of a man.

"You again?" I whispered loudly.

He shushed me. "Have you not learned?" he said quietly. "Our caretakers are vigilant. Any disturbances are handled quickly and efficiently. Do you know what I risk coming to your bed?"

"So why do you come?" I asked. "To rub it in my face that everyone considers you, Martín Ramírez, a great artist!"

"Shhh! How do you know it's me?"

"Because I've studied everyone here, and unlike you, my powers of observation are carefully trained. I may not be able to see your face, but your posture is exactly that of the man I saw drawing those childish scribbles today. It's enough to drive a person insane!"

"That's not my fault. Who am I to dispute their judgment? At the last hospital I was at, I hardly had a bed to sleep on. Sometimes I'd sleep on the hard pews in the ward chapel. But here we got it good. They even have arts and crafts. At the old hospital that would've been unthinkable. I always liked drawing. Beats working!"

"Drawing is work," I said.

"No, it's not," he said. "Drawing is fun. It's like playing. I feel like a kid again. Instead of killing myself at some job in the hot sun, repeating that day in and day out, I get to stay here, indoors, and have fun doodling. Is it my fault Dr. Pasto thinks everything I make is a masterpiece?"

"Yes, it's your fault. If you had any integrity at all, you would tell him you have no idea what you're doing and that he should quit making a fool of himself."

"But why would I do that? I'm allowed to sit and draw all day, undisturbed. You noticed how everyone has his chore. I haven't been assigned one in years. I don't lift a finger. I draw, I look through magazines and cut out pictures, I keep to myself, and I get a roof over my head and three square meals. That's not so bad for a man my age."

"Well, I still think it's ridiculous that your work is in museums and being sold in galleries and that professors bring their students to study you and you don't even know how to draw."

"But that's not my fault. If you had any sense, you would sit quiet, draw your pictures, and maybe Dr. Pasto will like your stuff, too. What you did today, trying to shove your picture in his face, that's only gonna get you in trouble. I already told you about the shocks."

"The shocks are supposed to be helpful," I said. "I'm even thinking that maybe I need another round to get me out of this rut I'm in. Today the doctor asked me if I was an artist and I told him I wasn't and now I can't get the idea out of my mind."

"Well, who cares whether you're an artist or not. Look at me; I just make my drawings and everyone says that I'm an artist."

"It's not so easy."

"Seems to me that tomorrow morning when we're done with breakfast, you go and sit down at the arts and crafts table and you start drawing, and be the artist you claim to—"

"But that's just it! Do you know how insulting it is, to be an artist, an artist following in the footsteps of Gustave Courbet, to sit at an arts and crafts table surrounded by crazies drawing with crayons of all things. Give me charcoal, give me oils, at least! It's an insult to sit at the arts and crafts table—that's what it is."

"But you don't have any other option. If you want to make art, you have to sit at the arts and crafts table with us crazies, as you say. If you insist on being a great artist, too great to actually sit down and make pictures when you're given the opportunity to do so, well then, by all means, play checkers and cards and stare out the window with the others."

"I have to get out of here, Martín," I said. "I have to get back to my studio in New Mexico."

"Then tell them what they want to hear. You're under seventy-two-hour observation. If they feel as though you're no harm to society or to yourself, they will let you go. You're not making too good a case for yourself. Don't insist on your sanity. Don't insist on anything. Either that, or contact your family and they can sign for your release."

"I don't want my family to know I'm here. They can't know—wait a second, I thought you said that here they make the sane insane? That there's no way of getting out of here, that the only way to remain sane was to act insane?"

"Yes, I said that."

"But now you're telling me all I have to do is tell them what they want to hear and they'll think I'm sane enough to leave."

"Yes, but that's easier said than done."

"What do you mean by that? I'll tell them anything they want to hear if it means I can gain my freedom."

"Good for you, then. Make sure the next two days are the quietest, sanest days of your life." And then I felt him rise from the bed and disappear into the darkness.

The next forty-eight hours, I kept to myself. I spoke to no one except when addressed, and I preferred to nod rather than speak aloud. I followed instructions. I made my bed. I brushed my teeth. I washed my face and was especially diligent behind my ears. I wore my hospital robe with the sash securely tied. I sat in a chair near the window with legs crossed, arms crossed, and I merely observed those around me as though I were sitting in a park passing a long afternoon with nothing else to do. When my name was called and Mr. Stanley took me to another session with the doctors, I ignored all of his snide comments and antagonisms. "Haven't acted up lately, beaner bomber," he said. I smiled. "You speak fancy for a Pancho," he said. I nodded. He pinched me right behind the neck as he directed me down the hall. I winced and bit my lip to prevent myself from crying out.

In my interview, as Martín instructed, I insisted on nothing. When the doctors repeated all the questions they had asked before, with slight twists and variations, I responded again with the answers of a sane man, meaning this: I said no to just about everything, and I offered absolutely no elaboration. I had learned my lesson: in their eyes, sane men offer no elaboration because they have nothing to prove. Insane men offer too much. Why? Because the stakes are so high. Their lives depend on that elaboration. Martín had said that telling them what they wanted to hear was easier said than done, but once I got going, once I knew my freedom depended on stringing together a few lies and denials, it was simple, and for once, my mouth complied. I didn't crack a smile.

The doctors seemed quite pleased with my improvement. They deemed the electrotherapeutic shocks successful. They said it was just the boost I needed. I had been sinking, but a life vest had been thrown my way, and now I was back aboard ship. They all jotted notes on their clipboards with great enthusiasm. The art historian told me that they would continue to observe me for the rest of the day and night, and if I felt okay I would be allowed to leave. I would no longer be a charge of the state. I thanked him, and shortly after, Mr. Stanley arrived to return me to the recreation room. He was quiet now, subdued. I was no longer worth his antagonisms. I would be gone soon, a civilian, a peer he could pass on the street.

Once back in the ward, I returned to my seat in the corner. I crossed my legs and arms and observed my fellow patients, waiting for the minutes and hours to pass, for the night to pass, for the morning to come and my freedom to arrive. I tried not to observe Martín, who was busy at his drawing table, making line after endless line. I tried not to watch the patients busy at the arts and crafts table; their activity only reminded me of my inactivity. I knew that the minute I picked up a crayon and a piece of paper and started to draw I would be sucked into their world. I couldn't do that. I had to return to my studio, I had to return to making my art. I had to make my way to Paris. I was an artist, a true artist, a great artist, and I had to believe that again . . . for at that moment my renunciation was still ringing in my ears. "Are you an artist?" they had asked. "No, I'm not," I had said. I was close to regaining my freedom, but I felt I had entered a different kind of prison.

When Lawrence in his brown-checkered slacks and loafers sat next to me and asked if I was ready to demonstrate that I was better than Martín Ramírez, I didn't take the bait. I just shook my head.

"I was thinking about what you said yesterday," Lawrence said, fixing his thick-framed glasses. "You know, about realism and how I disagreed that more real meant better when it came to art, and how when I saw your drawing of Wilcox's ear—which was quite remarkable—I thought to myself, 'Now, there's something there.' I had never thought about Wilcox's ears before. They were merely deformed, difficult to look at. But the way you rendered those ears brought them to life, told a story. You, your drawing, gave a permanency to Wilcox's ear. He may be made of flesh and bone and destined for dust, but your drawing will tell the story of that poor man for generations."

I realized then the depths of my misery and how deeply affected I was by my denial. Just a short while before, his flattering comment would've had my chest swelling with pride. I would've been putty in his hands, desperate to hear more words describing my greatness. But I was unmoved. I could hardly care that he recognized what I wanted others to recognize in my work: a steely-eyed record of life that would live forever. Instead, I told him the truth. "It's not so permanent, Dr. Kelson. Ramírez himself cut it up and collaged it onto one of his masterpieces."

Lawrence began laughing, and his face turned red. "Forgive me for not telling you outright that I am a doctor. I am supposed to observe the new patients discreetly."

"No problem," I said, and turned back to observing the floor. Lawrence extended his hand to shake mine. "Well, good luck out there," he said.

We shook hands, and I realized that he had been my last test. I was almost there. That night I waited for Martín to return to my bedside. I don't know why I expected him. Was I waiting for more advice? Maybe now that I was leaving, he had no advice to offer. His words were meant for those doomed to remain at DeWitt State Hospital, while I was almost among the living. I fell asleep and dreamed of the outside world. In my dream, I wondered where I would go. I was walking out the gates, and I couldn't figure out whether to turn left or right. Where would right lead me? Where would left? For a second I entertained the idea that Reies would return for me, abandoning his wife and child so that the two of us could travel the country proselytizing, I his best convert and exemplary man of God. But in truth, that life no longer appealed to me. Just the thought of it made my feet hurt. I could hardly believe that I had spent so long at his side.

Then Ella entered my mind, and I dreamed that she had found me and was ready to lead me back to the TSSS factory and my studio, our den of sin, artist and muse. But then I thought about it, really thought about it, that studio in the middle of nowhere that resembled Van Gogh's bedroom in Arles, but far from a place of creativity. Northern light or not, supplies galore or not, I felt no desire to return there. For what? To live with a woman who did not love me, who cared nothing for my artistic talent, who had her own dreams, none of which over-lapped with mine? And if I wasn't there with Ella, then I would be alone, and the thought of traveling a thousand miles to be alone in the middle of nowhere did not seem worth the effort.

No, I would have to strike out into the unknown, heading left or heading right, or maybe even straight ahead, because in my dream I was now at a crossroads. But no matter how hard I tried to go left or right or straight ahead, it was as if my legs had stuck in the ground, and the dream took a nightmarish turn. Day turned to night and I was still stuck at the gates, and the air became cold and without a jacket I started shivering, and then the rain started to fall and I was quickly drenched, and if that wasn't enough the wind picked up, and yet I couldn't move to save my life.

I awoke, my pajamas drenched with perspiration. I rose in bed and looked to my left and saw all of my roommates sleeping soundly. Then I looked across the way and saw more patients sleeping soundly, dreaming sweet dreams, not in the least bit concerned whether they were going left or going right or where they would find shelter when the rain and the cold came. I understood that with free-dom came responsibility, and even though I had spent all that time following Reies around, exposed to the elements on a daily and nightly basis, he still led the way. If I was cold, it was because Reies decided it should be so, and there was comfort in that. On my release, I would be the one making the decisions.

Where to go? Where to live? What to do at any given moment? Maybe Martín was right. For an artist who just wanted to make his art and not think about anything else, not a worldly care in his head, the hospital provided that benefit. You awoke when they woke you up, you put on your clothes when they placed clothes in front of you, you left your sleeping area when they escorted you to the cafeteria, you ate what they gave you to eat, and then for the rest of the day you remained in the room where they told you to remain. A simple equation, really. If only the hospital was full of easels set up with primed canvases, and instead of crayons and markers they had oil paints and brushes, and instead of robes we were given artist smocks, then it would be a respectable place for an artist to spend his days. But it wasn't. It was a crazy house, a loony bin, a sanitarium for the insane, and I didn't want to be crazy, loony, or insane. I just couldn't, for the life of me, figure out a way of making the masterpieces that were my destiny to create.

I must've fallen asleep at some point, because suddenly one of the orderlies was rustling me awake. A little startled, I blubbered, "Where? What—I—" He shushed me and whispered that he had been instructed to escort me to the processing office. I rose from bed and he handed me a robe. I pulled it around me, feeling a little chill. He found my slippers and placed them at my feet. "Thank you," I said, enjoying the special treatment. "Hurry," he said curtly. "I don't want to wake the others." We walked out of the ward and down a long dark hall. At the end of the hall, he knocked on a door, and a second later it opened. Mr. Stanley was standing there, as large and as pink-faced as ever, but instead of his usual grin and a snide remark, he looked at me as though I didn't exist. "Good morning, Mr. Stanley," I said. He didn't acknowledge my greeting. He grunted something at a man who sat behind a counter stacked with boxes.

"Outpatient?" the man asked.

"What else?" Mr. Stanley mumbled.

"Sign here," the man said, placing a clipboard on the top of the counter. Mr. Stanley pushed the clipboard toward me.

"Be right back to get his stuff," the man said.

"Hurry," Mr. Stanley said. "It's cold out here."

"It sure is," I said. "Will I be getting a jacket?"

Mr. Stanley heard me now. He scoffed. "What do you think this is, Montgomery Ward?"

"It's just I don't have a jacket and it is a little chilly."

"Welcome to the real world," Mr. Stanley said, rubbing his hands together for warmth. He then cupped his hand around his mouth and blew into them. I mimicked him. He told me, "Sign your release," and pointed at the bottom.

I signed the paper. By that time the man had emerged carrying a box. "Didn't bring much," he said. "You can change in the bathroom right there. The slippers are yours. The gown and robe you got on belong to the state."

He handed me the box and directed me to the bathroom. As the door closed behind me, I heard him say, "Leave 'em in the box. The box belongs to the state, too!"

I peered inside and found the remnants of my previous life: a pair of khaki pants with holes in the knees, frayed to the shins, and twine that replaced the broken zipper and button; a long-sleeved plaid shirt that Reies had insisted I wear when my old shirt snagged on a rose bush and was hanging on me by just the collar; and a pair of loafers with holes in the toes that I didn't remember possessing. Underneath my clothes was a stack of letters—Enrique's poems. After I changed, I secured the folded pages in my back pocket. I neatly folded the hospital clothes and placed them in the box, and then carried it out of the bathroom. I placed it on the counter and looked for Mr. Stanley, but he was nowhere around.

"Where'd Mr. Stanley go?" I asked.

"Back inside. Morning is starting. You're free to go."

It took me a moment to understand. He'd said it so nonchalantly.

"Free to go?"

"Yep. Just walk outside." And he made a gesture of walking with his fingers.

I took a hesitant step toward the door. I still wasn't sure if he was serious. But he wasn't paying attention to me anymore. He was reading something on a clipboard.

"Will I know how to get out of here?" I asked.

"Yep, just follow the path out the gates," he said.

I walked out the door and down the path toward the front gates. I stiffened when I saw a guard on duty, thinking that I would have to explain my presence and tell him what the man had said about being free to go, and if there was a mistake I completely understood and was happy to return to straighten things out, if need be. But he didn't even look at me twice. I was cold in my tattered pants and old shirt. I wished they had at least let me take the robe. I would have to find a jacket. Where would I find a jacket? Would I have to buy one? Where would I get the money? And once I started thinking about money, I couldn't help but think about a job, and then once a job entered my mind it wasn't long before I said to myself, "I'm back where I started!" And I thought of Enrique working all those jobs for me, sacrificing himself around the clock so that I could draw and paint my masterpieces, and how I had squandered that time. I had produced nothing, nothing worth saving, nothing that remained.

"What a waste," I said as I passed through the wrought iron gates. I now faced the crossroads of my dream. I looked to my left, then to my right, then straight ahead.

"Where to?" I said aloud.

I walked to my right and found a bench. I pulled out Enrique's poems. I read a few. I found one that he had titled "A Callus on My Hand," and another "Hours Spent Hating Coal." I found the one about the two artists living above the mechanic's garage who spent their nights talking about their love of the light at dusk, the colors of the seasons, and the surreal magic of dreams. Tears came to my eyes. "Enrique," I sighed. Enrique, my friend, the poet. Enrique who wrote poetry. Enrique who is dead. Enrique who died too soon. Enrique whom I abandoned.

Enrique the true genius. Enrique the artist. And me, I was nothing. I was alone. I was abandoned. I was without a jacket. I was afraid. I who lost Ella. I who lost Enrique. I who followed Reies into the abyss. I who didn't want to leave that bench. I who was afraid. I who said he was not an artist and became sane. I didn't want to be sane. I preferred insanity to the fear I felt then. The fear that all my dreams had come to naught, that all my life had led to this, me, shivering, alone on a bench in a place I didn't know, afraid of what was out there, afraid of continuing, of fighting, and ending up in the same damn place, no farther for my efforts, no closer to my dream, no more an artist than the rest of ill-begotten humanity.

I rose from the bench. I approached the guard. "Excuse me," I said. "Sorry to trouble you, but it seems that I left without saying goodbye to Dr. Kelson, and I would feel awful if I wasn't allowed to speak to him again."

"What's your name," the guard said, dialing the telephone.

"My name? Well, I'm surprised you don't recognize me. Maybe you're more familiar with my work. I'm quite a well-known painter, you know—"

"Your name, sir?"

"Gustave Courbet," I said, and my stomach growled. I wondered what we were having for breakfast that morning.

PART IV

The Last Prophet—Oscar Zeta Acosta

CHAPTER EIGHT

The years passed quickly at DeWitt State Hospital. Looking back, I can hardly account for them. I entered in 1950. I left when DeWitt closed in 1972. I watched Martín Ramírez's stature rise. I couldn't hold it against him. I even admired his growing body of work, if only because he had a body of work. I had none. I could never bring myself to pick up a pencil or paintbrush or crayon. Don't feel bad for me; I don't seek sympathy. In some ways those years were the happiest, most contented of my life. My dreams of Paris over, along with my aspirations of joining the ranks of Courbet and Millet and Corot, I learned to enjoy days of leisure. I picked up chess. I played checkers. I played a mean game of bridge. I won a lot of cigarettes playing poker. I adopted the quirks, anxieties, and compulsions of my fellow patients, my friends. I fit right in. I never considered myself completely crazy, but I felt so at home among the crazies that I figured I had to be at least a quarter or a third.

When Martín died in 1963, Dr. Pasto stopped coming and so did his students, and so did his artist friends, and along with them my hopes of being discovered. What would they have discovered? A man who talked a lot about his unrealized creative potential. A man who described masterpieces never painted. A man who gave a lot of pointers, but no demonstrations. I would not pick up a pencil, a brush; I would not join the arts and crafts table. I simply lived in past glories that never existed.

My first meeting with Oscar Acosta was as unmemorable as meetings went at DeWitt. I had met a hundred men like him. There one day, gone the next. Who knows what they suffered from? A frightened wife or parent had committed them, or maybe they had committed themselves; they needed time to rest, to reflect on life while wearing a paper-thin hospital gown, to have a soothing conversation with a bespectacled gray-haired doctor; and then they were released, just as I had been released. But most never returned.

It was 1959, my ninth year at the hospital, and I had long settled into a routine. I woke, I dressed, I ate my breakfast, and then I played chess until lunch. After lunch, I played poker or bridge and took breaks to walk around the arts and crafts table and offer critiques and suggestions for improvement, which of course were never heeded. I didn't critique Martín's drawings. I tried not to look in his direction. I remembered our late-night conversations—the only words we ever exchanged—when he told me that he wasn't an artist, and that it wasn't his fault Dr. Pasto thought so highly of his drawings. Martín's self-assessment was wrong. He *was* an artist. He taught me that. An artist wasn't determined by the quality of his work, the mastery of his medium; no, an artist was determined by one thing only and that was making art. So I gave him that, but in exchange I refused to look his way. I did try to engage Dr. Pasto, but the man was impenetrable. It was a fast trip to solitary if I so much as said hello. Eventually, I let the two of them be. One would think that at a state hospital in the middle of the California foothills I would at least be the resident artist. But I wasn't. That was Martín. As I said, I was known as a mean bridge player.

When Oscar met me, according to him, I wasn't playing bridge. I was talking to myself in the corner. He didn't know what I was saying exactly except that it had something to do with paint application, the merits of impasto over glazing. Because I was talking to myself, he didn't mind interrupting.

"You Mexican?" he asked me.

Again, according to him, I responded, "See voo play, Fransuey."

"French? You aint French, pendejo. You're as Mexican as I am."

"You were born in Mexico?" I asked.

"No, I was born in El Paso."

"Well, we're countrymen. I was born in La Trampa, New Mexico. Not a day's trip away."

"Why'd you say you were French then?"

"My great-grandfather was French. He was a soldier in Emperor Maximilian's army."

"A fucking traitor, that's what he was. Probably got shot by a firing squad. Are you a traitor to your race? Ashamed of who you are?"

According to Oscar, I ignored the question and asked him what he was doing at DeWitt.

He answered with a long rant against religion and white women. He told me how he had been in Panama with the air force and become a preacher converting Indian heathens into good Christians. After about a year of that he realized he didn't believe what he was preaching anymore. But once you start preaching, he explained, you can't just stop one day and tell everybody you were wrong. So he kept converting the heathens even when he was just as much a heathen as they were. Then he explained that the only reason he was in the air force to begin with was because his girlfriend's parents wouldn't accept him because he was Mexican. They'd gotten it into their daughter's head that he wouldn't amount to anything, and somehow that led him to enlist, which was a mistake because it didn't bring him any closer to marrying his "Miss It." In fact, he told me, his voice becoming emotional, she married some "wop dago" as dark as him.

But he did get to travel. When he came back from Panama and was discharged—honorably, he made sure to add—he suffered a breakdown. He didn't know where his life was going. He had lost his white girl, his religion, and his life's direction, and that was troublesome because he had always assumed he was destined for something great. He was going to be somebody, but he was no closer to being that somebody than when he was "a mocoso rubbing his pito" in Riverbank. He started cracking up, his nerves were shot to hell, and so he checked himself into a hospital in Modesto. He thought the doctors would be able to help him, but they didn't do much. The only thing that gave him any comfort was meeting his future wife, Betty, who was there too. Now, three years later, they'd just had a baby, little Marcos, and Oscar was no closer to finding his calling in life. Something about having a son made the idea of this unbearable. He didn't want to be a deadbeat old man. He wanted to be an example for his son, someone to look up to. Then he finished his story by saying that life was just one long fucking trip.

Apparently, when he finished his story I told him mine, going all the way back to my father's murder, my mother abandoning me, my exploitation of Enrique, our ill-fated trip to Los Angeles, my studio at the TSSS factory, my rapturous and doomed love affair with Ella, my spiritual tutelage under Reies López Tijerina, and ending with how I'd given up my dreams of becoming an artist. The fact that Ella, my own "Miss It," had left me troubled him greatly. He tried convincing me that I should go after her, but I told him that I didn't see the point of loving someone who doesn't love you. We debated that for a while; he seemed to think that was exactly who you should love because it made life interesting. I said it made life painful, and he agreed. "Interesting *and* painful," he said. Then I told him that I'd rather life be a little less interesting and could do without the pain. "Well, that's why you're talking to yourself in a corner and telling people you're French," Oscar said.

"I wasn't talking to myself—" but then I stopped because I realized that I probably was talking to myself, a common enough tic among my fellow patients. I then offered Oscar a convoluted explanation about the nature of tics in a place like DeWitt. First, I'd see a fellow patient do something; then I'd start to worry so much that I would end up doing it, that I would purposely do it to keep my sanity. In a ward full of men with awful tics, this could be exhausting, and oftentimes I couldn't keep my adopted tics straight. Luckily, Oscar changed the subject back to what I learned was his favorite topic of conversation: one's origins.

"So why do you say you're French when you're Mexican?"

"I don't say I'm French. I was practicing my French. And like I told you, my great-grandfather was a soldier in—"

"Yeah, yeah, I heard you."

"I'll have you know," I said, "that I'm often mistaken for being French."

"By who? These crazies around here. You're as Mexican as Pancho Villa!"

"Pancho Villa? What are you talking about? I'm nothing like—"

"I'm just kidding, man, calm down. Not Pancho Villa, but you're still Mexican. Me, I'm always getting mistaken for something else. I always tell people I'm a goddamned redskin and if I get drunk enough I'll take their scalp."

"Why would you do that?"

"Why? Because fuck 'em. They can't tell a Mexican from an Indian from a Filipino because they don't care to, because we're all the same to them, just brown baby-makers. You know what your problem is?" he said, poking me in the chest with his fat finger.

"My problem? I'm perfectly content. You're the one who committed yourself to the hospital just yesterday."

"You're in the same damn place."

"Yes, but I've been here for almost ten years, willingly, happily—"

"Don't lie to me; you ain't happy. You maybe think you're happy, but you were supposed to be a great artist and now look at you."

This hit me deep. I had said as much to myself over the years, but in a far different tone. I had said "now look at you" with an uplifting lilt; Oscar meant it as an insult.

He continued: "Yeah, man, that's your problem, you don't know what you are. You thinking you're French when you're nothing but a dirty stinking Mesicun like me, and if you just embraced that"—he lifted his arm and smelled his armpit—"you'd be an artist again."

"Seems to me like you're talking about yourself, Oscar. You don't even know me. I am who I am and that's it."

"...that's your problem, you don't know what you are.
...you're nothing but a dirty stinking Mesicun like me
and if you just embraced that
you'd be an artist again."
He lifted his arm and smelled his armpit.

"I do know you. I know you better than you know yourself. You're lost. I'm lost. Ever since I was a little kid I just tried to do right. I was an A student, star football player, band leader, student government, and yet when it came down to what I wanted—just a white piece of ass to call my own, God knows how much I loved her—I couldn't have her. Why? Because a big brown Indian like me doesn't get shit in this world."

"But you already said you found another white piece of ass to call your own," I told him, "and now you have a son, and I think that things are really looking up for you. But to think that somehow what you're going through applies to me, you're just simply mistaken."

"You're an artist," he said. "I'm an artist, too. A writer. That's what I've decided. I want to be a writer. I'm gonna be the greatest writer who ever lived, and one day when I'm famous and I got shitloads of money, I'm going to come find you here, and I'm going to set you up in a studio and buy you paints, and then I'm going to find you a show in a big-time gallery, and I'm gonna make sure all my famous friends buy your paintings, and then you, too, will be the famous artist you were meant to be. But on one condition."

"What's that?" I asked, hesitantly. My heart had started to beat. I had to remind myself that this was a man who had just checked himself into a mental hospital, and that his dream of being a famous writer was as much a long shot as me entering the Paris Salon.

"I want you to admit that you're just a dirty stinking Mesicun, and I want you do this"—and he smelled his armpit again, inhaling deeply as though his body odor were some magic elixir. Then he started laughing boisterously, a harsh cackle, and he slapped me on the arm and called me a big pendejo. "You should see the look on your face!" he managed to say through his laughter.

The next day Oscar was gone. I never thought I would see him again. Our conversation about being a dirty stinking Mexican wasn't any stranger than the many strange conversations I'd had over the years. Most of my conversations were strange, incomprehensible, and it was only with Dr. Kelson, Lawrence, that

I was really able to have a lucid dialogue. Part of the problem was that all of my fellow patients wanted to have conversations with themselves; so even when they were talking to you they were still talking to themselves, and in that way, my conversation with Oscar was no different. He was talking about what ailed him and trying to apply it to me because he wanted to dwell on himself and himself only.

I should mention one last detail about my exchange with Oscar. Feeling as though he had made a fool of me, I decided to make a fool of him. When his seventy-two-hour observation period was over, and he was waiting to be escorted out of the ward, I went to my bed and underneath my mattress I pulled out Enrique's poems. I walked back to Oscar and placed them in his hands. "Dirty stinking Mexican, huh? Well, read these," I said. "And weep at your mediocrity."

Oscar glanced at the first page, which was my favorite poem about the two artists living above the mechanic's garage. I wanted to see his face drop, I wanted to see his face turn green with envy, I wanted him to realize that no matter how much he wrote, how much he dedicated himself to his art, he would never measure up to my genius friend Enrique, my personal Baudelaire. But Oscar was a far more serious and generous man than I had given him credit for.

"Hey brother, these are for real," he said. Then he turned to the next page. "Damn," he said, letting out a long whistle as he read the first few lines. After several more poems, he said quietly, almost a whisper, "What the hell you got these stuffed underneath your mattress? These should be shared with the world."

Then the orderly appeared and barked, "Ready, let's go!" as if he had been standing there the entire time. Oscar handed me back the loose pages. As he was escorted away, he turned around to look at me, his dark manic eyes opened wide. "You're a genius, too. Maybe you ain't a painter, but you're a poet. When I get some dough, I'll come back and get you! I swear on my kid."

And before I could clarify that I wasn't the author of those poems, Oscar was gone from my life. I would soon forget him and our conversation. I would even forget the sting of being called a genius for an art that wasn't mine. Good for Enrique, I thought; he deserves the recognition. Then I placed his poems back underneath the mattress, where they would remain until my release. They would stay in my possession until Oscar found me thirteen years later living at my mother's in Albuquerque, when he promised to find a publisher for Enrique's poems, which he still thought I had written.

Yes, my mother eventually found me. As she later explained, after years of not hearing from me, she figured that my sister was probably right and that I had ended up in a mental hospital. So she wrote every institution in New Mexico, then every one in Arizona and Texas, then every single one in Colorado, Nevada, Utah, and finally California, starting in the south and moving up north, until she got word that I was safe and sound playing board games all day at DeWitt. Though I was a little peeved that my sister assumed I'd ended up in a mental hospital and not abroad in some far-flung bohemian community, I was touched that my mother had gone through such effort to find me. Still, I wrote back a long letter explaining that I was at DeWitt only because I chose to be there and that it beat the doldrums of mechanical labor. I told them I had more time to dedicate toward my artwork, all the art supplies I needed, and over a hundred models with nothing to do all day but hold a pose for me. I didn't have the heart to admit that they'd been right, that my art career had sputtered and failed and ended in renunciation.

My mother's tone was more conciliatory. Mr. Buenrostro had died, leaving her a widow. She was lonely and sad and had no one to keep her company in the gigantic house that had once been full of laughing children. Now those children were grown up and had either moved across town (my sister Lourdes) or moved out of town (my half siblings). Lourdes was so busy keeping Mr. Buenrostro's various businesses alive and thriving that she hardly had time for a visit. So it was just my mother and the cats, a dog named Luna, and Mr. Buenrostro's belongings, which she didn't want to touch because she wanted to preserve his memory. Such a good man, such a good man, and he always wanted what was best for you, she wrote. At the end of the letter she said, "Maybe you remember our little house in the backyard. Well, it's absolutely empty. Maybe you'd like to come home and take care of your mom, and you could live and work in that studio in peace and I wouldn't dare bother you, except to offer you ham sandwiches if you were hungry and lemonade if you were thirsty."

It was tempting, but I resisted. I couldn't just go rushing back as if the years hadn't scarred me. Why wasn't I offered the little house years ago? I read through the lines. *Yes, I'll take care of you, Mom, now that all you really need is a companion, and not someone to actually take care of you, meaning, provide for you* (after all, Mr. Buenrostro had left her well taken care of). *Yes, I'll take care of you because I have nothing better to do. Yes, I'll take care of you because you were right all along. I wasn't an artist, I was just a son shirking his duty who didn't want to work and who still doesn't want to work, but what does it matter when you're all set up in a nice house on a quiet street with neatly manicured front yard and a back house for wayward sons. You don't need me to be anything, not an artist, not a worker, not anything, just someone to fill the lonely space of your waning years.* That's what I read in her letter, and that's what I couldn't give in to. I had principles, after all. Or not principles, but rather, pride. But that was short lived. Who was I kidding? All I had to do was look around to know that pride meant little when you called DeWitt your home. So I didn't write back, and I thought she had forgotten about me again, disappeared from my life as she had done so many times before. But then one day I was told I had a visitor.

I hadn't ever had a visitor. I expected to be escorted in shackles to a room with mirrors that were actually windows, just as I'd seen in a movie the ward had voted to watch. "This isn't prison," said Mr. Stanley's replacement (Mr. Stanley had retired by then), whom I called Mr. Stanley as well, much to his annoyance. He led me out to the garden, which we were able to visit for short periods of time in the spring and summer, and he instructed me to sit on a dust-covered bench. He told me to stay put, and then I watched him walk toward the administration building. I looked around, breathed in the cool autumn air, and wondered who it could be. After all these years I still hoped that somehow Ella would have a change of heart and manage, miraculously, to find me. I pictured our reunion, our passionate embrace, our cries of desperation for the years lost to stubbornness and distance. I imagined her young and plump and full-breasted and full of ardor, and my hands began to tremble with nervous anticipation. So I was a little disappointed when in the distance I saw a small, gray-haired woman walking slowly toward me, slouched, her gait a little unsure on the uneven path.

"Mom?" I called out.

She didn't answer. The old woman just kept walking toward me, squinting her eyes as though trying to determine if I really was her son. When she was five feet away, she stopped and said, "It's you!" and opened her arms wide and held them raised as if she were going to flap them and fly away. "Come here! Hug me, I'm your mother and I've looked for you for so long," she cried.

Her directness startled me. After so many years I expected at least a preliminary conversation, but I felt compelled to rush toward her. Leaning down I placed my arms around her midsection, more to keep her upright than to share a heartfelt embrace. She wrapped her arms around me and rubbed my back, and I felt and heard her kissing the top of my head. "So many years," she said. "Why? Why so many years?"

I didn't mince words. "Isn't this where you wanted me all along? As far away from you as possible? Mr. Buenrostro made it very clear I wasn't to upset your nerves!"

"Not upsetting my nerves is one thing, but disappearing for twenty years is quite another."

"Twenty years?" I asked incredulously. I had never really done the math.

"Yes, twenty years."

At that moment, I realized that two decades had passed since I'd given up my dreams of being a great artist. They had passed in two blinks of an eye. All my defining memories came from a period of only ten years. Memories to fill volumes. And yet, in my twenty years at DeWitt I had no significant memories to speak of. It was a time one glossed over, summarized—I did this, I did that, and I played a

The old woman just kept walking toward me...

"Come here!

Hug me, I'm your mother and

I've looked for you for so long," she cried.

lot of board games and bridge in between—and all because it was a life without passion, without hopes, without dreams, without meaning. If twenty years had passed, that meant I was in my midforties. My mother, as I could see, was old, a widow twice over. My sister, who was a child when I last saw her, was all grown up, apparently a captain of industry. If I stayed at DeWitt, the rest of my life would pass just as the last twenty had, quickly and unmemorably. Is that what I wanted? I didn't think so. But I wasn't sure. Change was difficult for me, especially after so many years of relative inner peace. So I told my mother, "I'm really quite happy here."

"Here?" she cried, backing away from me. "This place is horrible, my son. This . . . this . . . this—is a place for the insane."

It pleased me that she didn't think I belonged.

Mr. Stanley's replacement soon walked over to us and announced that my paperwork was ready. "Paperwork?" I exclaimed.

"Yes, your outpatient paperwork?"

"Outpatient?"

"Yes, you're being discharged. DeWitt will be closing soon and patients will either be released to family or placed in other facilities."

This was news to me. I was aware there had been no new patients for some time, but I never questioned why. Maybe I assumed the outside world had stabilized and found its equilibrium. Well, I had found my equilibrium on the inside, and the thought of now being on the outside filled me with dread. But I looked at my mother, her gray, almost white hair and wrinkled face, her eyes sad but also happy, an aura of loneliness about her, and I decided that I would brave the outside world if it meant providing comfort for her in her final chapter. I would let bygones be bygones—a phrase I'd picked up from a fellow patient who mumbled it for hours on end—and not abandon my mother in her time of greatest need.

This thought inspired me, and before I knew it I had gathered my belongings, including Enrique's poems from underneath my mattress, said goodbye to friends, most of whom blurted out "Goodbye!" as if I were merely going to the bathroom and would be back in five minutes.

"No. Goodbye!" I said, "As in *goodbye!*"

"Goodbye!" they called.

I glanced one last time at the arts and crafts table, which had fallen on hard times in recent years, its supplies meager, participation at a minimum, and I felt a certain pride for never having succumbed, never having stooped to mediocrity. For twenty years I had maintained at least that strand of dignity. I may have given up on Paris, given up on art entirely, but I hadn't become a hackneyed hobbyist, a weekend watercolorist, a patient whiling away the hours until death.

I felt a stirring inside of me. Maybe my artistic ambition had simply lain dormant. Now, two decades later, I felt a rumbling, a bubbling, a gurgling—literally—as I realized that my insides were about to erupt. I rushed to the bathroom, tucked Enrique's poems securely under my arm, pulled down my pants, and relieved myself of twenty numb years. To my mind, it was a symbolic shit, and afterward I felt lighter, freer, ready to face whatever might come my way. When I emerged from the bathroom, several of my old friends called out, "Hello again!" I didn't bother to explain that my last goodbye had really been the last, that I was leaving forever and that we would never see each other again.

I took one final glance at the ward and sighed to myself, "Twenty years." Then I turned and walked down the hall, found my mother, and we walked out of DeWitt State Hospital together, and this time, holding my mother's arm, I kept walking.

We arrived in Albuquerque by bus. My mother kept asking me, "Can you believe how much everything has changed?" I looked around and realized that the ward television had kept me surprisingly well abreast of the outside world. Nothing shocked me. That is, until I saw my sister Lourdes waiting for us in a big black shiny Cadillac. When my mother informed me that my sister would be there to pick us up, I couldn't help but picture a child in a yellow summer dress doing pirouettes. But she was a woman now. She had grown, and by that I mean she had put on at least two hundred pounds since our last encounter.[18] Wearing a black funereal dress, taking up the driver's seat and then some, her ample arm resting on the sill of the open window, her first words to me after twenty years were, "Well, if it isn't the famous artist."

The long bus ride had tired me, and I didn't have the energy to respond. Instead, I wearily thanked her. For what, I don't know, and she just chuckled, her extra chin jiggling with her. I sat in the back. The car smelled strongly of her fruity perfume. My sister talked the entire time, listing off all of her achievements during my time away, all the properties she owned, all the money she'd made, all Mr. Buenrostro's businesses that she had transformed into thriving companies.

"What about the TSSS factory?" I asked.

In the rearview mirror, I saw her eyes squint as if she had to dig deep to recall the place. "That's right. Where you lived! I remember now. Oh gosh, the workers there were always threatening to strike. We ended up razing the camp and selling the factory."

---

18. Ernie writes: "This couldn't be further from the truth. My mother is a petite woman and always has been." Without Ernie's note, we would have no reason to question our narrator's description. But his correction makes us wonder what else could be fabricated and to what extent it matters. In our current age, we place high value on nonfiction and memoir for its supposed "truth," but we need not look further than ourselves, our faulty memories, our prejudices and biases, our need to make sense of and understand what can't be understood with absolute certainty to realize that "truth" is only an approximation. Does this mean I don't believe in objective facts? No, I just rigorously consider my sources. I'm reminded of a statement by Gabriel García Márquez: "In journalism just one fact that is false prejudices the entire work. In contrast, in fiction one single fact that is true gives legitimacy to the entire work. That's the only difference, and it lies in the commitment of the writer. A novelist can do anything he wants so long as he makes people believe in it." Which makes me consider our narrator's illustrations in a new light. At first, I didn't know what to make of them—I'm no judge of artistry—but I see now that just as novelists can do anything they want so long as they make people believe, an artist, in a way, has an even greater power to convince. I trusted our narrator when he said his sister Lourdes put on two hundred pounds because the drawing gave me irrefutable proof: *this* is what she looked like. I now must go back through the illustrations, checking to what extent they subconsciously helped me visualize, and therefore believe, an otherwise unbelievable, far-fetched or fantastic scene.

The TSSS factory was razed.

I imagined my sister at the controls of a bulldozer toppling my studio...

a mountainous pile of rusted tin, broken glass

and weathered wood... I the only one left to sort through the ruins.

My sister.

I couldn't help but picture a child in a yellow summer dress doing pirouettes.

But she was a woman now. She had grown...

"You did?" I said. I imagined my sister at the controls of a bulldozer toppling my studio, then the neighboring shack where I first saw Ella in the windowsill, and then the next shack, and the next, and the next, the row of shacks falling to the ground like dominoes. I pictured a mountainous pile of rusted tin, broken glass, and weathered wood. It was an image I carried with me as I settled into my new life. Who could deny that my past was now rubble? Every last person was gone, I the only one left to sort through the ruins.

As my mother promised, I had my little house in back, a bleached white adobe structure with red tile roof that matched the larger home in front, where my mother shuffled from room to room doing who knows what. She would bring me meals and watch me eat, and she would talk about Mr. Buenrostro and what her children were up to. She would speak about my half siblings as though they had no relation to me, as if I were just boarder in back. Soon she brought out her own food as well, and we would eat together. She would look around my room, which was little changed since my arrival. Accustomed to the hospital ward, I didn't think to decorate or put up pictures of my own. The place was fine as it was. I had my bed, a little television, and plenty of room both inside and outside to pace back and forth, a habit I picked up years ago from my friend Harrison, though he claimed to have picked it up from me. My mother never asked me any questions. Then one day, looking around the mostly empty room, she asked, "Are you lonely here?"

"Lonely?" I asked.

"Yes, do you miss your friends?"

I told her I didn't, and that was the truth. They had been gone too many years. I had grown accustomed to having them in memory only: Enrique, Ella, Reies, even Martín. My mother looked at me with sad eyes, and I wanted to tell her not to project her loneliness onto me. But I held my tongue. A few weeks into my stay, after I had spent countless hours either pacing or watching television, my mother knocked on my door and instead of bringing me the baloney sandwich with mayonnaise and lettuce that I had requested, she carried in a black hardbound sketchbook and a pack of pencils.

"These are for you," she said. "You need to occupy yourself with something or you're going to just wither away. You're still young, my son."

I didn't have the words to respond. I stared at the sketchbook in my hands, then shifted my gaze to the pencils as though these were foreign objects, new and incomprehensible.

My mother burst into tears.

"What's wrong?" I asked.

"It's just that you've lost the will to live! You're a ghost! You've lost your spirit!"

"My spirit?"

"Yes, your spirit. You were always so spirited. You were a boy, a young man who knew exactly what he wanted in life. You were so determined. Sure, you had your peculiarities, but at least you had your dreams. I always loved that about you!"

"You did?" I asked, slightly stunned.

"Yes!" And she rushed over to me and wrapped her arms around my neck. "Oh, why did you disappear? That place ruined you! That place took the life out of you. We could've helped you!"

There was a time when I would've questioned this skewed version of history, which held that she had no part in my banishment, which held that I had been the one to abandon rather than the other way around, but her tears were so genuine, slipping down her cheeks in large drops, and her embrace so forceful, practically choking me, that I kept my mouth shut. My mother wasn't my enemy. At one time, yes. She had been misguided. She believed, as all mothers do, that sons are meant for them and them only, and every other calling is secondary. My art was secondary. But now, she wanted what I had been to return. This shell,

My mother carried in a sketchbook and a pack of pencils.

"You need to occupy yourself with something or else you're

going to wither away.

It's just that you've

lost the will to live! You're a ghost!

You've lost your spirit!"

"My spirit?"

this ghost of a man, pacing back and forth all day, mumbling to himself (she claimed), doing nothing and going nowhere, obedient and peaceful—this was not the son she wanted.

But how could I explain my defeat twenty years ago when I gave up everything except my steadfast refusal to join the arts and crafts table? I couldn't. So I thanked her for the sketchbook and the pencils, and then I reminded her about the baloney sandwich. I also asked if it would be possible to procure some cigarettes. She wiped her tears and told me she'd call my sister. That afternoon I heard a car honking its horn. I peered over the fence and saw my mother slowly walking toward my sister Lourdes's shiny black Cadillac. Lourdes remained in the car, as she always did, her fat pasty arm resting on the windowsill. She handed our mother the cigarettes and quickly drove off.

The sketchbook remained untouched. The pack of pencils too. I knew nothing would come of opening them. I wasn't afraid of the blank page. It was the enemy I knew, the enemy that had defeated me too many times, and so I chose to keep my distance. My mother kept encouraging me to draw something. She asked that I draw a picture for her to put up in the house. She brought me a photograph of Mr. Buenrostro and asked that I draw his portrait. Perhaps one day, she hinted, I would even consider painting his portrait in oils, and she'd find a beautiful ornate frame like the kind that hang in museums and she would place the painting over the mantle. I took the photo of Mr. Buenrostro and pinned it to the wall, but staring at his youthful, smiling face depressed me. Not because he was dead but because he appeared so self-satisfied. So I took it down and placed it in a drawer next to the blank sketchbook and unused pencils.

CHAPTER NINE

One afternoon I heard my mother's knock on the door. "Come in," I yelled over the blaring television. I was watching a game show that featured a ticking clock and lots of buzzers. The door opened, and my mother entered followed by a large, dark-skinned man with a wide flat nose and curly jet-black hair. I turned back to the game show.

"A friend is here to see you," my mother said.

"We met at DeWitt years ago," the man added.

I glanced back at him. His skin was as smooth as a baby's, and he towered over my mother. He looked vaguely familiar.

"We only spoke a little bit, but you—you showed me something that I haven't been able to forget."

I knit my brow. "You got the wrong guy," I said. "I never showed anyone anything. I never had anything to show."

My mother turned to the large man, and they murmured words to each other. I couldn't hear because of the game show and its incessant ticking clock and buzzers. I rose and turned down the volume. I glanced at my mother. She was looking at me with the same sad eyes that she always looked at me with now, eyes that said, "What happened to you?" Then she turned and walked out of my little house, leaving me alone with the large visitor.

"Remember, you showed me your poems, your brilliant poems!"

"I don't write poetry," I said.

"Yes, you do. You showed me your work. A whole manuscript that you pulled out from under your mattress. You told me you were a great artist, and I told you I was going to be a great writer and that when I was famous I was going to come back for you. Well, I'm famous now. Look!"

He reached behind and pulled out from underneath his shirt two books and tossed them onto my bed. I glanced at one and saw a photo of my visitor starkly contrasted on a brown cover. He wore a tank top. His arms were crossed, and he had a pained look on his face. "*The Autobiography of a Brown Buffalo* by Oscar Zeta Acosta," I recited.[19] "Who's the Brown Buffalo?"

"That's me," he said, pointing to his chest. "Oscar Zeta Acosta, the Brown Buffalo. And *remember,* I promised you that when I was famous I was going to come and introduce you to my famous friends and set you up in a studio and buy you paints and canvas? That's when I thought you were an artist."

I looked up at him, confused.

"Goddamn!" he cried. "You really did lose your mind." He proceeded to recount our exchange from beginning to end, and slowly it started to come back to me. As he spoke, I seemed to recall a slimmer, short-haired version of the man before me. At some point, his dark manic eyes met mine, and I remembered.

---

19. Lorraine writes: "Ernie was lucky my phone had died when I first read this at 2am because I wanted to call and wake him up. *The Autobiography of a Brown Buffalo* was my favorite book when I read it my freshman year of college. By my senior year, I considered Oscar Zeta Acosta to be a sexist pig, but by the time I picked it up again in my thirties I was a little more forgiving. I don't know—I guess I just knew too many Oscars, insecure and wounded cabrones whom I still loved anyway. At least he was honest about his flaws. I also admired the fact that he managed to write books in addition to being a lawyer for jailed Chicano activists. But what always struck me as tragic was that he disappeared without a trace in Mexico in 1974." Lorraine is right: Acosta's disappearance remains a mystery, and I have been waiting for this moment ever since Ernie first wrote in his introductory letter that his uncle had something to do with Acosta's death. Could it be true? Could the mystery surrounding his disappearance finally be solved? In my excitement, I have abandoned my scholarly caution, not to mention my previous note about the veracity of this story and whether it matters or not. It does matter. I want it to be true. I want to know what happened to Oscar Zeta Acosta.

I recalled shoving Enrique's poems into his hands. He began speaking passionately about the poems, remembering a good deal of what he had read in those few short minutes.

"I've never been able to forget those lines," he said. "I need to see them again."

"So that's why you've come?"

"I went all the way back to DeWitt, and they told me where to find you. A promise is a promise."

"What promise?"

"I just told you. That when I was famous I was gonna help you out."

"You're famous? How come I never see you on television?"

"I'm not television famous, pendejo, I'm just regular famous. A lot of influential people know who I am, let's put it that way. I ran for sheriff of Los Angeles. How 'bout that? That's a whole lot of people who know my name. Even more people know me as the Samoan lawyer in that bastard Thompson's book—*Fear and Loathing in Las Vegas*—you hear of it?[20] I told that asshole I ain't Samoan, goddamn it. But he wanted all the credit for himself. Don't matter. I got my two books, and I'm about to start my third. The greatest Chicano novel ever written. That's what I'm going to write, if I haven't already. But this next one will be better than the first two. I just need help doing it, you understand? I need the help of the greatest insane poet who ever lived!"

I nodded, but I didn't understand. Then it donned on me that he still thought I was the author of those poems.

"Whose help do you need?"

20. Hunter S. Thompson gets credit for inventing "gonzo" journalism, a style typified by the journalist discarding any notions of objectivity and becoming part of the story if not the center of the story. But Acosta had been writing this way for years in Chicano publications such as *La Raza*. In fact, Acosta claimed to have coauthored Thompson's famous *Fear and Loathing in Las Vegas*. To what extent the authors collaborated, borrowed, or stole from each other is lost in both figures' penchant for outrageousness and self-mythology. That being said, Thompson became a key figure in twentieth century popular culture; Acosta, on the other hand, as Thompson's three-hundred-pound Samoan attorney Dr. Gonzo, became little more than a sidekick, or rather, a footnote.

"Yours, cabrón! Who else would I be talking about? We need an adventure, you and me. I'll write, you'll write, we'll share our words, and all along we'll be creating the stories as we write them. We are going to hit the road."

That was the last thing I wanted to do. Still, politeness compelled me to offer a legitimate excuse. "But I'm an artist. A painter. I need my studio, my paints and canvas." I opened my dresser drawer and pointed to the black sketchbook and pencils as evidence. "As you can see, I'm really quite happy where I am."

His eyes bulged as though this notion were preposterous. Then he looked around the room, shaking his head. "Seems to me like you got your studio right here and you haven't done much with it, have you? Your mom already told me. All you do is sit back here all day watching game shows and soaps. You're going to waste away. But with me, you won't. We're gonna go on that adventure. Now, where are your poems? That's the first order of business. We gotta bring those to my friend in Los Angeles and find you a publisher. You're gonna be famous, too!"

I wanted to tell Oscar right then and there that I hadn't written the poems, but something prevented me from doing so. Instead, I slipped my hands underneath my mattress and found the stack of Enrique's poems. It had been years since I'd read them. I saw the first lines of my favorite poem, the one I used to read over and over that told of the two friends living above the mechanic's garage. I felt a pang in my chest. Oscar approached me, and before I knew it he had removed the pages from my trembling hands and begun reading the words aloud. "This is genius!" he kept stopping to say.

Soon I was slumped onto my bed, tears pouring down my cheeks. I curled into a fetal position, as though if I just made myself small enough I would enter a void, no, a portal transporting me back twenty-five years when Enrique was still alive. Oscar didn't stop until he had read every single poem, and it was only then that he seemed to take notice of my state. He got down on his knees.

"Watchu doin', man? You losing it or what?"

"Those aren't my poems," I blubbered.

"What? I can't understand you. Turn around."

I felt his hands on my shoulder and thigh, and he unfurled me from my comforting ball. I tried to resist, but my strength was no match for his powerful hands.

"Look, man," he said. "I came to get you, and I'm not leaving without you. If you stay here you're going to die. Look at this place. You're living like an old Mexican woman. You're still young. You still have genius inside you. And I need to have you by my side, to feed off your energy. And you need me, because otherwise you're nothing but . . . but . . . this, a blubbering baby living with your mom."

"But I told my mother I would take care of her in her old age, provide her company."

"Well, that's not what she told me. She told me she was tired of having to make meals for you all the time. She asked if I knew any broads to get you out of the house, or even better if I knew any who would be willing to marry an old crazy like you. She told me that she'd rather rent out the back house and get a few extra dollars a month."

I should've been more skeptical. It didn't sound like my mother at all, certainly not the gentle gray-haired widow she'd become. It sounded like Oscar. But my mother's long-ago abandonment had scarred me to the core, and it didn't take much to believe the worst things about her. So I rose from my bed and wiped the tears from my eyes.

"She said that?" I asked.

"She did, man. I was surprised. What kind of mother says stuff like that about her own son. But who am I to judge? Look, you and me, we don't have to take it. We just hit the road together. We write, we check out some bars, we screw some broads, then we wake up the next morning and write some more, and when we feel like it, we hit the road again."

Oscar reached out his hand for my own. Mine disappeared into his, and he shook it wildly. "Call me Brown Buffalo," he said. "And we gotta think up a nickname for you, all right? Now grab your stuff."

"I'm ready," I said. Except for the poems I didn't have anything to grab.

"No change of clothes?" he said.

Oscar didn't stop until he had read
every single poem,
and it was only then that
he seemed to take notice of my state.

"Whatchu doin', man?"

You losing it or what?"

"Those aren't my poems," I blubbered.

I shrugged. "I'm used to this," I said, fingering the texture of my flannel shirt.

Oscar looked around the room as though it wouldn't be right to leave without taking at least something. "What about that there in the drawer? Your sketchbook."

I shrugged again. "I don't even use it."

"Well, on this trip you will," and he bounded over and grabbed it along with the pencils. "You're going to write, you're going to draw, and you're going to wish you had another pair of chones to change into, believe me."

We hit the road without saying goodbye. I was upset at my mother for asking Oscar to take me off her hands, and I wanted to prove a point. She was already tired of cooking my meals, already weary of my presence? Did I offer her nothing? Did she prefer a boarder who would entertain her—is that what she wanted? Well, now she could find one. I was off her hands. We quietly walked around the side of the house. Oscar's gigantic silver car was parked on the street, and as we got in, I slammed the door shut. I didn't mean to, but the door was lighter than expected.

"Attaboy!" Oscar cried. He started the car and slapped the dash. "What do you think of this beauty? Just bought it. A '63 Impala. Pretty good for a mocoso from Riverbank, eh?"

When he peeled out I was thrown back against the seat. He cackled loudly and cried, "We're doing it!"

When we arrived on the outskirts of Albuquerque, Oscar told me that he had made everything up about my mom, and he was just now feeling remorseful because he was imagining if it were his mom and he had left without a word goodbye.

"What? You mean she didn't say any of that?"

"No, of course not. I just threw it out there to convince you to come with me, and you took that bait. But now I feel bad. You got her number? I'll give you a quarter to call her when we get to the next gas station."

"No, I don't have her number. I never left the house; I had no need to call her."

Taking his eyes off the road, Oscar reached into the back seat and rifled through some papers. "Here it is, I think," he said, scanning the paper.

"The road!" I cried, clutching the door handle for security.

He ignored me. "This is what they gave me at DeWitt," he said, handing me the document. "This is how I found you. Next pay phone, you be sure and call your mom. I'm worried about her."

"Oh, you're the one worried!"

Several miles down the road we came to a filling station, and I practically leaped out of the car. I imagined my mother worried sick, Lourdes already at her side, consoling her, telling her that it was for the best, that I was never to be trusted, that I was better off far away from them. I called the number in DeWitt's records, and after several rings my mother picked up.

"Hello?" she said.

"Ma, it's me!"

"Oh, hello," she said, not a trace of surprise in her voice.

I explained to her that my visitor had tricked me into going on a trip with him. I didn't tell her that the trick had been at her expense. She was quiet the entire time. I kept waiting for a sob, tears of relief that I was safe and would return to her soon. When I finally heard a sniff, I asked her, "Are you crying?"

"No, just sniffed, that's all," she said.

"Oh," I said. I waited for some sign of alarm. Receiving none, I began to describe Oscar's plans to take me on a trip of debauchery, booze, poetry, art, broads, intellectual discussions. I said I wanted nothing to do with it. I had made a promise to be by her side in her waning years, and I would not break that promise. We had already lost too much time. When I finished there was silence, and I thought she was still processing just how close she had been to losing me all over again. I regretted telling her about the proposed debauchery. An old woman's nerves shouldn't be tested so.

"Ma? You okay?"

Finally, she answered. "My son, don't take this the wrong way. But I think you should go on this trip. This trip will be good for you—"

"You want me to go with him?" I cried shrilly. "You did want me gone?"

"Shhhh, listen. Listen to me. I don't want you gone. I want you to return whenever you're ready. But I told you before and I'll say it again, you've spent too many years just doing nothing, and you spend your days here just watching television. I can't help but remember the boy you once were, so full of dreams and ambition."

"Those dreams are over. And I've found peace. That's why I sit around doing nothing. I'm at peace."

"At peace like a dead man. But you have so many years ahead of you to be at peace. Peace is for old women like me."

"I want to come home," I said defiantly.

"Go with Oscar; he seems like a nice man. Decent, respectful. He's famous."

"Famous? Did he tell you that? Have you ever heard of him?"

"No, but what do I know? He said he wrote books. He said he wanted to publish your poetry."

"Mom, I don't write poetry. It's not even mine. It's Enrique's."

"Enrique? Your poor friend from years ago?"

"Yes, they're his poems that he wants to publish. He just thinks I wrote them."

"Well, then do it for Enrique," she said, and she hung up, or at least I heard a click. I couldn't believe my own mother would hang up on me; so I kept talking loudly, pleading my case, demanding she explain *what* exactly I should do for Enrique. Only when I paused to catch my breath did I hear the dial tone.

While I was on the phone, Oscar had purchased a case of beer and a bottle of tequila. He was waiting in the driver's seat, his left hand on the wheel, his right hand clutching an open Budweiser. He handed it to me. "This is for you," he said. "Take the edge off."

I took it from him. The can was cold. "Cold," was all I could think to say, still somewhat in shock over the phone conversation.

"Fuck yeah, it is," and he reached down between his legs and pulled out a beer for himself. Cracking it open, he raised the can to mine. "Salud! To our trip!" he said.

"Do you know what my mom said?"

He shook his head and took a long swig. I could hear the beer as it passed through his throat all the way down to his expansive stomach. "No, what did she say?" he gasped.

"That I should go with you."

"Atta mujer!" he cried. He turned the key and the car revved up and we were back on the road. "I wasn't going to take you back anyway. I didn't come all this way not to have you by my side."

The beer tasted good. I had never been one to purchase alcohol. It wasn't something I thought to do. I hadn't imbibed much before DeWitt, and of course, once at DeWitt I hadn't touched the stuff. So really, it had been a good twenty-five years since my last beer, if I was counting the ones I drank while completing the preparatory notes of the billiard hall and its patrons. My head felt lighter, and my heart did, too. Once I was done with one beer I asked Oscar if he would allow me to have another one. He laughed and reached down between his legs to pull out another can.

"Throw your empties in the back. We'll clean up later. I don't believe in littering the homeland."

I turned around and noticed five empties already back there. Had Oscar drank that many so quickly? I sipped my second one, not wanting the lightness in my head to overwhelm me. I already wanted to lay my head back, close my eyes, and smile. My mother was right. I needed this. I needed an adventure, and I needed to have a companion like Oscar, the Brown Buffalo, to guide the way. Never mind that he was chugging beers like water.

"You're thirsty," I said.

"You bet I am!" he said. "I need something stronger, though." And that was when he instructed me to open the bottle of tequila and to take the first drink.

I reached for the bottle, made a show of inspecting the label, and twisted off the cap. I hesitated before drinking, wondering if I should find a cup or glass, but Oscar nodded at me. "Go ahead," he said, grinning from ear to ear. I meant to take a small sip, but in trying not to place my lips on the rim I poured the tequila straight into the back of my mouth and much more than intended. I started coughing violently, completely unprepared for its vileness. Sudden nausea and a horrible burning in my throat replaced the good feeling from a moment before.

"Hand it to me," Oscar demanded. "I didn't know you were such a lightweight. What kind of Mexican are you?"

"I've been in a hospital for twenty years."

Oscar started laughing. "That's right, I forgot."

I wanted to stay awake, but my head started to spin and my eyelids grew heavy and soon I fell asleep. When I awoke we had entered a city. Oscar was driving slowly down a main thoroughfare.

"Where are we?" I asked. I had a sharp pain behind my right eye and my mouth was parched.

"El Paso."

"El Paso?"

"Yeah, we'll stop here for the night."

I noticed he was looking from side to side and reading signs. "You looking for a motel?" I asked.

"Naw, I'm looking for a bar. We're outta beer and tequila."

"We're out?" I asked. I looked in the back seat. Beer cans were everywhere. "The tequila, too?"

He handed me the bottle. "For the last hour I've been trying to get one last drop out of that. See if you have any luck."

It didn't take us long to find a bar. I was surprised Oscar was still standing, but he seemed in full control. I was the one struggling. The ache behind my eye had spread to the whole right side of my face, and my legs and feet felt heavy. I wanted to be back in my little house watching television.

The place was empty except for a few old-timers slumped over their beers at the far end of the bar. Behind the counter was a pale blond woman with a weathered face and a cigarette hanging from her lips. She didn't look happy to see us. I was surprised when she came over and asked what we wanted in perfect Spanish.

Oscar looked to me to respond. I looked to Oscar to respond. My Spanish was rusty. Except for Martín Ramírez, most of the Mexicans at DeWitt spoke English. I distinctly remembered that my mother used to speak Spanish, but on my return she and my sister and half siblings communicated only in English. So it had been a good decade since I'd uttered a word in Spanish, and I saw no need to start right then and there at a random bar in El Paso.

"Da me una cervayza y un shot of tequila—dos of each for mi amigo y yo," Oscar said.

As we waited for the bartender to return, Oscar asked, "You don't speak Spanish?"

I explained that I was out of practice.

Oscar leaned on the countertop and stared straight ahead, a distant look in his eyes. When the bartender brought our drinks, Oscar took his shot and then downed his beer before I even had a chance to size mine up. He ordered another round for himself.

"You drink like a fish," I said.

"Like a Brown Buffalo," he corrected. "*You* drink like a fish."

I changed the subject. "If we're going to Los Angeles, how come we came south to El Paso."

"Who said we're going to Los Angeles?"

"You did. *First things first, publish the poems,* you said."

Oscar pulled out a napkin and then reached for a pen in his pants pocket. He drew two dots. "This is Albuquerque," he said. "Where I picked you up. This," he said, pointing to the other dot, "is Los Angeles." Then he drew a line south, then west, then east, then farther south. He drew a loop, then another loop, a circle, a square, a line west, and then finally a line up, a few more loops on the way, until he reached the dot representing Los Angeles. "This is our route."

"That doesn't seem to be the most direct route."

"Exactly."

"What do you mean 'exactly'? Do you not want to reach Los Angeles?"

"Someday, sure. But first we're going to write our masterpieces."

"What masterpieces?"

"The ones we're going to write."

"The ones we're going to write?" I was growing exasperated.

"Yes."

"I don't even write! I'm an artist. I *was* an artist. What am I going to do while you write?"

"Of course you write."

"No, I don't. I don't write."

"So you gave up writing. Goddamn. Then draw if you don't want to write."

"I don't draw either," I said.

"Sure you do."

"I can't draw anymore. I can't draw, I can't write, and if I had my druthers I'd prefer not to take the route you've drawn on this napkin."

"Your druthers," Oscar said, chuckling and shaking his head. "You are something else. Here—" and he reached for another napkin—"I want you to draw something right here. Quit being a pendejo." And he placed the pen in my hands.

I held the pen and looked at the blank white napkin. Whether it was the alcohol, the new surroundings, or Oscar's presence, for the first time in a long time I actually wanted to draw. I wanted to cover that napkin, I just didn't know with what.

"Put something down," Oscar said, as though divining my thoughts. "Anything, it don't matter. Whatever the hell is inside you, let it out. Don't even think."

I moved the pen closer to the napkin, slowly, as if I were pushing against an imaginary force. Finally, the pen reached the napkin, a trace of blue ink shattering the white abyss. My heart was pounding and my headache was gone. I moved the pen across the napkin, the blue ink charting its course. First up, then right, then left, then around. I didn't think about what I was drawing, I just kept the pen moving. I pressed harder. I moved off my barstool so that I stood over the napkin. I lost myself in a swirl of movement, and all along I could hear Oscar encouraging me. "Thattaboy, thattaboy," he kept saying. "Let it out, put it on that napkin." So I kept going and going. I felt my lungs full of breath and my heart beating against my rib cage. My entire arm moved, and where my arm went my body followed. When the pen moved right I moved right, when the pen moved left I moved left, when the pen swirled, I swirled. I didn't want to stop. Oscar didn't want me to stop. But the napkin was only so big. It could only contain so much drawing, let alone so much pressure.

"Cut it out!" I heard someone say. "Cut it out; you're drawing all over the counter."

I stopped drawing. My chest was heaving. I looked up through bleary eyes. I had been crying.

"What's wrong with you? Drawing on the counter like a crazy keed."

It was the bartender. She looked horrified, first at me, and then at the counter. I followed her eyes. The napkin was in shreds. I had bored a hole directly through it. Whatever I had drawn was now lost. I had also drawn on the counter, my pen going entirely though the napkin, but I'd also unwittingly moved beyond the napkin, lines going this way and that across the wood counter weathered by years of beer spills.

"How am I going to get reed of dat?" she asked.

I struggled for an answer, still reeling from the act of creation.

"Get rid of it?" Oscar answered her. "Get rid of it, are you crazy? Do you know who this man is? He's a famous artist. Everything he touches sells for thousands of dollars, and here he's graced this piece of shit dive and you want to get rid of his drawing? Just goes to show you, people don't know good art when they see it. He's just upped the value of this entire joint. You could sell this in a gallery for more than a year's pay and you're asking us to get rid of it."

"Well, what is it then?" the bartender asked, taking a closer look at the counter.

"What is it?" Oscar said. He turned to me. "The lady asked *what is it*."

I was about to answer that I had no idea when Oscar told her, "That piece is called 'The dark swirl of my conscience at midnight in El Paso.'"

The bartender peered closer. She took the tattered napkin and placed it where it had been on the counter by matching up the lines. "I think I see it," she said. "So is he really famous?"

"You better believe it. Watch. Tape this thing off so no one messes with it, and next time you got someone in here with an ounce of culture ask them if they know who did it, and I bet they tell you without thinking twice."

"How they going to know it's authentic?" she asked.

"He'll sign it," Oscar said, and he turned and put his hand on my shoulder. "Maestro, would you do the lady the favor of signing your masterpiece?"

I still held the pen in my hand. I had been listening to their conversation through a fog. All I wanted was to find another surface to draw on. I was grateful that Oscar had made me bring the sketchbook. I would commence another drawing immediately. A barrier had been surmounted, and it had been as simple as encountering someone who would force me to cross it.

I took the pen and signed the countertop. Then we turned and walked out of the bar. I heard Oscar say, "Can't believe it, man. Your crazy ass draws on the counter and we end up getting our drinks free." He patted my back and said, "Let's go find another joint."

268

The drawing began there. I started with a lot of dark swirls of my conscience. I didn't know what to draw, and yet when I placed my pencil to paper, the pencil moved, and did so largely in a circular motion. At first Oscar was enthusiastic. He called it my "Conscience" series, but after a long day of driving, half the sketchbook filled, he said, "Can you knock off with your damn pencil swirls and drive so that I can sleep for a few hours?"

"This is my conscience—you said it yourself."

"That's not your conscience, man; that's just you not knowing what the hell you are or what you want to draw." His voice was sharp and irritated.

"What's gotten into you?" I asked.

"I'm tired of looking at you hunched over that sketchbook and moving your hand in circles as though you're drawing the fucking Sistine Chapel."

I stopped the swirls and thought for a moment. It was true. I didn't know what I wanted to draw. "You're right," I told him.

"Course I am. Now take over the wheel; I can't drive another mile."

I told him I didn't know how to drive.

"What? Are you kidding me? I'm sure as hell not going to drive the entire way. Take over and I'll show you."

It took about an hour, and Oscar cussed a lot, but learning to drive wasn't so hard. Just a few jerks here and there. It was a vast, empty stretch of road, and once I got the feel for easing off the clutch while pushing down on the gas, we were off. And once we were off, I asked Oscar what he meant when he said that I didn't know who I was or what that had to do with not knowing what I wanted to draw. But Oscar wasn't listening. He had pulled several pills from his pocket, and then he reached into the back seat and grabbed a beer. Before I knew it, he had downed the pills, drank the beer, and was reaching for another one.

"What are those?" I asked.

"These will help me concentrate," he said. After polishing off the second beer, he reached again into the back seat, but this time pulled out a notebook. He took a pen from his front pocket and without hesitating started writing. I had never seen someone write so fast. The pen looked small in his large hands, and it moved at breakneck speed from one side of the page to the other and then down. I already felt comfortable enough behind the wheel to peer over and try to read what he was writing, but I had little success. His hand kept getting in the way. I only stopped when I veered off the road and kicked up a sandstorm. Oscar didn't even notice. His eyes never left his notebook. He was in a trance. I envied his concentration.

I turned my attention back to driving. We were somewhere in Mexico. It was hot and dusty, and the desert stretched on interminably. I was enjoying myself. I didn't know where we were going, but it felt good simply to move. I had spent so many years in one place that I found the open road refreshing. I asked Oscar where we were headed, and without stopping his writing, he pulled out the map he'd drawn at the bar and pointed, "More or less like this." With the road offering little diversion, I glanced at the back seat and saw Oscar's books. I reached for the one about the Brown Buffalo. I held the steering wheel with one hand and the book with the other, and found that if I kept one eye on the page and one eye sort of on the road ahead, I could keep the car straight. I started reading. It felt strange to read about Oscar writing about himself at the same time that he was sitting next to me in the car, presumably writing about himself. I looked over to see if Oscar disapproved of my reading while driving, but he seemed to have drifted off to sleep.

In the first few chapters, I learned more about my companion than I had in our time together thus far. There he was for the whole world to judge: all his insecurities about his fat body, hallucinations about his shrink, failed sexual exploits. He even wrote about masturbating in the shower with soap. I read about his childhood, too, and all the humiliations he had experienced in Riverbank, for being fat, for being Mexican, and even for having a small penis. I wanted to ask him about that. Why, if this was his book, about him, the hero of his own story, didn't he invent that he had a large penis? I answered my own question: the fur-

I held the steering wheel with one hand and the book with the other.

I started reading.

It felt strange to read about Oscar writing about himself

at the same time that he was sitting next to me in the car.

ther I read, the clearer it became that this book was a confession.[21] This is what happened to me, he was saying; this is how I became the person I am today. Oscar awoke from his brief slumber and resumed writing manically in his notebook as though to make up for lost time. I looked over at him and thought to myself, "If it's as simple as writing down whatever the hell happened to you in life, then couldn't I do the same, but just draw it?"

At once I was awash in ideas of what those stories would be. My father's murder of course. My days trying to draw my father's uncooperative workers. My days in the La Trampa schoolhouse, misunderstood by everyone. My days thumbing through *The Great Book of French Painting*. I could draw my days in Albuquerque, deemed unfit for service, running errands and exploring the city. I could draw my meeting with Enrique, our blossoming friendship, our ill-fated sojourn to Los Angeles and the ensuing brawl, our days above the mechanic's garage. And that was all before I met Ella in the windowsill. I had so many memories; how could I draw them all, an entire lifetime?

I wanted to start immediately. I pressed on the gas. We had to get somewhere, anywhere, quickly. Suddenly the endless desert became oppressive, its vastness a great impenetrable wall. Night fell, and Oscar, unable to see the page any longer,

21. Again, it's necessary to point out the blurring of fact and fiction. Both of Acosta's published books—*The Autobiography of a Brown Buffalo* and *The Revolt of the Cockroach People*—are novels, or described as semi-autobiographical fiction. All writers write what they know, and all readers want to know to what extent the story is based on real life—it's only natural. So maybe I'm simply reminding myself that I can't confirm the veracity of our narrator's account: after all, he lived a largely solitary life, those he knew have passed away, I can't possibly interview others to verify his story, and he, as a narrator, has confessed to differing versions of his own account. I must keep in check my desire to believe this story is fact, to think that I am really following Oscar Zeta Acosta in his final days. But what does our narrator gain from inserting himself into this mystery? Oscar Zeta Acosta is yet another notorious, enigmatic figure from Chicano history who matters to me (and Lorraine, lest I forget!), but to whom else? Acosta has occupied my thoughts ever since I first read him as an undergraduate and felt that, finally, here was a man as flawed and insecure as I was. He was manic in life, yes, but he was just as manic on the page, and despite his books' flaws, his language soars. Earlier, I wrote that Chicano literature is un-Dostoyevskian, but the work of the Brown Buffalo comes close.

was forced to rest. He instructed me to turn on the headlights. The car was quiet without the sound of his pen and hand dashing furiously across the page. I heard a deep sigh, and then he said, "It's all shit."

"What is?" I asked.

"Everything," and I thought I heard his voice crack. I looked over to see if I could make out his face. Was he crying?

He didn't elaborate on what he meant by everything or why it was all shit, and the silence was heavy, so I decided to tell him about my epiphany. How, like him, I was going to tell my life story, but I was going to draw it instead. He didn't respond. I looked over, peering closer and closer, my eyes adjusting to the dark, and saw that he had fallen asleep. I sighed. Ours was the only vehicle on the road. The night was black. For reasons I can't explain, a feeling crept over me that I was alone in the car, and that I was escorting a dead man to his place of rest. I kept driving until I couldn't keep my eyes open any longer. We arrived on the outskirts of a small town with one street lamp. I parked, and after some fiddling with the key, I managed to shut off the engine. Before long I was asleep.

I awoke to a rooster crowing on the hood of the car. It was morning. I rose with a start, a painful crick in my neck. Oscar was still asleep. A group of schoolchildren in matching blue sweaters passed by and stared at us, smiling and laughing, and then shortly after an old man in white peasant pajamas sauntered by astride a donkey. He stared at us with an utter lack of interest, as though he frequently crossed paths with two men asleep in a shiny silver Impala. The rooster crowed again. Oscar didn't stir.

"Oscar," I said. My stomach growled. "Are you hungry? Want to get something to eat?" Nothing. "Oscar," I said a little louder. I reached over and placed my hand on his shoulder and shook it gently. "Oscar! Brown Buffalo! Oscar, wake up!" His broad face was heavy and slack; his gigantic body slumped into the corner between the door and the seat. I shook his shoulder harder now, but he didn't budge. A woman across the street pushed a cart selling tamales. My stomach growled again. I was famished. I rolled down the window and beckoned her over. She looked alarmed, but I pointed to her cart and said, "Tamales?"

"You want tamales?" she asked. "How many do you want?"

I almost told her "cinco," but I held up five fingers instead. She counted out five tamales and placed them in a plastic bag. She handed it to me along with a few napkins and told me the price.

I remembered I didn't have any money. I looked over at Oscar, dead to the world, and I knew that getting at the wallet in his back pocket would be impossible. Thinking that maybe he had some cash stored in the glove compartment, I reached over and opened it. Out fell a poorly folded map, a baggie of pills, a baggie of dried crumbly herbs, and a gun. I heard the woman gasp, and as I turned to her she pushed her cart away.

"Wait," I cried after her. "I need to pay you!"

In my rearview mirror, I saw her hurry down the street. She approached another woman and started pointing at us. The other woman's eyes grew wide in shock or fear, and then the two of them marched off. I could only assume that it was to tell someone else about the contents of our glove compartment. I started up the engine, eyeing the baggie of pills and the gun and wondering if Oscar had involved me in my first illegal act, the transport of drugs. Technically I'd stolen the tamales, too. After a few false starts, the car lurching forward before stalling, I drove out of the dusty pueblo and kept checking the mirrors to see if anyone was following. The town disappeared into the desert. I ate two tamales and saved three for Oscar. I was sure that when he woke up he would be starving.

I drove and Oscar slept. I had never in my life seen someone sleep so deeply. I turned on the radio. I turned it up loud. I sang along to the music, poorly on account of not knowing the words. I tapped my hands against the steering wheel in accompaniment. I honked the horn at men on donkeys and stray dogs and women carrying bundles on their back. Then I ran out of gas. The Impala sputtered and died in the middle of the road. I tried to wake Oscar but to no avail. I got out to find help, walking a hundred yards in one direction and then a hundred yards in the other, until I decided it was best to just lean against the car with my arms crossed. The sun was beating down on me. I imagined us stranded for days with only three tamales to sustain us.

Finally, a truck driver hauling pigs came by and asked if something was wrong. After much gesticulation and pointing and acting out, I made the man realize we'd run out of gas. He had some in reserve and poured the contents of a gigantic rusty container into our tank. I then told him through the universal gesture of empty pockets that we had no money. He was furious, and I thought for sure he was going to siphon the gas back out of our tank. That was when I offered him the gun. He pointed the gun at me and demanded the herbs as well. Who was I to argue and end up dead in the desert? Oscar slept through the whole ordeal. I drove off, waiting for him to wake up and tell me where to stop, where to turn, what was next on our itinerary. At some point we lost radio reception, and after a long stretch of willing the static to go away, I turned off the radio, my only source of entertainment. That was when I noticed Oscar's notebook on the floor near his feet. I wondered what he had been writing so furiously, leaving him practically comatose.

I reached for it, keeping one hand steady on the wheel. With the notebook on the seat between us, I turned the pages until I found his most recent entries. Glancing back and forth between the road and the notebook, this is what I read:

"I am accompanied by a madman, a crazy, a lunatic, a nobody except for the simple fact that he writes on par with Rimbaud, I swear to God. No one would believe me, but I have his poems here to prove it. Words that spring from the page to brutalize me, that slap me back and forth, that reach down and take my heart and squeeze it until I cry for mercy, words that are like a kick in testicles, in the gut, and a punch in the face beating you into submission, grabbing the back of your head and making you stare into a dank rotten puddle of muck until you find the beauty, the beauty, the enchanting beauty of life! How does he do it? How does he do it? I keep asking myself. This guy driving a car for the first time in his life, this guy mumbling to himself, who has spent twenty years in a madhouse and doesn't think twice about it, this man who has no idea who he is, who's ashamed of who he is, who has no sense of his history, who is ashamed to speak his mother tongue, who isn't crazy like the crazy pill-popping drug-fueled alcohol-soaked fuckers from Frisco, but actually crazy, certifiably crazy. I'm crazy, I'm the craziest person I know, but at the same time I'm the sanest person I know. I've searched deep down into my soul for years. I know who I am inside and out. And that's come at a price, after a lot of pain and suffering, and it's only now that I stand before you as the Brown Buffalo, lawyer and writer, defender of mi gente, proud warrior of the Chicano people, that I can look back and see that everywhere I've been, everywhere I've traveled, everything I've tried to be and have been rejected from, every humiliation, has led me to this higher state of consciousness. I am the Brown Buffalo! And beside me is my opposite. A man who has traveled nowhere, who has insulated himself from the brutal world, who has been lost inside his head for fifty years, who is as far from a Brown Buffalo as you can get. He's nothing but a Brown Pendejo . . . and get this, he thinks he's French! But he has the only thing that I want more than anything in this world . . . goddamn can that loco pendejo write."

It continued in this vein for another ten pages. Essentially diminishing me, listing off my tics, my inability to see beyond the tip of my nose, but praising my writing to the high heavens. Not my writing. Enrique's writing. He ended with, "If this pendejo couldn't write, I would ditch him on the side of the road."

I was offended. I didn't like his assumptions about what I'd seen or what I'd lived. I had also spent a lifetime knowing myself. He could be a proud warrior of his people, whoever they were, but my people had mostly shirked me, so I was alone to do as I pleased. Clearly he found my presence insufferable. Well, I found him insufferable! But I was in his car, following his plans, and now that he'd dragged me on this adventure I was prepared to continue. He thought he was the Brown Buffalo; well, I was something, too. I just had to figure out what that was. My anger momentarily abated while I contemplated nicknames for myself, but they were all variations of Brown and some animal. I didn't want to copy him. I wasn't even that brown, verified when I held up my forearm and compared it to Oscar's. I also didn't want to be an animal. But there I was, contemplating the Brown Eagle, the Brown Hawk, the Brown Rattlesnake, the Brown Bear, the Brown Wildcat, the Brown Panther. None seemed to fit. If I had to be an animal, I guess I would like to be a monkey, but that's only because monkeys are close to humans, and when it came down to it, all I really wanted was to be what I was, a human. Why the hell would anyone want to be a buffalo?

I finally gave up on finding myself a nickname and concentrated on Oscar's other criticisms. For one, I stepped on the gas. Apparently, while he was writing, I was keeping a pace of thirty-five miles per hour on the empty stretch of highway. He was too engrossed in his writing to say anything, but he complained in his notebook. So I brought the Impala up to forty-five miles per hour, which for a novice felt plenty fast.

I also now knew for sure that if I told him I wasn't the author of those poems, he would abandon me. I decided that if a genius was what Oscar wanted at his side, then I had to prove myself, and the only way to do that was to display what genius I did have, not for writing, of course, but for art. When we stopped next, I decided, I would pull out my sketchbook and draw my complete life history, *my* autobiography. Then Oscar would know two things: I was an expert drafts-man, an artist of unflinching realism, and I had lived lives and had the stories to prove it. Of course, deciding to do something and actually doing it were very dif-ferent matters. I at least knew myself that well. But the biggest issue was more practical: once I got going I knew I wouldn't be able to stop, and all I had was one sketchbook, which was already half full with the "Dark swirls of my con-science." I was mulling this over when Oscar finally woke up, which he did as though he'd only nodded off the minute before.

"Damn, aren't we ever going to stop?" he asked. I yelped in surprise.

As if on cue, the car began to lurch forward and sputter. We'd run out of gas again.

"Shit, I'm surprised we made it this far," Oscar said.

That was when I explained that we hadn't actually made it that far, that we had run out of gas a hundred or so miles ago, and that I had traded his herbs and gun for several gallons of gasoline.

"You did what?" he asked, his eyes bulging. He immediately opened the glove compartment and gasped when all he saw were the pills and the map. "You gave away my marijuana, you idiot! That's the only thing keeping me alive."

"The baggie of herbs?"

"Yes, why did you give that away?" he cried. He pulled at his oily black hair and then wiped the sweat off his forehead. Then he began rubbing his nose with the palm of his hand as though he wanted to grind it into his face. "Oh my fucking god, pendejo, I wish I had that gun right now, I'd shoot you between the eyes."

I let him cool off. I figured he was grumpy after his long nap. By the time he walked around the car and kicked the tires several times, I'd noticed in the distance what looked like a small town. "Let's just push the car, it won't take long," I told him. "We'll get to the town by nightfall."

Oscar squinted his eyes and looked into the distance. "I don't see anything," he said.

"It's a town, I'm telling you. My eyesight is very good."

We began pushing, and I was relieved when the speck I saw in the distance took the form of a church spire. I had had my doubts. But getting there by nightfall was overly ambitious. When we arrived on the outskirts of town it was well past midnight, and Oscar was still cursing me for trading away his gun and marijuana for nothing more than a few measly gallons of gas. "Why didn't you just wake me up, goddamn it?" I explained for the hundredth time that he had been dead to the world for at least a day and a half.

On Oscar's orders, the first thing we did, even before finding gas, was look for a bar. It didn't take long. The place was called Las Botas de Mi General. An accordionist stood outside practicing his scales. He stopped to whistle at our Impala, which we'd pushed to the side of the dusty road. We entered the bar and found men in cowboy hats playing billiards and cards and two couples dancing near a jukebox. Oscar pulled out the wallet that hours ago would've made my life much easier and paid for shots of tequila and several beers. He began drinking right away, and when I didn't start drinking fast enough, he ordered me to. "Come on, drink up!" I didn't protest. I burned my throat with the tequila and took several gulps of beer. I found myself desperately craving my mother's lemonade. When my throat recovered, I explained to Oscar that while he was asleep I had been blessed by an epiphany.

"And what was that?" he asked, the annoyance still in his voice.

"I need to start drawing my autobiography."

"But you're a poet," he said.

"Well, I want to be an artist, and you'll see—"

"Not this again," Oscar said, sighing. "Quit trying to be something you ain't. You're a poet, a poet who also happens to be a big pendejo, but you're not an artist; otherwise you'd have drawn something other than swirls."

"I can draw something other than swirls!" I said, slamming my hand on the countertop. I surprised myself. I must've surprised Oscar, too, because his eyes grew wide and a smile crept onto his face. "Attaboy," he said. "Let it out. Show me you're a man!" He placed his hand on my shoulder and shook it. "Show me you're angry!"

"I can draw something other than swirls," I said, calmer this time.

"So do it then."

That was when I explained that I had only half a sketchbook left.

"So?"

"I know that once I start I won't be able to stop. I don't want to stop."

"So?"

"Therefore, I need ample unfilled sketchbooks ahead of me."

"That's all you need?" he asked, sipping his beer and then taking another shot. It must've gone down wrong, because he began hacking loudly.

"Yes," I said.

"I tell you what. I got twenty notebooks in the trunk. I get ten, you get ten. I was going to use all of them, but we'll be in Mazatlán soon and we can pick up more. Sound all right?"

I nodded, but I was unsure. Notebooks were not sketchbooks. "Do these have lines on them?"

"Course they do. You gonna use that as an excuse? We're in the middle of God knows where. You think we're going to find an art store? Take it or leave it. An artist uses what he has."

I digested this for a moment. He was right. I was ready now. And if the sketchbooks were notebooks, then that's what they had to be.

After stocking up on liquor for the night, we left the bar and returned to the Impala. We pushed it down the road until we came to a motel. A group of musicians loitered outside, accordions and guitars in hand. They played a note or two as we passed, and an old man in a reedy voice asked if we'd like a song. Oscar walked right past them and into the motel clerk's office. When he emerged, he informed me that we had the room for three days.

"We're going to stay here for three days?" I asked, looking down the dark empty street. The town rivaled the TSSS factory work camp for dilapidation and dustiness.

"You said you were ready to start drawing."

"Yes, but—"

"No excuses," Oscar said. "It starts now."

And by now he meant literally right now. He seemed to forget that I had been driving while he had been sleeping for a day and a half. Not to mention the strain of pushing the car for so many miles. Not to mention the alcohol making my eyelids heavy. No, Oscar was ready, so that meant I had to be ready. He looked at me as if this were the last chance I was going to get before he gave up on me completely. We entered the small motel room. When the light flickered on, two cockroaches scurried under the bed. It was musty and hot, and the plaster walls were crumbling. We turned on an oscillating fan, but the neck only went right, then left, then right again before dying with a slow whir. There was one queen bed with a yellow and rust floral-patterned comforter, a metal folding table and metal chair, and a wooden dresser. Oscar told me that I could use the table; he was going to write standing up at the dresser like Hemingway. He was also going to write without a shirt because it was hot as hell. He struggled to remove his shirt. His body was big; his breasts were like a woman's, and his smooth hairless skin glistened with sweat. I kept my shirt on, and it wasn't long before it was damp with perspiration.

Oscar brought ten notebooks to my table and kept ten for himself. "We won't leave here until we've filled these. How about that?"

I didn't want to say it, but I had to say it because I knew that my eyes weren't going to be able to stay open much longer. "I'm really tired, Oscar."

I expected him to look at me with utter disappointment, but he didn't. He merely reached for his back pocket and took out a baggie of pills. "These will help," he said.

"What are they?" I asked.

That garnered me his look of utter disappointment. He didn't answer. He just took out three, then reached for his bag and pulled out the bottle of tequila he had purchased at the bar. "Don't drink the water," he said. Then he turned away, his back like that of a giant slippery whale, and walked to his dresser-desk, picked up a pen, opened his notebook, and began writing. I watched him for a while. I imagined that he was writing about me, complaining, telling his future readers what an absolute pain I was to have around. I decided I would show my future viewers what a pain he was to have around. I opened my notebook, picked up a pencil, and before I knew it I had placed pencil to paper. Except instead of drawing Oscar in all his slippery fatness, I became a slave to the lines in the notebook. I fell into my old habit of describing what I intended to draw rather than actually drawing. I wanted to stop, but at the same time I told myself that preparatory notes were a part of my process and that the more I wrote, the more I described, the more groundwork I laid, the faster I'd begin actually drawing.

I continued, filling one page after another describing Oscar the Brown Buffalo huddled over a dresser, shirtless, his brown skin glistening in the room's dim light, writing in a notebook with a pen much too small for his massive hands. I made five separate preparatory descriptions of Oscar. When I started the sixth, the sound of his pen rushing across the notebook suddenly stopped.

"It looks like you're writing," he said. "I thought you were going to finally draw."

"I am drawing!" I blurted out, louder and more defensively then I intended. I was in the middle of a particularly important detail, tracing the shape of his oblong belly button.

"Let me see then," he shouted back. He was smiling. I think he liked seeing me upset.

"No!" I said. "You work on your thing, I work on mine."

He chuckled loudly and muttered something about me being crazy. He returned to his writing. The pause was enough to break my momentum. I felt the long day of driving, the miles of pushing the car, the tequila and beer taking their toll. My legs ached and my back felt stiff. My head felt heavy and my eyelids heavier. But what was I going to do? Crawl over to the bed and fall asleep? Show Oscar that I didn't have what it took to be a serious artist? Give him a chance to peek at my preparatory notes before they became actual drawings? No, I couldn't fall asleep. But the pills Oscar had left on the table were my only hope of staying awake. The pills and the tequila. The dimly lit motel room. Two artists working at their craft, sweating profusely. Was this the adventure my mom had in mind?

I placed two pills underneath my tongue, then took a swig of tequila that burned all the way to my heart. I picked up my pencil. I turned the notebook to an open page, and I started to tell my story. My life. But through images. Or rather, through descriptions of images. The truth is I didn't know whether I was writing or drawing or scribbling or actually reliving the events as they happened. The pills took effect quickly, and they were powerful. I lost track of time. I lost

I filled one page after another describing Oscar the Brown Buffalo

huddled over a dresser, shirtless, his brown skin glistening in the

room's dim light.

"It looks like you're writing," he said.

"I thought you were going to finally draw."

"I am drawing!"

track of everything. It was like having an epileptic attack, except the loss of control felt amazing, and there was no blacking out. In fact, it was the opposite—my consciousness was heightened. I couldn't turn the pages fast enough.

When I finally awoke from my spell, my ten notebooks were filled, and I wanted more pills and more notebooks. I looked up to find Oscar asleep. He was still standing, though, his buffalo head cradled in his arms on top of the dresser. I called out his name, but he didn't wake up. I tried to stand, but my back and legs were stiff. I cried out in pain as I attempted to stretch. I could barely uncurl my hand from around the pencil. I slowly walked over to Oscar and shook him. "I want another notebook, Oscar. Oscar?" He didn't move.

He had stacked nine notebooks on the dresser and was asleep on top of the tenth. I thumbed through them to see if any were blank, but they were filled. I tried to remove the book he was sleeping on—perhaps it was still empty—but couldn't free it. I shook his shoulder and called out his name again. I shook harder, and this time he slipped off the dresser and collapsed against the wall, bringing the lamp crashing down with him. He fell to the ground with a gigantic thud. I was already apologizing and begging forgiveness when I realized he was still asleep. I would've assumed he was dead, but his broad chest was rising and falling. I checked his last notebook. It was almost filled as well. I looked at Oscar on the floor. I wasn't going to get a fresh batch of notebooks anytime soon.

I decided to lie down on the bed. My back was killing me, and the pain had crept up into my neck. I situated the pillow underneath my head, which eased my discomfort a little. I stretched my legs out as far as they would go, and that felt good too. Then I stretched my arms out like Jesus on the cross, and that felt even better. Finally comfortable, I thought of all the preparatory notes I had written and wondered which descriptions I would draw first. The logical choice was to start at the beginning and throw myself into my childhood memories, but I also thought that maybe I should start with the most impactful experiences, my father's murder for one. I wanted to ask Oscar his opinion, see what called out to him

THE LAST PROPHET—OSCAR ZETA ACOSTA

most. But that would have to wait until he woke up. My eyes grew heavy. I decided there would be no harm in closing them for just a few minutes, maybe an hour, however long Oscar remained asleep. I wouldn't open them until the next day.

According to the police report, the neighbors had heard Oscar's body crash against the wall and then fall to the ground with a wall-shaking thud. They alerted the motel clerk, who came to our door and knocked, first normally, then louder, and finally banging on the door and demanding we open it. When we didn't, he brought his key and entered our room. He found Oscar dead on the floor, his tongue out, and then he turned and found me, also dead, prostrate on the bed. Of course, we were only in a deep sleep after two, maybe three, pill-fueled days of filling notebooks. But the clerk thought we were dead, so he called the police.

When the police entered our room, they were prepared to find a crime scene. What they found, according to Oscar, was him awake, in the shower, masturbating. Guns drawn, they scared the shit out of him. He responded as any mocoso from Riverbank would, by hollering his head off in Spanish and English until they got the hell out of the bathroom. I slept through this exchange, as well as when the cops started slapping my cheek and telling me to wake up. This is all according to Oscar, who came out in a towel, telling the cops to get the fuck out of the room. They didn't take too kindly to this, and that was when the motel clerk, who was waiting in the doorway, saw Oscar's baggie of pills poking out of his pants pocket. This was all the small-town cops needed to arrest us both; apparently they thought I was high on the stuff, because who else could sleep through such a disturbance? When I finally woke up, Oscar and I were sitting in a jail cell with our belongings beside us. Confused, disoriented, and groggy, I couldn't figure out what had happened. That was when Oscar recounted the above.

"But what about our notebooks?" I asked.

"Forget them," he said. "They're gone."

"Forget them? But all that work!"

"We'll never see our stuff again. They'll hold us here, and by the time we get back to the motel our stuff will be gone. My Impala too, goddamn it!" He banged the back of his head against the cell wall.

"But what about Enrique's poems?" I cried. "They're in the back of the car."

"Whose poems?"

"Enrique's!"

"Who is Enrique?"

"The poems, his poems," I said, imagining Enrique's words lost to the world. My voice grew weak. "You said we were going to get them published."

"Those aren't your poems?" Oscar asked.

"No," I mumbled, closing my eyes and covering my face with my hands. I didn't want to look at the dingy jail cell with its crumbling walls, I couldn't accept being incarcerated while Enrique's poetry was being taken on a joyride. I heard Oscar rapidly breathing in and out of his nostrils as though about to hyperventilate. Curiosity compelled me to look up. He was looking at me cross-eyed, his nostrils flaring.

"What?" I asked.

"You didn't write those poems?"

"No, I told you, my friend Enrique wrote them years ago. They were sent as letters to me—"

"So why the hell am I traveling with you, stuck in a Mexican jail with you? And not with Enrique? Where the hell is he? He's the genius!"

"He's dead," I cried.

"He's dead? For how long?"

"For too many years," I said. I started to cry, more out of fear of Oscar than anything else. He kept looking at me with manic eyes as though he could kill me with his stare alone.

"I knew you weren't a genius," he growled. "I knew it. I just knew it. I couldn't make sense of it. Those poems spoke to me. The only one you can speak to is yourself."

"We just met," I said. "You hardly know me."

Oscar's eyes narrowed. He looked at me with disgust. "I get it now," he said. "You're the artist he writes about, the friend. The two of you lived together."

"Yes," I said.

"Now I know you better than I thought."

"What do you mean?"

"You're in every one of those poems. Hell, every line."

"I know," I mumbled.

He didn't talk to me for the rest of our incarceration. We were let out that afternoon, though our pills were confiscated. We returned to the motel and found the Impala intact and as shiny as ever. Our notebooks were on the hood of the car, untouched. I started to cry all over again, relieved that my promise to Enrique could still be fulfilled. We would publish his work. It was also a relief that Oscar now knew I wasn't the author of those poems. It wasn't my intention to deceive him; he just never gave me a chance to explain. But my admission only widened the gulf between us. He looked like he wanted nothing else but to make me disappear. I gave him an out. I told him that in the next city he could drop me off at the bus station. I would head back to Albuquerque and be out of his hair. But I would go only on the condition that I could keep my ten notebooks.

"You can keep your goddamn notebooks," he said.

This pleased me, but Oscar's face was frightening. Who knew how close the nearest city was, and he looked like a man capable of violence at the slightest provocation. So I kept quiet and tried not to fiddle with the door handle or bounce my knee. We drove in silence until Oscar asked me, "So no one knows that those poems exist?"

"No, he wrote them just for me," I said.

"You two queers?"

"We were each other's only friends."

Oscar chuckled. "Poor fool."

That was it for the rest of the way to Mazatlán, except for a short pit stop in a small town because Oscar wanted to find a pay phone. He didn't tell me whom he intended to call, and I didn't ask. When he got back into the car, his mood had darkened even further.

On arrival, we went in search of a bar. But first Oscar opened the glove compartment and rummaged around and pulled out another baggie of pills.

"Well, that's lucky," I said. "They didn't think to look in here."

"Pendejos," Oscar grunted. He took out two and placed them underneath his tongue. He didn't offer them to me, but he did hand me the keys. "Hold these" he said. The sun had just set, and I could hear the sounds of crashing waves in the distance. By now I wasn't so keen on returning to Albuquerque with barely an adventure to show for it. I thought maybe if I proved to Oscar that I could be a fun companion he would forget that I wasn't the author of those poems. Maybe then I could stick around long enough to start on my autobiographical series and display my own genius. I was surprised to find my desire undiminished. It had only lain dormant.

I embraced the reveler's role. I ordered the beers this time and several shots of tequila, lining them up all in a row and making sure each one was poured to the brim. Unconsciously, I started speaking Spanish to those around me, and after a few drinks my tongue lost its rust. I even called over a few women who had been eyeing us. I ordered drinks for them, too.

All along, Oscar remained staring at his large hands, his face fixed in a gloomy, hardened expression. He didn't even answer when two of the buxom girls with painted cheeks put their arms around him and asked, "What's wrong, good looking?"

I had a girl, too, copper-skinned with bright red lips and large gums, which I discovered when she smiled at me. I informed her that I was an artist and my friend here was a writer and that we were traveling through Mexico writing and drawing our adventures. She demanded that I draw her and her friends. After all, weren't they now part of our adventure? I couldn't deny this, but I had to confess that I had already filled ten notebooks and was all out of paper. She called over a snot-nosed boy and gave him a few pesos. She explained that he was her son. He would run and purchase a notebook from the corner store. Ten minutes later, the boy was back and I had a new notebook. I opened it up right away, and my lady friend, bubbling with excitement, insisted on sitting next to me. I wanted to explain that first I had to write a few preparatory notes, but when I looked at her face, her eyelids painted blue, her brown cheeks painted red, and her gleeful smile, I didn't have the heart to disappoint her.

"Draw them, draw them!" she cried, pointing at Oscar and the two women who were having little success raising his spirits. Then she whispered into my ear, "You can draw me later."

I began drawing Oscar and his companions.

"It's so light! I can't hardly see it!" my lady friend cried.

So I pressed the pencil harder.

"Oh, I can see it now, it's wonderful! Keep going!" she encouraged.

I traced the contours of the figures. I drew the women first, much to my lady friend's delight. She recognized them immediately. Then I drew the background— the empty tables, the crumbling walls, a bald light bulb—then moved on to the foreground—the bottle of tequila, the tumbler, the glass ashtray. My lady friend was practically through the roof with excitement as she watched the scene before her replicated on paper. Finally, I moved on to Oscar. Oscar and his large body, his large breasts and stomach, his large arms, his thick neck, his broad jowls. I could avoid his face for only so long. Finally I confronted it—first his flat wide nose, then his pursed lips, then his dark burning eyes—and it was there that I saw the face of a man lost, a man in pain, a man utterly disappointed with life.

When I finished my drawing, I allowed my lady friend to show it to her friends, who oooed and awed. She then paraded the drawing around the bar, holding it up for everyone to see. She even showed her snot-nosed son, who

My drawing of Oscar Zeta Acosta shortly before his death...

it was the face of a man lost, a man in pain,

a man utterly disappointed with life.

"It's wonderful!" my lady friend exclaimed.

smiled and said, "It looks just like them!" And then he asked when I was going to draw his mother, which led my lady friend to repeat the question in a much more provocative tone. I was made to understand that this drawing session would take place behind closed doors. I rose from my seat, took another shot, and began dancing with the woman. Meanwhile, my new notebook was being passed around the room. Everyone was so nice and congratulatory, and some even requested drawings of themselves. It felt so good to hold my lady friend close, even though her kid was still watching us with snot streaming down his face, that I lost track of everything, including Oscar. I didn't realize he had risen from the table and walked out of the bar.

I didn't discover his absence until the woman suggested we find a place better suited to that special drawing session. I turned to tell Oscar that I would be leaving his side. I almost thought he'd be happy for me. He didn't have to worry about my ability to have an adventure. We could carouse together. But when I turned to the table, he was gone, and the two women who'd been at his side were leaning back in their chairs, sharing a cigarette and wearing the same bored expression. "Where'd my friend go?" I asked them. They shrugged.

"Don't worry about him," my lady friend said, putting one hand on my neck and the other hand through the buttons of my shirt. I could feel her fingers on my hot sticky skin. I momentarily imagined our entire bodies pressed against each other. She kissed her son goodbye and told him to go to bed soon. Then she told me, "Pay the bill so we can go."

That was when I realized I needed to find Oscar. "My friend has our money," I said as I rushed out the door. I looked for the Impala and found it still parked down the street. Oscar wasn't there. I looked left up a dark street, then right toward a cluster of lights and what looked like the sails of boats. I could hear the crashing waves and the sounds of sea gulls. The air was different, thick and salty. I had never been to the ocean, but before I could contemplate that fact, I heard a commotion at the bar and someone cried out, "He left without paying! Get after them!"

I hurried to the right, keeping in the shadows, and breathed a sigh of relief when I thought I saw Oscar's large frame in the distance. The streets were quiet except for a drunk's blubbering lament and a group of musicians heading home for the night. I lost Oscar for a moment, but then I saw him out of the corner of my eye, heading down a long, dark pier.

"Oscar," I cried out, immediately shushing myself, afraid that I would alert our pursuers.

I drew closer to him. He was slowing down. At the edge of the pier I saw Oscar's shadowed form stop. I moved closer, the waves drowning out my approach. He held something in his hands. A stack of paper. Were these his writings? No, he only wrote in notebooks. It occurred to me that he must have Enrique's letters. What was he going to do with them?

He took out a lighter and held it to the edge of one of the pages. A tiny flame flicked out.

"No!" I cried. "No, don't!" I rushed forward, stumbling on the pier's rough wooden planks. Two small fishing boats bobbed up and down on either side of me. Oscar turned, but didn't seem concerned that I was there. He held up another page and the lighter's flame swallowed it, too. He threw the burning page into the water.

"What are you doing?" I cried. "Stop this! Those aren't yours to destroy!"

"They belong to nobody," he said. "No one knows they exist, and no one ever will."

"They belong to me!" I cried. "He was *my* friend!"

Oscar was quiet for a moment, and then said, "You don't deserve them. Your friend died a long time ago. He's dead, and nothing can be done to bring him back. He doesn't care if his poetry lives or dies."

"Yes, he would've! He deserves to be remembered!"

"You should have thought of that a long time ago. But you couldn't see his genius. He killed himself for you. I can see it in every poem. He killed himself because he loved you, because he believed in the world as you saw it. He would've done anything for you, and you—what did you do, pendejo? You abandoned him, thinking yourself more important, your quest worthier—"

"Yes! You're right," I said. "I didn't treat him as he deserved. All I cared about was myself. So I'm an egotist, but so are you!"

"No, I'm not. I live my life for others. I've sacrificed my life for the people—"

"That's not true and you know it. All you care about is yourself. Why else would you destroy these poems?"

Oscar was silent again. "What a brilliant faggot," he muttered. "He's too good. It's too painful. Every poem . . . it tears out my heart."

"Then why destroy them?"

"Because I'm tired," he said, shuddering. "It's just like what happened when I was in the service and preaching about Jesus and the gospels to them goddamn Indians in Panama."

"I'd love to hear more," I said, inching closer. I wanted to grab the pages out of his hand. "But how about you hand me those poems first."

"I was the best damn preacher until I stopped believing what I was preaching," he continued. "But you can't just stop between one day to the next. So I kept preaching even though I knew I was a liar and a phony. Same thing happened again. I thought the Brown Buffalo was going to lead the Chicano people to the promised land. But the Brown Buffalo doesn't exist. Only I do. And I'm tired of people. All people. I'm tired of myself. I'm tired of you. I'm tired of trying to be a part of something . . . I've spent all my life trying to be a part of something bigger only to discover over and over again that I'm all alone."

"You're not alone. I'm here with you—"

This made him laugh. A hysterical, frightening laugh that quickly morphed into a sob. He tried to choke it back and shook his head violently as though to rid himself of the emotion. After a moment he said, "Earlier today I called my son, and I told him that I was gonna hitch a ride back on a fishing boat. I don't want to be here anymore."

"Then let's head back. We'll head straight to that publisher in Los Angeles you mentioned, drop off Enrique's poems."

"I can't even bear to make the drive—"

"I'll drive, it's not a problem."

"I don't have any masterpieces in me," he said.

"Okay, but about the poems you have right there—"

"I thought—I thought that if I'm not going to be the leader of my people, then at least I'd be the greatest writer they ever produced.[22] But there's no greatness in me. I know that now . . ."

"I understand what that feels like, believe me, but that doesn't mean you destroy someone else's work. Now, just hand me Enrique's poems and we can talk about this over a few more drinks."

"I just want to forget everything," he said, and with that he took a fistful of pages and lit them on fire. I couldn't take it anymore. I rushed toward him and leaped for the burning pages he held in his hand. But he raised them, forcing me to jump on his back and try to hoist myself higher. But the most I could do was hold onto his neck and try pulling him down. I heard him gag. I pulled on his neck harder. "Let go," he managed to say.

"Drop the pages!" I cried.

---

22. Acosta's two published works have the feel of being written in a cauldron. Some critics would say they were dashed off in haste. Perhaps so, but the frenzied style he cultivated took years to develop and isn't as imitable as one might think. I do wonder, though, what Acosta's subsequent work would've looked like had he lived. The Brown Buffalo calmer, older, wiser, his prose style more refined—would the work be "better," or was his genius a product of his tumultuous time? I find it comforting that Acosta, like I in my younger days, sought to write the great Chicano novel and failed. We should all be so tormented by that ambition, by the inevitable failure. Until the day that champion is crowned, I will open every Chicano novel hoping to find greatness. Ernest Hemingway once talked about getting in the boxing ring with his literary masters, Turgenev, Maupassant, Stendhal, avoiding a bout only with Tolstoy. It's too macho a metaphor for me, but it will have to do: I will rest only when I know that our literature competes in the ring with giants.

The burning pages dropped from his hand and fell onto the pier, disappearing into the white flame. "No!" I cried. "Why did you do that?"

He tried to wrest me off, but I was enraged. We struggled. His elbow slammed into my cheekbone. I fell onto the planks. Oscar stepped back and tripped over my leg. He teetered, and then toppled, a post momentarily breaking his fall. I heard a gigantic splash. I scrambled to the edge and waited for him to pop out of the water. I waited and waited. By the time I realized he wasn't coming back to the surface, it was too late to run for help, too late for me to jump in after him. I couldn't even swim. I kept waiting, and waiting, expecting Oscar's giant buffalo head to emerge. But nothing.

At first, I thought justice had been done. He had tried to destroy Enrique's poems. He had tried to erase Enrique. But when I scooted over to the stack of pages that hadn't burned, I saw that the words were typed. Enrique's were all handwritten. I skimmed through the first few fragments. These weren't Enrique's poems—these were Oscar's! He had been destroying his own work! I rushed to the edge of the pier and stared into the pitch-black water, thinking that if justice had *not* been done, that if Enrique's poems had never been in danger, Oscar would rise from the depths. But he never did.

I was a wreck for several days. I didn't know what to do. I found my lady friend at the bar and apologized for running off. I explained that I had nothing but a baggie of pills to my name. Then I told her what had happened at the pier, and that I was ready for whatever punishment came my way. She could alert the authorities if she so wished. But she was surprisingly unfazed. She told me that I shouldn't worry, that there were probably a thousand bodies in the bay, and that no one knew who we were or even that we were there. Soon the body would disappear into the sea. She kept trying to console me by telling me that I would never be caught.

"But I've killed someone. I've killed my friend . . . I mean, he was sort of my friend."

"It was an accident. You will never be caught, don't worry, my love, and give me another one of those pills, won't you?"

She seemed to really enjoy the pills. When I told her I didn't have enough money to pay my bar tab, she explained that she'd take a few pills to the owner. When I told her that I didn't have any money to eat, she took another few pills and returned later with some cash and a plate of steaming tacos. When I finally decided to leave town, but didn't have any money for gas, she took the rest of the pills and returned with enough money to last me several trips.

"Don't worry, you'll never get caught," she said, still not understanding that it was my conscience that troubled me. I had blood on my hands, all because a man tried to destroy the evidence of his failures and frustrated ambitions.

Enrique's work remained safe in a neat little pile in the back seat. I brought it to the front seat. His poetry was my only companion. I decided that when I got back to Albuquerque, I would send off his manuscript immediately. I had been too close to losing it forever. The world had to learn of Enrique's genius. I couldn't hold onto it as if it were written for me and me alone. It belonged to posterity, and I had to ensure it got there.

I drove the same route back to Albuquerque, passing through El Paso. When I returned to my mother's house in my shiny car, she didn't ask how I'd ended up with it or where my big buffalo friend was or how my adventure had gone. Maybe she saw the answers in my face. She knew not to bother me with questions about the loss of my youthful spirit. She sensed that it was best to leave me be. I returned to my room, shut the door, and turned on the television.

EPILOGUE

I never attempted to draw or paint again. I don't count the chicken scratches found among these pages. They are just the scribbles of an old man trying to remember. No, I had finally learned from Oscar's example, his tortured soul. He had said that he was tired, and I understood his exhaustion. Hadn't I reached that point as well? Hadn't I already learned that lesson once? Isn't that what compelled me to commit myself to DeWitt so many years ago? So much turmoil and insecurity. It wasn't worth the fight. I should've counseled Oscar better. I should've told him to let it go, his dreams and ambitions, to forget all this nonsense of masterpieces. Instead of jumping on his back, I should've invited him to Albuquerque to live in the little house with me. We could've spent our days watching game shows and soaps. Together we could've taken care of my mother in her waning years, kept her company while she brought us lunchmeat sandwiches and lemonade. It was too late for Oscar, but not for me. I vowed to find peace and never relinquish it until the end of my days, regardless of who stopped by.

And Enrique's poems?

I tried, my friend. I tried.

I sent them to publishers large and small. I started in New York and moved west. I received one rejection after another. No comments. No encouragement. Nothing. Finally, some assistant editor offered me a tip, suggesting I send the manuscript to a publisher of Mexican American literature in Berkeley, California, which I did. Months later, the publisher wrote back, rejecting the work, saying that "although the work has clear literary merit, the insular nature of the poems doesn't aspire to represent the true spiritual potential of the Chicano community."[23] I didn't even have time to absorb what this might mean because the publisher also apologized for misplacing the copy of the manuscript. "A copy?" I screamed to the heavens. So certain that whoever held it in their hands would instantly know its value, I hadn't even thought to make copies. I had failed Enrique once again. I had been entrusted with his work. He had sent me the poems, and I, the steward of his genius, had doomed him to a fate he didn't deserve: oblivion. Say the word aloud, feel its wretchedness on your tongue, and know that he deserved so much better than a friend like me.

I kept expecting his poems to show up, that maybe someone someday would find the manuscript in a file box and know where to send it. I gave up on that possibility when my mother sold the house and moved to California, following my sister Lourdes, who convinced her to put me in a home for the old and sick but not sick enough to commit. Which, of course, is where I am now. Which is where I've been for a long time. Which is where I finally found the lasting peace, not to mention the typewriter, as well as the pens and the paper, to tell my story

---

23. I have addressed this point before, but it bears repeating until I'm blue in the face: we deprive our literature of its true potential whenever we expect it to fit or conform to our expectations. Jorge Luis Borges wrote in his essay "The Argentine Writer and Tradition" that "the nationalists pretend to venerate the capacities of the Argentine mind but want to limit the poetic exercise of that mind to a few impoverished local themes, as if we Argentines could only speak of *orillas* and *estancias* and not of the universe." Are there Chicano themes? Certainly, but can we not also speak of the universe? How many Enriques have we deprived or been deprived of because we couldn't reconcile the themes of the work with the author's surname and background. Borges, in the same essay, makes the argument that the reason English literature is dominated by the Irish is because of their very differences, their ability to know English culture while having enough distance from it to allow for innovation. Benjamin Alire Sáenz, in his essay "I Want to Write an American Poem," also makes the connection between James Joyce's ambivalence toward the English and Sáenz's own Chicano ambivalence toward the language of this country. We are too often made to feel alienated from our language(s), ashamed of what truly makes us unique, when we should embrace our inner Joyce and turn literature on its head.

as I lived it, in bits and spurts, a rush of memories and then no memories, years fully lived followed by years that passed by without so much as a whimper or a dream or a hope of anything else. I have no regrets.

That's not true. I regret everything, all of it, every single year of my life. How I wish it had been so different. But when I look back I can't see it being any other way. My life, that is. I guess there's something to be said for accepting that. I never became the great artist I thought I would be. Okay. I never made it to Paris. Fine. Courbet and Corot and Millet will be remembered, and I will not. As it should be. I abandoned Enrique, my only friend, and I couldn't satisfy Ella, and I disappointed Reies, and I didn't measure up to Martín, and clearly, I wasted my best years at DeWitt, and I killed Oscar, a man already hell-bent on destruction. Okay to all of it. I accept every last misstep and failing. But what still keeps me up at night, what disturbs the lasting peace I've found, is the sincere wish that somehow you—and by you I don't mean humanity, I mean you, the reader of my story—could've glimpsed the masterpieces I held in my head. The masterful paintings only I could see. Because then it would all make sense, all of it, every preparatory note, every developmental sketch, every false start, every excuse, every failure to do what I was set on this earth to do. Just a glimpse, that's all, and you would've understood.

But indulge me one last time. I will save you the tedium of my preparatory notes. I will save myself the embarrassment of another pathetic scribble. Just imagine. Imagine this as a painting. An old wrinkled man with thinning gray hair seated on a wobbly wooden chair, hunched over a typewriter that rests on his bed, tapping away. His form is lost in shadow as the day loses its light. The sky is visible through the window behind him, brilliant hues of pink and orange. Maybe he's crazy. Maybe he's a third crazy or a fourth crazy. Maybe he's not crazy at all. What matters is the hope he had in him. The room grows dark, but still he types.[24]

24. Ernie writes: "According to my mother, it became too difficult for my grandmother to take care of my uncle on her own. Putting him in a rest home was their only option. When I asked her why we never went to visit him, she said, 'Your uncle was just a shell of a man. There was nothing to visit.' I told her she should read the manuscript, but she refused. 'Do you hate your brother?' I asked her. 'Hate is too

strong of a word,' she said. 'When he disappeared, who do you think had to fill the void? One day he returns as if he'd just gone out for a carton of milk and I'm supposed to embrace him with open arms?' I told her, 'He's family.' She laughed at this. 'Madmen only have themselves,' she said."

Lorraine writes in response: "If nothing else, in sharing your uncle's story, Ernie, we get to share Enrique's story, too. His poems might be lost, but he doesn't have to be. Your uncle doesn't have to be, either. These two kids, even Ella wherever she ended up, lived outside of history, they had no world to call their own. They wanted in, you know, they wanted their lives to matter. Maybe they didn't exist then, but they exist now. I believe that."

But do they exist, Lorraine? Will their story be heard? Will anybody care about an artist who hardly created, who spent the greater part of his life institutionalized, or about a long dead poet whose poems are lost to us?

I found myself thinking a lot about Ernie's note, in particular what his mother said about madmen only having themselves. The first modern novel, *Don Quixote,* was about a madman trying to square his fantasies with reality. Rather, his fantasies became his reality; so it was the outside world that had to square their reality with his. Our narrator, too, had his fantasies, but he was very much aware that "reality" was inescapable. Could his story have been any different? In the 1940s and '50s, could a Mexican American from the mountains of New Mexico really have made a life as an artist? How about now, in the 2020s, can a Chicano "gain entry," as our narrator described it, into the art world? The literary world? Mainstream consciousness? He dreamed of Paris because he dared to dream big and had no other models to follow. What models and pathways do our young artists follow today? I don't know; I am too far removed to have my finger on the pulse of today's creatives. But I do know this: Ernie's mother, Lourdes, is right. Madmen only have themselves, and to be an artist is to be part or maybe entirely mad, and to be a Chicanx artist is to exist on the periphery, the margins, which means we are all madmen dangling at ends of the earth. No, generalizations are risky and I have already offered too many. I will speak only for my younger self, who dreamed of becoming a great novelist: I have often if not always felt that my dreams were too big for the box granted me by fate.

About the Author

Maceo Montoya is an author, artist, and educator who has published books in a variety of genres, including three works of fiction: *The Scoundrel and the Optimist, The Deportation of Wopper Barraza,* and *You Must Fight Them: A Novella and Stories,* which was a finalist for Foreword Review's INDIEFAB Book of the Year award for short stories. Montoya has also published two works of nonfiction: *Letters to the Poet from His Brother,* a hybrid book combining images, prose poems, and essays, and *Chicano Movement for Beginners,* which he both wrote and illustrated.

Montoya's paintings, drawings, and prints have been featured in exhibitions and publications throughout the country as well as internationally. He has collaborated with other writers on visual-textual projects, including Laurie Ann Guerrero's *A Crown for Gumecindo,* Arturo Mantecón's translation of Mexican poet Mario Santiago Papasquiaro's *Poetry Comes Out of My Mouth,* and David Campos's *American Quasars.* Montoya is currently an associate professor in the Chicana/o Studies Department at UC Davis where he teaches courses on Chicanx culture and literature.